'Oh, Rachel! I do

Rachel regarded

demanded. 'Have

Has either of us ever taken a calculated risk?'

Marion's expression changed also. 'Rachel!' she said wonderingly, surprised by the intensity of her sister's manner.

'Well, have we?'

'I suppose not.'

'I've done my duty and you've done yours. We have both done what was expected of us, always and without question. And what has it brought us? I rattle around in a big old house; I shall never marry – oh, don't pretend you think otherwise, because we both know the truth. You live with a man you cannot love and who will never give you the children you want so desperately.'

'Oh, please, Rachel! Don't!' cried Marion.

'But it's the *truth*, Marion. High time we faced facts.'

'I have Pip –' Marion began.

'Pip is a *dog*,' Rachel reminded her sharply. 'I am talking about *love*. If this young man loves you . . .'

'Of course he doesn't love me! Don't say such things.'

'Then why are you so afraid of meeting him? Oh, come on, Marion, let's take a risk. Let's have some excitement. Shouldn't life offer just a little more than we have already?'

A DUTIFUL WIFE
Pamela Oldfield

SPHERE BOOKS LIMITED

For Muriel, Eric, John and Carole,
with love

A SPHERE BOOK

First published in Great Britain by Michael Joseph Ltd 1989
Published by Sphere Books Limited 1990
Reprinted 1990 (four times), 1998

Printed and bound in Great Britain by
Clays Ltd, St Ives plc

ISBN 0 7474 0495 X

Sphere Books
A Division of
Little, Brown and Company (UK)
Brettenham House
Lancaster Place
London WC2E 7EN

CHAPTER ONE

'What on earth is happening?' Amelia demanded irritably. 'Why have we stopped?'

'I don't really know. There seems to be some kind of hold-up.'

Ralph lowered the window, letting the cold November air in to the landau, which made his mother snuggle deeper into her fur collar. After a quick glance up and down the street, he raised the window once more and settled back into his seat with a puzzled expression on his face.

'There are a lot of people milling about,' he told her, 'and even more policemen, and further up ahead there are Life Guards.'

'Life Guards?' Amelia's eyes were narrowed as she regarded her son. 'They're expecting trouble, obviously. Perhaps we should tell Johnson to find another route.'

Even as she spoke, the coachman approached the window which Ralph lowered for the second time.

'Something going on ahead, ma'am,' he reported. 'Could be nasty. Lot of noise up towards the square – shouting and suchlike. I'm afraid we might be stuck here for some time.'

'Go back then, Johnson,' Amelia instructed him. 'My sister May is expecting us and she frets so if we are late.'

'I don't know if I can go back now, ma'am. Too many vehicles pulling up behind us, and all in the same boat.'

Ralph muttered, 'Damnation!' and his mother gave him a vexed glance which he ignored.

'Should I try and find out what's happening for you, ma'am?' The coachman was obviously eager to satisfy his own curiosity, but Amelia shook her head. 'You can't leave the horses unattended,' she told him.

'I'll go,' said Ralph and before his mother could protest, he jumped down from the landau and began to dodge between the numerous carriages and carts until he reached the pavement, which was equally crowded with pedestrians. As he made his way towards Trafalgar Square, Amelia sank back into her seat with an exasperated sigh.

Johnson remained in the open doorway. Greatly daring, he said, 'It's been brewing up for some time, ma'am – the trouble, I mean.'

'Yes, it has.' She nodded absent-mindedly.

'Those sort have to be kept in their place. Trouble-makers, the lot of them.'

When she did not contradict him he took this as encouragement and rashly ventured a further remark. 'That bit of bother last year,' he said. 'The riot. That shows you the kind they are, ma'am. The papers called them scum of the earth, and that's exactly . . .'

As his words registered in Amelia's brain she turned on him a look of such coldness that he faltered into silence, wondering what he had done to offend her.

'They were *starving*,' she told him. 'They had no work, no money, no homes. Unemployment is a terrifying spectre if you have a wife and family to support. Have you ever thought of that, Johnson?'

He shook his head, cursing his runaway tongue. Now he was in for one of her lectures!

'If you had a wife and children who were dying for lack of food, what would you do, Johnson? Let them die, or try to alert the proper authorities as to the desperate nature of your situation?'

'Oh, that, ma'am,' he said hastily. 'I'd never really thought about –'

'Ah!' she cried triumphantly. 'That's the whole trouble, Johnson. Nobody really *thinks*. The poor won't just go

2

away, you know – not simply to oblige the rest of us. You are fortunate, Johnson; you have a job.'

'Yes, ma'am.' A sullen look settled over his face and he tried unsuccessfully to think of something to say that would bring the homily to an end. Still, at least he was sheltered from the worst of the cold wind standing at the side of the coach, whereas perched up on his box it caught him full in the face. His cheeks were already reddened and his lips were chapped. Soon it would be chilblain time, he thought, but what would she care? Her fingers never got cold, nor her feet neither. It was all right for some! She was a fine one to go lecturing him; rich folk were all the same. He avoided her eyes.

'All those people want,' she went on, 'is somewhere to sleep at nights, and if the best they can manage is a bench in Trafalgar Square then who are we to begrudge them that?'

She glared at him, and he felt an answer was required.

'There's lodging-houses, ma'am,' he suggested cautiously.

'Lodgings cost money and they haven't got any. Don't you understand? No money means no lodgings, and that means no roof over your head. I cannot make it much plainer. Do you see what I'm driving at, Johnson?'

'Yes, ma'am.'

'Well, I should hope so.'

At that moment a burly man came up to Johnson.

'What the hell's going on along there?' he asked, and the coachman took the opportunity to move out of Amelia's view. She closed the door and promptly forgot him. It appalled her to imagine what was happening in the Square and she prayed that the violence of '86 – when thousands of rioters had rampaged through the West End after a battle with the police and army – would not be repeated. It seemed likely that 1887 would see another such disaster.

Amelia Gaunt, née Thripp, a wealthy widow with

only one son, was one of the concerned few who cared about the misery of her fellows. She spent a considerable amount of her own money in attempting to ameliorate their lot, contributing regularly to the Lord Mayor's Fund, to a fund for distributing blankets and to another for the provision of hot soup. Tireless also in the extraction of money from her wealthy friends, today she was on her way to visit her elderly spinster sister, May, who – she believed – had more money than sense and would never live long enough to enjoy it all. Since May had no family, Amelia was very much afraid she might bequeath her wealth unwisely and was determined to separate her from as much of it as possible before she died and left it to a cats' home. Such was Amelia's personality that few could resist her for long. May, she was sure, would prove no exception.

For a while she remained deep in thought, rehearsing what she would say to her sister, but then her attention was caught by a slight scuffle outside. She glanced out and saw Johnson trying to turn away a young girl carrying a basket of matches over one arm.

'We don't want your fuzees,' the coachman was telling her. 'Now hop it before I box your ears – d'you hear me?'

The girl mumbled something, her voice high and plaintive, and the coachman swore under his breath. 'Look, she doesn't want your fuzees because she doesn't smoke a pipe nor a cigar, neither. She's a *lady*, see?'

Amelia opened the door and stepped down to the road.

'How do you know that, Johnson?' she asked. 'I might want some fuzees. I might decide to take up smoking a pipe. Yes, I think I may well do so. In fact I –'

She stopped abruptly as the match-seller turned to her and in spite of her natural good manners could not repress a gasp of dismay, for the lower left side of the child's face was swollen to such a degree that her nose

4

was pushed sideways. The girl mumbled something, but the swelling rendered her words unintelligible.

Johnson looked embarrassed. 'I tried to get rid of her, ma'am –' he began, but Amelia silenced him with a wave of her hand and addressed the girl herself.

'What is the matter with your face?' The girl hung her head. 'Answer me, child! Is it an abscess or toothache or what? If it's an abscess, it should be lanced. Is it painful? Yes, of course it must be; you must be in agony with a face like that. Speak up – or at least nod. You've got a tongue in your head, haven't you?'

Hastily the coachman intervened. 'It's "phossy jaw", ma'am,' he told her. 'I've seen it before, it's from the matches.' He turned to the girl. 'Am I right?'

She nodded and he looked pleased at this corroboration of his diagnosis.

'"Phossy jaw"?' Amelia repeated. 'What in heaven's name is phossy jaw? You are making no sense, Johnson.'

'Begging your pardon, ma'am. It's because of the phosphorous they use in the matches – it's poisonous, you see, and if it gets into your jaw it rots it all away. Eats into the bone, you might say.'

'Good heavens!' Amelia's dismay deepened into concern.

'She'll lose her jaw most probably,' he went on cheerfully.

'Lose her jaw!' Amelia was horrified. 'But there's a cure, isn't there? She must be cured. Lose her *jaw*? What a terrible prospect; she cannot be more than ten or eleven.'

'I expect she's been dipping,' said Johnson. 'Plenty of folks do it. They dip the match ends into the phosphorous and the fumes go up their noses or into their mouths.'

'But surely she's too young to be at work?'

'Oh, she won't work in the factory, ma'am – most likely been working in some back room somewhere. Anyone can make matches.'

5

'But that's scandalous!'

She took a closer look at the girl's face and asked sternly, 'Have you been dipping matches? Is that it?' The child nodded.

'"Phossy jaw",' repeated Amelia. 'It's quite disgraceful.' Suddenly she said, 'I'll have some matches. A dozen packets – no, make it two dozen – and here's a shilling.'

Seeing what he imagined to be her error, Johnson murmured, 'The proper price is fourpence-halfpenny, ma'am.'

'Then I shall pay an *improper* price!'

Eagerly the girl tumbled the required amount of matches into Amelia's cupped hands and watched as she then tossed them on to the seat of the carriage.

'What's your name, child?'

The answer was unintelligible.

'This is the most terrible thing I've ever seen,' whispered Amelia. She put the coin into the girl's hand, but said warningly, 'You are to stay here, do you understand? Don't go away. I shall speak to my son about you.'

The oddly assorted trio stared at each other for a few moments until Ralph conveniently reappeared.

Johnson said thankfully, 'Ah, here's Mister Ralph. What news, I wonder?'

However, Amelia had lost interest in the cause of their delay and turned at once to her son.

'Do look at this wretched child, Ralph. See this awful swelling? Phosphorous has attacked her jawbone. We must see what we can do to –'

But Ralph interrupted her. 'There's serious trouble coming, Mama. We are advised to leave the area. Several constables are being sent down this way to deal with the traffic and I think the best thing we can do is to –'

'Ralph! You're not listening.' Amelia caught him by the arm. 'I said, look at this child's face! It's unforgivable.'

Ralph glanced at the girl and his brows contracted

briefly, but he went on, 'This is no time for worrying about a match-girl's face. Johnson must try to turn the landau round, so that as soon as they have cleared the road sufficiently we can get away. It looks very ugly, Mama. Some of the crowd have staves and pockets full of stones. The Grenadiers are all along the parapet of the National Gallery. There's going to be an unholy row. The press are everywhere – notebooks at the ready – and they say the Life Guards are there too. The balloon is likely to go up at any moment.' As Amelia hesitated he urged, '*Please*, Mama! For God's sake, get back in the carriage.'

He turned to the girl. 'And you be off now.'

She turned to obey, glad to escape the eagle eyes of her generous customer, but Amelia had other ideas.

'No,' she said. 'She must come with us; she must see a doctor.'

This dire threat obviously terrified the girl and she immediately ducked under Ralph's arm and tried to run away. However, Johnson saw a chance to restore himself to his employer's good books and he darted forward to take hold of her arm. She struggled so violently that some of her matches spilled on to the road.

Ralph tutted impatiently. 'You can see how unwilling she is,' he told his mother. 'Do, please, let her go. Dr Reid was not very pleased with the last lame duck you sent to his surgery. He certainly won't welcome this . . .' Catching the look in his mother's eye, he added '. . . person'.

'The doctor gets paid for what he does – and handsomely, too,' Amelia reminded him. 'He cannot expect to be allowed to pick and choose his patients.' To the girl she said, 'Get into the carriage at once. I shall take you to the doctor, who will do something for your jaw.' As the child still hesitated, she gave her a slight push and said, 'Oh get along, do! No one is going to hurt you.'

Forty minutes later they reached No. 16, Queen Elizabeth Walk, and Johnson was told to wait while the girl was taken into the house for a cup of tea. She found it difficult to drink. Amelia had intended to give her sandwiches and cake also, but it was clear to everyone that the unfortunate child would find these equally difficult to cope with.

'She can't eat properly and she can't talk,' said Amelia. 'What kind of future does she have – even supposing she lives long enough to *have* a future?'

'I don't know, Mama,' Ralph replied, 'but frankly I don't think you should have spirited her away like this. Suppose her parents are looking for her? They will expect her to be on her normal round.'

Amelia gave her son one of her most withering looks and said, 'There are times when you can be very obtuse, Ralph. I sometimes wonder whether we speak the same language. If I didn't know better, I would suspect you of being a changeling. Now, please listen, I have to take Johnson and call on May; she will be wondering where I am. You will call a hansom, please, and take this poor wretch to see Dr Reid on the usual understanding that I shall settle the account. *When* the doctor has seen her – and not until then – she must be taken home. We don't want her wandering unfamiliar streets. I have to go now. Oh, and remember we are dining out tonight.'

'Are we really?' He did not pretend enthusiasm. 'Where are we going?'

'Sir Edward Somers.' He groaned. 'And please be ready on time,' she went on before he could voice any objections. 'You made us late when we went to the Fosters, and you know how I hate unpunctuality.'

'Mama . . .' he began, but she had gone with a swish of skirts and a vague wave of her exquisitely gloved hand. Ralph would do as he had been instructed not only because he knew better than to try to argue with his mother on such a matter, but also because the match-girl repelled him and the sooner the doctor gave his verdict

8

the sooner he could be rid of her. Privately Ralph thought it very unlikely that anything could be done to help her, but his mother was an unfailing optimist and would not be satisfied until she had a professional opinion.

He hailed a cab and bundled the girl into it, relieved that she offered only token resistance. 'Sixty-eight Harrington Hill,' he told the driver, 'and quick as you can.'

*

Marion Reid, née Napier, glanced at the clock on the mantelpiece. 'He'll be home soon,' she said.

The King Charles spaniel who lay curled in her lap opened her eyes lazily, then closed them again. Marion fondled the dog's ears, wishing she could look forward to her husband's return and wishing even more that she could love him as she had done when they had married nine years ago. Nevertheless, a daily recitation of his good points could not revive the affection she had once felt for him, nor could she ever reconcile herself to her childlessness.

Dr Gilbert Reid, twenty years her senior, had originally lodged with her family. At twenty, Marion had been shy and lacking in self-confidence, and uneasy in the presence of men of her own age whom she found unpredictable, even silly. She had been impressed with Gilbert's poise and courteous manner. When he began to show an interest in Marion her mother had encouraged his attentions, and she persuaded herself that she was in love with him. When he proposed, only her sister Rachel objected to the match; but assuming this to be prompted by a natural sisterly jealousy, Marion ignored her advice to refuse him. She was longing for a home of her own and all the responsibilities which that entailed; a new way of life; a husband and children to care for; a new circle of friends. Home was all she knew and she wanted to widen her horizons. They had married in 1878 and her expectations had largely been realized. Marriage to a successful doctor brought her most of the things that a Victorian wife in her position might expect – an attractive home, a comfortable income, agreeable companionship. Gilbert Reid was a well-respected member of the community and as his wife, Marion was held in similar esteem.

'People envy me,' she told Pip and shook her head, bemused by the idea. 'He loves me in the only way he can, and God knows I would love him if I could.'

To their small circle of friends their marriage appeared quite normal, and only to Rachel had she confided that the relationship was now purely platonic. Only Rachel knew that she could never have Gilbert's child. It was the bitterness of this realization and the reason behind it which had finally driven a wedge between husband and wife. Gilbert refused to discuss the matter and would not even consider adoption as a way out of their difficulties.

Five years ago he had bought her the little spaniel bitch on whom Marion lavished all the loving care she should have given to her children. Sometimes she thought that if only she could blame Gilbert she could release some of the grief that filled her heart, but that was not possible for he was a victim also. She sympathized and made excuses for him and showed him every consideration. No, she could not blame him. For both of them, the tragedy was that she no longer loved him.

With a sigh she smiled at the spaniel. 'Do you want to go out, Pip?' she asked.

A short yelp of excitement answered her and she kissed the dog's head, tipped her gently on to the floor and then made her way out of the morning room and along the passage to the kitchen. Here Mrs Cobbett was preparing dinner with the help of Kitty, the housemaid.

Marion opened the back door and Pip flew up the garden path barking extravagantly at nothing.

The housekeeper laughed. 'One of these days she'll

find something out there to bark *at*,' she said. 'That'll surprise her.'

Marion nodded absent-mindedly while in the garden Pip stood beneath the pear tree, barking hysterically at a bird which flew away in apparent disgust at this unnecessary outburst.

Today was Tuesday and they were having sweetbreads with asparagus, followed by 'tipsy cake' which was one of Gilbert's favourite desserts. The only way she could please him was through his stomach, Marion thought resignedly, but his expanding waistline was proof of the success of her efforts in that direction. On Thursdays, she did the cooking herself because Mrs Cobbett had the day off.

'Pip!' she called. 'Come off that flower-bed at once!'

The spaniel had probably buried a bone there, Marion thought. She had too many bones – she was spoilt – so that the dog was a little overweight too. With a sigh, she turned back from the door and walked across the kitchen.

Mrs Cobbett glanced at the large clock which hung on the wall. 'The master's late,' she remarked. 'They take advantage of his kind heart, I reckon. Keep him listening to their grumbles.'

'I expect so,' agreed Marion, pausing in the doorway which led to the hall. 'Call Pip indoors in a few moments, will you, please, but keep her in the kitchen. I'll collect her later when we have finished our meal.'

'I will, ma'am,' said Mrs Cobbett cheerfully.

Marion went back to the morning room and took up her sewing. She was edging a pillowcase with a narrow strip of white lace, but after a few stitches she let it fall into her lap and stared ahead with unseeing eyes.

'Oh, Gilbert . . .' she whispered, but at that moment the front door-bell rang and she heard Kitty scurry along the hall to answer it. There was a small exchange and then a knock at the morning-room door.

'There's a young man to see the doctor, ma'am,' Kitty informed her. 'He's got a girl with him.' She lowered her voice confidentially and added, 'She looks horrible, ma'am. Her face is all swollen up and her nose –'

'That will do, Kitty!' Marion told her sharply. 'How many times do I have to tell you that it is not part of your duties to pass comment on the doctor's patients? Anyway, they are too late for the surgery today; you know that as well as I do. You should have told them to come back in the morning.'

'I did tell them, ma'am, but the young man wouldn't take no for an answer. Said tomorrow's too late; said his mother would skin him alive or some such thing.'

'Well, really!'

Kitty sighed wistfully. 'He's ever so handsome. Speaks well, too – not a bit like the girl, who kept mumbling and tugging to get away.'

'Tugging to get away from what?'

'From him, ma'am – like she didn't want to come here and he was forcing her. All ragged, she is, and . . .'

'Ragged?' Marion thought rapidly. It sounded like another of the wretches that Amelia Gaunt frequently sent to Gilbert for help. Gilbert did not particularly relish her waifs and strays, but he charged her extravagantly for curing their various ailments and she paid promptly and without demur. Amelia Gaunt was a valued client and the young man might be her son who had recently returned from a tour of Europe.

'Ask them to wait,' she told Kitty reluctantly.

Now dinner would be late, she thought crossly, and that would put Gilbert in a bad mood – not to mention Mrs Cobbett, whose culinary efforts would not now be enjoyed at what she considered their peak of perfection.

Kitty hurried off to deliver the message and Marion heard a complaining mumble as the girl was hustled unwillingly into the waiting room across the hall. After a moment, curiosity overcame Marion's usual discretion and she went into the waiting room to speak to them herself.

'My husband is out on his rounds . . .' she began, but faltered a little as she caught sight of the girl.

The child's dirty ginger hair was cut short in uneven chunks and stuck out round her head like the bristles of a brush. Her body was filthy, her feet were bare and, as Kitty had so bluntly put it, her face was horribly misshapen by a large swelling on the left side of her jaw. It was a relief to turn back to the young man whom Kitty had also described accurately. Marion thought she could detect the elegant Gaunt features in his boyish face – Amelia's very bright blue eyes, fine blond hair and firm well-shaped mouth.

'I'm so sorry,' he said, 'but my mother insisted, and she's used to getting her own way. I'm Ralph Gaunt. We found this poor child near Trafalgar Square selling matches, as you can see.' He indicated the basket to which the girl clung like a drowning man. 'Our coachman says her condition is "phossy jaw" – that is, caused by phosphorous which is used in the making of some kinds of matches. I told Mama that it's most unlikely anything can be done for her, but she was adamant that we try so here we are. I threatened little "Miss Matches" here with the direst punishment if she runs off before the doctor sees her!'

He wagged a reproving finger at the girl and said, 'Remember what I told you; it's for your own good. So no nonsense.' Then he smiled suddenly and the match-girl, embarrassed by the attention of such a good-looking man, raised her basket to hide her swollen face.

'I'm sure Dr Reid will do what he can,' Marion replied. 'I expect him to return from his rounds at any moment, although the surgery is actually over for this evening.'

The young man held out his hand and she took it briefly. 'Thank you,' he said. 'My mother will be in touch, I don't doubt, to hear the verdict. She thinks very highly of your husband. Oh, and my mother was most emphatic that "Miss Matches" should be taken back to her home. Perhaps your husband would be kind enough to put her in a hansom and charge it to our account? I asked her where she lived, but couldn't understand what she said. But now I must dash – please do excuse me.'

When he had gone, Marion hesitated outside the waiting-room door. Experience had taught her that people such as the ragged child were not to be trusted. A baker with a horrific burn on his arm had once absconded with a small clock, and on another occasion a pregnant orange-seller had stolen the mat from inside the front door!

Amelia Gaunt's protégées were notoriously light-fingered, but at least she paid for whatever they stole. This one would prove no exception, thought Marion, but to be on the safe side she decided to send in Kitty to sit with her. She was on the point of summoning the maid when she heard hoofbeats outside and a carriage rolled to a stop. Gilbert was home.

Gilbert Reid was the youngest of three sons born to a prosperous ironmonger and his wife. As a child he had shown great intelligence and the headmaster of his school had taken a keen interest in him. When he announced at the age of twelve that he wanted to be a doctor, his parents had been surprised but not too disappointed since the older boys were already involved in the family business and his presence there would not be missed. The question of finances, however, threatened to become a major stumbling block until the headmaster, a childless widower, offered him free tutoring in Greek, Latin and Mathematics. He then put up half the £200-pound premium necessary for Gilbert to be apprenticed to a local doctor by the name of O'Rourke. Gilbert stayed with him for three years – by which time he was ready to apply to begin his medical studies – and following the advice of Dr O'Rourke he spent the next two years at Meath Hospital, Dublin, and two more at Edinburgh; there he finally took and passed his final examinations and became a fully qualified physician. On moving to London, he went into partnership with a Dr Grant in Kingston, who also held a consultancy at Guys Hospital. This meant that he was frequently away from his practice, which eventually became Gilbert's responsibility, and when Dr Grant was elected to the hospital as a full-time member of staff, Gilbert took over the practice in its entirety.

Although his career was moving predictably upwards, his personal life was not very satisfactory. Gilbert had no time to look for a wife, and it was not until he was nearing forty that he considered the advisability of marriage. Marion was the younger of his landlady's two daughters and to him she seemed eminently suitable as a wife, being of a mild disposition as well as reasonably attractive and refined in appearance. He had offered her security and a home of her own, and had been rather surprised when she appeared to return his affection and accepted his proposal of marriage. Two years later he bought a larger practice and they moved into No. 68 Harrington Hill and set up home there.

By this time he was confidently expecting to be invited to join the staff at Guys Hospital, but to his great disappointment this did not happen. Although Gilbert Reid's qualifications were admirable, his somewhat austere manner and lack of cordiality made him a difficult person to get to know and colleagues at the hospital did not warm to him.

This unexpected setback in his career, combined with the lack of physical satisfaction in his marriage, made him outwardly taciturn and inwardly resentful, although he tried hard to hide his feelings from Marion so that she did not suspect the extent of his growing unhappiness.

Now when Marion greeted him with the news of his unexpected patient, he managed to bite back the angry comment which sprang to his lips. A few moments later he went into the waiting room and beckoned the child to follow him into the surgery, which she did with great reluctance. He sat down at his desk and motioned her to stand before him; she was dirty and she smelt horrible, and he had no intention of allowing her too near until it was absolutely necessary.

'How long have you had that swelling?' he asked, drawing a pad of paper towards him and reaching for his pen, 'A week? A month? A year?'

She shrugged and then shook her head.

'You can speak, can't you, child?'

She mumbled something which was unintelligible, but which answered the question for him.

He made a note on his pad and went on, 'How old are you? You must have some idea. Hold up your fingers.'

The girl held up all her fingers and both thumbs and he wrote: '10 yrs. Undersized.'

Again he asked, 'How long have you had that swelling? A year?' She shook her head. 'Do you know how long a year is? It's twelve months. Have you had it as long as twelve months?'

The child looked round for a way of escape, but Gilbert said, 'You will be going home soon. Don't worry; we don't want to keep you here. Have you ever had toothache?'

At last a nod.

'And did you have the tooth removed?'

A shake of the head.

'You've been working with matches, I suppose?'

Another nod.

'Dipping them in yellow phosphorous?'

Yes, she had.

'Come round here, child, and open your mouth as far as you can. Oh, I know it hurts.'

After a brief examination of her mouth he wrote: 'Inflammation buccal mucosa' and sighed heavily. Feeling along the jaw-bone, his practised fingers gentle, he found what he had expected – minuscule knots of bony tissue. To the notes on his pad he added the words: 'Sequestra present'.

Then he waved her back to her place on the far side of his desk and considered her case dispassionately. Her breath was offensive, her jaws and gums swollen; no doubt there would be damage to the jaw-bone itself. Extraction of some of the teeth would give some immediate relief, but would almost certainly lead to an extension of the diseased area. Eventually the whole jaw, both upper and lower, could be affected. Removal of diseased bone would prolong the agony, and if extensive would be painful and lead to severe disfigurement. At some stage septicaemia would undoubtedly occur and this would lead to her death. There was no simple cure for 'phossy jaw' and none that was guaranteed. The disease was an abomination.

He pointed to a chair in the far corner of the room and continued to make notes on the pad. The case was arguably operable, but he wondered if this would be a kindness.

'Damnation!' he muttered.

There was a surgeon at the London Hospital who would undertake the operation, but the girl's chances of survival were slight. She was undernourished and probably possessed a poor constitution. No doubt Amelia Gaunt would pay for the treatment, but the fee would go to the surgeon concerned. Was it all worth the effort, he wondered, or should he allow the wretched child to go her way without further interference? Sometimes, he thought irritably, the do-gooders of the world had much to answer for.

He wrote rapidly. A full report must be sent to Mrs Gaunt with his bill.

At last he pushed back his chair and stood up, and as he did so he noticed a suppurating weal on the girl's right leg. After a closer look he went to his medicine cabinet and took out a large jar containing a white paste; from this he filled a smaller pot. At least he could do something for the unfortunate creature.

'Now, we'll send you home,' he told her. 'You do know where you live, I suppose?'

An eager nod was followed by an unintelligible mumble.

He hazarded a guess. 'Bow?' No, she indicated.

'Spitalfields? Finsbury? Hackney? Whitechapel? Ah!' He could not, however, discover the name of the road or number of the house, so sending her home by hansom was out of the question. He would take her there himself and charge Amelia Gaunt for the cab fare, which would effectively pay for his time. He was eager to be rid of the child; her misfortune depressed him.

*

Fashion Street was a dreary row of ill-kept and dilapidated houses. A few provided places of work for tailors and seamstresses, but most of them were used as common lodging-houses while No. 38 was no better and no worse than the properties on either side of it. The crumbling brickwork was grey with years of soot, and only a few flakes remained on the door to show that once it had been painted brown. The wooden window-frames no longer fitted and thus allowed access to wind, rain and snow. The glass in the ground-floor window was cracked, but someone had pasted strips of newspaper over the worst of the cracks to prevent further disintegration. The door-knocker had long since been pawned and would never be redeemed, but when the doctor rapped on the door with his knuckles it swung open smoothly enough.

The fair-haired young woman who opened it regarded him with a mixture of surprise and suspicion. Prosperous-looking men in smart coats and well-polished shoes were rare in the neighbourhood, but this one was holding her sister Ellie by the arm and Meg did not know what to make of it.

Gilbert saw a young woman in a shabby blue dress. A coarse and very dirty apron was tied round a narrow waist, while an untidy mass of fair curls framed a face which was saved from plainness by a pair of large hazel eyes.

Meg saw a man of average height, with a firm mouth, smooth complexion and eyes of a strangely pale blue. She had seen worse, she decided.

'I am Dr Reid. Is this your daughter?' he asked while the girl wriggled to free herself.

'Daughter!' Meg glared at Ellie. 'Blooming sauce! She's my sister. What the 'ell you been up to, Ellie?' she demanded. 'If you've got yourself in trouble, you'll have more to come from me –'

Gilbert released the girl's arm and at once she darted past her sister and disappeared into the shabby recesses of the house, still clutching her basket of matches.

'She's in no kind of trouble,' the doctor interrupted, 'except that particular trouble which has affected her jaw.'

Meg thought rapidly. If her sister had done nothing wrong, then why had this posh chap brought her home – and was there a copper or two to be made out of it somehow?

He introduced himself and explained briefly about the girl's meeting with the Gaunts and her subsequent arrival at his surgery.

'Well, it's very kind of you, doctor,' she said, recovering her poise. 'I really dunno what to say and that's the truth.' She tossed her head and flashed him the special smile she reserved for her clients. To her surprise he responded with a nervous smile of his own.

'The jaw is quite seriously affected, I'm afraid,' Gilbert told her.

'It's toothache!' Meg interrupted him.

'Toothache?' he echoed. 'You don't really believe that. The girl's jaw is –'

'I tell you it's toothache,' Meg insisted.

'It's phosphorous necrosis,' he said firmly. 'The condition might be helped by surgery; there is a surgeon at the –'

'She don't need no surgeon.'

'You'd call it "phossy jaw",' he said.

She lowered her voice. 'No, I'd call it toothache. Look, you people mean well, but I don't trust hospitals and I don't want no one doing operations on Ellie.'

'It can prove fatal.'

'That's my worry. I'm not letting anyone cut up Ellie, so you can save your breath.'

He shrugged. 'It's very tragic,' he said. 'There must eventually be legislation –'

'Ledges–what?'

'Legislation – there must be laws passed – to prevent that kind of disease, but if and when it comes I fear it will be too late for your sister.'

She gave a careless toss of her head. 'Laws is always too bloody late for our sort,' she told him.

'I am afraid I have to agree.'

Flattered, Meg began to relax. A gentleman agreeing with her was heady stuff and her thoughts began to turn to more familiar matters.

She could smell a delightful mixture of expensive cigar smoke and scented soap and although he was old – well, knocking on for fifty most likely – he was not unattractive and she wondered if he liked women. She had never 'obliged' a gentleman. Now that *would* be a lark! Not to mention the possibility of a sixpence maybe instead of the usual threepence. She gave him a bold stare and saw at once that he had registered the meaning of her special smile. Ah! Quick on the uptake, was he? That was a good sign. His mind would be ticking over by now and soon the rest of him would follow suit!

'You live here alone?' he asked.

'No such luck . . .' She bit back the word 'ducks' and said 'sir' instead. 'Couldn't manage the rent on our own. No, there's me and Ellie; then there's my lodgers Alf Berry and his wife, Sal, and their kid. Alf, he sells groundsel and stuff for birds. You know, birds in cages – linnets, larks and things. They eat it. He does turfs, too, for the bottom of the cages. You got a bird, sir?'

At this point in the conversation Ellie reappeared and stood beside her sister.

'No . . . we haven't,' said Gilbert. 'My wife has a small pet dog.'

So he was married, she thought. Pity. She adjusted her fantasies to fit in with this new information. Still, plenty of men were married, but that didn't stop them from patronizing girls like her.

He looked from Ellie to Meg. 'About your sister's jaw,' he said again. 'I'm afraid it *is* phosphorous necrosis and it will almost certainly get worse as time goes on. It *may* affect the right side of her face as well.'

Meg said, 'I don't want to talk about it.'

'The damaged bone could be cut away.'

'Cut away?' Two pairs of startled eyes met his.

'It has been tried,' he assured them hurriedly. 'I have a colleague at the London Hospital – a most eminent man – who specializes in –'

Ellie burst into loud sobs and Meg hugged her protectively as she glared at the doctor.

'No one's going to cut out nothing!' she declared. 'You hear that, Ellie? No one's going to touch you, so for God's sake stop hollering.'

Gilbert decided he had done all that could be expected of him in the circumstances and drew a small pot of ointment from his overcoat pocket. 'This ointment will help to heal the wound on her leg.'

'Oh, thank you, sir,' Meg hesitated. 'But how much is it? I don't think . . .'

'There's no need to worry about payment,' he assured her. 'As I told you, Mrs Gaunt has generously offered to meet any expenses. She really is a . . .'

But Meg had suddenly seen her chance. She gave the still sobbing Ellie a push back towards their room, then turned to face Gilbert.

'Oh, no, sir!' she protested, her voice vibrating with righteous indignation. 'That would be charity, that would. We may be hard up, but we never had a penny what we hadn't earned. Even poor folks has their pride, sir, although this Mrs Gaunt means well and no disrespect to folk like her. It's just that . . .' She wished that she looked a little more alluring; she didn't expect clients in the middle of the day and was mortified to realize that she was wearing her old blue dress and her hair had not been combed.

'There's really no need –' he began.

'But I'd like to repay you' – she gave him an intense look – '*the only way I know how* – you taking an interest in Ellie and bringing her home and all that.'

'It wasn't too far,' he said and she noted that his voice was now rather hoarse.

She knew intuitively that he understood exactly what she was suggesting and was longing to accept her offer! Well! This *was* a turn-up for the books – if only she didn't let him slip away, if only she could land him!

'Think! Think, damn you!' she told herself. 'Use your wits, Meg Swain. This could be your lucky day.'

'I suppose you wouldn't accept a cup of tea,' she suggested desperately. 'There's only me and Ellie here right now so . . .' She paused and after a long hesitation, he said, 'I think it would be churlish to refuse. Thank you, Miss . . .'

'Swain, Meg Swain. Then come along in, Dr Reid.'

She led the way into the room which served as both bedroom and kitchen. Palliasses and blankets were piled in one corner; there was a card-table in the middle of the room with four chairs standing round it; a deep sink was piled with unwashed crockery and clothes bulged from every drawer of an ancient chest. Threadbare curtains hung at the windows and a kettle was suspended above a small fire. As they went in, Ellie leaped to her feet and mumbled desperately.

'No one's going to cut you up, Ellie,' Meg told her. She took a coin from a tea-caddy on the mantelpiece. 'You just run down the road, there's a love, and get a couple of pies for our supper.'

Ellie mumbled again.

'Well, herrings, then,' Meg answered sharply. 'I don't care what you get – just go.' She tossed her the coin, which Ellie caught.

'And don't hurry back,' Meg warned her. 'You know what I mean.'

Ellie looked surprised, but then nodded vigorously and went out banging the front door behind her.

Meg smiled at her visitor and then busied herself with the teapot, two chipped mugs, sugar and milk.

They sipped in silence for a while, then he put down his mug with hands that trembled.

'Did I understand you to mean . . .' he began. 'You are willing – I mean – what exactly do you do, Miss Swain? To earn your living, that is?'

Meg shrugged. 'I do what you think I do. Oh, you want me to spell it out, do you? Well, then, I'm a lady of the streets. Been at it five years now.'

'Five!' he gasped. 'But how old are you?'

'Eighteen. Ah! Now I've *really* shocked you. Yes, I started just before I was thirteen. Left home at eleven because I hated my father. Tried selling in the streets – wash-leathers, nutmeg graters, candlesticks, stuff like that – but folks didn't like buying from a girl. I don't know why. I was nigh on starving at the end of a year, but then I met this young man – Harry Hobbs, his name was. He had three other girls and they showed me the ropes, so to speak. There's ways and means. Then one day he got killed on the way to the Three Feathers. Tried to stop a pair of runaway horses, but they dragged him along and he fell under the wheels. So from then on we was on our own.'

'Terrible!' he said. 'An appalling story.'

Meg shrugged again. 'It's not so bad,' she told him, 'when we get to meet real nice gentlemen like you.' She smiled provocatively, her head tilted to one side. 'Giving satisfaction to a real gentleman . . . well, that's hardly work in my book. That's pleasure.'

He dropped his voice to a whisper. 'I've never been with . . . one of your kind. You understand?'

Meg gave a light laugh. 'Bless you, sir, that's no problem. I get all sorts of gentlemen, you'd be surprised.' She tapped her nose meaningfully. 'Don't give it another thought.'

'But I have to tell you something,' he told her. 'I am not . . . that is, I'm afraid I am a . . .' He swallowed and she nodded encouragingly. 'I am not a gentle lover, not gentle at all. In fact . . .'

Oh no! thought Meg. A bully-boy! Wasn't that just her luck! Her smile, however, did not waver. 'I'm used to all sorts,' she said briskly. She would charge him extra.

'But you don't understand,' he began. 'When I . . . I mean, my wife . . .' He shuddered as his voice sank to a whisper and then trailed off altogether.

'Don't tell me,' she begged silently. 'I'll find out soon enough.'

'That's the trouble with wives,' she told him. 'They can be very delicate. Us lot, we're made of sterner stuff, we have to be. Don't worry. You'll see.'

'I'll pay,' he offered. "I'll pay you well.'

Meg thought frantically. How far could she push him, she wondered. If it was to be a 'one-only' she must get as much as possible. On the other hand, if it wasn't too much he might come back! A rich regular! That was every street-girl's dream. Inspiration came to her. 'Make me an offer,' she said coyly and began to toy with the top button of her dress.

'I don't know,' he said helplessly. 'I have no idea. A shilling, maybe? No, no, perhaps a florin?'

Meg nearly swooned with excitement. On a good night she would have five or maybe six clients at three-pence a time. That was a bob and a tanner at the most.

She gave him a shrewd look, drew a deep breath and took a chance. 'You're nearly there,' she told him. 'Double it, and you've got yourself a bargain!'

With an impudent toss of her head, she began to unfasten the row of buttons which ran down the front of the dress. She did not normally take off her clothes – five minutes in a corner of a dark alley was all she offered for threepence – but this was different. This was the chance of a lifetime and she wanted to make the experience one that the doctor would wish to repeat. He was also looking very ill-at-ease and must be coaxed into the deed. She wriggled out of the dress and tossed it aside. Beneath it she wore a single flannel petticoat and this, too, she removed with a flourish. Her close-ribbed stays were none too clean, but she could see that the doctor was not in a critical mood.

Gilbert could not take his eyes from the spectacle of a strange woman removing all her clothes. Her casual manner astonished him, for he had always been careful never to watch his wife undress for fear of offending her.

'Going to unlace me, then?' Meg asked, but he shook his head. His conscience was telling him in no uncertain terms to leave before he did something he would live to regret. Another part of his mind, however, held him en-thralled.

Meg unlaced her stays and tossed them on top of her dress and petticoat; then she removed her boots, until finally she stood incongruous in nothing but black woollen stockings. She sat down on a chair and stretched out her legs, which were short but shapely.

'Pull them off, ducks!' she told him. 'They won't bite you.'

Gilbert's throat was dry. 'I don't think . . .' he said hoarsely.

'Go on!' she insisted. 'Be a devil! Don't you want to see me in the altogether?'

But even now Gilbert backed away. 'I think I'd better go,' he whispered. 'I'm sorry but this is impossible . . . really, quite impossible. I cannot – dare not . . .'

Seeing her golden opportunity slipping away, Meg tugged frantically at the pins in her hair and shook out her blonde curls.

'Come on, doctor,' she wheedled. 'You like me, don't you? You won't regret it, I promise you that. You'll be . . .'

Somehow Gilbert managed to tear his gaze away from her naked body and turned to fumble for the door handle. The business-woman in Meg abruptly asserted herself. 'Oy!' she cried. 'You can't go now! Not now you've seen me in the buff! You owe me for that, if nothing else.'

But he had gone and she swore furiously as she heard him clattering along the bare boards of the passage. The front door slammed behind him.

Disappointment overwhelmed her. 'You bloody old fool!' she screamed. 'Gutless! That's what you are – a useless, gutless, apology for a man!'

She aimed a kick at the pile of clothes which lay in the middle of the floor and one of her boots flew across the room to land on top of the palliasses. 'A stupid, gutless old fool!' she mourned, torn between grief and rage. 'I should have known. Your sort are all the same – sodding useless!'

Meg remained in the middle of the deserted room, her hands on her hips, cursing him and shaking her head at the vagaries of fate. A moment ago she had had a rich client within her grasp, but now he was gone and she had not a penny to show for it.

'Bloody men!' she grumbled.

For a moment she stared moodily after him, but then with a sigh she bent to the pile of clothes and from the pocket of her dress extracted a small piece of broken mirror. Holding this up at arm's length she peered into it, turning this way and that as she considered her shape with approval. Suddenly she heard a knock at the front door and her heart leaped.

'Let it be him!' she muttered. 'Please, God, let it be him!'

Hastily abandoning the mirror she pulled on her petticoat and, clutching her dress to her to cover her breasts, she flew along the passage.

When she opened the door she was delighted to discover that her prayers had been answered. The reluctant doctor stood on the step staring at her speechlessly and without a word of reproach she pulled him quickly inside away from prying eyes and closed the door. She was by no means the only prostitute in Fashion Street, and she had no intention of losing him to anyone else.

'I'm ever so glad you changed your mind,' she told him sweetly as she led the way back to her room with a song of triumph in her heart.

*

Ten minutes later, when it was all over, her mouth was badly bruised and there were deep scratches on her back and shoulders. Her whole body ached and her legs trembled.

Avoiding her eyes, he tidied himself and smoothed down his dark hair. Then suddenly he gathered up her clothes and threw them to her.

'For God's sake cover your nakedness,' he told her.

For a moment he watched her, then sank down on to a

chair and covered his face. 'What on earth have I done?' he whispered. 'Oh God, what have I done!!'

Meg, pulling on her clothes, watched anxiously. If he left without paying . . .

'You owe me,' she told him. 'Four bob, that's what you said.'

'Yes, yes. Here . . .'

He pulled a handful of coins from his pocket and without looking at them tossed them into her lap. She counted them incredulously. Nine shillings and sixpence! She'd suffered much worse for far less, she reflected.

'I'm so terribly sorry,' he began. 'So desperately ashamed. I did warn you . . . I just seem to lose control. I can't . . .'

Meg pulled on her stockings, oblivious to his protestations of remorse. She was planning how she would spend the money. First she would buy something nice to eat, a real treat. Then some new clothes. Or maybe a set for the mantelpiece – two vases and a matching clock all made of china. She could get them secondhand for as little as a shilling if they were chipped, and what did that matter? If she bought them brand spanking new, they'd soon *get* chipped.

The prospect of a grand spending spree had almost driven from her mind the recent pain she had experienced. Gilbert was still muttering apologies when she finished dressing and glanced up at him hopefully.

'When are you coming again?' she asked him. 'You'll always be more than welcome.'

CHAPTER TWO

By the time Sally came home an hour or so later, Meg had recovered from her ordeal and could talk about it with convincing bravado. Sally sat amongst the blankets, feeding her baby and listening with rapt attention to Meg's highly exaggerated account of her afternoon caller. Sally was small and dark, with pale skin and eyes that looked too large for her pinched face. The baby was undersized and cried a lot.

'Gave me the best part of half a sov,' Meg told her. 'Ever so handsome, he is, and very grand in his ways. Talks with a plum in his mouth and smells like an earl or a duke. I wouldn't be surprised if he *was* an earl or something.'

'You said he was a doctor,' Sally objected. 'Make up your mind, Meg.'

'Well, he is a doctor, but what I mean is he must come from the gentry. You could tell. Perhaps his father's an earl.'

'I didn't think the gentry went round beating people.'

'He didn't beat me . . . not what you'd call "beat".'

'He's given you a puffy-looking mouth.'

Meg tossed her head. 'You don't understand men,' she told her loftily.

'I hope I never have to understand that sort of man!'

'Oh, we are superior, aren't we!' snapped Meg. 'Just because you've got a man of your own. Well, don't be too cocky, ducks, because who knows what Fate's got in store for *you*? Your precious Alf might get knocked down by a horse tomorrow and then how'd you earn your living? You with a baby an' all.'

Sally's mouth tightened, but she made no reply and Meg went on with her whitewash of the doctor.

'Some men are made that way. They don't mean any harm; they can't help it. It's their animal natures, the beast in them — anyway, who cares about a puffy mouth if he's handing out half-sovs as though he's made of money! I hope he comes back for more, then I shan't need to work for a few weeks. Might even buy myself a new titfer or a pair of boots, and Ellie could do with some new things.'

'Well, it's a bloody hard way to earn money, that's all I can say,' retorted Sally, who was aggrieved to think that her Alf could wear himself out all week and not earn more than five shillings. Meg had a knack of falling on her feet, she thought enviously. Once she had been *given* a gold watch by a sailor who was very drunk, and on another occasion she had managed to steal a silver snuff-box while her elderly client was sleeping off the effects of his indulgence.

Meg touched her mouth gingerly and winced. 'Another day or two and this'll be gone down,' she said hastily, 'and then I'll be laughing. Half a sov! You're just jealous, Sal Berry.'

'Don't kid yourself!'

As Sally moved the child from the left to the right breast, Meg stood up carefully.

'I'm off round to Dora's,' she announced. 'Tell Ellie I won't be long. She's making herself scarce, buying herrings, though I must say she's taking her time over it. Tell you what, I'll treat us all to some eels tonight when Jack comes round. How'd that be? Not too proud to share in my good luck, are you?'

Sally's tired eyes lit up at the promise of an unexpected treat. 'Course not,' she said quickly. 'It's ever so kind of you, Meg. Alf loves eels.'

'Eels it is then, ducks.' A thought struck her. 'I'll get pea soup for Ellie; she'll never manage eels with her mouth. I'll send Fred round with a scuttle full of coal, too, if I see him. Cheerio!'

She left the house bruised in body only, for her spirits were soaring with her new-found wealth and the possibility of more to come. If *only* he would come back, she'd make him an offer – he could be the only one if he'd pay her regularly. Of course she knew his conscience was troubling him right now; that was only natural, being the first time, but he'd soon come to terms with the idea and then he'd want more, she was sure of it. Like a kid with a new toy, he'd been.

If only he'd got enough gumption to keep quiet and not go confessing to his missus like that other fool had done – Marcus Something-or-other, the undertaker. He'd been a promising catch, although he didn't exactly throw his money around like this one did, but he had paid over the odds and looked like being a regular until his conscience caught up with him. Then he'd confessed to his wife and she'd come storming round. Meg shuddered at the memory of that fight. Some women were worse than men, she reflected. Still, a doctor's wife was hardly the type to go in for fisticuffs. Too ladylike by far, probably, but she would certainly put an end to her old man's visits if she ever found out and that would be a shame. No, if the doctor played his cards right no one need be any the wiser – and Meg Swain would be in the money! Meg had had enough of scrimping and making do. Being rich, she thought, would make a nice change.

'Don't do anything hasty,' she warned the absent doctor. 'Keep your mouth shut and we'll all be laughing.'

In spite of her aches and pains she walked jauntily, the route to her cousin's so familiar that her feet took her along Chicksand Street and down Bakers Row without any conscious effort on her part. Her newly-acquired wealth burned in her pocket and her mind was considering a variety of ways of spending it.

She stopped to buy a drink of her favourite peppermint water and later invested in a pennyworth of brandy balls which she knew were Dora's favourite.

Maybe she would pay a shilling or so off the rent she owed – that would keep the landlord quiet – and she would get her best jacket and Ellie's boots out of pawn. The prospect of seeing the jacket again cheered her enormously, for it had a black velvet collar and she always felt good in it.

'If the thieving old whatsit hasn't sold it,' she muttered. He was so quick off the mark. As soon as the time was up the goods went into his window or were sold to the elderly Jew who ran a second-hand clothes shop.

A voice interrupted her thoughts. 'Penny for 'em, Meg.'

She recognized the grimy face of Eddie, bent double beneath the weight of a huge hod of coal. Greeting him, she produced a shilling.

'Drop us some in on your way home,' she told him, 'and no slack. Last time it was rubbish.' She hurried on, ignoring his excuses. Poor old Eddie, he wouldn't last much longer, she thought, with his rotten lungs.

Lifting her skirts as she crossed the dirty streets, she elbowed her way through the crowds which spilled out of the pubs on to the pavement, with a cheeky reply for a man who accosted her. At last she left the main street and turned right.

Dora, her cousin, lived two miles away in Hewlett Road and worked at the Bryant and Mays factory in Fairfield Road. At nineteen she was a year older than Meg, with thick dark hair, a pert nose and a plump but shapely body. The two girls had been close friends since childhood. Now Dora worked as a matchbox filler; on piece-work rates in a very good week she could earn more than eight shillings and was always lending money to her less fortunate cousin.

She opened the door and was surprised to see Meg. As soon as the two girls had exchanged greetings Dora asked, 'What's wrong with your mouth?'

'Had a bit of a barney with one of the girls,' said Meg airily, for she had practised the lie on the way over. 'Nothing to fuss about.'

'Who won?'

'I did, believe it or not!' Meg produced her purse with a flourish. 'I've come to settle up,' she told the astonished Dora. 'Every single penny! What do I owe you? Get the paper.'

Dora led the way up the stairs. She was small, with pale golden-brown eyes, and she wore her abundant hair pulled back into a bun on her neck; her manner was calm, but underlying it was an instinctive wariness. Her small attic room was shabby but clean. Now she was ironing, so a folded blanket covered the small table and was in turn covered by a threadbare piece of scorched sheeting. A pile of newly-ironed clothes rested on a nearby chair and several other garments waited their turn in a wicker basket on the floor.

Dora found the scrap of paper on which Meg's previous loans had been noted down and added it up.

'I hate to tell you, but it's over a pound,' she said. 'You've never got that much, surely?'

Momentarily chastened, Meg had to admit that she had not.

'What's half of it?' she compromised. 'I'll give you half now and half when my gentleman client calls again.'

'Gentleman client!' cried Dora, wide-eyed. 'You never have!'

'Well then, I have,' Meg told her triumphantly. 'Well, as good as. Give me that list, Dor.'

She checked the total. 'One pound, two shillings and threepence.' She hesitated. 'Tell you what I'll do; I'll give you two bob now and the rest later.'

'That'll do,' said Dora, who had never expected to see

any of the money again. 'Two bob it is.' She wrote it down and Meg handed her a florin.

'So you really have got a gentleman client,' Dora went on. 'Well, Meg. I have to hand it to you. You are a goer!' She stowed the money in the pocket of her apron and reached for the flat-iron which was heating in front of the fire. Then she shook out a crumpled petticoat and laid it across the table.

'You talk,' she instructed. 'I'll iron.'

Soon both girls were sucking the brandy balls Meg had purchased on the way over and the tale was being told for the second time that day.

*

When Gilbert eventually returned home Marion looked at him in dismay. His face was flushed, beads of perspiration stood out on his forehead and his hands trembled.

'Gilbert! Whatever is the matter?' she asked. 'Are you ill?'

'I do feel rather hot,' he replied, avoiding her eyes.

'You look terrible. Perhaps you've caught a chill?'

He seized on the suggestion gratefully. 'Yes, yes, that will be it. The weather's changed for the worse and I was not prepared for it. Don't worry, my dear. I'll have a brandy. That will calm . . . warm me.'

She helped him to remove his coat, shook it to remove the worst of the creases and hung it up on the hallstand.

'Go on in and sit by the fire,' she said. 'I'll pour your drink. You'll probably feel better after you've eaten. Sweetbreads in sherry; nice and light.'

Instead of obeying, however, he took hold of her hands and she felt him tremble.

'You *are* ill!' she exclaimed. 'Whatever can it be that has struck so suddenly?'

'Please, Marion, don't fuss. It's nothing serious, I assure you. It's just that . . .' His eyes burned into hers. 'Marion, you know that I respect you. You've never doubted that, have you?'

Her heart leaped uncomfortably. 'Of course not,' she answered. 'I've never doubted you, not even for a moment.'

'Even though we . . .' He shook his head, unable to find the words.

Marion felt a cold finger of fear, wondering what could have provoked this strange outburst. It was so uncharacteristic of Gilbert to reveal any emotion whatsoever; he prided himself on what he called his 'equable disposition'.

'And am I a good husband to you?' he demanded.

'Of course, Gilbert.'

He seemed to relax a little, reassured by her replies.

'I don't understand,' she told him. 'Why are you suddenly asking me these questions? What has happened, Gilbert?'

By way of an answer he pulled her closer and hid his face against hers. Marion was dumbfounded. Embracing in the hallway where they might be seen by the servants! After a moment he gently released her.

'I think I need that brandy,' he told her and led the way into the drawing room.

To her infinite relief he did not seem to pursue his line of thinking, but he was very quiet throughout dinner. Marion tried to draw him out on his day's work, a subject on which he was usually delighted to hold forth, but today he seemed unwilling to talk.

'That child,' she prompted. 'The one with the "phossy jaw". Where did she live? Presumably you found her home?'

He answered with a nod of his head.

'Was it very awful?'

'Ghastly!'

So that was it, she wondered? Had he been shocked by the grim surroundings in which the girl lived?

'And her mother?' she asked. 'What is she like?'

'She has no mother, only a sister. Her name is Ellie; the sister is Meg.'

35

'And is *she* a capable sort of person?'

'Capable?' Briefly he hesitated, then said, 'Oh yes. She's capable.'

'Then you must put the girl out of your mind, dear,' she told him. 'It's not as though she's alone in the world and has no roof over her head. In that respect, she's better off than many others. Gilbert, you must try to be more detached about your patients. You will make yourself ill if you let them upset you like this.'

Gilbert nodded again and she was pleased to see that at least his appetite was unimpaired. In fact, he had eaten more heartily than usual.

He sighed. 'Mrs Gaunt will not be very pleased, though,' he said. 'The sister insists that the girl has toothache and refuses to consider surgery. I should have expected it. They are so ignorant, these poor wretches; they have no understanding of modern medical procedures and an inbred horror of hospitals. Without surgery the child is doomed.'

'Well, at least Mrs Gaunt will be satisfied that you did all you could,' said Marion. 'If there is nothing to be done for the poor child, you won't have to go there again.'

He lifted his head sharply and there was a strange expression in his eyes. 'No, never!' he exclaimed. Incredibly she thought he was *afraid*. 'Never again, I swear it!'

Again that feeling of deep unease swept over her and there was a long silence. She laid down her knife and fork and he became aware for the first time that by contrast with himself she had eaten very little.

'Are you not hungry?' he asked with an attempt at normality.

'No. Gilbert, I'm worried about you. You seem so strange. Disturbed, even.'

'It's nothing. I'm recovered now. Please forget it.'

'Very well,' she agreed. 'We won't talk about it any more.'

'There is nothing to talk *about*!'

'Of course not. Shall I call Kitty to take away the plates?'

'Yes, please.' After a pause he said, 'I shall write to Mrs Gaunt.'

Marion gave up. It was obvious that while he was out something had happened to distress him, but equally obviously he did not intend to share the details with her. Reluctantly, she decided she must respect his wishes and made up her mind to press him no further.

*

Later that night while Marion slept, Gilbert lay wide awake, staring at the strip of ceiling illuminated by the flaring gas-light in the street outside. He thought miserably about the woman who slept at his side, recalling their disastrous attempts to consummate the marriage when his violence had appalled them both. After the first occasion he had sworn never to touch her again. Marion, however, had eventually recovered in both mind and body and had begged him to try once more. She had convinced him, against his better judgement, that his aggression would have diminished, but she had been proved wrong. The act of love, which in other men brought out tenderness, brought out in him a terrifying aggression which he had never suspected and which he was powerless to control.

After a third fiasco, Gilbert had made up his mind that the problem was insoluble and from that night onwards had never asked more from his wife than a chaste kiss. Despising himself for his failure, he tried to make up to Marion for the unhappy situation in which they found themselves. She had never reproached him, but he sensed her growing frustration and over the years they had grown inexorably apart so that now they were simply two people sharing the same home. Companions, certainly. Good friends, possibly. Lovers, never.

Before his marriage he had led a celibate existence, entirely engrossed in his work and eager for advancement. Marion had been the first woman with whom he had shared physical love. Meg Swain had been the second; her willing body and eager ways had betrayed him into adultery while his conscience cried out against the treacherous act, and now his emotions were chaotic. He was deeply ashamed, but exhilarated by what had taken place in that sordid room. Guilt was paramount, but he was conscious also of a deep satisfaction and, worst of all, a terrifying urge to repeat the experience. He had told the girl it would never happen again and he desperately wanted to believe that, yet all his instincts warned him that he had not seen the last of Meg Swain. He had not meant to hurt her and had not appreciated the extent of her sufferings until it was all over. Yet she had insisted that 'It was nothing' and had asked him to come back; had been prepared to offer herself up for two florins; and had *undressed* before him!

At least he had paid her generously, he thought, but took small comfort from the fact. With a heartfelt groan he turned on to his side, longing for sleep but unable to relax. He was a haunted man – haunted by a living ghost. Try as he would he could not rid himself of the memory of her face ... her pretty mouth spoiled, her eyes full of pain which belied the brave words. How many others had enjoyed her body, he wondered. He was so sorry for what he had done, yet he craved the incredible sense of release it had given him and, offered the opportunity, he knew he would do it again. Next time he would ... He pulled himself up short, horrified at this further proof of his weakness. Next time? Was there going to be a next time? He had committed adultery and adultery was a sin in the sight of God. He was a respectable doctor and devout Christian. How could he ever be reconciled to such outrageous behaviour when it was so wildly at odds with everything in which he believed? Another thought occurred to him. Suppose someone found out? He would be ruined. He sighed heavily and whispered, 'Never, never again!' but even as he uttered the words a small inner voice said, 'Just once more' and the prospect alerted every nerve in his body. As he closed his eyes in a kind of ecstasy, he knew in his heart that he was lost.

*

That night in Parfett Street, not so many miles away, Jeff Bannerman was still typing as midnight struck on the nearby church clock. The sound broke his concentration and he stopped, straightened his back and flexed his fingers. He did not notice the chimes during the daytime, but when he first arrived in England and took up residence in the upstairs room the clock had kept him awake at night for the first three weeks and he had been desperate for sleep. Then one Sunday night he had slept right through and from then on had had no further trouble. Mrs Coot, his landlady – elderly and somewhat frail – was glad to have such a personable young man in the house. In return for a modest rent she provided him with a breakfast and a Sunday dinner, and he carried in her coal and even undertook occasional minor repairs about the house, although he was not particularly gifted in this last respect.

In Mrs Coot's eyes, however, he could do no wrong and she talked at length – to anyone who would listen – about her American lodger and his new-fangled typing machine. She treated him like the son she had never had. Jeff found his life in London very comfortable, and was reassured that his decision to try his luck across the Atlantic had been a wise one.

He was a little below average height and there was not too much flesh on his small frame, but his boyish face wore an eager expression and his manner was friendly and outgoing.

Jeff had never considered any other form of employment and never would. He was a born journalist, relishing the excitement and enjoying the thrill of the occasional chase. Nothing was too much trouble; no distance too great. If there was a story to be unearthed, time and effort were of secondary importance. Consequently, he ate at irregular hours and made do with too little sleep. He had no wife and was convinced he did not need one.

He liked to tell people that he was a reporter for the *New York Times*; most of those he told were prepared to believe him and were suitably impressed. Only the discerning few realized that at twenty-two he was rather too young to be holding down such an elevated position in the newspaper world. The truth was that although he did send copy to the *New York Times* they rarely, if ever, made use of it. In fact, his father, Cyrus Bannerman, ran a local newspaper in his home town of Seattle and Jeff's journalistic efforts were therefore guaranteed publication. Cyrus had only one son and he wanted him to carry on the business, so was dismayed by Jeff's announcement that he wished to see the world – by which he meant Europe. After much argument it was agreed that Cyrus would finance a trip to England to last no longer than two years. He would pay Jeff's fare and make him a small allowance. In return, Jeff would write about 'the London scene'.

The evening papers had given a full and frightening account of the battle in Trafalgar Square. Some called it 'Bloody Sunday'; others declared the confrontation to be 'a blot on the Queen's Jubilee year'. The details were horrifying. Thousands of demonstrators had fought with the police. Life Guards and Grenadiers had assisted the police against the frustrated mob, who were armed with a variety of crude but effective weapons. The forces of law and order had eventually prevailed, but hundreds of the demonstrators had been arrested and many more had been injured. It was a miracle no one had been killed.

Jeff had had a bird's-eye view of the trouble from the top of a lamp-post where, clinging on at considerable risk to life and limb, he had watched the battle taking place around him. Unable to take notes, he had committed it all to his prodigious memory and was now transferring it to paper.

It was going to be the best piece of copy he had ever written and he worked in a fever of excitement. He had helped himself to the 'Bloody Sunday' tag invented by one of the English papers and he had figures, too. Editors were impressed by figures. Three hundred Grenadier Guards! And the same number of Life Guards. His words would bring the picture vividly to life. Over 150 people injured! Countless arrests. Tomorrow he would worm his way into the various court-rooms to hear the sentences. That would make the promised 'follow-up' – that and a description of the men's faces as they stood in the dock ... not to mention their womenfolk crying. With any luck, there would be a disturbance in the court: a woman fainting, perhaps, or better still a *pregnant* woman fainting. Or maybe a mother shaking her fist as her son was led away. A father hurling abuse at the magistrates would be good, too ... and possibly being arrested, also, for contempt of court. If not, he would use his fertile imagination.

Grinning suddenly, he bent again to his labours. This would definitely be his best piece to date, there was no doubt about it. London was the place to be, because England's capital city was in a state of deep unrest and anything could happen. France had suffered a revolution and there was no reason to suppose that England was immune to such upheavals. The thousands of poor were to England what the peasants had been to France and Jeff had seen them – ragged, starving, desperate. If the balloon was going up for England it would go up in London, and Jeff hoped he would still be in residence when it happened.

CHAPTER THREE

Dora reached up wearily to tuck back a stray strand of dark brown hair and smoothed her apron over her slim hips, a habit she had when she was tired. She was not pretty in the conventional sense, but her features were regular and she looked hopefully on the world through gold-brown eyes.

She wondered what the time was. It must be nearly dinner-time, she reflected hopefully, for Sid Patten the foreman was nowhere to be seen and it was well known that he liked to slip outside and 'wash his hands' before the bell sounded so as to leave all of his dinner break free to enjoy the ale in the nearby pub. Her head ached from the clatter of machinery and her legs ached from standing. The work was monotonous in the extreme, but Dora rarely complained. With her cousin's dreadful example always before her, she was determined to stay in regular employment and knew that the best way to ensure this was to give the bowler-hatted foreman no cause to find fault with her. Sid Patten could be reasonable at times, but those times were few and far between and meanwhile he could be spiteful and small-minded if someone crossed him. Girls had been known to get the sack after tangling with him, and Dora tried never to give him the slightest excuse for criticism. Now, in spite of her aching legs, she bent industriously over her work-bench and applied herself to the task of filling matchboxes. Like the other five girls in her row, she wore a long apron and her hair was drawn back neatly and fastened at the back of her head as regulation demanded. In front of them were wooden trays full of empty matchboxes and hundreds of double-ended matches waiting to be cut before being packed into them. These boxes had been mass produced but when demand was high some of the girls would be required to make extra ones by hand; Dora much preferred that work, for she was quick with her hands and could make slightly more money that way than at her present job.

Parallel with her row were nearly a dozen similar rows, but here and there she could see gaps where no operator was at work, for it was now June and the demand for matches fell in summer. Some of the girls were already seeking casual employment elsewhere but Dora, who was considered one of the most reliable operators, was still at work. Later on in September more of the girls would take time off.

Dora sighed and straightened up, a hand to her back. The bowler-hatted figure had reappeared and soon Sid Patten was making his way towards her.

Zoe Bush, the girl on Dora's right, whispered, 'Watch out! Old fumble-fingers is on his way!' and she giggled while Dora hid a grin.

Sid Patten made his way along the rows until he stood beside Zoe. He was small but thickset, with a lopsided face and large moustache.

'There's matches on the floor, Miss Bush. Pick them up and quick,' he told her.

'Yes, Mr Patten. I'm sorry, Mr Patten.'

Zoe bent to collect them and as she rose to her feet she felt his leg move against hers and his hand slide over her thigh, but they both knew that she dared not protest.

He moved on to Dora and stood watching her nimble fingers. His glance showed him that there were no fallen matches, so he satisfied himself by standing as close to her as he could; then he reached forward to pick up a filled box and shook it.

'Empty them,' he instructed her.

Resignedly Dora tipped out the matches and waited

until he had counted them. Unable to find cause for complaint, he tossed the empty box back on to the pile and allowed the matches to drop into her outstretched hands.

Dora said nothing, although she was mortified by his actions, because she fully understood why he had done it.

'So, have you changed your mind?' he asked in a low voice.

'No, Mr Patten. I'm afraid not,' she said as firmly as she could.

His cold blue eyes glittered as his fingers closed over her arm. 'I should think again, if I were you,' he told her. 'I really would.' His large moustache brushed the side of her face as he leaned forward to whisper in her ear. 'You could do a sight worse,' he said. 'You'll have another think if you know what's good for you.' Before she could answer he moved on and she saw his arm slide round the waist of a small blonde girl in the next row.

'Jesus to God!' muttered Zoe, who had overheard his whispered remarks. 'You'd best watch your step with him, Dora.'

Dora shrugged with a show of bravado she did not feel. 'He's a toad,' she said. 'I'm not scared of Sid Patten.'

'Well, you damn well should be!' Zoe told her. 'He's dangerous, you mark my words.'

'He's supposed to fancy me,' Dora reminded her.

Zoe snorted. 'All the more reason to go careful. The likes of him can turn real nasty if they don't get their own way.'

'Well, what am I supposed to do?' Dora demanded. 'Accept his offer? You won't get me going out with him, not even for a bite of dinner! More than my life's worth!'

Zoe giggled. 'I don't know about your life,' she said, 'but your honour wouldn't stand much chance! Greasy little toe-rag! I'd like to see him brought down, I really would.'

44

Here the conversation was brought to an abrupt halt by the bell heralding the end of the morning shift, and at once the vast room was transformed as hundreds of eager feet turned towards the doors and a welcome change of scenery. Within minutes, the place was almost deserted. Most of the girls looked forward to a break and went outside the factory in search of something to eat. Those who could not afford this small luxury took a slice of cold dripping toast, or maybe a hunk of bread and cheese, and ate it at the work-bench. Dora hung back until last to avoid another meeting with Sid Patten, but as she left the room the assistant overseer smiled at her. His name was Jerry Mills and he was the complete opposite of his colleague, being authoritative in a quiet way and liked and respected by the women.

'So, Miss Becket,' he said. 'Will we be losing you to the Kent hop-gardens later?'

She returned his smile as she shook her head. 'No, I'll stay on here if I can.'

'Be a bit of a holiday though, wouldn't it?' he persisted. 'The girls that go seem to enjoy themselves. They have a right old time, if you can believe all they say.'

Dora shrugged. 'I don't know if I'd like all the fields and cows and things. I've never been to the country. Have you?'

'I went as a kid with my Ma a few times and I loved it. We young'uns used to climb the trees and paddle in the river. Once we saw a rabbit.' He smiled at the memory. 'We had catapults, of course, and we'd shoot at the birds – never got any. I always bawled my head off when it was time to come back to London. The country's not bad at all; it's the country folk you have to watch. They're not so keen on the Londoners; they don't understand us. My Ma used to say "there's their ways and there's our ways" – that's how she put it. But the grass is lovely and so green, and it's all open and fresh and sort of clean. I reckon you'd like it.'

'Sounds as though you're trying to get rid of me,' Dora laughed. 'Going on about it like that!' She waited as he collected his jacket from the hook and pulled it on.

'No, no!' he protested. 'I don't want you to go. Just thought it might do you good – get some fresh air into your lungs.'

Outside the gates they parted company, for he lived nearby and had a wife who cooked dinner for him. Dora made her way along the street until she came across a pie-man besieged by factory workers and doing a roaring trade. From him she bought a couple of oyster patties which she consumed as she walked back towards the factory, still wrestling with the problem of the unpleasant foreman. He had asked her out 'for a bite' followed by a visit to a 'penny gaff', but neither of these prospects appealed to her in the slightest. The former meant at least an hour in his company; the latter meant a noisy evening in a dingy converted shop watching the bawdy antics of third-rate entertainers. To Meg they were 'a little bit of fun', but Dora shrank from the overwhelming vulgarity. Only once had she accompanied Meg and Sally to what the posters described as 'an evening of riotous fun and laughter', but she had come away heartily sickened by it. To attend such a performance was bad enough, but to go in the company of Sid Patten would be quite unbearable. Her refusal, however, had not been well received and she was afraid that she had made an enemy of him, which could lead to all kinds of trouble.

Dora did not particularly like her job at the factory, but she enjoyed the company of the other girls and appreciated the security of steady employment. If Sid Patten had her sacked she would be hard put to find work elsewhere and although Meg insisted that with her looks she could make a good living on the streets, the idea was abhorrent to her – though she was careful never to say as much to Meg for fear of offending her. If only she could meet a nice man, she thought wistfully. She would like to settle down and have a family, but in her experience nice young men were few and far between. Perhaps she should ask Jerry Mills if he had a brother, she thought, and went back to work with a cheerful smile on her face.

*

At No. 68, Harrington Hill, Pip lay in a small pool of sunlight in the hallway keeping one ear cocked for any sound which might suggest that her mistress was preparing to go out. Putting on her coat would be the best indication that something interesting was about to happen, or perhaps gathering up her lead. On most days she could count on a walk along streets full of fascinating sights and smells. On less frequent occasions, she found herself enjoying the heady delights of a park, though her memory and understanding of such treats was hazy. She was sure that once she had been taken to the seashore and had leaped among the wavelets, frantic with excitement, but that might have been a dream. Now she raised her head as the housekeeper came along the passage from the kitchen and greeted her appearance with a few wags of the tail.

'Well, Pip, you've found the best spot in the house as usual!' Mrs Cobbett told her.

The wag in Pip's tail increased so as to wag her whole body in response to this attention, but as soon as Mrs Cobbett had passed into the morning room the dog relapsed once more into watchful immobility. The sun was warm on her back and she tried to ignore the persistent bluebottle beating itself against the coloured glass panes in the front door. Gradually she relaxed into a peaceful doze, but before this developed into a full slumber she was awakened by the ringing of the front door-bell and was forced to leap to her feet, only half awake, to embark on the furious bout of barking with which she felt impelled to greet all visitors.

'Oh do stop it!' grumbled Mrs Cobbett as she stepped round Pip to open the door.

A young woman, little more than a girl, stood on the step. She was tidily dressed and her fair hair was neatly tucked away beneath a bonnet.

'Yes?'

Mrs Cobbett managed to inject a note of discouragement into the word for she did not approve of the doctor's less affluent clients who, in her opinion, lowered the tone of the place. They were, she felt sure, only tolerated as a sop to Mrs Gaunt, who in Mrs Cobbett's opinion ought to know better than to encourage them.

'I want to see the doctor,' the girl said firmly. 'I *must* see him!'

Mrs Cobbett's eyes gleamed with triumph as she answered, 'Well, you can't see him, because he isn't here.'

'I'll wait then,' said the girl.

'You can't wait because it isn't surgery hours. Come back again at six o'clock and we'll –'

'I'll wait.'

Mrs Cobbett was amazed by the girl's persistence. What were the poorer classes coming to, she wondered indignantly. The newspapers were right; they certainly were getting above themselves and would have to be put in their places with a firm hand. Give some people an inch and they'd take a yard!

She played her trump card and said, 'The waiting room doesn't open until five-thirty, so you'll *have* to come back later.' So saying she began to close the door, but to her surprise the girl thrust her foot in and held it open.

'And I tell you I'm staying,' she insisted. 'I won't be no trouble, but I won't leave here until I've seen Dr Reid.'

Mrs Cobbett glanced down. The girl was wearing men's boots!

'Wait here,' she said icily. 'I'll tell the doctor's wife

you're here, and perhaps *she* can get it into your head that you will have to come back this evening.'

A minute or two later Marion went out to speak to her, and for a moment the two women regarded each other curiously until Marion broke the silence: 'I understand you wish to see my husband?'

'I'm not leaving 'til I do.'

'Why can't you come back later like anybody else? I don't understand.'

'It's urgent.'

'In what way urgent? Are you desperately ill?'

'No, but I've got to see him.'

'But he's not here. My housekeeper tells me she has already made that perfectly clear to you.'

The girl tossed her head. 'If you won't let me in, then I'll sit on your step, but I shan't budge 'til he gets back.'

Marion regarded her helplessly, wondering how best to deal with the situation. She seemed most determined, yet she did not appear to be in need of medical attention. What could she possibly want with Gilbert? Presumably she was one of Mrs Gaunt's lame ducks.

'Are you connected with Mrs Gaunt?' she asked. 'Mrs Gaunt of Clissold Park?'

'*Her!*' the girl exclaimed. 'I'm not having any truck with the likes of her.'

'So you *are* connected with her.' Marion felt slightly reassured.

'Not so's you'd notice.'

'What's your name?'

This question appeared to alarm the girl who looked around her nervously, pursing her lips, and Marion saw doubt in her eyes.

'I'm nobody,' she told Marion sharply. 'Just someone who wants to see the doctor.'

'You can see him at six o'clock,' Marion repeated. 'It's only a few hours; if you are not ill, then you can wait that long, surely?'

49

Some of the girl's bravado had by now deserted her and she stood with furrowed brow, uncertain what to do next. Before she could rally her resources Marion repeated, 'Come back at half-past five and you will be the first to see the doctor. That really is the best I can suggest.'

The girl muttered something that sounded suspiciously like 'Miserable cow!' but Marion pretended deafness as she closed the door and leaned back against it.

Mrs Cobbett, who was still hovering in the background, said, 'Well, did you ever hear such a thing! Cheeky baggage! You're much too soft with them, ma'am. A box round the ears is what her sort needs.'

'They don't know any better,' said Marion.

In spite of her small 'victory' she was worried, for intuition told her that the girl was not ill at all. What, then, was her business with Gilbert? She would have to ask him later.

The housekeeper returned to the kitchen muttering indignantly to herself, while Marion looked down absent-mindedly at Pip who was staring pointedly at the front door and throwing occasional looks in her direction.

'Oh, Pip! You want your walk, don't you?'

The dog began to bark excitedly and Marion reached for her jacket and collected the lead from a hook on the hallstand.

'Come along then,' she said and opened the front door.

When she reached the end of the road a young crossing-sweeper darted forward with his hand outstretched for her penny. As he began to sweep a path through the filth that covered the road, Marion's interest was caught by two young women talking earnestly together on the far side of the road. One of them she recognized as her recent visitor; the other was an attractive darkhaired girl of about the same age. Had the girl called on

50

her companion's behalf, she wondered; but now the two were walking away, their heads still together, deep in conversation and unaware of Marion's presence. Marion crossed the road and then turned in the opposite direction. She must ask Gilbert what it was all about, she told herself, yet she shrank from the prospect. Something about the girl had disturbed her more deeply than she cared to admit, but forty minutes later when she returned home she still had not established what it was.

*

When he arrived back from his calls, Gilbert claimed he could make no more sense of the girl's visit than Marion had done, but she had the feeling that he was not being entirely honest with her.

'It sounds like Ellie's sister,' he said reluctantly. 'You remember – the child with "phossy jaw"?'

'Then you think she came about Ellie?'

'I really don't know. I'm a doctor, not a mind-reader. These people are odd creatures,' he continued. 'Unpredictable at the best of times.'

'I couldn't understand why she had made such a secret of her name.'

He shrugged 'I don't have the answers, Marion. We shall have to wait until this evening to find out.'

Five-thirty came and then six o'clock. The waiting room filled up with the victims of everyday ailments – a strained wrist, warts on the hand, an inflamed eye, abdominal pains. The patients sat in an uncomfortable silence, mainly ignoring each other's existence. A baby cried, an old man gasped painfully for breath, a middle-aged woman dozed. The girl did not put in an appearance and Marion was glad, for in a strange way she had felt threatened by her. Ridiculous, she told herself, but true nonetheless.

That evening – because they were busy – Marion acted as receptionist, handling the paperwork, handing out the prescriptions her husband had prepared and offering what reassurance she could with a cheerful smile and ready sympathy. Time passed and still Ellie's sister did not arrive.

While Gilbert was busy with his last patient, Marion made a quick visit to the kitchen and told Mrs Cobbett that if the girl ever called again out of surgery hours she was on no account to be admitted to the house. The housekeeper, with the doctor's best interests always at heart, agreed willingly.

*

May Thripp lifted her lorgnette and regarded her sister warily.

'School! School!' she exclaimed. 'That's all I hear. A school for ragged children? Really, Amelia, I do feel you are getting carried away.'

May was small and plump, with frizzed grey hair and blue eyes which had once been as bright as Ralph's.

'Nonsense,' said Amelia. 'It's a perfectly sound idea. Homeless children need homes and illiterate children need schooling. I shall provide both. You should be encouraging me, May, not behaving as though I have suddenly lost my wits. There are people in this city who have money to spare and you and I are among them – oh, don't plead poverty, May; it cuts no ice with me. There are other people, too, with the capacity to help those less fortunate. I shall give them the chance to use their money *creatively*.'

'You are making a speech, Amelia,' said May. 'Do stop it.'

Ignoring the interruption, Amelia went on, 'I shall start in a modest way and then expand as the finances become available. It will be a charity. No money that has to be repaid. Every penny must be donated. I have already looked into the question of fund-raising and it is quite fascinating. It will be an interest for you, May, and will give you something to think about. I thought that you and I should set an example by donating a thousand pounds each.'

'A thousand?' May's lorgnette rose again. 'Do my ears deceive me?'

'Of course not,' retorted Amelia. 'Your hearing is very good for a woman of your age.'

May bridled. 'Please don't use that phrase, Amelia. You make me sound old and I hope I shall live for a long time yet. A woman of my age, indeed! You really are becoming very outspoken; I don't know what Mama would say if she could hear you. She always said you were headstrong, even as a child.'

Amelia laughed. 'Then she would hardly be surprised to know that I am headstrong still.'

'You should have remarried,' May said with a sigh. 'A husband would have moulded you — made you more pliable and less inclined to flights of fancy.'

'I had no wish to remarry,' Amelia told her, 'and I certainly had no desire to be "moulded", as you put it. What do I need a husband for? I have plenty of money and I knew exactly how I wanted to bring up my son. Even you must admit that I haven't made such a bad job of it.' She looked affectionately towards Ralph.

'But of course. I'm perfect, aren't I?' he suggested.

'Not perfect, Ralph,' May told him, 'but you could be a lot worse. You should be married by now. What's wrong with you? Can't you find anyone good enough?'

'I can't find anyone rash enough!' he amended with a smile.

Amelia said sharply, 'Ralph is much too young to settle down, May. Please don't put ideas into his head. I shall need him to help me with my plans and I don't want him rushing to the altar. Now to revert to my school — you do see, I hope, the vast potential for good it would offer, and you must make up your mind to help me with it. I have thought it out most carefully and I thought we would start with just ten children —'

'Girls, I hope,' her sister put in firmly. 'Boys can be so horribly rough and rude –'

Amelia went on talking as though May had not spoken. '. . . so that we need to employ only one teacher. I'm sure we could find a suitable person if we make enquiries. Only recently someone mentioned an impoverished niece who had been well educated before the family fell upon hard times. She might do very well if I can remember who she is. I shall inspect suitable premises which must be easy to keep warm in winter so that a single wood-burning stove might be sufficient. I am thinking of calling it "The Queen's Jubilee School" as being most appropriate; of course the celebrations were last year, but the germ of the idea was in my head at that time.'

She paused for breath and Ralph waited hopefully. These long visits to his aunt bored him and he did hope that his mother's assessment of the situation was accurate, for she had been quite sure that 'the apple is ripe for picking' (May being the apple!) and that all her previous talks with her sister would have prepared the ground for this final revelation about the school.

May simply muttered, 'Hmm,' and then, undecided how to answer, said, 'Where is the tea? Janet is getting so slow that I think I shall have to get rid of her.'

Since she had been threatening to sack her elderly housemaid for at least ten years, Amelia made no reply but waited impatiently for her comment.

'A ragged school,' mused the old lady. 'I don't know, Amelia. The setting up of such places is not the problem, it's the day-to-day running that requires earnest consideration. Suppose you were to fall ill – who would be responsible for the management of the school? Who will raise the necessary funds after you've gone? You will not live for ever, Amelia.'

'I have thought it all through,' Amelia assured her, trying not to let her excitement show. Her sister was obviously interested in the scheme. 'We would set up a trust with the assistance of the bank manager to supervise the project, and we would elect a small committee on which Ralph would serve.'

'Hmm.'

Amelia looked at Ralph, who hid his surprise at her words. He correctly interpreted his mother's look to mean 'Say something helpful' and tried to think of something, but most of the salient points appeared to have been covered.

'Ralph, do be a dear and ring the bell again,' May asked him. 'I know it's Cook's day off, but it cannot possibly take half an hour to toast and butter a plate of tea-cakes. It really is getting beyond a joke.'

Amelia prayed for patience as her sister looked thoughtful.

'Would there be a strong link with the church?' May asked. 'I do think the presence of a man of God would have a most uplifting effect on the children – or should have. Mind you, some of those godless wretches . . .'

'May, it's exactly because they *are* godless that they need our help,' Amelia insisted. 'And yes, certainly, there will be links with the church, very strong links. I have mooted the project with the Reverend Albert Craythorne at Holy Trinity and . . .'

Suddenly Ralph had a brainwave. 'Why don't we call it the Weston Jubilee School?' he suggested. 'I think that has a very fine ring to it, don't you, Mama?'

Amelia looked at him in astonishment, stunned by his perspicacity. 'I most certainly do,' she agreed.

Harold Weston was the man May should have married but he had died of consumption a week before their wedding day.

They waited breathlessly for May's reaction. A soft blush of emotion swept into her faded cheeks and her eyes glowed.

'The Weston Jubilee School,' she whispered. 'Now, I wonder . . .'

'Or the Harold Weston Memorial School,' Amelia suggested, 'because perhaps, by the time it's opened, we really will be too late for the Queen's Jubilee. Oh yes! Wouldn't that be the most marvellous memorial! The Harold Weston Memorial School! And you would have to open it, May, and unveil the plaque.'

Again they waited as May, deeply moved, fumbled for her handkerchief and wiped away a tear. 'Forgive me, I'm a sentimental old fool!' Then she nodded. 'My poor, dear Harold. Very well then, Amelia, I will help you with your school. Harold would have wished it; I am sure he would.'

Amelia flashed her son a look of deep gratitude before moving from her chair to drop a light kiss on her sister's cheek.

'Thank you, May,' she began. 'I'm sure you'll . . .' She paused as running footsteps sounded in the hallway and a young scullery-maid burst into the room without knocking. Her face was pale and her cap was crooked.

'Oh, ma'am!' she cried. 'It's Janet, she's in a swoon. I just come in from the yard and there she was on the floor, and the plate's broke and there's tea-cakes all over the place! It gave me such a turn . . .'

By the time they reached the kitchen Janet was beginning to recover consciousness and insisted that it was nothing but a dizzy spell, but May decided that she must see a doctor. Janet Neace had been with her for thirty-five years. Nowadays she was slow and full of rheumatics, but she had come to a house as a young widow soon after May's bereavement and the similarity in their situations had created an unspoken bond between them. May could not imagine the house without her.

'Now, where is the nearest doctor?' May wondered aloud. 'I have never needed one in my whole life, thank the Lord. What about your man, Amelia? Reid, is it? Could we send her there?'

'Of course. Ralph can take her round at once while we finish our discussion.'

Ralph groaned inwardly but said nothing. His mother was very fond of finding little jobs for him to do and was constantly volunteering on his behalf, but as he helped the old woman out to the carriage his face brightened. It had occurred to him suddenly that he might see the doctor's wife again.

*

Ralph Gaunt was not a selfish young man; he was simply rather spoilt. His father had died within a year of his birth and his mother, a very wealthy widow, had flatly refused suggestions that she should look for another husband and insisted on bringing up her son according to her own inclinations. He had had the best education and had shown great artistic talent, so he had been sent to Italy for a year. This had whetted his appetite for further travel, so that after a few months back in England he had departed once more for an extended trip to Europe. Life was good to Ralph Gaunt. He was good looking, having inherited his father's slim build and his mother's delicate colouring. He had a charming manner, strongly laced with natural confidence and a ready wit, so that his contemporaries enjoyed his company and elderly relatives doted on him. The world was a happy and rewarding playground and he tried not to take life too seriously.

This attitude was the only bone of contention between mother and son, for Amelia thought him sadly lacking in social conscience. When she upbraided him on the subject, however, he laughingly insisted that her own conscience was quite large enough for both of them.

Young women appeared to feature very little in his life except as casual acquaintances, and Amelia was hopeful that she would have her son at home for a few more years. Meanwhile he was back in England once more and they must soon explore the various possibilities of a career, for although there was no need for him to work his mother insisted that he must occupy himself usefully. Despite his talent he showed no real interest in becoming an artist. Amelia told herself that they would have to think about it later, for she had more important things on her mind at present.

*

When Ralph and Janet arrived at Harrington Hill Dr Reid was at home, and although the surgery was not due to start for another hour he felt unable to turn away one of Mrs Gaunt's protégées. While he took Janet into his consulting room, Ralph was left alone with Marion Reid.

Today she was wearing a dark brown skirt and frilled white blouse which together emphasized her neat figure. She had fine brown eyes and good features and her dark hair waved naturally around her face. If her manner were not so strained she would be quite attractive, he thought. He looked at her boldly, deliberately allowing his admiration to show in his eyes, and was amused to see that she made an almost imperceptible movement away from him. She appeared to be on the defensive – but from what? Most women were flattered by his appraising stare, but the doctor's wife seemed startled by it. She was obviously much younger than her husband and Ralph wondered what she had found attractive about Gilbert Reid, who looked much older than her and was beginning to lose his hair. Probably he had never been a handsome man, and now he was past his prime.

Ralph smiled at her. 'I feel I should apologise for all these untimely visits,' he told her. 'Your husband is very long-suffering.'

'Please do not concern yourself,' she replied. 'Your mother is a generous, kind-hearted woman and I'm sure my husband is pleased to be of service in any way he can.'

They regarded each other for a moment; there seemed nothing else to say and because Ralph was afraid she

58

would leave him alone in the waiting room he said quickly, 'My last visit here was some months ago. Do you recall the little waif with the deformed jaw? Poor wretch. I'm ashamed to say I could hardly bear to look at her.'

She nodded, her expression serious. 'My husband was very sorry he could not help her. He did make further enquiries, you know, and it made him very angry because these people are well aware of the risks. The factory at Fairfield has a room set aside for dentistry but the workers hate it, of course, and when they're due for treatment they stay away. Everyone knows that "phossy jaw" is a real risk, but they prefer to take a chance.'

'On the premise that it always happens to someone else?'

'That's right. They *joke* about it.'

'Good heavens!'

'It's tragic.'

He nodded, searching his mind for a more cheerful topic with which to delay her further. If only he could make her smile . . . or laugh! He would like to see her face wearing a more cheerful expression, but although he was rarely at a loss for words in the company of women today the easy phrases eluded him and he could think of nothing at all humorous to say.

At that moment, however, a small King Charles spaniel bustled into the room and with a quick movement the doctor's wife stooped to pick her up. As she hugged the dog to her, Ralph patted it.

'So you've decided I'm *not* a burglar,' he said to the dog. 'You barked most ferociously when we arrived.'

The smile he had hoped for now lit up Marion's face and made her almost beautiful.

'Don't take it personally,' she said. 'Pip barks at everyone. She's a good little watchdog and tries to protect me, so I can't bring myself to scold her. Do you have any pets, Mr Gaunt?'

'A cat,' he told her, 'but I must admit that it does not

59

figure very largely in our affections. It's an independent creature and only condescends to return home when hungry. I am not a cat lover, I'm afraid.'

Marion dropped a light kiss on top of the dog's head. 'I wouldn't be without Pip for all the tea in China,' she confided. 'She is such wonderful company and so affectionate; she really loves me, you know.'

So, thought Ralph, she is starved of love!

As he stroked the dog he allowed his hand to brush Marion's arm, but she appeared not to notice his touch.

'Pip sleeps at the bottom of the bed,' she went on. 'She has a basket in a corner of the room and goes to sleep in it most dutifully, but when I wake up in the morning there she is at the bottom of the bed!'

'You lucky little dog,' he said, ruffling Pip's fur and allowing his fingers to touch Marion, this time on the hand, but she merely hugged the dog once more and put her back on the floor.

'How old is she?'

'Six. But I don't think that's old for a dog, do you?'

He shook his head emphatically. 'These little dogs have a good long life-span,' he invented. 'Don't worry. You will have Pip around for many years yet.'

Another smile lit up her face and suddenly, inexplicably, he longed to take her in his arms and swing her round so that her feet left the ground; to make her helpless with laughter. He would give her a dozen dogs, he thought, if that would make her happy.

A thought occurred to him and he asked casually, 'Do you have any children?'

The light faded at once from her face and the closed-in look returned as she shook her head. 'It just wasn't meant to be,' she said, as though she had used the phrase many times before. 'I would have liked . . .' She stopped, confused, and sighed, then apparently decided she had already said too much. 'You must excuse me now,' she told him. 'I have to speak with my housekeeper.'

'And will you then come back to me?' he asked, allowing the most subtle inflexions to give the innocent words greater significance.

He saw at once that she had recognized his ploy. 'I'm afraid not,' she said. 'I have to supervise dinner. I'm sure you will excuse me.'

When she had gone, Ralph considered with some amusement what, if anything, he had learned from their brief conversation. He deduced from the haunted look in her eyes that she was not a very happy woman, but before he could give the matter further thought the doctor came into the room with a small pill-box in his hand and Janet trailing disconsolately behind him.

'I have told Mrs Neace she is to go straight to bed and take things easily for a few days,' he said to Ralph. 'Rise at lunchtime – something like that. And she must take these pills. Tell your aunt there is nothing terribly wrong, but we are none of us getting any younger.'

He gave the old woman a reassuring pat on the shoulder and put the pill-box into her hand. She looked anxiously at Ralph, who said heartily, 'Well, that's a relief, Janet, isn't it? Nothing for you to worry about.'

Both men knew that she was probably worrying more about the prospect of losing her job than about the state of her health, but Ralph knew he must leave that side of the matter to his aunt. He thanked the doctor again and said, 'Please send the bill to Mrs Neace's employer.' Then he took Janet's arm. 'Now we must get you home,' he told her. 'Then you can go straight to bed – doctor's orders!' And, ignoring her protests that she was 'fine', he helped her into the carriage and they were driven away.

*

The following morning Marion wrote to her sister:

I was so pleased to receive your letter. It seems an age since one of your familiar envelopes appeared on

61

the mat. It always brightens my day to hear from you. I am glad your bronchitis is improving. I think the sunshine has obviously helped. Biarritz was certainly a good idea. What a pity you cannot afford to spend a winter out there. If you could, I think your troubles would be over, at least as far as your chest is concerned.

Thank you for your invitation to come home, but I cannot accept. I am not always needed, but on occasions the surgery fills to overflowing and Gilbert cannot manage single-handed. If only he would take on temporary help. It is flattering to believe I am indispensable (his words, not mine!), but I would so like to see you. He has suggested that you might come here. Now that poor Papa has gone, there is nothing to keep you in Kingston except your beloved plants and your new housekeeper could surely minister to them for a few days? You insist that you are not lonely, but I do so hate to think of you all alone in that big house with no one but the servants. Do think over my suggestion that you sell it and buy something smaller closer to London (and to me!).

Write back soon and say that you will come. We would have quite a lot of time together, and if I am helping Gilbert with the surgery you could amuse yourself with a good book or the piano – or take Pip for a walk and earn her undying devotion! I know you are not fond of Gilbert, but he has been very pleasant to me lately. (Not that he was ever unkind, but he has never been a demonstrative man.) Last week he bought me a bunch of roses! I was speechless with surprise.

Anyway, do think about the invitation. I would so enjoy your company.

Pip sends her love and so do I.

Your loving sister,
Marion.

She sat back in the chair and imagined her sister moving around in the large, gloomy house where they had grown up together. Rachel had stayed at home to nurse both parents through their last illnesses and was now alone. She had never married and probably never would, for she was seven years older than Marion and took after their father with his plain features and sallow complexion. She alone had warned Marion against marrying Gilbert (on the grounds that he was too old for her), but Marion had allowed herself to be persuaded by her parents that with dedication she could make the marriage a success. They had always been close as children, with Rachel playing the part of the protective elder sister. Their two brothers, both older than Marion but younger than Rachel, had died in an outbreak of whooping-cough and their father had never recovered from the disappointment of losing both heirs. His daughters were made aware of his indifference; Rachel had resented this deeply and they had quarrelled frequently as she grew older, but when he was widowed she had stayed at home to care for him. Later she had nursed him through a prolonged illness until his death early in 1887. For her part, Marion had longed for children of her own and marriage to Gilbert had seemed to offer her that. Since the marriage however the two sisters had spent very little time in each other's company. Now Marion reflected that it would be good to see Rachel again.

She glanced down at Pip who lay beside her chair, head resting on paws. 'Would you like Rachel to come and see us?' she asked and the tail wagged dutifully.

As Marion rose to fetch her coat the front door-bell rang, immediately followed by an impatient banging which sent Pip out of the room and along the hallway in a frenzy of excitement while Marion followed, a slight frown on her face.

'Who was that?' she asked Kitty, who was closing the front door.

Kitty turned, grinning proudly. 'Please, ma'am, it's a parcel for Pip!' she said, holding out a peculiar ring-shaped package about seven inches in diameter. It was wrapped in brown paper and resembled a large dough-nut.

'What on earth . . .' Marion exclaimed as she took it wonderingly.

'A boy brought it,' Kitty told her. 'An urchin boy. Then he just ran off laughing.'

Pip's name was on the parcel, followed by the address, but there was no clue to the sender.

Marion regarded it uncertainly and Kitty asked hope-fully, 'Aren't you going to open it, ma'am?'

'I suppose so.'

As she did so, a folded note fell out and Kitty bent to retrieve this. Inside the wrapping paper Marion found a brand-new dog collar of pale brown leather decorated with gold-coloured studs; on a small brass plate attached to it Pip's name and address was engraved.

'Oh, ma'am, it's lovely!' cried Kitty. 'Oh, do put it on her, ma'am. Oh, Pip! You *are* a lucky dog.'

Marion knelt down, calling Pip to her, but as her fingers removed the old collar her mind was racing. Who on earth could have done such a thing? Not Gilbert, certainly, and it did not seem the kind of thing Rachel would do considering she was not particularly fond of ani-mals.

Pip was revelling in the attention she was receiving and, as soon as the new collar was fastened, she pranced about the hall while Marion and Kitty made suitably admiring noises. Marion took the note from the maid and unfolded it.

Dear Pip, [she read]. I am sure your mistress has warned you about accepting gifts from strange men, so I will confess my identity and trust you will accept the enclosed from your devoted admirer, Ralph Gaunt.

Marion felt her cheeks burn. Ralph Gaunt! 'It's from a friend, Kitty,' she said. Without understanding why, she did not want to reveal his name.

'A friend?' Kitty's disappointment was obvious but Marion hardened her heart. If she decided not to tell Gilbert (although why she should do this was not clear to her) she would not want the servants to know.

'No one you know,' she elaborated, then felt annoyed with herself for behaving so stupidly.

'I see, ma'am,' said Kitty, her tone of voice suggesting otherwise.

As the maid bent to fondle Pip, Marion cursed her own excessive caution. Suppose Ralph Gaunt should call again and refer to the collar in front of Kitty? Kitty would then wonder why Marion had lied about it and might then assume . . . It was all too ridiculous for words! Why hadn't she simply said, 'It's from Mr Gaunt,' and laughed it off? That would have been the most natural thing to do.

'Well, Pip, you are a pretty girl,' said Kitty. She straightened up and went on, 'May I take her to show Cook?' Marion nodded, but all the excitement of the gift had been spoiled by her foolish over-reaction. 'Marion, you are such a fool!' she told herself.

Back in the morning room she sat down and re-read the note, observing as she did so that her hands were shaking.

'Oh, this is absurd!' she muttered, but in her heart she knew exactly why she was alarmed. Ralph Gaunt had sent a gift to Pip because he could not send one directly to *her*. On his last visit he had deliberately allowed his hand to brush against her while pretending to fondle the dog; she had known it intuitively, but at the time had refused to acknowledge it even to herself. She had also seen the challenging look in his eyes and had fully appreciated the nuance of meaning he had given his apparently innocent question: 'And will you then come back to me?' His attentions had at once flattered and disturbed her.

Since her marriage she had been entirely faithful to her husband and had never given a second glance to any man, although she had frequently considered how infinitely more full and satisfying her life might have been with a different partner.

Glancing down at the note once more, she smiled at the wording. He had been very clever, she would grant him that. 'Accepting gifts from strange men'. Surely she was accepting the gift on Pip's behalf? And 'Your devoted admirer' – was he really suggesting that he was *her* devoted admirer, or was she reading too much into an innocent gift sent merely to amuse her? She was angry with herself for half hoping it was not the latter. After all, she argued silently, there was nothing wrong with being admired. Gilbert ought to be pleased that another man was paying her such a compliment – if that *was* what he was doing.

'Ralph Gaunt,' she whispered, 'why did you do this?'

She thought about him – the way his blond hair fell across his forehead and the bold look in his blue eyes. He was a very attractive young man. A sigh escaped her. She must tell Gilbert for he would see the collar . . . unless she took it off again, but then Kitty would notice and might pass comment on its disappearance.

Restlessly, she rose and moved across to the window, wondering if the delivery boy had had to report back to the sender of the gift, and if so had Ralph Gaunt been in the immediate neighbourhood? Her eyes widened suddenly as a new thought struck her. Was he out there now? Carefully she lifted the edge of the curtain and looked quickly up and down the hill. There was no sign of him and she did not know whether to be pleased or sorry.

'Why?' she exclaimed aloud. 'Why did you do it?'

And how was she to thank Ralph? Would it be proper to write a note? She hardly knew him, yet it was necessary to thank him for the collar which had obviously cost a considerable amount of money.

When Gilbert came home she waited for an opportune moment and than said casually, 'You will never guess what happened today. A present came for Pip – a collar from Ralph Gaunt. Wasn't that nice of him?'

Gilbert frowned. 'A collar for Pip?' he echoed. 'How very odd.'

She managed a smile although her mouth felt tight with nerves. 'I thought so too,' she told him. 'He *is* fond of animals, I suppose. Should I answer the note, do you think?'

'What note is that?'

'Oh, he sent a funny little note addressed to Pip.'

Gilbert snorted derisively. 'Ridiculous!' He frowned as though the matter was already irritating him. 'Just write a brief note to thank him. Collar, indeed! You'd think he would have better things to do with his money. Mind you, his mother is to blame. She worships him; anyone with half an eye could see that, it's written all over her face when she looks at him. If he had to *earn* his money like the rest of us, he would think twice before wasting it on dog collars.'

Marion found that her heart was beating faster than usual. She *could* answer the note!

At the first opportunity, she escaped to her room and took up pen and paper. She had thought long and hard about the wording of a possible reply and now it was speedily committed to paper.

Dear Mr Gaunt,
   My mistress has allowed me to accept your kind gift, for which I offer heartfelt thanks and a hope that on some future occasion you may see how well it looks on me.

Your affectionate friend,
Pip.

As she slipped it into an envelope, Marion wondered

about the last line of the note. Would he consider that an invitation to call again? And if he did, would she object? She shrugged slightly and told herself, 'The whole thing is absurd. I shall put it out of my mind as soon as the letter is safely in the pillar-box.' At least it would be something amusing to tell Rachel, she reflected. Together they would have a good laugh about it and there the matter would end.

She looked down at Pip. 'You see what trouble you have caused me?' she said, then bent to hug the dog so fiercely that Pip was forced to squeal in self-defence.

*

Meg had given Sally sixpence to make herself scarce, taking Ellie and her own baby with her so that Meg could talk to her 'gentleman client' privately. A week had passed since, accompanied by Dora, she had tried to contact him at his home. Now that he had finally put in a belated appearance, Meg's well-rehearsed phrases flew out of the window as she countered his furious accusation that she had dared to approach his home.

'Well, what if I did?' she cried. 'That stuck-up wife of yours refused to let me in! Refused point blank. Who the hell does she think she is, high and mighty madam! I very nearly told her a thing or two. Oh yes! I could wipe the smug look off her face if I wanted to!'

Gilbert caught her by the wrist. 'If you ever dare to tell her about us . . .'

'You'll what?' she challenged.

'I'll have you thrown into prison!'

'Oh yes? And on what charge, may I ask?' She jerked her arm free and glared at him defiantly. 'What have I done what's criminal – that you can *prove*?'

'I shall think of something,' he told her. 'It would be your word against mine.'

'Oh, ta very much!' She almost spat the words. 'Oh, that is nice after all I've put up with from you.'

'I've paid you well, damn you!'

Suddenly remembering the news she had for him which was to ensure her an income for many years to come, Meg made an effort to control her temper. She really must not ruin her chances at this late stage, she told herself. In spite of Dora's advice to the contrary, she had allowed her pregnancy to proceed in the hope that the doctor, as a respectable and God-fearing man, would be prepared to support his child and the mother in reasonable comfort. So far he had been very generous, but how much more generous might he be with a child to support? Meg had visions of a rosy future in more salubrious lodgings paid for by the child's father. A rich man's *mistress*! The word had a magical ring to it.

So now she bit back the flow of angry words and forced a smile instead, as she laid one hand placatingly on his arm and looked into his eyes beseechingly.

'Oh, please don't let's quarrel,' she said. 'Look, sit yourself down and . . .'

But it appeared that he was not to be so easily mollified, for he ignored her and remained standing, his expression grim.

'I have no wish to sit down,' he told her coldly. 'I want an explanation. I want to know why you expressly defied my instructions, which were most explicit, to stay away from my home. I told you when I first started coming here that my wife was never to hear of it, so for you to force a confrontation like that was unforgivable.'

'I truly didn't mean no harm by it,' she insisted, her tone even more conciliatory.

The truth was that she had done it partly out of devilment, partly out of curiosity to see the house where he lived and partly to impress Dora. Also she had wanted to see the doctor's wife and be seen in return. The meeting, although not entirely successful, had been a bit of excitement.

'I knew she wouldn't know me from Adam and she didn't, did she?'

'She was rather suspicious,' he said. 'My wife is not stupid. You took an unnecessary risk when there was no need at all for such a visit.'

Meg took a deep breath. 'But there *was* a need. I wanted to tell you a bit of good news.'

He drew his brows together, puzzled. 'Good news? What could you possibly tell me that would be good news?' he asked.

Meg felt a flutter of fear. She had taken a terrible chance and if he took her news the wrong way it would all be over. Earlier she had been so sure but now, face to face with him, she was suddenly doubtful. She crossed her fingers.

'How'd you like to be a father?' she asked him.

Her attempt at jauntiness failed miserably and her rapidly beating heart frightened her. As she waited for his reply, her worst fears were realized; his face stiffened and the colour drained away, leaving him white and shaken. He opened his lips but made no sound. Meg could not bear the silence nor the look of horror on his face.

'A kid of your own!' she cried desperately. 'A son and heir – all men want a son and heir.'

Without allowing his gaze to leave her face, Gilbert groped for a chair and sat down heavily. 'A child from all that pain? Oh, no! It's too horrible! It's obscene!'

'How d'you mean, obscene?'

'It's out of the question. A child! Oh, no! Never!'

He considered her body, which showed little change. 'You might be mistaken . . .' he began.

'Well, I'm not! I've just moved the button on my skirt – see here!'

He shook his head, averting his eyes.

Meg managed a tight-lipped smile. 'Some girls don't show much. My Ma never did.'

'I won't allow it!' he whispered harshly.

Meg tossed her head. 'Bit late for "won't allow it".

I'm having a kid and it's yours. Oh, for Pete's sake, Gilbert! I thought you'd be pleased!'

He lifted his head and she was shocked by his expression. 'Are you out of your mind?' he demanded hoarsely. 'The prospect of *you* bearing *my* child is utterly preposterous. You must get rid of it at once. You must know someone – your sort always does.' As she made no answer he cried, 'Do you hear me, you wretch? You must *not* have the child.'

'I heard you,' she said sulkily. 'There's no need to carry on like that.'

He looked up, suddenly brisk and to the point. 'If you don't know anyone, I shall have to make some discreet enquiries – dear God in heaven! You women are supposed to know better. How on earth could you let such a thing happen?'

'That's right, blame me,' she grumbled. 'You men are all the same.'

She was playing for time before she had to tell him that the pregnancy was well advanced and that the usual methods of abortion were no longer suitable. He would not dare insist on what would almost certainly be a most dangerous operation, in case something went wrong and she died. When the facts came to light, he would then be faced with criminal charges which would ruin him.

He stood up and began to pace restlessly to and fro and Meg watched him nervously.

At last she said, 'Let me make you happy. Let's have a bit of fun the way you like it.'

To her dismay he stared at her as though she was mad. 'Poor Meg,' he said with a shake of his head. 'You really have no idea. You are the most stupid little –' He choked back an ugly word. 'For God's sake keep quiet, and let me think of someone who can help you.'

In spite of her good intentions, Meg bridled immediately.

'Help *you*, you mean, you miserable hypocrite!' she

cried. 'Don't try and make out you're thinking of me, because you're just thinking of yourself! Men! You're all the bleeding same. Get a poor girl into trouble and then there's hell to pay. Anyway, how d'you know I want to get rid of the kid? I might *like* kids. Fact is I *do* like 'em, so there!'

Suddenly he grabbed hold of both hands and pulled her roughly towards him, his eyes steely. 'You are not to have that child!' he shouted. '*Never!* Try to get that into your empty little head. The idea is impossible – out of the question.'

'You bastard!' she exclaimed vehemently, wriggling to free herself. 'Let go of me before I start to yell!'

The threat had the desired effect and he at once released her, but she saw that the word she had used had been an unlucky choice.

'A bastard,' he whispered. 'That any child of mine should bear that unspeakable epithet. I would not wish that on my worst enemy.'

'Well, then, why not *marry* me?' Meg taunted. 'Make an honest woman out of me, and that way you can give your son a name. All you have to do now it get rid of your wife.'

She ducked too late to avoid his hand, which struck her a stinging blow across the left side of her face.

'Perhaps that will teach you to mind your tongue!' he shouted, beside himself with fury. 'Leave my wife out of this. You are not fit to lick her shoes!'

Meg, resentful but wary, moved back a few steps before delivering her trump card.

'Well, maybe not, but *I'm stuck with the kid* and she's not. There's no getting rid of it! You've had your fun and now you're going to have to fork out for it. So put that in your bleeding pipe and smoke it!'

For a long moment they regarded each other furiously across the few yards of threadbare carpet but then, with a tremendous effort, Meg's common sense prevailed. She knew that in the long run threats might not succeed and somehow she ought to appeal to his better nature. She could not allow him to walk out on her in the heat of an argument, because if she did she might never see him again and that would certainly not solve her problems. Having made her plans very carefully, now – through her own stupidity – she had come within an inch of losing everything. With a low moan she burst into loud sobs and sank down on to the floor, presenting what she knew to be a most piteous spectacle.

'Oh, God help me!' she wailed. 'What's to become of me if you won't help me? I was relying on you. I *trusted* you. I was good to you, wasn't I? I let you have your way and never reproached you no matter what hurt you done me! Don't desert me. Please don't desert me!'

She looked up at him with tears streaming down her face and as she had expected, his heart was touched by her tears and reluctantly he reached out to take her hands and help her to her feet again. He handed her a spotless white handkerchief and told her to stop crying and she almost held her breath.

Much though she would have liked him to take her in his arms, she knew that would be expecting too much. Instead he stared out of the window and the silence lengthened between them.

'Of course I shall not *desert* you,' he said at last. 'But I must have time to think. I shall get in touch with you soon, but only if you agree to stay away from my house. If you are ever seen near Harrington Hill again, I swear you will regret it. My wife is to be spared the knowledge of this ghastly business. I don't yet know what to suggest, but I shall think of something.'

Meg gave him a watery smile. 'You're ever so kind,' she sniffed. 'You're a real gentleman.'

'A gentleman?' He laughed mirthlessly. 'Oh no! I can no longer class myself as a gentleman. A fool, perhaps . . . Oh, Meg! You stupid girl! Why didn't you tell me before it was too late?'

'I was scared,' she whimpered. 'I thought you'd cast me off and I couldn't bear that. I love you . . .'

He shuddered. 'Love! What do you know about love? You don't know the meaning of the word.'

'Oh yes, I do,' she argued. 'And anyway, what about you? You're supposed to love your wife.'

Gilbert frowned. 'My poor Marion, I've done her a most terrible wrong. My God! I can scarcely believe it.' He looked round the shabby room with an air of incredulity, as though wondering how he came to find himself in such surroundings.

'I must go,' he said abruptly.

She began to stammer. 'Oh, but we haven't – I thought we would . . .'

He gazed at her sadly. 'No,' he said. 'Never again. If I had known . . . if I had ever anticipated such an outcome . . .' He shook his head.

'But the money . . .' she faltered. 'I ought to be drinking milk and suchlike to build myself up.'

'You are not going to have the child,' he repeated stubbornly. 'I shall think of something. Here, take these.' He gave her a handful of coins and turned to go. 'And remember,' he warned, 'keep away from Harrington Hill and my wife, or I shall not answer for the consequences!'

*

On the same day, Amelia and Ralph stood in the large front room of an old house situated next to an undertaker's. Together they inspected it with critical eyes, but it was the fourth of such properties they had visited that week and Ralph, unlike his mother, was finding it difficult to sustain his flagging enthusiasm for the task in hand. Plans for the Harold Weston Memorial School were now going ahead and Amelia was in her element, but Ralph found the daily excursions tedious beyond measure. The trouble was that he could not look at them with the same detachment as his mother and had to imagine himself as one of the potential inmates, which depressed him.

While Amelia hurried from room to room exclaiming over the advantages and disadvantages, Ralph could only nod or shake his head in agreement. According to his mother they were too large, too cramped, too dilapidated or too expensive for she was as hard to please as though she intended to live there herself. *That*, she insisted in answer to his mild complaint, was the criterion she had set herself.

In vain he suggested that to a homeless street urchin the most spartan environment would seem like a palace. Amelia simply waved his objections aside and carried on with her search.

Glancing around this particular room with distaste, he waited for his mother to explain why it was totally unsuitable, although to him the reasons were patently obvious. The window-pane was broken, cobwebs festooned the ceiling, patches of green mould disfigured the walls and there was a musty and all-pervading smell of tom-cats.

When, to his surprise, she made no comment, Ralph broke the silence.

'Ghastly!' he exclaimed.

Amelia rounded on him. 'It is a lot better than the last place,' she pointed out. 'It would need a few pounds spent on it, I admit, to make it habitable, but it has the great advantage that the room above this one would convert into a dormitory. May would approve, I feel sure.'

Ralph shook his head. 'Mama, are you certain that living-in is such a good idea? I really do have my doubts. A school where they learn sums is one thing, but taking over their lives completely – isn't that asking for trouble? I'm wondering if you are getting carried away with enthusiasm and should be prepared to walk before you run.'

'I have explained it to you before, Ralph,' Amelia

answered, unperturbed. 'The children must be properly able to take advantage of their opportunity. How can we expect the poor wretches to study during the day if they are wandering the streets all night, without shelter? How can we expect their minds to function properly if they are starved of nourishment? No, they must live in. I have quite made up my mind. It simply means a larger building and one or two extra staff.' She screwed up her face in concentration as she mentally measured out the room. 'This room would take ten desks and the teacher's desk could go there.' She pointed. 'The stove there, and the cupboard there.' She looked around, weighing up the possibilities. 'It would have to be whitewashed and thoroughly cleaned, and perhaps a good linoleum on the floor.' She gave a quick, satisfied nod.

'The Goya could hang there,' Ralph suggested, 'but where should we put the Rembrandt?'

Amelia was not amused. 'Don't be flippant, Ralph,' she admonished him. 'I've told you before that it does not suit you.'

He smiled. 'I was only trying to help,' he assured her.

'I don't know why I bring you,' she said, but she spoke with an affection she could not entirely hide.

After further consideration she pointed. 'Through there is another room which I think would serve as a dining room with a small kitchen area partitioned off.' She led the way to a dark room which smelt abominable and lacked any window. 'What do you think?' she asked. Without giving him time to answer, she stabbed the air four times. 'Large table, dresser, cooking range, cupboards. So on and so forth.'

'Brilliant!' said Ralph. 'Has anyone ever told you, Mama, that you are incredible? Such vision! Such –'

'Now, the upstairs room,' she went on as though he had not spoken. 'At present we have to reach it from outside, but I shall have the stairs enclosed, naturally.'

'Naturally!' agreed Ralph with a wry smile as he

followed his mother outside and up a rickety flight of steps. Amelia unlocked the door and threw it open with such a flourish that the lower of the two rusting hinges broke and the door sagged drunkenly on the one that remained.

'Mama!' shouted Ralph delightedly. 'You don't know your own strength!'

'A new door,' she said serenely. 'Remind me to add it to the list.' Quite unabashed, she propped open the door more securely and led the way in.

'The beds,' she pointed again, 'will go there; and there behind a screen, I shall put the matron's bed, a small chest of drawers and possibly a small table. It is most important that the girls are properly supervised. There is a smaller room off this one that will do for her sitting room. Yesterday I saw a large swing mirror which might do very well for the dormitory.'

'A mirror, Mama? You will make them vain!'

Amelia adjusted her hat and said, 'Nonsense! They must learn to take a proper pride in their appearance. Neatness and cleanliness must be thoroughly taught, or they will slip back into their old ways as soon as they leave us.'

'You talk as though this is it,' said Ralph. 'Do I understand that you have finally made up your mind?'

'You do and I have.'

Ralph's bantering tone disappeared. 'Then, seriously, Mama, I congratulate you. It will make a really splendid home.'

Pleased with his praise, she smiled and patted his arm.

'Thank you, dear. I think it will do very well.'

He kissed her lightly. 'And if you ever turn me out, I shall probably move in here myself!'

CHAPTER FOUR

The following day found Jeff hard at work once more. On his left the typed sheets lay scattered untidily on the table and on his right a forgotten cup of cocoa stood untasted. As a knock sounded at the door, he glanced at the cocoa guiltily, snatched it up and drank with his eyes closed. When it had all gone, he set down the empty cup, wiped his mouth with the back of his hand and called, 'Come in!'

Mrs Coot's face appeared round the opened door.

'Still working!' she chided with a shake of her head. 'I said to myself, "surely that young man's not still working?" I heard you start this morning – six-thirty, it was, because I looked at my clock. "He's never working already," I said to myself, but you were. And now it's nearly eleven and you haven't stopped yet. It can't be good for you, working all the hours God sends the way you do.'

Jeff waited until she paused for breath, knowing from experience that it was useless to try to interrupt her. She either did not hear or did not want to hear.

'I'm doing a piece on this article in *The Link*,' he told her. 'I expect you've read it? It's about the girls at the Bryant and May match factory in Bow.'

Mrs Coot shook her head disapprovingly. '*The Link*!' she snorted. 'I don't hold with that sort of paper. Stir up trouble, that's all they do. Radicals – that's what my late husband used to call them papers. "I won't have those radical rags in my house," he used to say. As if we haven't got enough trouble without them stirring up more. Not that he was much of a reader; he didn't have the learning I had, bless him. I was lucky. I had an uncle – Uncle Freddy, I called him – and he taught me to read. Should have been a schoolmaster, only he died of his lungs. Radical rags is trouble.'

'Maybe, but I guess there's a lot of truth in what they say,' Jeff told her. 'Some of the girls are working for four shillings a week. Four shillings! Can you imagine! With a shilling or more for their rent, what does it leave them to live on? Coal and food and that's about all it'll stretch to. White slaves, it calls them, and I should say that's a pretty accurate description. They have a tough time, too, according to this.'

'Maybe and maybe not,' said Mrs Coot. 'You can't believe all you read in the newspapers – begging your pardon, you being a journalist and all that. But you know what I mean, I'm sure.'

'Sure I know,' he told her, 'but I aim to find out for myself this afternoon. As soon as I've finished my preliminary paragraph, I'm off to Fairfield Road to ask for an interview. First-hand experience, Mrs Coot – you can't beat it.'

'An interview?' She looked suitably impressed.

He nodded. 'I shall ask to speak to one of the managers, someone in charge, and I shall ask him outright about the claims in this article.'

Mrs Coot regarded him with obvious admiration. 'Well, rather you than me,' she assured him. 'They won't be feeling too cheerful after that article.'

Jeff laughed. 'Don't worry about me. You get used to that kind of response. What you need most in this business is a thick skin, and mine's thicker than most. You know what they say about "sticks and stones"!'

Mrs Coot said, 'I came to see if you wanted another cup of cocoa. I'm making one for myself and Mrs Hubbard next door. Poor old soul; she likes a bit of company since her husband died.'

She picked up the empty cup and Jeff said, 'That

went down very well, Mrs Coot, and I wouldn't say no to another.'

Satisfied, she hurried away and Jeff returned once more to his typewriter.

*

As Mrs Coot had predicted, those in charge at the Fairfield factory were not at all pleased to see him, but agreed reluctantly that one of the managers would give him a short interview. The offending article in *The Link* had caused great embarrassment, they told him, but Mr Alfred Hunnicut would answer a few questions. The exchange was to prove shorter than Jeff expected.

Mr Hunnicut sat behind his desk, his face impassive, his plump hands clasped on the desk-top in front of him.

Adopting what he hoped was an earnest expression, Jeff asked, 'Mr Hunnicut, is it true that the match-girls are only earning four shillings a week – and if so, isn't that extremely low?'

The manager considered his answer carefully.

'That is true of some of the girls,' he said. 'Some do not put in regular appearances and so do not earn as much as others; they have family problems and they stay away. Others – I have to say it, Mr Bannerman – are idle, or they turn up late and leave early.' He shrugged.

'I see. Then you are saying that any worker who puts in a full week will earn more than four shillings?'

'Certainly. In most cases that is so.'

Jeff scribbled furiously. 'Then is this summer abnormal in some way?' he asked.

'Yes, it is. Obviously the demand for matches falls every summer – a seasonal fluctuation – but what usually happens is that many of the girls take time off anyway to go hop-picking in Kent. They look on it as a kind of holiday. Others leave to work in the jam factories.'

'And that isn't happening this year?'

'No. The harvests have been poor and there is very

80

little of that kind of employment. Since we have to spread what work there is between all the workers who remain, therefore they have to do fewer hours.'

'Ah! Light is dawning!' said Jeff, still writing.

'So you see, we are not the ogres that *The Link* would have people believe,' concluded Hunnicut.

'No, indeed.' Jeff turned the page with a disarming smile. 'Now the article suggests that your company has put up a statue to Mr Gladstone and that –'

'We have, and a very fine statue it is, too,' Mr Hunnicut interposed sharply. 'You will find it in Bow Road.'

'And is it true that your workers were forced to contribute a shilling each out of their wages towards the cost of its erection?'

The manager's mouth tightened. 'I have no information on that point,' he said. 'I am afraid I cannot help you.'

'Mr Hunnicut, the article also alleges that some of the girls are badly treated by the foremen. Is that possible, do you think?'

Mr Hunnicut took up a pencil and began to scribble on a corner of the paper which lay in front of him. 'I should think it most unlikely,' he replied. 'I have heard nothing of any such claims.'

'Are you the person they would complain to?'

'Not directly, but I would most certainly hear of it.'

'Has Bryant and May ever had any serious unrest, Mr Hunnicut?'

'Not to my knowledge. And, I venture to suggest, we never will because our girls are very happy here. We take good care of them and there are welfare facilities.'

Jeff was puzzled. 'Welfare facilities?' he echoed. 'How do you mean, exactly?'

'We have our own dentists to ensure that the risk of phosphorous necrosis is kept to a minimum.'

'The risk of *what*?' Jeff asked. 'What is kept to a minimum?'

'Phosphorous necrosis. It is the erosion of the jaw-bone, Mr Bannerman. Phosphorous fumes can damage the jaw-bone – but only if they are allowed into the jaw by means of dental caries. Our dentists ensure that all our workers have regular checks. Our facilities are the most modern in the country, and we are justly proud of them.'

In spite of himself, Jeff was impressed. He wrote rapidly and at length, then closed the notebook and smiled.

'I wonder if I could be allowed an interview with one of your girls, Mr Hunnicut? Just to get a balanced . . .'

The manager rose quickly to his feet. 'I am afraid not,' he said. 'It is most unlikely that anyone would want to lose time, you see. I'm sure you understand that time is money to them. And on the matter of time, Mr Bannerman, I think you have taken up enough of *mine*. So I shall have to wish you good day.'

Jeff rose to his feet, but Mr Hunnicut went on, 'I hope I have convinced you that we are not the monsters we have been made out to be, and that we do have the girls' interests at heart, no matter what *The Link* may choose to suggest to the contrary. Is it too much to hope that you will give our side of the matter as much space as *The Link* has given to the other side?'

Jeff tucked his notebook into his coat pocket. 'I'm afraid I can only present the facts to my paper,' he told him. 'The editor decides how much space to allot to each article and they often do a pretty good hatchet job but . . .' He spread his hands helplessly. '*I'll* treat you fairly, Mr Hunnicut. There are always two sides to every question and I'm grateful to you for all your help.'

As they shook hands, Jeff added, 'I can find my own way out.' Mr Hunnicut had no intention of allowing him to roam around the factory unescorted, however, and he sent for a junior employee to accompany him to the main factory gates.

Quite by chance the timing of Jeff's departure proved very convenient, for as he left the factory he discovered the workers spilling out onto the streets at the end of their shift.

'So you won't allow me to talk to the girls,' Jeff muttered to himself as he approached the first woman who passed him.

'I'm a reporter on the *New York Times*,' he began, but she hurried on, calling back over her shoulder that she had a family to look after. The next one he went up to shied away nervously at the prospect, declaring that it was more than her job was worth to talk to him.

After several similarly abortive attempts, however, Jeff finally found a young girl who paused long enough to consider his request and actually agreed to be interviewed.

'But not here outside the factory,' she told him. 'I'm not that daft.'

His spirits soared. A personal interview with one of the downtrodden factory hands! It would read very well.

'There's a pie-shop on the corner,' he suggested. 'They also sell puddings. Suppose I buy us both steak and kidney pud? How would that be?' As she hesitated, he added, 'That's what you English like, isn't it?'

'You're not English, then?' she asked. 'I thought you sounded a bit foreign.'

'American,' he told her. 'I'm working for the *New York Times* and I've just interviewed your Mr Hunnicut. He was very helpful.'

He thought this information would help to overcome any lingering doubts she might have on the wisdom of accepting his offer.

'We'll talk as we eat,' he told her firmly and before she could refuse he took her by the arm and led her across the road in the direction of 'Stan's Pie Shop'.

The shop was a small one with six tables each seating two people. A wooden counter ran down one side of the narrow room and the wooden tables were ranged along the other. Behind the counter a short elderly man bustled to and fro, pausing only to shout orders into a speaking-tube which led to the kitchen. Jeff and Dora found an empty table and settled themselves on the rickety seats and Jeff ordered steak and kidney pudding twice, with bread and butter and two mugs of tea.

Only then did he take the time to study the young woman who sat opposite him and he decided that he liked what he saw. Smooth brown hair framed a round face and a neat mouth revealed surprisingly even teeth. Dora's brown eyes were wary, but her manner was friendly enough.

'Are you going to tell me your name?' he asked with a smile.

'If you're going to tell me yours!'

'I'm Jeff Bannerman.'

'I'm Dora Becket.'

He held out a hand across the table with exaggerated gallantry and she shook the finger-tips, smiling.

'In America we believe that steak and kidney pud is the staple diet of the Londoner,' he told her. 'Would you go along with that?'

She laughed. 'Maybe – but don't forget oysters, pea soup and sheep's trotters, jellied eels and pork pies! Anyway, what's the . . .' The unfamiliar word 'staple' daunted her and she substituted 'favourite food of people in America?'

'Would you believe pork and beans – the cowboy diet.'

Dora grinned. 'Sounds very dull. So, why aren't you in America then, eating pork and beans?'

'Because I'm a newsman. I go where the news is and I happen to believe that right now it's in England.'

'But why? What's happening here that's so special?'

He stared at her. 'You really mean you don't know?'

She looked at him uneasily and asked, 'Don't know what?'

'Why, the revolution, of course! The whole world's waiting for it – and high time, too.'

Dora frowned, but was saved from the need to answer by the arrival of two steaming plates, each one heaped high with meat and suet crust and a mountain of mashed potatoes, all smothered in thick brown gravy. Her eyes opened wide in delight at the glorious sight of so much food.

'It's ever so kind of you,' she told Jeff. 'This is a real treat for me, I've never eaten in a shop before.'

He stared at her in astonishment. 'Never?'

'Never.' She shrugged. 'I buy what I want from the street-sellers. They're much cheaper and my Ma used to say, "Why pay extra just to sit at another man's table?"'

He considered this homespun philosophy. 'She was right, I guess – but then if everyone thought like that the pie-shop owners would be out of business and starving. You see,' he leaned forward earnestly, 'that's the thing about money – it has to *circulate*. At the moment it's not circulating properly in this country. A few rich folk have most of it, and the poor folk have nothing.'

She looked at him seriously for a moment and then said, 'This pudding's scrumptious.'

They both laughed. 'I can take a hint,' he told her. 'No lectures until we've satisfied the inner man.'

He patted his stomach to explain the reference, thinking it was a shame that someone so attractive should be both poor and ignorant. They ate in silence for a while, during which time the remaining tables had filled up and the man behind the counter had redoubled his efforts in order to keep his customers happy. When at last Jeff deemed it a suitable time to begin his 'interview', he asked her to tell him about her work.

Dora considered before replying, her head on one side.

'It's not exactly *hard*,' she said, 'though it's long hours – but then we don't mind that too much, for there's plenty would be willing to step into our shoes. At least we've money to keep ourselves. What I do is cut and pack matches into boxes. Sometimes I make the boxes. Once I worked in the dipping room, but I didn't care for that much although I did have a lad to help me. I wasn't in there long – just until they got another man.'

'And are they kind to you, Miss Becket?'

The question surprised her. 'Why, should they be?' she asked.

'Why not?' he countered. 'Surely a happy worker is more productive than one who is unhappy?'

'I don't rightly know,' said Dora. 'I suppose they're fair, most of them. There's one foreman I don't care for – but then no one does. He's got wandering hands, if you know what that means.'

'I can guess!'

'But then there's Mr Mills – Jerry, his name is, but we don't call him that to his face. He's a real gentleman, he is, a respectable married man. Everyone likes Jerry.'

She forked a mouthful of pudding into her mouth, ate it with great relish and said, 'This is very tasty. It's really ever so kind –'

'So, what do you think of all these strikes?' he interrupted her. 'Coal-miners, dockers – where's it all going to end?'

She shrugged. 'Don't ask me. But it's hard on their families,' she said. 'There's a girl at work –'

'But do you *approve* of strikes?'

'Approve? I don't know. I've never thought about it.'

'Would *you* go on strike, Miss Becket?'

Another forkful of food was arrested half-way to her mouth and she regarded him with sudden caution. With her narrowed gold-brown eyes she looked, Jeff thought, like a wary animal.

'Why should I go on strike?' she demanded. 'I get paid regular. I do my work and mind my own business. What are you asking me about strikes for? I never said I wanted to go on strike, did I?'

Seeing her obvious alarm, he smiled reassuringly. 'Of course you didn't. I was only wondering because of what it says in the article in *The Link*.'

'I don't know anything about that. What does it say?' She had stopped eating altogether now and was watching him with growing unease.

'Just that Bryant and May are bringing in Scottish labour, which means that all the wages will go down.'

'Go down? Who says?'

'They *suggest* they will go down.'

Her eyes darkened in dismay at his words. 'Who's this "they" you keep on about?' she demanded.

'The writers of the article.'

'Well, how do *they* know? I don't believe it.'

She did not tell him that in fact there *had* been a sudden influx of workers down from Scotland and that there *had* been rumours. It was Jeff's turn to shrug and for a while they resumed their dinner in an uncomfortable silence.

Dora finished first and wiped her plate with what remained of the bread, soaking up every drop of gravy.

'Did you enjoy it?' he asked.

'I did.' She looked at him with a troubled expression. 'But I wouldn't have come if I'd known you were going to go on about strikes and things. How do I know you're a newspaper man? How do I know you're not one of these agitators we hear so much about?'

'An agitator! Of course I'm not.' His indignation was obviously genuine.

'Well, you're agitating me,' she told him.

He laughed, but hastily smothered his amusement. 'I didn't mean to,' he assured her. 'Truly, I didn't. I just wanted your views on the current situation. There's so much unrest . . .'

Dora tossed her head. 'Well, I'm not "unrested" so you can just leave me out of it. I do an honest day's work and I don't know anything about strikes, and if dockers and people want to strike that's none of my business.'

She made as if to rise and, sensing that she was poised for flight, Jeff put a restraining hand on her arm.

'Please, you can't go yet,' he said. 'We haven't finished the meal.' She hesitated, as he had hoped she would. 'I think there's jam tart. You're not full, surely?'

'I don't know,' she said doubtfully. 'Is this really an interview? You're not writing anything down. How will you remember what I said? You might write something I didn't say; you might write lies.'

'Why should I do that?'

'You might say I want a revolution when I don't.'

'But lots of people do!'

'Well, Mr Bannerman, I'm not lots of people. I'm Dora Becket and I don't get mixed up with stuff like that. I've got a job and I've got self-respect. I don't walk the streets like Meg. I've got my pride. So you just remember to put all *that* in your blooming newspaper!'

'I will,' he said quietly and she sat down again, her face flushed.

'Who's Meg?' he asked, deciding it would be prudent to steer the conversation into a different channel.

'My cousin. Meg Swain.'

'And she's a . . . a street-walker?'

Dora flew to her defence. 'What if she is?' she demanded. 'Lots of girls are. That's all there is for some if they can't get jobs.'

Jeff tried to keep his gaze steady, but inwardly he was suddenly bubbling with excitement. An idea had occurred to him. Suppose this chance meeting with Dora Becket led to a whole series of interviews with a selection of London's unfortunates! Perhaps he could talk to this Meg – and perhaps he could find a discontented docker and a coal-miner. The possiblities were endless, but if there was going to be a revolution these were the people – the disenchanted poor – who would rise up in their thousands. He could imagine the headlines. And he, Jeff Bannerman, would already have his contacts!

He became aware that Dora was leaning towards him. 'Are you listening, Mr Bannerman?' she demanded. 'Or am I talking to myself?'

'I'm sorry. Of course I'm listening,' he lied. 'Go on.'

'I said, "Are we having jam tart?" because if not I'd best be going home. I've some washing to do and then –'

'If I could walk home with you . . .' he began, intrigued at the prospect of seeing where she lived.

'Walk me home?' She looked doubtful. 'And then what?'

'Nothing. I just thought I could finish the interview as we walked. I swear I have no ulterior motive.'

'No what?'

'No dishonourable intentions towards you.'

'I should hope not,' she told him with a toss of her head.

'Do I look the type who would take advantage?' he asked.

She considered the question seriously, inspecting him with a thoughtful expression. 'Probably not,' she conceded, 'but Meg says all men are the same under the skin – all after one thing, if you'll pardon the expression.'

'Do you think Meg's right?'

She sighed. 'I hope not,' she told him.

Suddenly they both smiled and Jeff said, 'We've wandered a long way from the match factory. I'll order the jam tart.'

It came covered in thick yellow custard and while they ate it Jeff asked her about Annie Besant.

'Never heard of her,' said Dora.

'But you must have done!' he protested. 'She was outside your factory gates a few days ago, talking to the Fairfield workers. You could hardly have missed her.'

'Oh, I saw *her*,' Dora agreed. 'Was that Annie Besant? Funny hair, all short and curly, and a red tammy on her head. And a red tie! Is that her name, then? Annie Besant?'

'That's it. She's a radical thinker and she writes articles for *The Link*. It's a halfpenny newspaper which has been going a few months now. Ever heard of it?'

'No. Why should I?'

He shrugged and then, as a thought occurred to him, asked casually. 'Can you read, Miss Becket?'

'Of course I can blooming well read!' She glared at him. 'I've been to school and I can read. I don't care to, but I can if I feel like it. I can add up and take away – and I know about kings and queens and geography. You think that because I work in a factory I'm ignorant, is that it?'

'I'm sorry.' He gave her a quick smile. 'How's the jam tart?'

She grinned. 'Nice – and the custard's hotter than hell!'

Jeff surrendered himself to the delights of Stan's tart and watched Dora devour hers.

Ten minutes later, deliciously replete, Dora allowed him to escort her home. On the way he told her about his own family and worked hard to restore her confidence in him.

When at last they reached Hewlett Road, Dora stopped outside No. 36. Seeing the way her companion surveyed the sunless street, she said, 'There's plenty worse streets. It may not be Park Lane, but at least we're near the park.'

'Which park?' He looked surprised.

'Victoria Park. It's less than a mile from here. Up the road, over Skew Bridge – that's the canal – and across the green.' She grinned suddenly. 'There's two bathing pools – for men. They swim starkers. When we were kids, we used to try and creep through the trees to spy on them. That was a favourite trick. Or the boys would nip in and pinch their clothes!'

'Starkers? That's nude, I take it?'

She nodded. '"In the buff" or the "altogether" –

whatever you like to call it. There's a pub down Wick Lane called the White Lion. The far end of the park, that is. They had a running track and my Pa used to fancy himself as a runner – ran against a Red Indian called Deerfoot and lost. But we never heard the end of that race; my Pa used to tell everyone he'd run against a Red Indian. So, Mr Bannerman, don't turn your nose up at Hewlett Street.'

'I'm sorry. I didn't mean to.'

Dora resisted the temptation to show him her room.

'I won't ask you up,' she said, 'because I've got things to do. But thank you for the meal. I ate too much, but I don't care. I shall remember it for a long time.'

'I enjoyed your company.' He grinned ruefully. 'I'm sorry the interview's ended. Why aren't you going to invite me in? Don't you trust me? Has Meg turned you against men?'

'It's nothing to do with Meg,' said Dora. 'I just keep myself to myself, that's all.'

He wondered what would happen if he tried to make her change her mind, but thought better of it. He had always been too impatient, according to his mother. 'You always rush your fences!' she had told him on numerous occasions and he knew she was right. He said lightly, 'This Meg sounds interesting. I'd like to meet her.'

'Well, you can't. She's got herself into enough trouble already, so she won't be looking for any more by talking to the newspapers.'

He was immediately intrigued. 'What sort of trouble?'

'The usual. A man.'

He nodded. 'I see. So that's why you're so wary.'

'No, Mr Bannerman. I've *always* been wary. That's where Meg and I are different.'

They regarded each other with that strange dichotomy of feeling which strangers have for each other at such moments – the need to end a fragile, barely developed relationship and the reluctance to let it go.

Dora said, 'I hope your article turns out all right – and that you've remembered it all the way I said it.'

'If I need to refresh my memory I know where you live, don't I?'

He hoped she would take the hint and say that he would be welcome, but she merely smiled again.

'Goodbye, Mr Bannerman.'

'Goodbye, Miss Becket.'

He watched her open the door and close it behind her and then he walked back along the street, his thoughts whirling.

CHAPTER FIVE

Gilbert Reid's day was tightly structured. It began with
breakfast which he shared with Marion at eight o'clock,
and this was followed at nine by the first surgery of the
day which lasted until ten-thirty when the door was
closed. By eleven-thirty his waiting room was usually
empty and he was free to set out on his rounds to visit
those of his patients who were too sick or infirm to leave
their homes. He normally expected to be back by one
o'clock at the latest and then lunch was served. The
afternoon was free until the second surgery began at six
and this was followed by another, but hopefully shorter,
round of visits. If he was lucky, he would be home again
some time between eight-thirty and nine o'clock.

On the 24th of June he and Marion sat at breakfast,
the day's post between them on a small silver tray.
Marion finished reading her letter from Rachel and
looked up with shining eyes.

'Gilbert, she's coming! In two days' time! Oh, I can
hardly believe it. It will be so good to see her.'

Gilbert smiled. 'I'm so pleased dear. It will do you
good to have some company.'

She glanced down at the dog who lay in a pool of
sunlight beside her chair and said, 'Do you hear that,
Pip? Your Aunt Rachel is coming. Isn't that wonderful!'

'Someone else to spoil you!' observed Gilbert, but he
too was pleased at the news. He felt that he was a poor
companion at the moment and hoped that a visitor in the
house would ease the constraints which were developing
between himself and Marion. He was well aware that

Rachel had not approved of his marriage to her sister, but he had never let that knowledge give him a sleepless night. For his part he did not dislike her – in fact he had seen her only rarely because her duties to her parents had kept her in Kingston. Now that those duties had ended, she would doubtless wish to visit Marion occasionally and he had no objection.

A fortnight had passed since his last metting with Meg Swain had thrown his thoughts into turmoil. He had vowed never to visit her again and had tried to discover someone who would abort the child but without success. He was half-convinced that conception had not taken place as early as Meg suggested, and suspected her of exaggerating the nearness of her time in order to pressure him into agreeing to pay maintenance for the child. He did not trust her to stay away from his home and was dreading a reappearance. Somehow he managed to perform his medical duties but the strain was showing, he knew; Marion was uneasy about him, asked frequently what was wrong and had encouraged him to confide in her. The temptation to do so was immense, but he knew that any vestige of love which might still exist between them would be irrevocably lost if she ever learned the truth. To deny his wife children and then father a child by a prostitute was quite unpardonable.

'Gilbert!' said Marion.

He became aware that Mrs Cobbett was staring at him. 'I was asking if you want any more toast, sir,' she said.

'No, thank you.' He consulted the clock on the mantelpiece. 'I have a letter to write,' he told Marion. 'I don't want to be disturbed.'

As she nodded and smiled, he was relieved to notice that the news of Rachel's visit had brought a sparkle to her eyes.

Upstairs in his study, he sat down at the bureau and, taking out a sheet of notepaper, he wrote:

Dear Meg,

   I have been unable to find anyone willing to undertake the operation which I have suggested for you, and in view of this I am forced to consider any alternatives. Perhaps it might be possible for the child to be adopted. I will look into this possibility . . .

He threw down the pen and leaned back in his chair. Who would want to adopt a child brought into the world by such a pathetic creature? It was a forlorn hope. If only it would die at birth! That would solve all their problems. Hundreds of infants did die, but Fate would no doubt ensure that this particular one survived and lived to reproach him for many a long year!

Perhaps he could find an unscrupulous doctor to ensure that it *did* die! But no – the risk to himself was too great. He might be betrayed and that would amount to conspiracy to murder. It was madness even to contemplate such a dreadful course of action.

As another thought struck him, a cold sweat broke out on his skin. How could he have been so stupid as to consider writing to her? A letter in his handwriting and bearing his signature would link his name with hers. Suppose it were found, or suppose Meg could not read and decided to show it to someone else! Snatching up the letter he tore it angrily into shreds before finally committing it to the wastepaper basket.

He must take a firm hold on himself, he knew. If he allowed himself to crack under the strain he might do something foolish. Whatever happened, he must keep his nerve. But if he could not write to the wretch then he would have to visit her, and the thought appalled him. If only *she* would die!

Suddenly, he cried out, 'No!' He was thinking wildly again; letting his imagination run riot.

'Meg Swain!' he groaned. 'I wish to God I'd never set eyes on you!'

But wishing could not undo the harm he had done; he must face up to his responsibilities and find an acceptable way out for all concerned. Suppose he did agree to maintain the child? Could he bear to know that a child of his, his own flesh and blood, was growing up in the gutter? No, it was impossible. Damn Amelia Gaunt, he reflected savagely. If she had not assumed responsibility for that wretched Ellie, he would never have met Meg Swain.

'Damn her to hell! The meddling busybody!' he groaned, his head in his hands. For a long time he sat defeated, but eventually he straightened up and stared at the pen. Meg must not be allowed to do anything rash that would precipitate a storm. He would have to make one last visit.

Meanwhile Marion had finished her breakfast and was preparing to take Pip for her morning walk. She snapped on the spaniel's lead and opened the front door. Outside the sun was already very warm and promising to be hot later in the day.

Pip tugged and fussed and managed to wind her lead round Marion's legs so that she was forced to stop and untangle herself. As she did so, she looked at the collar Ralph had sent and a smile touched her lips. If she was honest with herself she had hoped he would make some further contact, but he had not done so. Perhaps it was just as well. He was a very attractive young man and she ought not to be thinking about him at all.

Having walked Pip for the best part of ten minutes, she then turned back and had nearly reached her own front door when she became aware of raised voices and saw Kitty arguing with a young woman. As she drew closer, she recognized her and her heart missed a beat.

Kitty turned towards her mistress, her face flushed and furious. 'How am I supposed to whiten the steps with this baggage sitting on them?' she demanded. 'I've asked her politely and she won't budge, so I've told her to go and that won't shift her. I'm late as it is and the last thing I need . . .'

She fell silent at a glance from Marion and they both looked at the hunched figure on the steps.

'I think I recognize you,' Marion told her. 'Why won't you move? What are you waiting for?'

Meg ignored her and continued to stare resolutely ahead.

'My maid has work to do – don't you understand? If you want to see the doctor, the waiting room is open.'

Still no answer.

Kitty burst out, 'I've told her that already, ma'am, but she just sits there staring and won't say a word.'

Marion tried a different approach. In a friendlier tone she said, 'You're Ellie's sister, aren't you? The little girl my husband tried to help?'

Meg's lips twisted into a sardonic smile but still she did not speak, nor did she raise her head.

Kitty asked, 'Should I fetch the master, ma'am – or maybe a constable?'

Marion hesitated to take the latter step but was disturbed by the girl's attitude; she behaved as though she had a right to be there.

'I will have a word with Dr Reid,' she said and hurried indoors.

As she entered the study and caught sight of Gilbert's face she thought, not for the first time, that he looked ill. There were lines on his face which aged him and his eyes were unnaturally bright.

'My dear,' she began, 'I hate to trouble you but do you recall that young woman, Meg Swain?'

He started visibly. 'What about her?'

'She came here once before . . .'

'I know. What now?'

Marion was taken aback by his brusque manner. 'She's sitting on our steps,' she told him, 'and refuses either to move or speak. She really is most odd. I wonder if she is quite right in the head, yet she looks normal enough. Would you see if you can make her understand, Gilbert? Kitty is making such a fuss because she can't get on with the steps, and I don't want all the neighbours to take an interest – you know how they are.'

To her surprise, Gilbert did not at once rise to his feet. 'No,' he said after a moment. 'Leave her there. And tell Kitty to leave the steps.'

'Leave the steps?'

'Yes, leave them. It won't be the end of the world if the steps are not cleaned.'

'Then you don't want to speak with her?'

'I don't think so.'

'But, Gilbert, if she is ill –'

'There's nothing the matter with her,' he broke in.

'But how on earth can you know that? Is *she* one of your patients? I did not know.'

'Of course not,' he said without looking at her. 'I tell you there is nothing wrong with her and that's an end to it.'

'Then perhaps it's Ellie,' Marion suggested. 'Perhaps Ellie is in trouble of some kind and . . .'

She stopped as Gilbert's mouth tightened. 'I tell you there's nothing wrong with her!' he repeated. 'Nothing. Leave her alone. I won't speak with her and I do not want to hear another word on the subject.'

He turned back to the papers on his desk and Marion, with fast beating heart, slipped from the room. She had just closed the door behind her when Kitty ran up the stairs, a look of triumph on her face.

'She's gone, ma'am! Suddenly upped and . . .' As Marion put a warning finger to her lips, she dropped her voice to a whisper and went on, '. . . took herself off.'

'Did she say anything?'

'Not a word! I think it was me mentioning the constable that did it. Scared her, I reckon.'

'Maybe,' said Marion slowly.

'Anyway, she's gone. Shall I finish the steps, now, ma'am?'

Marion nodded and Kitty, hoping to prolong the excitement a little longer, commented, 'Rum do, though, ma'am, wasn't it? Her so determined to stay.'

'Yes,' said Marion distractedly and although Kitty waited hopefully for a further comment, she could make none. When the maid hurried off to do the steps Marion followed her downstairs and found Pip scurrying around still trailing her lead. As she bent to take it off her thoughts were racing.

'Gilbert Reid,' she muttered, 'you are hiding something from me, and that something involves Meg Swain. I suspect that young woman is not the innocent she pretends to be.'

*

By nine o'clock there were seven people in the waiting room. As the doctor walked through into the surgery he greeted them courteously and somehow managed to force a smile to his unwilling lips; from one or two of them he received a mumbled 'Good morning' by way of reply. He had recovered a little of his composure, for Marion had told him that their unwelcome visitor had departed, but as he seated himself behind his desk and rang the small hand-bell for his first patient his heart was still thudding uncomfortably.

Mrs Peters, a large woman, waddled into the surgery; Gilbert waved a hand to indicate a chair and she sat down heavily.

'It's me gut,' she announced. 'Whenever I eat. Here . . .' She placed a large hand on her right side. 'Doubles me up, it does. My old man says it's indigestion, but I don't reckon so.'

Gilbert nodded, but he did not hear a word she said. Instead, he saw Meg Swain as he had seen her that first day, unlacing her stays with that provocative look in her eyes, her pink tongue outlining her lips seductively. In spite of himself he saw her naked, her flesh firm under his hands, her pale hair tousled over rounded shoulders. Even now the memory proved a potent aphrodisiac and he moved uncomfortably, thankful for the desk that screened the lower half of his body from the gaze of Mrs Peters.

'My God!' he thought desperately. 'How can I still want her after all that's happened!' Dare he risk another visit? And if he did not go to see her, what would she do next? He had never imagined that she would defy him in that way and her appearance on the steps of the house had frightened him immensely. She was becoming a nuisance – no, worse than that. She was becoming a *threat*!

If only he could decide on a suitable course of action . . . but he floundered helplessly, out of his depth, powerless to solve the problem.

Becoming aware that Mrs Peters was looking at him expectantly, he made an effort to concentrate on the matter in hand.

'Like I'm caught in a vice,' she repeated. 'A vice that's getting tighter and tighter. Sometimes I'm doubled up with the pain, and then for no reason it just goes off and I'm right as rain until the next time.'

Gilbert looked at her and tried hard to concentrate. 'And does this happen after a meal?'

She tutted impatiently. 'I've just *told* you, it happens any old time, day or night. Sometimes it wakes me up in the early hours . . .'

A stupid, fat old woman, thought Gilbert, and with uncharacteristic callousness he despised her. Once a humane man, he now found that his patients mattered less and less. All he wanted was to be rid of them so that he could devote time and energy to the problem of Meg Swain which loomed so large and threatened to ruin all he held most dear.

'I'll give you something to ease it,' he told her abruptly and rose to cross to the medicine cabinet.

'But aren't you going to examine me?' she demanded.

'There's no need.'

'But surely . . .' Her affronted tone made it quite clear that she felt she deserved more of his time.

'You described the symptoms very adequately,' he told her firmly.

'Then what is it?' she persisted. 'What have I got? Is it serious or what?'

'No, it's not,' he told her. 'Dyspepsia – that's the medical term for it.'

She looked at him with awe and repeated it carefully. 'Dyspepsia. Is that so? Well, I knew it wasn't indigestion – not with these dreadful cramps, it isn't. Well, well! Dyspepsia. I'll never remember that, doctor, so would you write it down for me, please?'

'You'll remember it,' he told her. He was mixing a white mixture in a small flask and when it was ready he shook it well, poured it into a large bottle and inserted a cork. Having scribbled a dosage on a white label, he stuck this to the bottle.

'That will be sixpence,' he told her. 'Take one teaspoonful first thing in the morning and again last thing at night. It should last about three weeks. Wait for another week after that and then come to see me again. That will be one shilling all together.'

She fumbled in her purse and looked up in feigned surprise. 'I think you'd better send me an account, doctor,' she said. 'I don't seem to have that amount on me. I've just been to pay my rent and –'

He cut short her excuse. 'Next time will do, Mrs Peters.' Anything to be rid of her, he thought irritably.

She rose to her feet with difficulty. 'Dyspepsia,' she repeated, half to herself. 'Well, who'd have thought it!'

He looked at her dispassionately. 'It's really quite common,' he said with the merest touch of sarcasm.

'Send in the next patient as you go out, will you, please?'

And he watched with relief as Mrs Peters waddled out of the room, unaware of the malignant tumour already discernible within her intestine which, within the next six months, would reduce her to half her present weight before finally causing her death.

*

Just before midday Marion was busy in the spare room making up a bed. She smoothed the patchwork quilt she had finished the previous Easter, plumped up the matching cushions which adorned the nearby chair and looked around her with a critical eye. The room smelled strongly of camphor, but she would cut some roses on the day of Rachel's arrival. The ornate brass bedhead gleamed as did the base of the large oil-lamp which stood on the chest of drawers. Much of the patterned wallpaper was hidden by an assortment of framed prints and three of her own water-colours. A hip-bath stood in front of the fireplace and the floor was covered with what had once been a brightly coloured Turkish carpet but was now pleasantly faded. Kitty had laid a fire in the grate – screws of paper, a handful of kindling wood and a scattering of small coal. However, the scuttle stood empty and Marion tutted to herself. Kitty was not usually so forgetful, but presumably the distraction of Meg Swain's untimely appearance had been partly to blame. As she reached out a hand to pull the bell-rope the front door-bell rang, and going out on to the landing to see who it was she was astonished and delighted to see Ralph Gaunt being shown into the morning room.

As she hurried down the stairs Kitty said, 'It's Mr Gaunt, ma'am, to see the doctor.'

'Did you tell him the doctor is out on his rounds?'

'Yes, ma'am. He said he'd speak with you if that was possible.'

'Thank you, Kitty.'

She went into the morning room with one hand outstretched in greeting and found Ralph standing by the window. He turned and grasped her hand firmly, holding on to it for just a fraction longer than was necessary.

'My husband is out . . .' she began, but he smiled broadly.

'I know,' he told her. 'I waited on the corner until I saw him leave the house.'

Marion felt the colour rush into her cheeks. 'But why . . .' she stammered, 'if you wanted to see him . . .?'

'Not quite correct,' he replied. 'I do have business with your husband, but I also hoped to see you.'

Marion searched her mind for a witty answer but could not think of one so said instead, 'Well, here I am. You see me.'

He held up an envelope. 'I do have a legitimate reason for being here. This letter for your husband is an invitation from my mother about her new school. She wants to put forward Dr Reid's name as consultant to the school and would like to discuss it with him. I understand he would be paid a retainer on the condition that he is available to minister to the children or staff when needed.'

'I see. I imagine my husband will be happy to consider it.' She accepted the letter. 'I will see that he receives it the moment he returns from his rounds, and I'm sure he will send your mother a prompt reply.'

For a moment they looked at each other in silence and then Ralph said in a lower voice, 'I looked for you last week – on Thursday and again on Friday. I thought you might be taking Pip for a walk and I meant to ask if I could join you. But I must have chosen the wrong times.'

Marion was silent, so he continued, 'Do you walk Pip at regular times, or just when the spirit moves you?' She gave him an appealing look, but he hardened his heart and persisted. 'Is morning or afternoon the best time to catch you?'

'Mr Gaunt . . .'

'Please call me Ralph.'

'Oh no, I couldn't! Really, I –'

'Not even between ourselves? When we are *alone*?' His eyes denied his mocking tone.

'Alone? But we never are. I mean we shouldn't . . .'

He laughed gently, amused by her discomfiture. 'But we are alone now, aren't we? And you are quite safe.'

Pip whined noisily at his feet and he bent down to pat her. 'Perhaps *you* will be kinder to me,' he said. 'What do you think, Pip? Should your mistress call me Ralph, or would that be too terrible?'

When Pip barked Ralph smiled up at Marion. 'She approves the idea wholeheartedly.' He stood up. 'What a discerning animal. Ralph it is, then.' He put his head on one side and gave her a comic look.

Marion thought that to have objected further would seem churlish. 'Just occasionally then,' she hedged. 'But really, Mr Gaunt, you –'

'Ralph!' he reminded her. 'And may I dare to call you . . .' He shrugged, his hands spread helplessly. 'I don't know your name, do I?'

By this time Marion had overcome her confusion. 'It's Marion,' she told him, 'but please don't talk about us being alone together. My husband would be horrified if he knew.'

'But if I just *happen* to meet you out walking Pip, I may call you Marion?'

'*If* we just happen to meet.'

'I shall see to it that we do!' he assured her.

Baffled, Marion glanced away, afraid that her eyes would reveal that she found the prospect exciting. 'Forbidden fruit!' she thought and then was immediately ashamed of herself. With a moment of insight she saw that he was playing with her, but he *was* only young and

Amelia Gaunt's son and so she considered him harmless.

'Pip looks very smart in the new collar,' he said.

'Yes, she does. It was very generous of you.'

He smiled. 'It was my pleasure. Thank you for suggesting that I might call to see it *in situ*, so to speak. That *was* the suggestion in your note, was it not?'

'It was *Pip's* note,' she reminded him with exaggerated innocence.

'Oh, but of course! How silly of me.'

Marion shook her head. 'This is all too ridiculous,' she laughed.

'But such fun, Marion! Don't you agree?'

With an effort she looked straight into the blue eyes. 'As long as it doesn't go too far,' she temporized.

'It will only do that if we allow it – if we both *wish* it.'

'But I don't,' she stated.

When Ralph staggered back, clutching at an imaginary knife in his heart, she was forced to laugh at his antics in spite of herself.

'You won't take anything I say seriously,' she protested.

'That's because you haven't said anything I want to hear.'

'Please, Mr Gaunt –'

'Ralph!' he corrected again.

'Probably I never will,' she told him. 'Now, I have things to do . . .'

'You want me to go?'

As she hesitated he said, 'Say it and break my heart.'

'Mr – Ralph, I mean – I do think you should leave now.'

'Your wish is my command, O mistress!'

Suddenly she cried, 'Oh please stop! I know you are only amusing yourself with me –'

Further words were suddenly rendered impossible as he stepped forward and kissed her. To Marion it seemed an eternity before they parted and then she gazed at him with an incredulous expression.

'Oh, Ralph,' she whispered faintly. 'That should not have happened.'

He looked equally stricken, and for a long moment they stared at each other in disbelief until Ralph recovered his powers of speech.

'I ought to go,' he said. 'Please say that you forgive me?'

Not trusting herself to speak, she could only nod. A moment latet the front door closed and with a great effort she resisted the temptation to run to the window for a last glimpse of him. For some time she remained panic-stricken, but at last she bent to scoop Pip into her arms.

'Oh, Pip!' she murmered. 'Whatever have we done!'

*

Several days later when Dora arrived at the factory she was surprised to find the girls in a state of great alarm, and even more surprised when Zoe grabbed her by the arm and hurried her into a corner where two of her friends were engaged in earnest conversation. They looked so worried that Dora felt an immediate thrill of apprehension.

'What's the matter?' she cried.

'They're *sending* for people,' Zoe told her in a loud whisper. 'Asking questions and trying to get them to sign a paper. Jenny Hill says we've got to be careful what we say or we'll get the sack!'

'But why?' cried Dora. 'What have we done?'

One of the other girls piped up. 'They want to know who told *The Link* all that stuff they put in the paper – you know, that day when Annie Besant came outside the factory gates. All that stuff they printed about us getting fined and everything – calling us white slaves.'

'White slaves!' giggled the other girl. 'My Pa thought that was a scream. "You, a white slave!" he said to me. "You'd never do something for nothing, you wouldn't!" He thought that was really a laugh.'

Zoe rounded on her fiercely. 'Well, your Pa doesn't know what he's talking about. He doesn't work here and we do. Why shouldn't we get more money, like Annie Besant says? Perhaps we *are* slaves and don't know it. You wouldn't say "No" to another shilling or two at the end of the week, would you?'

Trying to make sense of what they were saying, Dora asked, 'But what exactly do they want us to sign? Are we –'

A familiar voice broke into the conversation as Sid Patten appeared beside them. 'You're paid to work, not gossip,' he told them sharply. 'Get to your benches at once and start earning your money.'

The girls hurried to their benches without another word. Aware of impending trouble, they were reluctant to be singled out for any reason, but when he had moved on Zoe leaned towards Dora and said, 'You notice he didn't threaten to fine us for wasting time like he usually does. That's because of that man who came round yesterday. Jerry Mills says he was an inspector.'

'Inspector of what?'

'How the hell do I know!' Zoe snapped. 'I don't know everything, do I? I'm just telling you what Jerry Mills said. He said they're not allowed to fine us any more; not allowed to dock our money.'

'What, not ever?' It sounded too good to be true.

Zoe shrugged. 'I suppose not ever. Ask him yourself if you don't believe me.'

But glancing up, Dora saw Sid Patten's eye upon her and hastily reached for another coil of matches.

Half an hour later the dreaded moment arrived when Sid Patten told her to go to the manager's office. Her heart sank at the prospect and she obeyed with leaden feet.

Once in the office, she looked round in awe at the imposing mahogany desk and the walls covered with photographs and pictures. Then shrewd brown eyes stared into hers as she stood before the manager, her hands clasped nervously behind her.

'Now then, Miss Becket,' he said, 'have you ever heard of Annie Besant?'

Dora took a deep breath and decided there was no point in lying. She had tried never to lie and she wasn't going to start now.

'Yes, sir,' she said. 'I saw her outside the factory a few days ago.'

'And what did she say to you?'

'Nothing, sir. Not to me because I didn't stop to listen – but I did see her. She had a red hat on.'

'And you are sure you said nothing to her? Nothing at all?'

'No, sir. Nothing, I swear it.'

'And you like working here, Miss Becket?'

Oh Lord! A trick question! thought Dora.

'Yes, sir,' she said cautiously. Well, that was true enough.

The manager was regarding her sternly. 'Do you know what Annie Besant wrote in *The Link* about girls like you?'

Dora hesitated. She only knew because Jeff Bannerman had told her, but she certainly did not want to bring *him* into the conversation. It appeared now that to have talked to anyone, particularly a 'news man', might prove to have been a dangerous mistake.

'I've heard things,' she parried. 'Bits and pieces, like. Everyone's talking about it.'

He consulted a sheaf of papers on his desk. 'I see you have a very good record,' he told her. 'One of our best workers.'

Dora could not resist a feeling of pleasure at this praise and said, 'Thank you, sir.'

'Would you agree that you are well treated here?'

Panic flared at another difficult question. Dora told herself to think carefully before she answered.

'Mostly,' she said at last and saw a flicker of annoyance cross his face.

'What exactly does that mean?' he demanded.

She took a deep breath. 'I mean sometimes the fore-man – one of the foremen – doesn't treat us well. I don't want to say his name, but he picks on us for nothing when he's in a bad mood. Not like his assistant – not like Mr Mills,' she added quickly. 'He's very decent to us.'

'Would you like to sign a paper to that effect?'

Here it comes, she thought. Here comes the sack!

'About Mr Mills being decent, or about the other one *not* being –'

'To the effect that you are well treated.'

She searched her mind for a convincing reason why she should not agree to sign.

'I really don't like signing things,' she said and, aware at once how feeble that sounded, added, 'I don't think I ought to.'

'Is that so?' His tone was sarcastic. 'And why do you think that you ought not to sign?'

'I don't know, sir.'

'But if you agree that you are not ill treated or fined or –'

'Oh, but I have been fined, sir,' she broke in. 'Once for being late; once for talking back to Mr Patten, although I didn't think I was talking back, but he said I was and fined me a penny . . .'

He held up a hand and she fell obediently silent.

'I am not interested in those matters,' he told her. 'Fines should not have been awarded or paid, but that is now academic. There will be no more fines. The question now is that if what Annie Besant says is untrue – which it is – why should you be reluctant to put your signature to a statement which sets the record straight?'

She looked at him desperately. 'Has anyone else signed?' she asked.

'Is that really relevant?' he asked.

'Ah,' thought Dora, 'so they haven't!'

'We-ell,' She squared her shoulders metaphorically. 'We girls have to stick together.'

His expression hardened. 'I'm afraid I don't follow that line of argument,' he told her.

'Well then, sir,' she said desperately, 'if it's all right for one of us, it must be all right for the rest of us because we're all in it together, and if it's not all right . . .' Her voice trailed off. 'What I mean is, it's the same for all of us so if no one else has signed, then I won't either.'

'I'm disappointed in you, Miss Becket,' he said coldly. 'I was rather hoping you might have more sense than some of your workmates. In fact, I may say I was looking to you to set a good example.'

'I'm very sorry, sir, but I can't.'

He drummed his fingers on the desk for a moment, then selected a sheet of typewritten paper and pushed it towards her.

'There is still time to change your mind,' he suggested. 'Just read it through.'

'I'd rather not,' she said, averting her eyes. 'I am sorry, sir . . . sort of.'

For a long moment he looked at her without speaking and slowly shook his head. Then he waved a hand towards the door and Dora escaped into the corridor with an overwhelming feeling of relief which almost immediately gave way to doubts. *Had* all the others refused to sign? Suppose she was one of just a few who refused? Suppose those who refused to sign were sacked? Anxiously she made her way back down the stairs; half-way down she met Zoe coming up, escorted by Jerry Mills.

'What happened?' he asked.

'I didn't sign!'

He nodded, while Zoe grinned and held up a thumb in a gesture of approval, and Dora returned to her work-bench with a lighter heart. When dinner-time arrived, the girls gathered together in worried groups, comparing notes on their respective interviews and wondering what, if anything, would happen next.

'They can't sack us all,' argued Zoe. 'Not if we all stick together. But the thing is, *did* we all stick together or did some sign?'

Annie, one of her friends, said fiercely, 'They'd better not have signed or they'll have me to deal with!'

'Well, we aren't exactly ill-treated . . .' Dora said slowly.

Three pairs of eyes swivelled towards her, full of suspicion.

'You never signed?' cried Annie. 'Dora Becket! If you did –'

'Course I didn't sign!'

'I bet no one signed,' said Zoe. 'We may not be ill-treated, but it's not exactly a picnic, either. I dropped a large hint about old fumble-fingers, but he didn't want to hear. I'd really love to see Sid Patten get his come-uppance! If only we'd thought of it – we could *all* have grumbled about him and then maybe they'd have sacked him to keep us lot sweet.'

'Well, we didn't,' said Dora.

'Pity.'

Another group of girls swept up to them excitedly and one asked, 'Did any of you sign?'

The four of them shook their heads determinedly and the others moved away satisfied to ask the vital question elsewhere. Zoe, Dora, Annie and Vi regarded each other earnestly.

'We must stick together,' Zoe repeated, 'whatever happens.'

Vi looked at her apprehensively. 'Like what?'

'What's going to happen?' Dora asked.

'How do I know? retorted Zoe.

'I daren't get the sack,' said Annie. 'My Pa won't half wallop me if I go home without a job.'

'It won't come to that,' Zoe assured her, and on that hopeful note they turned their attention to their dinner.

Later that afternoon Sid Patten sidled up to Dora and whispered, 'Have you heard what they're saying?'

Dora turned quickly. 'No. What?'

'They're going to make an example of someone.'

'How do you mean, an example?'

'I mean like getting the sack,' he told her, 'but it's only a rumour – you know how these things start.'

Her heart thudded. 'Why are you telling me? It's not me, is it?'

'Course not. Could have been though, but I put in a good word for you.'

'I don't believe you!'

For a wild, panic-stricken moment she wished she *had* signed their wretched paper. But Sid was shaking his head. 'I'm only kidding. I told you, it's just a rumour and maybe it's wrong.'

But the following day the rumour became fact when one of the girls in another department was accused of disobedience and promptly dismissed. The news ran round the factory and at dinner-time a group of girls plucked up courage and decided to ask for her to be reinstated. As they trooped back downstairs every eye was on them and when one of the girls shook her head, a roar of dismay went up. So the threatened retaliations had started! With one accord, everyone abandoned their work and milled together, each girl worried in case she was to be the next victim. In vain the foreman remonstrated with them, urging them to calm down and resume their work. Before anyone knew what was happening the girls had closed ranks and a heady feeling of strength and solidarity overwhelmed them. If they acted as one, it must surely turn out well. Safety in numbers! If they banded together they could not fail.

'One goes – we all go!' cried a voice from the crowd and this was quickly taken up by hundreds of others.

After that, there was nothing else to do but walk out and that is precisely what they did. The match-girls were on strike and no one was more surprised than they were.

*

Amelia sat at her writing desk and frowned at the paper she held in her hand. Glancing at her from behind *The Times* Ralph smiled to himself. Try as he would – and he did try very hard – he could not take his mother seriously. He had grown up with the impression that she was a lovable eccentric and that is how he still saw her. Generous-hearted and public-spirited certainly, but eccentric with it.

'Are you sure about the strike, Mama?' he asked. 'I see nothing about it in *The Times*. Perhaps you were mistaken?'

His mother glanced up irritably. 'Of course I am not mistaken, Ralph. I heard it from the bank manager himself and Mr Foster is not the kind of man to give credence to malicious lies or gossip. If Mr Foster says that they have walked out, then I am sure it is so.'

'And you condone such behaviour?'

'I neither condone nor condemn it,' she told him. 'I think it may be ill-conceived and I trust the poor wretches will not regret their action, but I am bound to say that I think they have shown great spirit. I shall try to buy a copy of *The Link* and read about it for myself. According to Mr Foster they were being badly paid and badly treated, and that is not a happy combination.'

'There are two sides to every question, you know.'

'Don't be trite, dear. It does not suit you.'

'But shouldn't you consider the management's viewpoint also? You must admit that they might be exaggerating. If *The Link* has anything to do with it . . .'

'*The Link* is a perfectly respectable paper, Ralph.'

'But it represents the Law and Liberty League, Mama, and you know the kind of reputation –'

'I know they do a lot of good, Ralph,' she broke in serenely, 'and someone has to fight for the underdog. That is what they are trying to do. Now please let me get on, dear. I am not in the mood for one of your arguments. You have no social conscience and you know it.'

She reached for another sheaf of papers and studied them in silence before throwing them all down with a gesture of exasperation.

'Oh, this is quite preposterous!' she declared. 'They must think I was born yesterday. Fourteen pounds – just to replace a few window-frames! It's daylight robbery and they know it. Well, they can whistle for it! I shall find someone else.'

When Ralph made no comment she asked sharply, 'Are you listening to me, Ralph? I said they can –'

'Whistle for it. I heard you, Mama. Who are these unfortunate "they"?'

'Russell and Croft, from Whitechapel. And Parsons are not much better; their estimate is nearly double – that does include a new front door and all the skirtings, but even so it is a ridiculous price. They must think I am made of money!'

He smiled. 'That's the trouble. They know you *are*, so they price the work accordingly. They know it's a charity fund, so they argue that a few pounds here or there –'

She bridled at his words. 'A *few* I would not object to "a few". What I do object to is this impudence – the assumption that I shall meekly pay up. Well, they will play a different tune when I'm done with them, for I shall call their bluff.'

'I am beginning to feel quite sorry for them!' Ralph told her with a smile.

'That will do, Ralph,' said Amelia with a snort of irritation. 'If you cannot converse sensibly, then I have nothing more to say to you.'

Unperturbed, Ralph resumed his reading while his

mother continued to mutter angrily over various estimates for work on the new school.

After a moment he said, 'Oh, by the way, I shall not be coming to Aunt May's tomorrow. I'm going to the Zoo.'

His mother nodded absent-mindedly and reached for her account book. Ralph waited because he knew she hated to visit Aunt May without him.

'I'm meeting a crazed Russian emigré,' he told her, 'and a defrocked priest.'

'Are you, dear?' Amelia picked up her pen and wrote furiously on one of the estimates.

'We are planning a second attack on the Houses of Parliament,' he went on. 'Guy Fawkes and all that.'

At last she glanced up. 'Don't be frivolous, Ralph.'

'Don't you believe me?'

'Of course not.'

'You're very shrewd, Mama. The truth is that I'm meeting a lady there.'

She regarded him vaguely, then said, 'I shall write to Parsons telling him what I am prepared to pay for the work and that will place the matter firmly in his hands. He won't dare to lose my custom. At least I don't think he will. If he refuses to see reason, then I shall make other enquiries, but I shall be disappointed. And those delays are so infuriating.'

'So please give her my love,' went on Ralph, 'and say that I shall see her again before too long.'

'Who, dear?'

'Aunt May.'

Paying him no attention, Amelia continued, 'And I shall sign it simply "Amelia Gaunt". He doesn't deserve a "Yours truly".' As she reached for a sheet of notepaper, Ralph slipped out of the room and hurried upstairs to take up a pen on his own behalf. After long deliberation, he wrote:

Dear Pip,

I wonder if you have ever had the good fortune to experience the delights of the Zoological Gardens? It is a pleasant place on a Friday afternoon and should you decide to join me there the day after tomorrow, I shall be most happy to show you round. Imagine parrots, monkeys, gazelles and lions! Not to mention fresh air, green grass and trees. There will also be an opportunity to meet other dogs of equal gentility and breeding. If you wish, by all means bring your mistress with you. I shall linger along the Parrot Walk around two-thirty and look forward to renewing our aquaintance.

> Your devoted admirer,
> Ralph Gaunt.

He smiled as he folded the note, slipped it into an envelope and went outside in search of someone to deliver it. Seeing a young lad, he beckoned him over.

'Here's threepence,' he told him. 'Take this letter to that address . . .'

The boy squinted at it uncertainly.

'Can you read?' Ralph asked.

'No, sir, but I can say my numbers. One, two, three, four, five, six –'

'For heaven's sake!'

The boy stopped. 'And my two times –' He began, 'Two, four, six –'

'Take this letter to Harrington Hill,' said Ralph patiently. 'To that number – see? Sixty-eight. A six and an eight.'

'Yessir. A six and an eight.'

'Ask if there is an answer. Do you understand? If there is an answer, you bring it here and I'll give you another threepence.'

The boy's eyes gleamed. 'Will you be here, sir? On this very spot?'

'No, of course not, but I shall be in this house.' Ralph pointed behind him. 'You ring that bell and hand in the letter to whoever opens the door, and I'll bring you another threepence. Do you understand?' The boy nodded. 'Then get along.'

Ralph watched him run along the street, his bare feet soundless, his ragged clothes flapping, and thought fleetingly, 'There but for the grace of God . . .'

He waited impatiently for the boy's return, but day gave way to evening and he did not come.

*

Mrs Cobbett took the letter into the morning room and handed it to Marion, who was sitting with her sister.

'A boy brought it, ma'am,' she announced. 'He wants to know if there's any answer – says there's threepence in it for him if there is. Proper little urchin, he is!'

Marion glanced at the envelope and, surprised, Rachel saw her face flush.

'It's not for me,' said Marion with a light laugh. 'It's for Pip!'

Hearing her name, Pip glanced up from her place by the window and barked dutifully.

Rachel looked puzzled. 'Since when does a dog get letters?' she asked as Marion tore open the envelope.

'This dog does; she has an admirer,' laughed Marion. 'I was going to tell you about it, but I haven't had time yet. See the collar she's wearing? That was a gift.' As her eyes skimmed the page her colour deepened.

Mrs Cobbett waited hopefully for enlightenment, but Marion folded the letter and pushed it back into the envelope. Then she crossed to the window and glanced at the boy who waited on the steps.

'Give him threepence, Mrs Cobbett,' she said, 'but say there is no answer.'

Hiding her disappointment, the housekeeper withdrew and the two sisters exchanged looks.

'What on earth was all that about?' asked Rachel. 'And why do you look so . . .' – she searched for the right word – 'so guilty! And so excited! Really, Marion – if you could see your face! What does it all mean?'

Marion handed over the letter and watched her sister's face as she read it. She could hardly credit Ralph's impudence, yet she found it flattering and somehow endearing. She saw that her sister was frowning, but suddenly Rachel's face broke into a broad smile.

'Marion Reid!' she cried. 'You've had a secret admirer all this time and never breathed a word about it! How could you be so sly?'

Marion laughed breathlessly. 'But Rachel, there was nothing to tell. It's Pip who has the admirer, not me.'

Rachel handed back the letter. 'You are not fooling me, Marion, and I doubt very much if you're fooling yourself! You have an admirer, so tell me about him. Is he young? Rich? Handsome? Tell me or I shall shake it out of you – the way I did when we were children!'

Haltingly, and with much prompting, Marion explained the story to date while her sister listened intently. When she had finished Rachel said, 'And Gilbert knows nothing of it?'

'Only that Ralph sent the collar.'

'And will you tell him about this note?'

'I don't know.' Marion looked at Rachel uncertainly. 'I ought to – and yet I am sure he'll be angry.'

'Then don't tell him,' advised Rachel promptly. 'After all, it's Pip's letter and Pip should tell him, not you!'

Marion laughed with delight. 'Rachel, you are so wicked! And you have the sauce to call *me* sly!'

'Wicked?' protested Rachel. 'Me? I'm not a married woman with a young and handsome admirer – you're the wicked one.'

Her forthright words sobered Marion abruptly. 'Oh, doesn't that sound terrible?' she exclaimed, dismayed.

'It sounds rather exciting to me,' Rachel confessed.

'But you haven't sent him an answer. Are you not going to the Zoo on Friday?'

'But that's tomorrow.'

'So?'

'I daren't!' said Marion.

They looked at each other like two conspirators, then Rachel asked, 'Do you really like him?'

Marion nodded. 'I was going to tell you, Rachel, I swear it, but I was trying to gather my courage. I was so afraid . . .'

Rachel smiled. 'Afraid I would tell you to send him packing?'

'Something like that. Oh, Rachel, it's only a bit of harmless fun – isn't it? I'm quite sure he doesn't mean anything by it. I am older than he is and there are plenty of rich young women so he could take his pick. I keep telling myself that as long as we both know it doesn't mean anything . . .' With a deep sigh she allowed the sentence to remain unfinished, and Rachel put out a hand and clasped hers sympathetically.

'You can't pull the wool over my eyes, Marion,' she said. 'You're in love with him.'

Marion jerked her hand away as she stared at her sister, genuinely shocked by the outrageous suggestion.

'In *love* with him? Certainly not! Oh, for goodness sake, Rachel, don't make matters worse than they are.' She stood up abruptly and moved to stand by the fireplace. 'I admit I find him amusing company and – and probably I think about him more than I should, but as to falling in love – I hope I would never make such a fool of myself! I expect he is just amusing himself with me. Isn't that what young men do? Flirt with married women?'

'I'm hardly the person to ask.'

If there was a trace of bitterness in her sister's voice Marion did not notice it. She read the letter again and then looked at Rachel. 'I suppose I shall have to show it to Gilbert,' she said.

'I don't think you should.'

'Don't you?' Marion looked at her hopefully.

'No – not if it's going to cause trouble between you.'

Marion whispered, 'Oh, damn! I really don't know what to do for the best.'

After a long silence Rachel assumed an air of innocence and said, 'Do you know, Marion, I've never been to the Zoological Gardens. Never. Isn't that sad?' Slowly their eyes met as she continued, 'Perhaps we could find time during my visit here. Perhaps we could go tomorrow – about half past two – what do you think Marion?'

Marion's face lit up. 'Perhaps we could,' she agreed carefully. 'Now, why didn't I think of that? I forgot how much you like animals.'

'All kinds,' Rachel agreed. 'All creatures great and small. Particularly *homo sapiens*!'

'Oh, Rachel! I do so want to, but do we *dare*?'

Rachel regarded her steadily. 'Why not?' she demanded. 'Have we ever dared in our whole lives? Has either of us ever taken a calculated risk?'

Marion's expression changed also. 'Rachel!' she said wonderingly, surprised by the intensity of her sister's manner.

'Well, have we?'

'I suppose not.'

'I've done my duty and you've done yours. We have both done what was expected of us, always and without question. And what has it brought us? I rattle around in a big old house; I shall never marry – oh, don't pretend you think otherwise, because we both know the truth. You live with a man you cannot love and who will never give you the children you want so desperately'

'Oh, please, Rachel! Don't!' cried Marion.

'But it's the *truth*, Marion. High time we faced facts.'

'I have Pip –' Marion began.

'Pip is a *dog*,' Rachel reminded her sharply. 'I am talking about *love*. If this young man loves you . . .'

'Of course he doesn't love me! Don't say such things.'

'Then why are you so afraid of meeting him? Oh, come on, Marion, let's take a risk. Let's have some excitement. Shouldn't life offer just a little more than we have already?'

'Rachel, I . . .' She fell silent under her sister's defiant gaze and for a long time neither spoke again. Then suddenly Marion held out her hands and Rachel took them firmly in hers.

'We'll go to the Zoo tomorrow,' Marion declared. 'I shall tell Gilbert when he comes home from his rounds.'

Rachel's face relaxed into a smile. 'Hide that letter,' she advised, 'and remember, the outing to the Zoo is my idea. You know what Grandmother used to say – a little treat for being good!'

Marion laughed as she reached for the matches. 'A little treat for being good!' she repeated. 'Oh, Rachel! You always did have a way with words!'

CHAPTER SIX

Dora stood at the wash stand and rubbed soap into the hem of her best petticoat. The chipped china bowl, covered in a pattern of tiny rosebuds, was the only item that she inherited when her parents died. The matching jug had been broken years before and the bowl was now partnered by a white jug banded with blue. The room itself was small, with sloping ceilings, and looked out on a sea of roof-tops and chimneys which stretched away into a distance softened by a pall of smoke which was broken occasionally by a church spire. Sunlight came in through a window which, though cracked, was kept clean by weekly washing since the soot ever present in the outside air soon dimmed the glass. Behind her on the wall was her one and only picture which she had bought from a pawn-shop for sixpence – a great extravagance on her income, but she had justified the outlay by considering it as a birthday present to herself. It showed a castle high in the mountains surrounded by trees and clouds, and Dora never tired of looking at it. Her other luxury, the bed, was a flock mattress on the floor in the corner. Most of her friends slept on a straw-filled palliasse, but Dora had aspired to something more comfortable. To pay for it she had worked at home making paper flowers long into the night and five of these flowers (roses of an unlikely red), remained in a small vase on the mantelpiece, providing the only splash of real colour in an otherwise sober room.

Dora liked the view best when it was raining, for then the grimy roofs were washed clean and, if the sun shone soon after, she was sometimes rewarded with a glimpse of a rainbow.

Hearing footsteps on the stairs, she groaned as she anticipated Meg's arrival, no doubt come to gloat over the fact that she was out of work. She opened the door to find her cousin, red-faced and out of breath, leaning against the wall outside.

'Meg! You look like a beetroot!' she cried. 'Come in.' Meg stumbled into the room, took off her coat and collapsed into the only strong chair, panting heavily, and it was a moment or two before she could deliver the first broadside.

'So, Dor, you're out on strike!'

'Looks like it,' Dora agreed mildly. 'Don't blame me. It just happened.'

'Not very smart, though.' Meg tweaked a ribbon on her hat and asked, 'How you going to live with no wages?'

Dora shrugged and went back to her washing. 'I don't suppose it'll be for long,' she suggested. 'Zoe doesn't reckon so.'

Meg snorted. 'What the hell does Zoe know about anything? Strikes me you could all lose your jobs and then you'll be in trouble and no mistake.'

'Oh, you *are* a cheerful soul!' Dora rinsed the petticoat in half a pail of water which she would use later to wash the floor.

'I'm only warning you for your own good, Dor. Now me, in my profession, I'll never be out of work. See what I mean? Factory work is so unreliable. One minute you're earning, the next you're out on your ear! What will you do if they don't take you back?'

'I don't know but I'll think of something. Our committee thinks that –'

Meg rolled her eyes in mock despair. 'Oh, you've got a committee now, have you? Much good that'll do you!'

'Well, someone has to speak up for us,' Dora explained patiently. 'Can't have all of us shouting at once. There's fourteen hundred of us.'

Meg's eyes widened. 'Strewth!'

'The committee is Mary Cummings, Mrs Naulls, Sarah Chapman and a few more – I'm not sure exactly.'

'Well, as long as they don't rope you in.' Meg wagged an admonitory finger. 'If you want my advice, you'll keep off committees. Honestly, Dor, I thought you'd got more sense than to get yourself into such a scrape.'

Dora turned on her irritably. 'Look who's talking!' she retorted, her tone scathing. 'You aren't exactly the world's brightest are you, Meg? Got yourself in the family way! I never thought I'd see *you* in such a scrape, so don't come all high and mighty with me, Meg Swain.'

Meg patted her hair. 'Ah, but I know exactly what I'm doing,' she said loftily, 'because I'm working to a plan. You're just following blindly on – a flock of sheep, that's what you lot are.' She watched aggrieved while Dora shook out the petticoat, draped it over a pole and then wedged the pole out of the window.

'So,' asked Dora when this was done, 'is that why you came round? To have a go at me about the strike?'

Meg produced a screw of paper and tossed it on to the table. 'Brought you some tea,' she said. 'Thought you'd be a bit short.'

Dora eyed it suspiciously, aware that Meg rarely made such gestures without an ulterior motive.

'Thanks,' she said. 'What do you want?'

'Oh, that's charming! That really is charming. What do I want?'

Dora waited resignedly. Her cousin had always been devious and she was hardly likely to change now.

'I want you to take a message,' said Meg, 'to His Nibs.'

'I won't!' said Dora.

'I'll have my tea back then.'

'Take it.'

Meg gave an elaborate sigh which was calculated to soften Dora's hard heart. 'Oh, go on, Dor!' she begged.

'Just this once. I'll never ask you any favour again, I promise. It's not for me – I wouldn't ask for myself, Dor. It's for the baby, because what's going to happen to the poor little sod? How can I look after a kid if I've got to work?'

Dora hardened her heart. 'Same way other folk do, I suppose.'

'You can be a real bitch sometimes, Dor. You know that?' A disgruntled expression settled over her normally cheerful features. Inspired, she added, 'If Ma could hear you now, after all we've done for you!'

Dora felt a small pang of remorse. 'I'm sorry, Meg . . .' she began and Meg, seeing the chink in her armour, took advantage of it. Her face crumpled and she put her head in her hands and managed a few sobbing noises. She would have liked a few tears but they would not come, so she had to make do with a prolonged bout of sniffling behind her fingers.

At last Dora said, 'Look, what exactly did you want me to –' but just then there was another knock at the door and they looked at each other in surprise.

'Who's that?' Meg asked.

'I can't see through the door, can I?'

'Then open it and find out.'

The open door revealed Jeff Bannerman, holding a posy of violets.

'Flowers for the fair,' he said and presented them to Dora with a broad smile.

'Oh, thank you!'

'Do I get invited in today?'

'Yes, come in.'

He caught sight of Meg and said, 'Oh! You've got company.'

Dora made the introductions and Meg brightened visibly at the prospect of someone new to talk to.

'So you're a newspaper man,' she said. 'I've heard all about you. I could tell you a tale or two if I was willing –

which I'm not. You haven't got a camera, have you? I've never had my picture took. Never.'

He shook his head, hoping that she would not stay too long for he was planning to write an article around Dora and had expected to find her alone: 'The poverty of a striking match-girl', from the horse's mouth!

He addressed himself to Dora. 'So, how are you making out?'

Meg giggled. 'I like the way he talks, Dor. "How are you making out?"' She smiled at him. 'It's easy to tell you're a foreigner.'

Jeff smiled politely and looked at Dora.

'I'm fine,' she told him.

Meg said, '*She's* all right, it's me that's got the problem. I've got no husband.' She looked at him hopefully. 'Want to write about me?' she asked, patting her abdomen. 'I could tell you tales. If you knew whose kid this was, you'd be surprised. If I was to mention a certain *duke* . . .'

Dora cried, 'Meg Swain! You fibber!' although nothing Meg did really surprised her.

'I really wanted to write about Dora,' said Jeff, 'because of the strike.' He turned to her. 'Did you know there's going to be a meeting on Mile End Waste on Sunday July the eighth and that –'

'July the eighth!' echoed Dora. 'But that's more than a week away. Surely we'll be back at work before then?'

Meg tossed her blonde head derisively. 'I wouldn't want to go back to work,' she declared. 'If I worked for those old scrooges, I'd never go back!' and she glanced surreptitiously at Jeff to see if he was impressed by her spirit.

Dora rounded on her quickly. 'It's all right for you – you'll never be out of work.'

'Well? What's stopping you from doing what I do?' asked Meg. 'It's a living, same as anyone else, it's no disgrace.'

'No thanks!' Dora muttered.

Her cousin's eyes narrowed. 'Well, you just watch it, Miss High and Mighty! You might be glad of a chance to earn a few bob my way if the strike does go on. You might have to come down off that high horse of yours and sell yourself, same as plenty of others. See how you like that!'

Jeff held up his hands imploringly. 'Ladies!' he begged. 'No harsh words, please.'

Meg's anger evaporated. 'Hark at him,' she giggled. 'We're *ladies* now!'

Jeff turned back to Dora. 'Annie Besant is going to persuade the newspapers to start a strike fund. You've all got to be at the Mile End meeting to register for your money. There'll be some important speakers – Cunningham Graham, the MP, and Clementina Black.' Seeing her puzzled expression, he added, 'You must have heard of her.'

'Well, I haven't,' said Dora crossly.

'No more have I,' agreed Meg. 'Who the hell is Clementina Black?'

'She's a Fabian, very wealthy and influential, and she's taking up the strikers' cause. Oh yes, and the Reverend Stewart Headlam will be there – and almost certainly Burrows.'

'I wish someone would take up *my* cause,' said Meg. 'I could do with one of them knights in armour what rides about on a white horse!'

'Sir Galahad!' Jeff suggested, but both girls looked at him blankly.

He stayed for a quarter of an hour, asking Dora questions and making notes, but when it became clear that Meg had no intention of leaving he was forced to make his departure.

When he had gone, Meg said, 'Honestly, Dor, you have all the luck. Now you'll be in the papers.'

'Only the American ones,' Dora reminded her. 'I

certainly don't want to appear in any of ours; I'd get into trouble.'

'Suppose he puts you in *The Times*!'

'Don't!' Dora cried, dismayed.

Over a cup of tea, Meg again asked Dora to intervene with the doctor. 'Tell him how much I love kids,' Meg told her. 'Say how you know I'll make a good mother and how I only do what I do because I've fallen on hard times. You could get round him, Dora, better than me.'

Eventually Dora reluctantly agreed to go to Harrington Hill and try to speak to Gilbert about Meg's plight.

Having finally won her cousin over, Meg rose to take her leave. 'Look, Dor,' she said. 'You know you can always doss down with us if things get really tough.'

The prospect of 'dossing down' with Meg was almost as unwelcome as the possibility of a week with no money for food and rent, but Dora was too polite to say so and thanked her for the offer.

'I may go down to Kent,' she said. 'Try to get some fruit picking – strawberries or something. I don't want to lose this room.'

'How can you go down to Kent?' Meg asked. 'You've got to be here to go to that meeting.'

Dora sighed. 'Oh yes, so I have,' she agreed. 'Oh dear, I'll have to think of something.'

'I've heard *that* before!' Meg told her caustically as, with a last shrug of her plump shoulders, she made her way heavily downstairs leaving Dora to close the door despondently behind her.

*

Next morning, true to her promise, Dora put in an appearance at No. 68 Harrington Hill and joined the four patients who were already there. The waiting room was small and bare and they sat along the walls on benches, trying to avoid each other's eyes. For a few moments Dora sat in splendid isolation against one wall, but then an elderly man joined her. He was small and wizened, his face was white and his skin waxlike. Dora hoped that his disease, whatever it was, was not infectious, for she had no desire to catch anything unpleasant on Meg's behalf. He wheezed heavily and continuously, one hand held to his chest, but he spoke to no one and his suffering were studiously ignored by his fellow patients.

Suddenly from beneath one of his trouser-legs a trickle of urine appeared and began to spread out across the linoleum which covered the floor. Immediately every eye was focused on it, but the old man himself appeared quite oblivious to what was happening. As the puddle continued to grow, eyes were hastily averted as it became obvious that someone must do something. Dora waited, but no one moved and at last she went out into the hall to look for help.

From behind one of the other doors she heard the sound of light laughter and taking her courage in both hands, she stepped up to the door and rapped sharply. It was opened by a woman whom Dora took to be the doctor's wife.

'I'm afraid there's been a bit of an accident,' said Dora. 'An old gentleman – I think he's wet himself. It's all over the floor –'

'Oh dear! It's probably Mr Bates, poor old soul. I'll call Kitty to mop it up. Thank you for telling me, Miss . . .'

'Becket. Miss Dora Becket.'

Marion looked at her carefully. 'Have I seen you before? Are you one of my husband's patients?'

Dora hesitated. 'No exactly. That is, my cousin is – sort of . . .'

'And your cousin is?'

Feeling trapped, Dora cursed her foolishness. She wished she had let someone else report the old man's problem, but it was too late now.

'Meg Swain,' she replied.

'And you have come here on your cousin's behalf, you say? To collect a prescription?'

'I'm not sure exactly.' Dora felt certain that the doctor's wife was giving her a penetrating look.

'And what is wrong with your cousin? Why doesn't she come herself?'

This wretched woman was asking too many questions and Dora, blushing under the cool scrutiny, searched her mind feverishly. 'She's in the family way – and not feeling too good,' she added.

'Ah! And is your cousin a married woman?'

'Not exactly,' said Dora, flustered.

'What are her symptoms?'

Dora invented wildly. 'Sort of cramps – and she feels dizzy – not all the time but some of the time.'

'And she can't walk?'

'It's a long way from Fashion Street.'

'She should surely have chosen a doctor nearer to her home. What made her choose Dr Reid?'

Dora wondered desperately if it was safe to mention Mrs Gaunt and decided that she would have to chance it. 'It was because of Ellie,' she explained, 'because of her jaw. Mrs Gaunt sent her to your husband and so Meg thought he'd be a good choice . . .' She fell silent.

'And no doubt hoped that Mrs Gaunt would meet the cost? Is *that* it?'

Dora could see no harm in letting her believe that and she nodded, but before the doctor's wife could make further comment another woman appeared in the doorway behind her and asked, 'Is something wrong, Marion?'

'No, no!' said Marion. 'A poor old man has tiddled on the floor, that's all.'

'Good heavens!'

'Oh, it's not the first time and it won't be the last. It's the failing muscles.' Turning to Dora she said, 'Thank you, Miss Becket. I'll see to it now,' and thankfully Dora escaped back to the waiting room.

A maid soon appeared with a bucket and mopped up the puddle, and another patient went through into the surgery. Ten minutes later several more people arrived and Dora's nervousness increased as she found herself hemmed in on every side. On her left, a woman held a baby which was covered in unsightly spots and screamed without pause. Opposite, a young man nursed a cut hand which was still bleeding profusely into a dirty cloth which had been wrapped around it. A small boy scratched his head incessantly and was cuffed by his father from time to time. At last Dora could stand it no longer and, jumping up from the bench, hurried out of the room to breathe deeply in the untainted air of the hallway. She almost ran to the door and let herself out into the street, infinitely relieved to be rid of her depressing companions.

'I'm sorry, Meg,' she said to her absent cousin. 'If you want to give him a message, you'll have to take it yourself!' And she made her way back up the hill, putting Meg's problem determinedly from her and concentrating upon her own.

*

The Zoological Gardens on a Sunday were a favourite haunt of fashionable people, but Friday found them relatively empty. Marion resplendent in slate blue and Rachel in grey sauntered casually along in the warm June sunshine, trying to pretend they were not looking for anyone in particular but simply admiring the scenery and enjoying the fresh air and open space. They had arrived at half-past one, had already inspected the big cats and the elephants and having studied the large map of the Gardens, were now making their way towards the Parrot House. Marion was determined to be a little late – but not too late, in case Ralph assumed they were not coming!

Not that they had said they *were* coming, of course –
as Marion pointed out more than once – for they had not
answered Ralph's letter, but if he was at the Zoo he
would surely find his way to the Parrot House in the
hope that Marion had changed her mind.

The sisters strolled arm-in-arm, admiring the fashionable people and wishing they had not eaten their lunch
so hurriedly. Rachel tried to smother another hiccough
and they exchanged conspiratorial looks.

'Whatever will he say when he sees we have left Pip at
home?' whispered Marion.

'What will who say?' Rachel asked with a reckless
disregard for her grammar.

Marion's mouth twitched. 'Oh, I forgot. We aren't
here to meet anyone.'

'Of course not,' Rachel insisted. 'We are here to look
at the birds. Remember, I have always been fascinated
by our feathered friends!'

'I'll try to remember,' Marion vowed.

'Oh look! Is that him?' cried Rachel, giving a slight
nod in the direction of a tall young man, but Marion
shook her head.

'He's slimmer and not quite so handsome,' she said as
a neighbouring clock struck the half hour. Then abruptly
she stopped, took Rachel by the arm and began to walk
back the way they had come.

'Marion!' protested Rachel. 'Where are we going?'

'I can't face him,' Marion admitted. 'Oh, Rachel, this
is too ridiculous. Whatever are we doing here? I should
never have agreed to come. Whatever will he think of
me? We must go home at once.'

'But what will Gilbert think?' asked Rachel. 'He'll
wonder why we're back so early. Oh, do pull yourself
together, Marion. Ralph can't bite you. And why should
he think ill of you? It was his idea, remember? And it's
not as though you are here alone. I am here to play
gooseberry and spoil your fun.'

Marion clutched at the idea gratefully. 'Oh yes, of course you are. I'm being silly.' She stopped, sighed and faced her sister. 'Do you remember when we were little and used to go to those awful parties? Mama would tell you to look after me because I always used to feel sick with excitement.'

Rachel nodded. 'Once you fainted!' she recalled. 'Do you remember? It was at the Hemmings girl's birthday party. You stepped inside the front door and fell down in a dead faint. I was so cross! They put you in one of the bedrooms to recover and I had to run upstairs every five minutes to see how you were. You quite ruined that party for me.'

Marion laughed. 'Oh, poor Rachel! I never thought about you, I was so busy being sorry for myself.'

'Well, if you're thinking of fainting today . . .'

'No, of course I'm not, but I have to admit I have butterflies in my stomach – very large butterflies. I feel the way I did when we missed the art lesson to pick bluebells!'

Rachel gave her arm a reassuring pat. 'Come on,' she said. 'We are going to the Parrot Walk to look for your nice Mr Gaunt – and don't bother to faint, because if you do I shall just keep walking and I shall have him all to myself!'

Five minutes later they found themselves at the end of a long tree-lined walk where lime trees, laburnums and larches provided a welcome shade from the afternoon sun. A wire had been strung from tree to tree and from it delicate wooden perches were suspended at intervals of three feet or more. On these perches a dazzling variety of parrots swung and squawked to the delight of an admiring crowd. Men, women and children had gathered to watch their antics – the men sober in dark jackets and toppers, the women brightly dressed with flowers and ribbons in their hats, the children looking unnaturally prim in starched shirts and frilled dresses.

Lost in heartfelt admiration for the exotic birds, Marion and Rachel almost forgot the purpose of their visit until a voice beside them said, 'Aren't they beautiful?' and they turned to find Ralph Gaunt beside them. As he took off his hat and gave a little bow, Marion felt a surge of excitement and was thankful that she still held her sister's arm.

'Oh, Mr Gaunt,' she began, 'allow me to introduce my sister Rachel who is visiting us . . .'

He gave Rachel a warm smile and said, 'A pleasure. May I presume to call you Rachel, since your sister has been kind enough to become Marion to me?'

'Of course,' murmured Rachel, charmed by his interest.

'Pip sends her kind regards,' Marion told him, 'but we thought dogs might not be allowed in the Zoo and then –'

Rachel broke in, 'And then we would have been turned away also.'

'How wise!' said Ralph. He turned to Marion. 'I didn't think you would come. You didn't answer my letter, but I thought I would take a chance and I'm so glad I did.'

Rachel remembered her role and said quickly, 'Marion thought we shouldn't come, but I have always been fond of birds – especially parrots – so I persuaded her that we should.'

'Then I have you to thank,' he told her, 'and I have two handsome companions for the afternoon. I insist that you take an arm each so that we do not lose each other in the crush.' He extended an arm to each of them and neither mentioned that the Parrot Walk was not as crowded as he suggested.

As they strolled together, admiring the birds and chattering light-heartedly, Marion could not recall when she had felt so absurdly happy. The feel of Ralph's arm roused in her so many exciting thoughts that she felt almost light-headed as they paused to admire a large Amazon parrot, resplendent in green plumage with yellow cheeks and a blue forehead. Next to him was a grey parrot from Africa which sported red feathers in its tail and Rachel, in her assumed role of bird-fancier, read out the details: 'Parrots have strong curved beaks with which they pull themselves from branch to branch. They live in large groups and eat nuts and fruit.'

They exclaimed together over the pure white cockatoo with its crest of yellow feathers which hung upside down from the perch, screeching for attention, and the pale green parakeet with the tell-tale black band round its neck which was daintily accepting a morsel of food from a young admirer.

The air was full of colour and sound as the birds bobbed extravagantly on their swings, delighting the eyes with their bold plumage and assaulting the ears with their raucous voices. When they had seen them all, Ralph led them to the bears and then the monkeys and chimpanzees. Both sisters demurred at the prospect of the snakes, so Ralph took them instead to the refreshment arcade where they sat at a small wicker table, sipping iced lemonade and nibbling almond biscuits. Ralph proved himself a wonderfully entertaining escort, amusing them with a feast of reminiscences from his Grand Tour and Marion – taking a quick glimpse at her sister's glowing face – was pleased to see that she too was enjoying every moment. Briefly she tried to imagine how it would be if she and Ralph were together without Rachel, but soon rejected the idea as unworthy. After all, had it not been for Rachel, they would still be at home and Ralph would be wandering the Gardens without them.

Suddenly another thought crept into her mind – suppose Ralph were to fall in love with Rachel? How could she begrudge Rachel *her* chance of happiness? Stealing another glance at her sister's flushed face she reminded herself that she had chosen Gilbert Reid and nothing could untie that particular knot. Ralph was simply a diverting companion and he must never be anything more to her than that. Deep in her heart she felt the first stirrings of guilt for her present happiness and wished that she and Gilbert could feel even a fraction of such pleasure in each other's company. How much better if her husband could provide such a response; if she too could bring him such joy; but the failure of the physical side of their marriage had eroded the rest of the relationship to such a degree that only mutual consideration and sterile courtesy remained. It was not enough for either of them, but she was helpless to ameliorate the problem. Their marriage had become a barren wilderness in which love and affection no longer thrived and where a passionate heart could only wither and die. For a wild moment she imagined herself married to Ralph Gaunt, sharing his life, caring for him. She thought how wonderful it would be to wake in the morning and find him beside her, his face soft in repose, his hair tousled on the pillow. This picture aroused in her a sudden desire which she had not experienced for many years and against which she closed her eyes as though in pain. Ralph would give his wife children; Ralph would be a warm and caring partner, a firm but loving father. He was the man she should have married, but what good was that knowledge now? She was married already to a cold-hearted stranger. At the crossroads of her life she had made a wrong decision and must now tread a lonely path.

Marion sighed deeply and became aware suddenly that both her companions were staring at her.

'A penny for them!' Rachel offered, while Ralph's eyes looked into hers with . . . was it compassion?

Startled, she stammered, 'What is it?'

'You look so sad,' he said gently. 'How can we make you smile again?'

She smiled at once with forced cheerfulness, shaking off her anguished thoughts as she glanced from one to the other.

'Have we seen everything there is to see?' she demanded. Ralph began to tick off the various animals they had seen and discovered that only the eagles had not been inspected, but on examining their map it became clear that to reach the eagles' eyrie they would have a very long walk and they decided unanimously to save the huge birds for a possible future visit.

'A shame,' said Ralph mischievously, 'since Rachel is *so* fond of birds!'

The two women exchanged guilty glances and then exploded into laughter. That Ralph had not been deceived did not matter any more; nothing mattered except that they had had a wonderful day.

Cheerfully they made their way out of the Gardens, and at last it was time for Ralph to hail a cab to take them all home. Squashed up together in the shabby hansom, Marion wondered what Gilbert would say if he could see them.

For the sake of appearances Ralph was dropped off first and the two sisters returned unchaperoned to Harrington Hill, where they descended from the cab and paid off the driver. As they turned to mount the steps Rachel said, 'We must be careful. Don't look so happy!'

'Do I?'

'Yes, you do,' Rachel told her. 'You look positively radiant. Remember you have only been to the Zoo with me!'

Marion nodded, but it was going to be difficult.

*

Later that evening as ten o'clock approached, Marion congratulated herself on the way she had behaved since their return, doing nothing that might arouse Gilbert's suspicions. It had been comparatively easy while there were three of them, but when the time came for them to retire to their respective bedrooms it became more difficult. To prevent any further mention of the Zoo, Marion decided to introduce another topic of conversation and her exchange with Dora Becket, earlier in the day, seemed an obvious choice.

'I spoke to one of your patients this morning,' she remarked as she sat at the mirror brushing her hair. Gilbert, sitting on the edge of the bed, glanced up from untying his shoelaces.

'And which one might that be?' he asked.

'A Miss Becket – at least, she isn't one of your patients but her cousin is. Do you remember Meg Swain, the sister of that poor little girl with "phossy jaw"?'

Although she sat with her back to Gilbert, she could see his reflection in the mirror and could not miss his reaction to Meg Swain's name. He straightened up abruptly and she saw a strange expression on his face which she could not recognize; then he quickly bent once more to his task so that his face was hidden from her.

'I don't recall a Miss Becket,' he replied. 'Are you sure you were not mistaken?'

'Quite sure. She told me she had come on her cousin's behalf – to collect a prescription, she said, only I must admit she looked rather uncomfortable and I soon found out why.'

Slowly he raised his head. 'Why?' he asked.

'Well, apparently the cousin is with child,' Marion told him, 'and she is having cramps and feeling sick, and having no husband is obviously hoping to encroach further on Amelia Gaunt's generosity; hoping she will pay for her treatment as she paid for Ellie's. I asked her why the cousin didn't come herself, but it seems she lives in Fashion Street and that's quite a walk in her condition.'

Gilbert made no comment and Marion climbed into bed. He carried his shoes to the door, opened it and put them outside for Kitty to clean in the morning.

'I did not see her,' he said, as he too climbed into bed and blew out the candle.

'I wonder why not,' mused Marion. 'Perhaps she thought better of it. Maybe I jolted her conscience with my remarks about Amelia Gaunt.' She thought for a moment and went on, 'Should she be having cramps? Is that normal in her condition?'

'I would not think so.'

'Well, since Miss Becket did not accomplish her mission we can no doubt expect a visit from Miss Swain herself. Is she married, I wonder?'

'It really is of no interest to me, Marion!' he said sharply. 'I do not want to discuss the woman any more.'

For a moment Marion lay silent, surprised by his tone, and some of her earlier suspicions resurfaced uneasily.

'What does she do for a living?' she asked.

'I said I did not want to discuss her.'

'*Is* she a woman of the streets, do you think?' He made no answer and at last Marion said, 'Poor little baby. Fancy being born to such a mother and to such a terrible life!'

Gilbert sat up suddenly and faced her. 'I told you I do not want to speak of her!' he said furiously. 'Can't you understand? My patients are my affair – *and* how I treat them *and* what I charge for that treatment.' His voice was tight with anger. 'Mind your own damned business!'

Marion, sick at heart, wondered why the luckless Miss Swain should provoke such an outburst. Try as she would she could think of only one explanation but that was so bizarre! So impossible! She stared helplessly into the darkness while Gilbert tossed restlessly beside her.

*

Dora arrived at the Mile End Waste ground to find a large and boisterous crowd already gathered in front of a makeshift stage, on which two men whom she did not know were in deep conversation with Annie Besant. She recognized most of her fellow workmates among the crowd, but at first she could not find Zoe or any of her friends so she wandered alone, astonished to see how many strangers had also decided to attend. On all sides she heard snatches of conversation concerning the strike, but try as she would she could not entirely share their obvious enthusiasm for the fight. She had chosen to live alone and would find it difficult to pay the rent, but few people, if any, would sympathize with her predicament.

A few chairs for the speakers had now been placed on the stage and the meeting began. A thousand pairs of eyes were focused on the platform as the first speaker rose to address the crowd, and the listeners strained their ears, determined not to miss a word of what was said. Dora paid close attention and learned that people called shareholders were making a great deal of money from Bryant and May, and that among these fortunate people were a large number of clergymen who were 'grinding the faces of the poor' and should be setting a better example. Dora did not quite see the significance of this point but it was obviously of great concern, judging by the angry murmurs from the crowd and cries of, 'Shame on them!'

A woman near Dora suddenly raised a fist into the air and shouted, 'Let them come and do our work! Let them see what it's like to be a white slave!' and there were a few ragged cheers which slowly grew into a roar of approval. Apparently encouraged by this, the speaker on the platform went on to discuss at length something called the 'ethics of shareholding', and then to denounce rich businessmen who were growing richer each day by exploiting the unfortunate match-girls who apparently lived in abject poverty and were very forlorn creatures.

Dora found this rather irritating since she did not see herself in that way, but she quickly repressed the ungrateful thought and concentrated on the speaker once more.

Suddenly someone whispered in her ear, 'I've got something for you, Miss Becket,' and she turned to find Sid Patten beside her.

'Whatever it is, I don't want it,' she hissed.

'You haven't seen it yet.'

'I don't want to, thanks very much.'

'You'll change your tune when you see it. Here . . .' He thrust a small package into her unwilling hand. 'Open it up and take a look. No girl in her right mind would say "No" to what's in there.'

Intrigued in spite of herself, Dora stared down at the roughly wrapped parcel; through the brown paper she glimpsed what looked like red leather.

'Go on! Open it, it won't bite you.'

She began to shake her head, but Sid's good humour seemed a very temporary emotion. He snatched the box from her and opened it to reveal a gold ring set with five opals.

Dora gasped with surprise and Sid's cheerful mood was immediately restored.

'Like it, do you?'

'Mr Patten, it's beautiful!'

'You can call me Sid.'

'But where on earth did you get it?' she asked, for even to her inexpert eyes the ring looked expensive and clearly was far beyond the means of anyone on Sid's wages.

He tapped one side of his nose and laughed. 'Ask no questions, hear no lies! Go on, take it. Try it on for size. It could be yours, if you play your cards right.'

'You mean it's stolen?'

'What if it is? It won't burn your finger, will it?'

Hastily, she shook her head. 'I'd rather not, thanks all the same.'

'Don't be so bloody daft!' he protested. '*I* didn't nick it, if that's what's worrying you. I got it off a mate – my brother Jack, if you must know.'

'And did he nick it?'

He put a finger to his lips and glanced round furtively. 'Course he did,' he told her, with pride in his voice. 'Rings like that don't grow on trees, you know. How else would he get it? He's not a bloody millionaire. Try it on. It'll suit your finger. I chose it specially.'

Her eyes grew wider. 'You mean there were others?'

'Others? Not half! My brother's a proper "Jack the Lad". Jack by name and Jack by nature! You'd like him – all the girls do. I done him a favour, so he let me have this on the cheap, like.'

'I'm sorry, Mr Patten,' said Dora, hiding her dismay as best she could, 'but I can't possibly take it.'

'Why not?'

'Because I wouldn't want to "play my cards right" as you put it. I just don't want to.'

'You don't know what's good for you,' he snarled. 'That's your trouble. One of these days you'll wake up to the fact that you're' – he tapped his forehead – 'just a stuck-up little madam! You think you're too good for the likes of me! You think you're so –'

Dora had no wish to antagonize him. 'I don't think we're suited, Mr Patten, that's all,' she told him.

He thrust his face close to hers. 'Oh, you don't? Well, that's your bad luck. There's plenty of girls with their heads screwed on right, not like you. I could take my pick from a dozen girls a damn sight prettier than you!'

'So why bother with me?' Dora cried. 'Choose someone with her head screwed on right. Give *her* your stolen ring and –'

But he clapped a hand roughly over her mouth. 'Cut that out!' he threatened.

She jerked away from him. 'Then leave me alone, Sid Patten. Once and for all, I'm not the one for you.'

He grabbed her arm so tightly then that she winced in pain and several people turned to see what was happening. Sid released her. 'You wait, you stupid little bitch! You just wait!' he told her in a furious voice.

For a moment they glared at each other, then he turned and a moment later had melted into the crowd.

More shaken than she would admit by the exchange, Dora tried once more to pick up the thread of the speaker's message. Annie Besant was outlining the match-girls' grievances – the deductions which had been made from their pay, the fines for trivial so-called offences. It was all true, Dora reflected. Maybe Annie Besant was right and they were being treated unfairly by their employers. The reference to heavy-handed charge-hands certainly rang a bell, she thought ruefully, if Sid Patten was an example; yet Jerry Mills, a fair man, was being tarred with the same brush. She wished she dared shout a protest on his behalf, but the thought of all the heads that would turn in her direction effectively kept her silent.

Soon it was the turn of their Member of Parliament and he spoke, among other things, about a Mr Bradlaugh who was going to ask a question in the House of Commons. He received a loud round of applause for his pains and was followed by Clementina Black. The mood of the crowd remained cheerful and supportive; although there were occasional dissenting voices, these were few and far between and quickly silenced.

Dora listened to them all, but she was waiting to hear about the strike fund and at long last these details came. The registration of the strikers was to take place in the Assembly Rooms and there in serried ranks with the rest of the match-girls, Dora later waited patiently until it was her turn to be presented to the presiding officers.

'Name and address, please.'

'Dora Becket, 36 Usher Road.'

'Married or single?'

'Single.'

'Factory occupation?'

'I'm a cutter-down. I fill the match-boxes.'

'What were your wages last week?'

'Seven shillings and sixpence.'

A ticket was given to her with a number on it and Dora looked at it with something approaching awe. Two hundred and seventy-four.

'Bring that with you when the strike pay is doled out. No ticket, no money, so don't lose it.'

'I won't!' she promised.

Apparently it was all over; it was almost an anticlimax.

Outside the Hall she found Zoe in triumphant mood. 'Weren't they grand!' she cried. 'All those people spouting off about us girls! They really mean to see us right.'

'I take my hat off to them,' Annie agreed. 'I never thought to hear anything like it. It's not until you listen to someone like that you realize just what we've had to put up with all these years. When that second man said about the employers telling lies about us – I mean, we'd never have known!'

'I wonder what we'll get,' said Zoe. 'I mean, will we get our usual money or a bit more?'

Vi said, 'More? You'll be lucky! A bit less, I reckon.'

Dora shrugged. 'Depends on how much they can collect, I suppose. Married women with kids will most likely get more than us single girls.'

Zoe grinned. 'Wish I was married! And talking of married, Dora Becket, did I see you and the horrible Sid with your heads together?'

Dora gave an exaggerated shudder and told them about the ring.

Zoe looked thoughtful. 'You could have sold it,' she told Dora.

'That would have paid your rent for weeks to come, strike pay or no strike pay.'

'What, get myself lumbered with old fumble-fingers?' Dora said. 'No thanks! Anyway, he'd half murder me if I sold it.'

'You could pretend you'd lost it.'

At this point they were joined by Jeff Bannerman and introductions were made all round. 'I guess that went as well as could be expected,' he told them. 'Are you girls satisfied?'

They all agreed that matters appeared to be going well and that they were in good hands. Around them the crowds were slowly dispersing and after a few minutes Zoe, Annie and Vi drifted away, leaving Dora and Jeff alone.

'So you've got your article,' she said.

He nodded. 'It'll be in the *New York Times*, I wouldn't wonder. How does it feel to be famous?'

'I'm not famous.'

'Oh, but you are. You're making history, Dora. Women on strike! Of course you're famous. How does it feel?'

Dora thought about it and then smiled ruefully. 'Not as good as I expected!' she answered. 'In fact, it frightens me at times.'

Jeff laughed and took her arm. 'You'll feel braver when you've eaten,' he assured her. 'I told my landlady about you and she says I'm to take you back for a bite of dinner. What do you say? She's a decent old thing.'

Dora was thrilled at the prospect of seeing Jeff's lodgings. 'I'd love to,' she told him.

As they made their way arm in arm across the grass in the direction of the road, they failed to see Sid Patten who was watching their departure with an expression of great animosity. If they had known what was going on in his mind, their joy would have given way to apprehension.

*

That same night the taproom of the Three Horsemen was hazy with tobacco smoke and the noise was deafening. An assortment of customers filled the room; some were leaning heavily on the bar, others swaying precariously on their feet, while a few slumped on the meagre seating which consisted of nothing more than planks of wood supported on iron legs. The floor was thick with greying sawdust which had seen better days and one or two dogs of indeterminate breed sprawled in positions of abandonment or stood with ears pricked, the epitome of watchfulness. The tapman kept a wary eye on known troublemakers as voices rose and fell and the inevitable arguments developed. Ribald jokes were greeted with loud guffaws of laughter, secrets were shared, rumours were started and racing tips were passed on. Large mugs of porter were downed freely and orders for more of the same dark liquid were bellowed across the bar by men who had already drunk more than enough.

About a quarter of the clientele were women – the young ones gaudily dressed in their best feathers and flounces, the older ones more soberly arrayed and beginning to fray round the edges. The jokes the women told were no less bawdy than those of the men and their delighted screeches assaulted the ears of their nearest neighbours and drew forth unflattering comments which only provoked further laughter.

In the midst of this unbridled hilarity Sid Patten and his brother sat with their heads close together. Sid, still smarting from Dora's rejection of his ring, was putting forward a proposition, but Jack's befuddled brain was finding it hard to comprehend.

'I just want to give him a little warning,' Sid told Jack for the third time. 'Or maybe a not-so-little one!' He laughed. 'Scare him off, like, let him know he's not appreciated. Know what I mean, Jack? We could do it, the two of us.'

Jack looked at him, his brow furrowed. 'Do what?'

'Christ Almighty!' Sid exploded. 'I've just *told* you. Why the hell can't you listen?'

'Told me what?'

'About this bloody little runt – Bannerman. Her fancy

man. I asked around a bit and it seems he's one of our American cousins! He's the one.'

'What?'

Sid brought his fist down so hard that every mug on the rickety table jumped into the air, spilling some of the contents. Grumbles arose all around, but Sid ignored them.

'Listen, damn you,' he insisted. 'I know where he lives and I want the two of us to knock him about a bit. We can wait for him one night – tomorrow, maybe – and bloody his nose for him.'

Jack made a superhuman effort. 'Can't do it tomorrow,' he muttered with a shake of his head. 'Got something on.'

'Like what?' Sid demanded truculently.

Jack lowered his voice. 'Like a job.'

Even Sid was shaken and his eyes rounded in reluctant admiration. 'Another job? You've hardly had time to get rid of the last lot of stuff. You want to watch it, Jack. You're pushing your luck, that's what you're doing. Tomorrow night? Bloody hell!'

Jack grinned, showing broken teeth that bore witness to many fights. 'You worry about yourself,' he advised. 'I'm a big boy now.'

Obediently Sid nodded. 'But Bannerman,' he persisted. 'We could make it Tuesday – is it on for Tuesday night?'

Jack straightened his back and looked at his brother. 'We could top him!'

Sid paled. '*Top* him? Christ no, Jack. Are you mad? Just rough him up a bit, like I said, to put him off the girl.'

Jack considered, then tapped his empty mug with a grimy finger. 'Buy us a drink and you're on!' he said. 'Tuesday it is!'

CHAPTER SEVEN

To Meg's great disgust, she went into an early labour in the small hours of the following day. With a minimum of pain and fuss and a straightforward delivery, she gave birth to a baby girl. The child was small but perfectly formed and, apart from a small cry of protest when slapped, appeared to take little interest in the proceedings. Exhausted and furious, Meg lay back while Dora washed the baby and Ellie made a pot of tea. Alf had taken refuge with the people in the next room, but Sally's baby slept in its makeshift crib in a corner.

Meg wiped the perspiration from her face. 'Why did it have to come so bloody early?' she demanded. 'I haven't got nothing ready and I haven't sorted His Nibs out. I was doing my damndest for the poor little perisher. Why couldn't it have waited a few more weeks?'

Ellie paused in pouring the tea to mumble something and Meg scowled. 'I never said it was the kid's fault, did I? I only said, "Why did it have to come so early?"'

'Oh, give it a rest, Meg, for heaven's sake!' said Dora. 'It's here and the worst is over, so stop moaning, can't you?' She looked pale and harassed. 'And stop calling her "it". It's a girl, so give her a name, can't you? You must have thought of some name you like.'

'Well, I haven't,' Meg answered sulkily. 'I told you, I wasn't ready to have it and anyway I wanted a boy. Men are always more interested in their sons. Oh, ta, Ellie.' She propped herself up on one elbow and accepted the 'life-giving' tea with a weary smile. 'You're a good kid. Saved my life, you have.'

Dora finished drying the silent baby and wrapped her

carefully in the threadbare blanket that would do duty as a shawl.

'You're a little fidget, you are,' she told the child with a smile. 'Let's give you to your Ma, shall we, so she can take a proper look at you.'

'Hang on a minute!' Meg protested. 'Let me finish me tea in peace.'

'I thought you'd be dying to see her now she's all cleaned up.'

'Well, I'm not,' Meg informed her. 'She's not going anywhere, is she?' She sipped the hot tea noisily while Ellie placed a mug in front of Dora, then she asked, 'Where the hell's Sal got to? She's been gone ages. I asked her to fetch the doctor, not emigrate to Australia!'

Ellie laughed, but the movement pained her swollen jaw and she quickly straightened her face.

'Maybe he won't come,' said Dora.

'He'll come!' Meg declared grimly. 'He'll come because he knows if he doesn't, I'll go round there and take his squalling brat with me!'

Dora rocked the child gently. 'You're not squalling, are you?' she said. 'And you're not a brat; you're a good little moppet.' She smiled at Ellie. 'Come and look, Ellie. Or should I say "Aunt Ellie"?'

Ellie proudly inspected the baby and nodded her approval. Then she said something to Meg, who considered the suggestion and translated for Dora's benefit. 'She says "What about Lizzie for a name?"' Lizzie Swain. No, Lizzie *Reid*!' She gulped down the last of her tea, put down the mug and held out her arms for the baby. 'Come on then, Lizzie Reid. Let's have a proper look at you.'

Dora placed the baby in her arms and gratefully took up her own mug of tea. Although it was Meg who had suffered the pains of childbirth Dora's own legs felt weak with shock and exhaustion, for she had been roused from her bed at quarter-past one that morning and summoned to Meg's bedside to share in the drama. Fortunately, Sally had known what to expect and had proved a tower of strength before departing to fetch Dr Reid, leaving Dora with Ellie as willing assistant. Now Dora sat down on a chair and watched with secret envy as Meg peered down into the face of her offspring.

'No,' decided Meg. 'She doesn't look like a Lizzie to me. More of an Ivy, or maybe an Ada. Ada Reid? Hmm . . .'

Dora was beginning to feel distinctly nervous at the prospect of the doctor's visit. She tried to think of an excuse to leave before he came (supposing that he *would* come), but since she was on strike her time was her own and she could not even plead a day's work ahead of her as normally would have been the case.

'I don't like Ada,' she told Meg. 'Lizzie is better.'

'Nora, then?' suggested Meg.

Both Ellie and Dora shook their heads.

'Pity she wasn't a boy,' Meg reflected. 'I could have called him Charlie, I love that name. You know – Bonnie Prince Charlie, like that teacher told us in history. Charlie Reid. Hmm . . .'

'*Swain*,' Dora corrected her. 'You'll get yourself into trouble, Meg, if you keep on saying Reid. You're not married to him and the doctor's not going to like it one bit.'

'Too bloody bad!' said Meg, with a defiant shake of her head. 'It's him as got me into trouble in the first place.'

'Come off it!' said Dora. 'You know you needn't have had it. You never had a kid before, so how come you get this one if it wasn't *meant*?'

Meg could not be bothered to deny the charge. 'If he has his fun he should pay for it!'

'I thought he had – and very generously, from what you told me.'

'Well, now he can keep on paying.' She had lost

interest in the baby and held it out to Dora. 'You take her. I want to smarten myself up a bit before His Nibs gets here.'

Dora took the baby and then, seeing Ellie's wistful expression, said, 'How about Aunt Ellie holding her for a bit? Sit yourself down, love, and I'll put her into your arms. Don't worry, you'll be fine.' She smiled at Ellie. 'I bet you'll be spoiling her before long, that's what aunties always do!'

Ellie was just holding out her arms for the baby when they heard footsteps on the stairs and for a few seconds everyone froze.

Meg was first to recover. 'Quick!' she cried. 'Give her back to me. How do I look, Dor? Damn and blast! I should have tousled my hair.' She snatched the child to her and arranged her features into what she hoped was a tenderly maternal smile.

The door opened and Sally and the doctor came in. Quickly Dora stood up and held out a hand to Ellie. 'We'll wait on the stairs,' she told Meg and gave Sally a meaningful look.

'Oh, me too,' said Sally and they all went out.

Left alone with the father of her child, Meg finally allowed her eyes to stray to his face, but what she saw there did not reassure her. His mouth was set into a hard line and his eyes were furious as he approached her.

'What the devil do you mean by dragging me over here at this hour?' he demanded.

Meg's smile faltered and disappeared. 'I needed you,' she told him plaintively. 'I was frightened and I was in agony. Who else could I send for?'

'I doubt you needed anyone,' he told her. 'Your kind are tough as nails. Look at you – started at just after midnight, so I'm told, and here you are barely five hours later holding the child in your arms!'

Meg allowed her lower lip to tremble slightly. 'Don't you want to know what you've got?' she asked him. 'It's a lovely little girl. I'm calling her Lizzie.'

'I am not interested,' he said curtly. 'I made that clear some time ago.'

'But she's your *daughter*!'

'If I ever have a daughter, she will be born to my wife! How dare you presume to call this scrap of humanity my daughter?'

'But she is!' cried Meg, her mind racing. It was all going to be much harder than she had expected. She had half hoped that the sight of his child would soften his heart, but this now seemed rather unlikely.

Gilbert was standing less than a yard away, clutching his black bag and looking as though he might depart at any moment, and Meg racked her brains desperately for some way to detain him. The longer he stayed, the more chance there would be that he would take an interest in the child.

'I've got an awful pain,' she told him, suddenly inspired. 'Like a knife, it is. Aren't you going to examine me? You're a doctor, aren't you? You can charge it to that rich woman. If it gets any worse and I have to get another doctor in, there'll be all sorts of awkward questions asked and I shan't know what to say.'

'You'll never be lost for words,' he told her bitterly. 'Your sort never are; you live off your wits.'

Meg's face crumpled ominously. 'Don't keep calling me "your sort",' she begged. 'You didn't call me that when you was pleasuring yourself; it was different then. After all I've put up with for you! It wasn't "your sort" then, was it? I gave you what you wanted and never complained, but then it was "good girl" and "brave little lass" and –'

'Oh, very well!' he interrupted hastily. 'I'll examine you and then I'll go.'

'And what then?' Meg protested. 'I mean, what about the kid? She's got to be fed and clothed. I'm not made of money.'

'You should have thought of that,' he told her bluntly, moving closer to the bed. 'Lay the child down somewhere.'

'Just take a quick look at her. Oh, you must!' She held out the baby and for a brief moment he glanced at it, but then she saw his jaw tighten resolutely.

'Lay it to one side,' he repeated and a great panic swept over her. It was not going to work out, she had made a fatal mistake. Real tears of frustration and anger spilled down her cheeks.

'Oh, Gilbert . . .' she wailed.

'Don't call me that.'

He took the child and laid it on the floor nearby; when he turned back his expression frightened her.

'Lie flat,' he said. 'Pull up your shift.'

He made the examination as brief as possible and two minutes later was washing his hands. 'As I thought,' he told her. 'The pain, if it exists, is in your imagination. So stop grizzling and face up to your responsibilities. You're a mother now.'

'And you're a father!' she cried. 'What about you facing up to *yours*? What about . . . Oi! Gilbert, you come back here!'

But he had gone.

Passionately she screamed after him, 'You selfish, arrogant, pig. You wicked, rotten – oh, I hate you, do you hear me? Gilbert bloody Reid! I hate you! I'll make you sorry for this!'

Tears blinded her eyes and her rage choked her into spluttering incoherence. She pulled the bedclothes up to her eyes and sobbed helplessly as Dora, Sally and Ellie came back into the room.

Dora knelt beside her. 'What happened?' she asked.

Meg raised her ravished face. 'He didn't even speak to Lizzie!' she wept. 'Not a single bloody word!'

A new sound filled the air – a thin, tremulous sound –

and they all fell silent. As though aware that her troubles were only just beginning, Lizzie screwed up her face and began to cry.

*

Gilbert's cab had waited outside as directed and he climbed in to it with a great sense of relief, for the sordid scene with Meg Swain had affected him deeply but in a most uncharitable way. There was no question, he told himself, of his ever setting foot in the place again. Hopefully the child would not live long; at least the law of averages weighed heavily against it surviving the first month. Born early and underweight into a careless, unhygienic environment, it must surely perish from neglect, accident or disease, and then his connection with Meg would be finally severed.

'Take me back to Harrington Hill,' he told the cabby, 'and don't hurry.'

No doubt Marion would be awake when he got home and would be curious, and he wanted time to think. He had been called out at inconvenient times before, but had never gone so unwillingly, and in retrospect he saw that he should have reacted in a more reasonable manner. He should have pretended that he had been expecting the summons and shown less reluctance to attend the confinement, but taken by surprise he had bungled the matter.

Now he shook his head, regretting his ill-considered behaviour, but how could he have guessed that the stupid little hussy would dare to send for him? Her words came back to him with startling clarity . . . 'when you was pleasuring yourself'! God Almighty! Had it ever been a *pleasure* to lie with that wretched creature? A release, maybe. Yes, it had been a physical release for his tortured body, but no amount of imagination could dignify it with the word 'pleasure'. He had experienced feelings of shame and degradation merely by being in such a dreadful district, while the knowledge of his own weakness – the frequent decisions to be done with it and the equally frequent changes of heart – had further contributed to his loss of self-esteem. No, he told himself bitterly, there had been no pleasure. He had been more like a man addicted to opium, unable to break himself of a vicious but self-destructive habit, and now he was paying the price for that lack of self-control. At least he would pay if Meg had her way and if the child lived . . .

His eyes darkened as the words echoed in his brain. *If* the child lived! Maybe he should make sure that it did *not* live. He would be doing the poor little wretch a favour, he argued, for the world was a harsh place for Meg Swain and her kind. What did the child have to look forward to? Her life would be made ugly by her miserable surroundings, and surrounded by the dregs of humanity she could not hope to rise above the poverty into which she had been born. She would doubtless become a drab like her mother. Did he want that for any child of his? In the dark interior of the cab he shook his head determinedly. Far better and *kinder* to put the child out of its misery while it remained blissfully unaware of its destiny. Yes, it would be a kindness, he told himself; a kindness to the child, and to himself and to Meg Swain who would be relieved of the burden of rearing a bastard.

Glancing round, he realized that they were nearing Harrington Hill. He leaned out and said, 'Keep going for another ten minutes.'

'Please yourself, guv!'

Please yourself! Yes, he would do just that, Gilbert thought defiantly. He would act in his own interests and be done with all weakness. With the child dead, he would close this awful chapter of his life and somehow make up to Marion for his infidelity. He admitted that she was a fine woman who deserved better; he owed it to her to save the situation and he must find the courage to do so. The notion that he would be doing it for Marion instead of himself pleased him, because it meant that any accusation of self-interest could not be levelled at him. Yes. He would ensure that the child did not survive, but he would do it for his wife's sake. Smiling faintly, he gave a small, satisfied nod.

The decision taken, his mind raced. It should not be too difficult to get rid of the child, for Meg would not rest in her quest for maintenance and when she contacted him again he would make one more visit to Fashion Street. He would take with him a 'sedative' for the child in the form of oil of bitter almonds – otherwise known as medicinal arsenic – and Meg in her careless, ignorant way would inevitably administer a fatal overdose. Almost certainly she would call on him when the child sickened and he would make out a suitable death certificate, releasing them both from blame and bringing the whole matter to a satisfactory conclusion. Once buried, the child would be quickly forgotten. Somehow, then, he must steel himself to stay in contact with Meg Swain for a little longer so that he could put the plan into operation; he must go back and pretend a change of heart. He would give Meg a little money to restore her confidence in him and would assume an interest in the child. Yes, that was the best way to go about it. He had been foolish to antagonize Meg, for he did not underestimate her and if she wished to make serious trouble for him she could do so very easily. To prevent that he must feign repentance for his insensitive behaviour and win back Meg's goodwill. Then, when the child was dead, he could part from her amicably.

'Yes, yes,' he muttered eagerly. 'Whatever happens I must not arouse any further ill-feeling.'

It must be seen as a sorrow to him that, just when he was beginning to take an interest in his daughter, she was taken from him. He would be *heartbroken* if that would please Meg. He swore under his breath. 'What a charade!' But it was a necessary one, and he must play his part well for the stakes were very high.

'Here we are, guv,' cried the cabby. 'Back home again. That's a guinea – and cheap at the price.'

'A guinea? Why, you swindling rogue . . .!'

'Double fare after midnight, guv.'

'That's preposterous!'

'Maybe, guv, but it's still a guinea and make it quick. I've got a home to go to, same as you.'

Unwilling to cause a disturbance in the street at such a late hour, Gilbert paid him, then ran up the steps to the house and let himself in.

As he had expected, Marion sat up as soon as he entered the bedroom. 'Don't light the candle,' he told her. 'I can undress by the light from the street.'

'I wasn't asleep,' she said. 'Are they well? Did the baby live?'

'Mother and child doing well,' he told her. 'A wasted journey, in fact. The child was born before I arrived and there were no complications.'

'And the baby? Is it a girl or a boy?'

'A girl. Underweight but apparently healthy.'

'Apparently?' She looked at him in surprise. 'But didn't you examine her?'

'Of course I did,' he lied quickly. 'She was fine.'

'I wonder what they will call her? Was the father there?'

'No. I've never seen him.'

'But you've been there so *rarely*, Gilbert,' said Marion. 'There must be a father somewhere. Let us hope that, for the baby's sake, he does the right thing by her. What was she like, Gilbert? The baby, I mean, not the mother.'

He shrugged. 'Like all babies.'

'Did she have any hair?' she persisted. 'What colour were her eyes?'

'Does it really matter?'

She pretended not to notice his lack of enthusiasm. 'Poor little thing,' she said. 'Maybe I could call and take some –'

Gilbert rounded on her sharply. 'You keep away from her, do you hear me? Keep well away. Call on her, indeed! The idea's ridiculous.'

'But, Gilbert,' she reminded him, 'I called on Mrs Allen when she had her little boy. You *encouraged* me to go. I took her some eggs and calves' foot jelly, don't you remember? I only thought –'

'Mrs Allen is a perfectly respectable milliner who has fallen on hard times. She is quite different. Meg – Miss Swain – is a whore!'

Although Marion had suspected as much, the word shocked her. Her husband was somehow involved with a prostitute! All her earlier suspicions flooded back.

'I didn't know,' she stammered. 'I'm sorry.'

'Well, you know now. She is a drab; the lowest of the low. I forbid you to even think of visiting her.'

'Of course I won't, Gilbert. Why are you so angry? It was simply a mistake on my part.'

He climbed into bed beside her and took her hand. 'I'm sorry,' he said, his tone conciliatory. 'You have such a kind heart and I know you mean well, but this time I must insist. The area where she lives is thoroughly unsavoury and no one in their senses would venture there, especially a lady. I, for one, hope that I shall never need to call there again. If you went there, you would be taking the most awful risk. You must understand, Marion, I say this for your own sake.'

'Yes, Gilbert.'

He leaned across and kissed her briefly. 'Forget all about them,' he advised, but Marion lay awake for a long time. To keep the spectre of her suspicions at bay, she tried to visualise the new baby, innocent and helpless, thrust among such dreadful people. A mother who was a street woman and a nameless father! What had the poor little thing done to deserve such a fate? Gilbert was right, she knew, and she must not pay a visit, but she was touched by the child's dismal plight and rebelliously searched for a way to help. At last a faint smile touched her lips as she saw a solution to the problem. She would send some nourishing food and perhaps a few articles of clothing . . . but she would do so anonymously.

*

Marion and Rachel enjoyed their week together. The time passed so quickly that Marion had toyed with the idea of suggesting that her sister extend her visit, but Gilbert's mood did not encourage her. Thus she and Rachel finally found themselves on the station platform reluctantly saying goodbye.

'And you will promise to come again?' begged Marion. 'Gilbert wasn't too unbearable, was he?'

'Of course not. He behaved very well towards me, considering that we don't like each other!' Rachel laughed. 'Mind you, if you'd married a certain other gentleman, I must admit you would be finding it much harder to get rid of me!'

Marion's face lit up at this reference to Ralph, but all she said was, 'He's a nice young man, isn't he? I daresay he will settle down one day and make someone a good husband.'

'And don't you envy that someone?' asked Rachel. 'I must confess I do.'

'He is very attractive,' Marion confessed, 'and such fun to be with. I don't think I shall ever forget those hours at the Zoo. It was so carefree, somehow, that I felt young again for the first time in years. Do you understand what I mean?'

Rachel nodded, then said suddenly, 'He's in love with you, Marion. I didn't intend to say anything, but perhaps I should.'

Marion regarded her sister with alarm. 'In love with me? Oh, Rachel, don't say such a thing!'

Her sister took her hand. 'But he is, Marion, and what is more I think you are half in love with him. Oh, don't bother to protest; it's written all over your face and it rings in your voice when you mention him – which is frequently.' Marion had opened her mouth to deny it, but Rachel went on relentlessly, 'I'm not saying this in any way to criticize you, but merely to warn you to be careful or you and Ralph will find yourselves in serious trouble. You in particular, Marion, because you have a husband and Ralph is unattached. For God's sake, Marion, be discreet. If you cannot, then you must give him up.'

'Give him up?' Marion protested indignantly. 'You talk as though we are lovers and you know that isn't so – far from it. We do like each other, I'll grant you that. Maybe we like each other too much, but we've done nothing wrong.'

'Not yet!' Rachel sighed. 'I wish I didn't feel so responsible,' she went on. 'If I hadn't persuaded you to meet him at the Zoo, matters might have stayed under control.'

'But they *are* under control,' Marion insisted. 'We simply enjoy each other's company and we would never go too far – you must know that.'

Rachel remained unconvinced. 'How do you know *what* you would do,' she asked, 'if your affection for him became passion? Oh, don't look so shocked. I am only saying this to try to save you from yourself. The fragile relationship you have now is exciting, and I envy you – yes, I admit that – but I worry for you in case it all turns sour. Ralph is young and impetuous, and for him it might be no more than another amusing flirtation.' As Marion began to protest, she held up a hand. 'Please let me finish. It may be more than that; it may go deeper. But whatever it is, it might not last and you might be badly hurt. I wouldn't want that to happen.'

A distant whistle warned them that the train was approaching and while people around them began to gather their luggage and round up straying children, Marion and Rachel regarded each other soberly.

'You should never have married Gilbert,' said Rachel, 'but you did, and you must not do anything which could jeopardize your marriage. There must be no scandal, Marion, whatever happens. I should not like you to cross swords with Gilbert, because he would make a most ruthless enemy.'

With a rush of steam and a squealing of wheels, the train drew alongside the platform and doors were thrown open. Porters with their barrows appeared from all directions, some to load outgoing luggage on to the train, others to unload for passengers arriving. All was pandemonium, making it quite impossible for the sisters to finish their conversation. Instead they hugged each other and then above the din Rachel said, 'Write to me, Marion. Tell me *everything*. And please do be careful!'

'I will,' shouted Marion, 'and you be careful how you answer my letters in case Gilbert reads one of them. And do come again soon – it's been so wonderful.'

A porter bustled up to relieve Rachel of her luggage and she followed him into the train, where he found her a window-seat and stowed away her bag. Looking down at her sister waiting on the platform and seeing her subdued expression, Rachel wondered if she should have remained silent on the question of Ralph Gaunt, but she was reluctant to let matters slide any further for Gilbert Reid was a hard man. Marion had made the wrong choice years ago. If she were still single she might have found happiness with Ralph Gaunt, despite the disparity in their ages, but now it was not to be. Hopefully, the liaison with Ralph would eventually wane without too much heartbreak on either side.

Now the train doors were being slammed shut and a few opened yet again to admit late-comers. A fat man settled himself in the next seat and Rachel returned his smile with a polite nod. As the train pulled slowly out of the station she watched Marion hurrying alongside until she could no longer keep up, and when she disappeared

into the crowd Rachel sighed deeply and settled back in
her seat with a heavy heart.

*

Amelia glared at the bed, which had a wooden headboard
elaborately carved with trails of twining ivy and bunches
of grapes.

'I am buying basic equipment for a ragged school,'
she told the salesman caustically, 'not furnishing a palace!
I can only suppose this is your idea of a joke, Mr Fisk!'

As his eyes met hers Mr Fisk – a small grey-haired
man – shrank further down into his high winged collar.
'But this is one of our less expensive lines . . .' he
faltered. 'You did say, madam –'

'I know exactly what I said,' Amelia informed him
coldly. 'I asked for some decent *low-priced* furniture. I
certainly do not intend to pay through the nose for
carved headboards, so you will kindly show me something
more suitable or I shall be forced to take my custom
elsewhere. And please hurry, Mr Fisk. You are wasting
my valuable time.'

'Well . . . we do have one with brass fittings . . .'

'No brass, thank you. I want a simple *truckle* bed. I do
not intend my girls to be pampered, but neither do I
expect them to make do with straw palliasses on the
floor. Don't you have any simple beds? For heaven's
sake, I am not asking for the moon!'

Mr Fisk clasped his hands nervously. 'We do not sell
truckle beds, madam,' he told her. 'There is no demand
for them. Perhaps you would care to talk to the manager,
our Mr Carter, who may be able to advise you?'

'Let us hope so, Mr Fisk.'

Mr Fisk's spirits plummeted as he led her to the
manager's office. In his experience, when a day started
badly it rarely improved. Tall, imperious women frightened him and it was with great relief that he delivered
Mrs Gaunt into the capable hands of his superior.

Mr Carter, large and rotund, proved very helpful. 'We have nothing in stock to suit your requirements,' he told her. 'Try the Curtain Road area in Shoreditch. You should find someone there who is willing to undertake your order.'

'I have no wish to *find* someone,' Amelia corrected him. 'I want the name of a reliable firm. Can you recommend anyone who will do the work at a reasonable price?'

'Certainly, madam,' he assured her. 'If you will give me a moment, I have details somewhere of firms with whom we have done business in the past. Now, let me see ...' He took up a large blue ledger and peered shortsightedly at the dog-eared pages. 'Ah, yes. There is an Albert Keer in Hoxton Street, who will supply furniture to order. He made us a larger than usual bed, I recall. I was only a lad at the time and to me the customer was a giant!' He chuckled at the memory. 'Six foot five and built like a heavyweight! You will find Mr Keers at number 12, next to a French polisher, if my memory serves me right ... and at number 35 are Samsons. Been there years, they have; they might help you. I'll make a note of these for you.'

'And is Samson as good as Keer?'

'Much of a muchness, madam.' He scribbled on a small sheet of paper, then leafed through the pages once more. 'There is Newman's, of course. They're very good; nice quality and they're quick. Yes, here we are. Number 4, New Inn Broadway. Do you know where that is? If not, I have a map in the drawer. Mind you, he may not still be there because he was quite elderly when we last had dealings with him and he was talking about retiring then, I remember, but he did do a good job of work. Took pride, if you know what I mean. We had a customer for a corner cupboard and the corner in question was not square. The actual angle was more than ninety degrees, because the house had been –'

Amelia interrupted him. 'I shall go to Mr Keer first,' she announced. 'Pray do not bother with any more names. You have found me three and that should suffice.'

He looked disappointed. 'There's a Mr East next to the baker in Hoxton Street. He's –'

'No, thank you.' She held out her hand for the paper. 'I am obliged to you for your help.'

'Glad to be of service, madam,' he assured her eagerly. (A customer who bought in multiples of ten was rare.) 'We have a fine selection of furniture,' he went on. 'Bedside tables, linen chests. For your own home, naturally. Much of our furniture is imported from Italy.'

'I shall remember.' She nodded her thanks, swept out of the shop and allowed Johnson to help her back into the carriage.

'Number 12, Hoxton Street,' she instructed him, settling back against the cushions.

As they bowled along towards Hoxton Street she was glad of the chance to think, for it had recently come to her notice that her son had quite obviously fallen in love. He sang about the house; was unnecessarily charming to the servants; sat around staring into space and could no longer be relied upon to remember anything she told him. Amelia did not want Ralph to be in love; she needed his help with the school and did not wish him to waste hours mooning over an empty-headed slip of a girl when his time, in her opinion, could be put to much better use. She blamed herself for allowing such a thing to occur, since her preoccupation with the school had blinded her to what was happening and now she feared it might be too late. She would have to speak to him about it. She was intrigued to know who it was who had found favour in his eyes, for they had done little entertaining lately and he did not move in a large circle of friends. He was neglecting his painting, too. She wondered if she should send him abroad again . . . but she did not want to lose him. She enjoyed his company and valued his opinions . . . or pretended to value them, for whenever their ideas clashed she invariably followed her own inclinations, but nevertheless it was pleasant to confer and she found the house empty when he was away. This morning she had asked him to accompany her to the furniture dealer, but he had declined saying that he had to write a letter. To *her*, no doubt, thought Amelia with a snort of disapproval. Somehow she should have prevented him from going to the Zoo, but she had not taken him seriously. A Russian emigré, indeed! Afterwards she realized that he had met the girl there, because she had recognized the look in his eyes when he returned. If only she had been paying attention, she might have invented a reason for his not going to the Zoo, but she had been so distracted by those rascally builders . . . She stared with unseeing eyes at the passing shops – bootmakers galore, a tassel-maker, a bookbinder. The grimy shop-fronts depressed her.

They came to a crossroads and turned right, narrowly escaping a collision with a totter's cart pulled by a donkey, and she tutted to herself. Johnson drove much too fast and she would have to speak to him about it. More bootmakers flashed by, an oilman, a milliner, a hatter and a coffee house. They passed St Monica's Church and the George and Dragon and pulled up outside No. 12.

'This is it, ma'am,' said Johnson, and with his help Amelia descended to do battle with Mr Keer.

*

That evening over dinner she tackled Ralph on the subject of his lady friend, being as usual brisk and to the point.

'You have met a young woman, I believe, Ralph. Am I to know her name?'

Deliberately Ralph put a forkful of potato into his mouth and she fought down her irritation.

165

'Her name is Marion,' he told her. 'Would you pass the gravy, Mama, please? This pork is on the dry side, I fancy.'

'It is nothing of the sort and you know it, but by all means swamp it with gravy if you wish.' She passed the gravy-boat and watched Ralph pour a liberal amount over his meat.

'Marion who?' she asked.

'Just Marion.'

'No one is called "Just Marion", dear. Don't prevaricate.'

'What I mean,' he said with a challenging look, 'is that I only intend to tell you her first name.'

'Why is that, Ralph?'

He gave a careless shrug. 'Let us say that the lady in question prefers to remain anonymous.'

So, thought Amelia, she was a lady and not a servant. So far, so good. How many Marions did they know, she wondered.

'And would you say that you are in love with her, Ralph? This lady Marion?'

His smile was mocking. 'Desperately so, Mama!'

'And how does she feel about you? Does she return your feelings?'

'I have never presumed to ask her.'

Better and better, thought Amelia. It was still what she thought of as 'early days'.

Lucy, the parlour-maid, came into the room and asked, 'Is everything satisfactory, ma'am?'

Ralph said, 'The pork is a little on the dry side . . .'

Her face fell. 'Oh dear. I'll tell Cook.'

'You will do nothing of the kind,' interposed Amelia. 'There is nothing wrong with it. My son is being awkward for reasons best known to himself.'

'Awkward?' he protested. 'I have had to flood the plate with gravy!'

He winked at Lucy and she hastily smothered a giggle,

but Amelia waved her away and when she had gone said wrathfully, 'You must not tease the servants, Ralph. They are not here for your amusement.'

'Lucy appreciates a bit of a joke,' he protested. 'You know she does; you know they never take me seriously.'

'Then they should, Ralph,' she responded. 'One day you will be master of your own house and you will want the servants to know where they stand.'

'Yes, Mama. I hear and obey.'

'Do not be flippant, Ralph.'

'No, Mama.'

She glared at him across the table. 'Being in love seems to have addled your brain,' she told him. 'I do not envy the young woman. Do you intend to bring her here to meet me?'

'Certainly not, Mama. You would terrify her.'

'Have you met her parents?'

'They are both dead.'

'Then she is an orphan.'

'Are *you* an orphan, Mama? Both your parents are dead.'

Amelia frowned. So the girl was a woman old enough for both parents to have died of natural causes. She was beginning to feel slightly uneasy and a sudden thought struck her. 'She is not married, I hope.'

'May I have a little more pork, please, Mama?'

'I thought you found it dry?'

'I like it dry.'

'You really can be very exasperating, Ralph, but since you are feeling so perverse I shall not ask you any more questions but will leave you to tell me in your own good time.'

She cut two slices of meat and put them on to his plate, but as he helped himself to more vegetables his good humour suddenly deserted him and his eyes were serious.

'Nothing can come of it, Mama,' he told her quietly. 'You need have no fear on that score.'

Her irritation vanished. 'She is *married*!'

He nodded.

'Then you must not allow yourself to love her!'

'It is too late, Mama.'

She laid down her knife and fork, her appetite gone, and for a long moment they looked at each other. 'I'm so sorry, Ralph,' she told him. 'Love can be the very devil.'

*

On Saturday night, just after eleven, Jack and Sid Patten swaggered along the Whitechapel Road having drunk enough but not too much. They turned left into New Road and right into Fordham Street and a few minutes later were in Parfett Street, looking for a conveniently dark corner from which to watch for Jeff Bannerman's return home. Sid had made it his business to learn a little of his rival's movements, and seeing no light in his room he was reassured that he was still out. His resentment of the young reporter had now hardened into loathing and he was eagerly anticipating the chance to 'spoil his looks'.

Parfett Street was broader than many in the area, but the darkness was intense. At the far end, where it joined the Commercial Road, a single gas-lamp flickered eerily making little or no impression on the surrounding gloom. Underfoot the cobbles were slippery from a brief shower of rain earlier in the evening, while overhead unseasonable clouds rolled across the sky threatening more rain and only occasionally allowing the moon to shine through.

There was little or no light coming from the windows of the houses, for these were the parlour windows and the rooms were only used on high days and holidays. Most of the inhabitants had gone to bed, but those not sleeping were ensconced in their kitchens at the rear of each house.

The large terraced houses fronted directly on to the

pavement, offering no place of concealment, so Sid and Jack were forced to huddle up against the wall in an effort to make themselves as inconspicuous as possible.

Jack clutched his stomach. 'That bloody porter – I reckon it was off. It's griping my gut something chronic.'

He unbuttoned his trousers and relieved himself against the nearest doorway. A passing couple gave them a hostile glance but, deciding discretion was the better part of valour, moved on without audible comment.

'Nosy bastards!' growled Jack and belched loudly.

'Never mind them,' said Sid. 'Keep your mind on the job.'

'Wouldn't I like to wipe the smiles off their smug faces!'

'They weren't smiling, Jack. Forget them, can't you?'

Nervously Sid looked up and down the road. 'Suppose a copper comes along? We stick out here like a couple of sore thumbs.'

Jack thought about it. 'You're right. We'd better squat down on the pavement and lean back against the wall'

'But suppose he . . .'

'He'll do sod all, believe me. He'll think we're drunk and turn a blind eye. They're not bloody heroes, you know. One copper against two of us? Huh! He won't want any trouble, so just act like you're blind drunk.'

Obediently Sid slid to the ground and Jack joined him. They assumed abandoned poses, heads lolling, legs sprawled.

'If he comes from the Fordham end of the road,' said Jack, 'we'll just jump up and grab him. If he –'

Sid stared at him in horror. 'Grab a copper!' he cried. 'Christ Almighty! Are you out of –'

'Not the copper, you numbskull; Jeff whatever-his-name-is! If he comes from the *other* end of the road, we'll have to make a run for it so as to get him before he reaches his door.'

Minutes passed and Sid's courage began to ooze away.

A rat emerged from a hole beneath a doorstep and approached them curiously, but Jack kicked out at it and it scampered off into the darkness. 'Bloody things. I hate rats,' he said.

Sid began to imagine the worst. It would all go wrong and they would be nabbed in the act by a policeman, charged and found guilty of assault and clapped into jail. Or transported! Australia was a long way away.

'He's not damn well coming,' he said at last. 'Let's give it a miss.'

'He'll come,' said Jack. 'Just give it time. You're so bloody impatient.'

'I tell you he's not coming.'

'Shut your trap!'

'But –'

'You're windy!'

'I'm not. I just . . . strewth! Here he comes now!'

Jeff was approaching at a brisk walk from the far end of the road so that the door of his lodgings was between him and the Pattens.

'Wait for it!' cautioned Jack as Sid began to scramble to his feet. 'If he's too far away, he'll skedaddle and we'll lose him. Wait . . . Now go for him!'

He sprang up with Sid behind him and the two men pounded towards Jeff, who realized too late that he was the intended victim. He turned and ran, but before he had gone ten yards Jack had grabbed him by the collar and, jerking him backwards, slammed him up against the wall, face first.

'Now, my lad!' he cried. 'Time you learnt a thing or two!' As Sid reached them Jack pinned Jeff's arms behind him and jerked him round to face his brother. 'Give it to him, Sid!' he shouted and, seeing his adversary helpless, Sid's courage returned and he began to punch Jeff around the face and chest. 'You keep away from Dora Becket!' he panted. 'She's mine. Understand?'

'In the guts, you idiot!' Jack urged. 'Wind the scraggy little blighter!'

In a desperate effort to defend himself, Jeff kicked out at Sid, but his legs flailed ineffectively as his enemy neatly side-stepped.

'You little runt!' Jack shouted. 'Kick my brother, would you? Let's see how you like it!'

He hurled him violently to the ground and began to kick him savagely, giving Jeff no chance to regain his feet. Sid joined in, but by this time several windows had been pushed up and one or two enquiring heads were being thrust out to discover the cause of the commotion. Someone screamed 'Police!' and someone else further down the road blew a whistle. Then a nearby door opened and a huge man lumbered out on to the pavement.

'What the hell's going on here?' he roared and more doors opened.

Jack decided it was time to go. 'Quick! Scram!' he told Sid. He jumped to his feet and glancing back, shouted again to his brother who, enjoying his work, was unaware of the danger.

'Sid! That's enough!' yelled Jack as another whistle sounded, heralding the arrival of a constable at the Fordham end of the road.

Sid, who had finally scrambled to his feet, discovered the large man bearing down on him with a poker. 'Jack!' he screamed. 'Help me!'

The man struck out at him and caught him an agonizing blow on the shoulder with the poker, causing him to stagger and almost fall. Then he closed in and grabbed him round the throat, but Jack was on his way back and almost at once he hurled himself at the legs of Sid's captor and brought him crashing to the ground where he lay without moving.

Sid stared at him, paralysed with fear. 'Oh, God!' he whispered. 'Oh, Jesus Christ, you've –'

With an oath, Jack grabbed his arm. 'Run, you bloody little fool, run!' he urged. 'You'll get us both nabbed –'

Almost as he spoke a constable appeared from Commercial Road and stood with his arms outstretched to block their path, but seeing *two* men approaching he hesitated and Sid and Jack took advantage of that split second to run round him, one on either side. The last tram was passing on its way to Tower Hamlets and they raced after it, with the policeman in pursuit. Jack managed to pull himself on to the rear platform where he stretched out a hand to his terrified brother, and in another moment they were both on their way to safety.

*

Behind them in Parfett Street Jeff was being helped to his feet and his landlady, in nightdress and curling rags, was wringing her hands in dismay.

'Mr Bannerman! Oh, poor Mr Bannerman!' she cried. 'Look at the state you're in. Oh, my good Lord!'

Willing neighbours helped him into the house and laid him on a sofa. His right eye was fast closing, his lip was split and bleeding, he ached all over and breathing was a painful business.

The constable from Fordham Road arrived and followed him into the parlour, his notebook and pencil at the ready.

'I'm all right,' Jeff muttered thickly through his broken lips. 'No bones broken. I'm not hurt, Mrs Coot. Truly, I'm not.'

'Not hurt?' she cried. 'What, with blood all over your face and that terrible eye! I'll get a towel and some water. Oh, my Lord!' She appealed to the policeman and neighbours. 'What is the world coming to, right outside his own lodgings? If a man can't be safe in his own street, well, I don't know. I just don't know.'

The constable thanked the neighbours for their help, took their names and told them he would be questioning them the following day; then he hustled them out of the house and turned his attention to Jeff, trying to determine the exact nature of his injuries for his report. It seemed that miraculously, as Jeff had said, there were no bones broken although he was severely bruised.

'Animals!' the constable remarked wearily. 'Senseless, brainless animals!'

He was still detailing the injuries when there was a knock at the front door and Mrs Coot admitted the wife of the large man who had gone to Jeff's aid with the poker.

'We can't rouse him,' she told them in great agitation. 'I think they've killed him. Oh, do come quick!'

The constable frowned, turned over the page of his notebook and went outside where the crowd had doubled in size.

The man, whose name was Albert Tredwell, appeared to be dead and a doctor was hastily called. He arrived ten minutes later and, after a brief examination, diagnosed a broken skull and severe concussion. An ambulance was ordered from the nearby London Hospital and a large vehicle like an oversized three-wheeled pram arrived ten minutes later; the unconscious man was securely strapped in and wheeled away to hospital.

When the constable eventually returned to the house Jeff's wounds had been treated by his solicitous landlady and he was sitting up in bed in his nightshirt, able to answer questions.

'No,' he told the policeman in answer to the first enquiry. 'They made no effort to rob me. It was because –'

'One thing at a time, sir, if you don't mind,' said the constable reproachfully.

'Oh, sorry.'

'And were the men concerned known to you, sir?'

'Not exactly, but I do know who –'

The constable coughed another warning and Jeff fell silent again. His head ached abominably and shock had set in, causing him to tremble all over. He longed to sleep, but this interrogation was obviously going to be very thorough.

'Did the assailants at any time produce or use a weapon or weapons of any kind?' asied the constable.

'No. Just their fists and feet,' Jeff told him. 'They didn't need anything else! One of them held me while the other one –'

'And there were two, you say?'

Jeff nodded.

'Now then, sir, could you give me a description of one or both of your assailants? Age, colour of hair and eyes, height, etc?'

Gingerly Jeff was examining one of his teeth. Suddenly, with a wince of pain, he held it up.

Mrs Coot gave a shocked gasp. 'Oh, no! Not one of your teeth! That's really too bad.' She turned to the policeman and added, 'Mr Bannerman has such lovely teeth. I've always thought that,' but he wrote solidly on, refusing to be diverted from the business in hand.

'The description, if you please, Mr Bannerman.'

Jeff seized his chance. 'One was called Sid. It must have been Sid Patten who works as a foreman or charge-hand at Bryant and May's match factory in Fairfield Road. He's about five feet six, thin, and was wearing a dark jacket and trousers.'

'Sydney Patten – would that be with a double T, sir?'

Nodding again, Jeff tried not to think about the dull ache low in his back where he imagined his kidneys to be. He tried to catch Mrs Coot's eye, but she was looking over the constable's shoulder, trying to see what he had written.

Jeff ploughed on. 'Miss Becket, a friend of mine, could give you a better description than I can. And the other one was called Jack. He's shorter, but thick-set . . .'

'Possibly charge-hand at Bryant and May's,' murmured the constable reprovingly.

Despite his discomfort and the loss of the tooth, Jeff was beginning to see the possibility of an article arising from his unpleasant experience. 'Low life in London' would make a good heading, he reflected. 'First-hand experience of the violence so prevalent in the streets of England's capital city.' He might even be able to tie it in to the current strike. He had used Dora's name in previous copy, so that would provide a link. But he needed an angle . . .

After what seemed an eternity the constable closed his notebook, bade them 'Good night' and left. Jeff was then tucked in by Mrs Coot and threatened with dire retribution if he should dare to set a foot to the floor before morning.

'Rest with a capital "R",' she told him firmly. 'My mother swore by it, God rest her soul. You've had a nasty shock and what you need now is rest. Tomorrow I'll bring you up something on a tray for your breakfast – something soft and easy to eat. Porridge or a coddled egg. Oh, your poor face! That young lady of yours will never recognize you.'

'It could have been worse,' said Jeff. 'I wonder how that man is – the one they took to hospital.'

'Dead, I shouldn't wonder,' said Mrs Coot.

'Dead!' Jeff sat up, gazing at her in horror.

'Well, you'd be dead with a cracked skull and whatnot. That's what he had, poor man.' She shrugged. 'That's what you get for being a hero – a cracked skull.'

She pushed Jeff back on to the pillows as he said hopefully, 'He might not be *dead*.'

'Pigs might fly!' she told him. 'But if he does die, why then it's murder and serve them right; I hope they swing for it. Knocking out your lovely tooth! Good job it wasn't a front one.' She blew out the candle and tiptoed to the door. 'Now remember what I said.'

Jeff, shocked by the news of the neighbour's tragedy, could only nod wretchedly.

'Rest,' she repeated and closed the door.

CHAPTER EIGHT

As the church clock struck eight, Ellie sat among the palliasses with baby Lizzie in her arms while in another corner of the room Meg, wrapped in a blanket, slept fitfully. Ellie kept nodding off and jerking herself back into wakefulness, for she had had a bad night – unable to sleep for the pain in her face and the worry of her unexpressed fears for the future. She knew her swollen jaw was not toothache, however hard Meg might try to convince her that it was, and she knew also that 'phossy jaw' could and often did kill people. So she guessed that she too was going to die, but was not at all prepared for such an eventuality. She did not know anything about being dead. She thought that maybe she would be a ghost and that was a frightening prospect. What exactly did ghosts do, she wondered. If she did not become a ghost what would happen to her and, more to the point perhaps, where would she be when it happened? She had heard of Heaven, but it sounded too good to be true or, if it did exist, too good for the likes of the Ellies of this world. She thought it most likely that rich people went to Heaven, and they would hardly want to rub shoulders with common street women or the sisters of such. She worried about her jaw for fear that it would still hurt after she was dead. Or did death take away pain? If it did, then it would not be so bad. And would she ever see Meg and the baby again? She supposed she would have to wait until they too died, but in Lizzie's case that might be a very long time.

Then there was her funeral . . . she did not like what she had heard of funerals. Being buried six feet under the ground would cut her off from everything she knew – and then there were the worms! But it would be nice if the pain went away. Perhaps when she was dead she would be able to speak properly again, so that everyone would understand her, and when the swelling had gone down she might be beautiful like Meg. Her own face had been misshapen for so long that she had forgotten what she looked like. Once she had borrowed Meg's piece of mirror, but her reflection had frightened her. If being dead meant being happy . . .

A loud banging on the front door broke into her reverie and also wakened Lizzie, who began to cry loudly and in turn woke Meg.

'What's up with her?' cried Meg crossly. 'Can't I have a doze without her ladyship having a go?'

Ellie mumbled an explanation.

'Someone at the door? Well, answer it then. Give her here to me and get a move on.'

A few moments later Ellie reappeared with a parcel in her arms and glowing eyes. She told Meg what had happened.

'What d'you mean, run off? Some kid just give you the parcel and done a bunk? Here, let's have a look.' Parcel and baby were quickly exchanged and Meg tore off the wrapping paper and string.

'Strewth!' she whispered. 'Take a look at this little lot!' There were five smaller parcels wrapped in tissue paper and tied with coloured ribbon. Meg looked up at Ellie in triumph.

'They're from him!' she exclaimed. 'They must be! He's had second thoughts. Oh, Gilbert Reid, I take back all I said about you. You've turned up trumps at last! Here, Ellie, put her down somewhere and we'll open them up together. One at a time – take it in turns, like. Christ! I'd like to see Sal's face when she knows, and Dora's too. They won't be quite so sniffy when they know it's all coming up roses!'

She handed the first parcel to Ellie who opened it with trembling fingers, the pain in her jaw temporarily forgotten. Inside she found an ivory teething ring with a small bell attached to it and handed this to Meg for her inspection.

'A rattle!' cried Meg. 'Now that *is* nice.' She handed it to Ellie. 'Give it to her ladyship, Ellie. Put it into her hand, and give it a shake for her – show her how it works.'

While Ellie did so, Meg opened the next package which contained a toy elephant about six inches long and carved out of mahogany. Meg considered it carefully from all angles. 'I'll sell that,' she announced. 'That must be worth a tidy sum – good, that is.'

Ellie protested at the proposed sale but Meg remained adamant. 'Lizzie don't want no elephant,' she explained. 'Better get a few bob for it and buy her something more useful.' But privately she thought that she might buy herself a new hat. 'Here, it's your turn now.'

She thrust another parcel into Ellie's hands. It contained a jar of honey, and within seconds Meg had taken the lid off and was dipping an exploratory finger into it. 'Ooh, it's lovely!' she told Ellie. 'You try it. Do babies like honey, d'you think? I reckon he meant that for me, to build me up. I think you and me'll eat that.'

While Ellie sampled it Meg opened the last two packages, one of which contained a sealed basin of beef broth jelly, the other a tiny bonnet made of fine white cotton and edged with lace.

Meg was beside herself with delight at these examples of what she took to be Gilbert's unexpected change of heart.

'Bring Lizzie here,' she commanded. 'Let's see how she looks in the bonnet. I suppose I could sell that, too, but then "His Nibs" might create. He'll expect to see her wearing it. Better keep it, but it's a shame.'

The bonnet proved to be much too big, but while

Ellie paraded the baby in her outsized bonnet, they reassured each other that in time Lizzie would grow into it.

Meg took the lid off the broth and looked at it doubtfully. 'Funny sort of broth,' she said. 'More like jelly, I'd say, but it says beef broth on the label. Still, it must be nourishing, mustn't it? Fetch a couple of spoons and we'll try it. All right – maybe it's *meant* for the baby, but she won't mind sharing. This'll do us *all* good. Here, Lizzie, love, open your mouth and see what your Pa's sent you.'

When, later that same evening, Gilbert himself arrived, Meg's elation increased a hundredfold and she threw her arms around his neck and hugged him.

'Oh, thank you. *Thank* you!' she cried. 'It was such a lovely surprise, I can't tell you! Me and Ellie was that thrilled! All them lovely things and the food and –'

His surprise was so obvious that she broke off in mid-sentence and her face crumpled.

'You mean it wasn't you!' she exclaimed. 'You didn't send them? Then who the hell was it?' Her disappointment was lessened by the knowledge that *someone* had cared enough to expend money on them. Gilbert would have been her first choice, but *anyone* was better than no one.

'Well, I must have a secret admirer!' she laughed, with a toss of her head. 'I thought sure as eggs it was you, you being the father and all that.' She tried to read his expression but failed.

'I sent you nothing,' he said, 'but my wife is interested in the child. I imagine it was her gift.'

Meg was astonished. 'Your wife!' she exclaimed. 'Your wife sending stuff to your baby! Who are you kidding?'

'Naturally she doesn't know,' he said stiffly. 'She frequently does give to deserving causes; she's a very good-hearted woman.'

Meg giggled. 'Am I a deserving cause, then? Well, I'm blowed! No one's ever called me that before, and

I've been called a few things in my time, I can tell you. A deserving cause! Hear that, Ellie? That's rich, that is.' She regarded him with her head on one side. 'So, why did you come then?'

He seemed to find his voice with an effort. 'You could call it conscience, I suppose. I thought perhaps I should see my . . .'

Meg supplied the missing word for him. 'Daughter,' she said. 'It's not a dirty word, you know. Aunt Ellie, show the doctor his *daughter*. Right bonny little lass, she is, and so good. Not a peep out of her most of the time.'

He took Lizzie, looked at her briefly and handed her back to her aunt without comment. Then from his pocket he took a small brown bottle and gave it a shake before handing it to Meg.

'I brought this for her,' he said. 'If she becomes at all fretful, give her a spoonful in water. If she cries –'

'She hardly ever does,' put in Meg proudly. 'Real happy little soul, she is, isn't she, Ellie?' Ellie nodded.

Gilbert went on, 'If she gets colic, then . . .'

'Colic? What's that?'

'Abdominal pains, stomach ache, gut-ache, or belly-ache – call it what you like. Or if she won't sleep at night. You can repeat the dose if necessary.'

Meg said, 'My Ma used to give us gin in a drop of milk. Gin's very soothing. Or Godfreys Cordial if she was feeling flush.'

Gilbert repressed a shudder. Godfreys Cordial, like penny sticks and a variety of opium-based pills, were notoriously lethal in careless, ignorant hands.

'This is better,' he told her. 'It's a superior cordial.'

'Well, thanks. That'll come in handy, I'm sure.' She put the bottle on the mantelpiece between a cracked mug and a jam-jar full of dead flowers.

'So, what do you think of your kid, eh?' she asked him. 'Right little cracker, isn't she?' He nodded and Meg bridled. 'Well, *say* so then! After all I've been through you could at least *say* something. I know she's a bit on the small side, but she'll grow.'

He nodded again but then, seeing her expression, searched hastily for words. 'She's . . . she's a nice child,' he said. 'Don't let her suffer. Remember the cordial; that would cost a lot of money if you had to buy it.'

As usual Meg was impressed by the mention of money. 'Special, is it? What you give to rich kids?'

'Yes, indeed.'

Meg grinned at Ellie. 'See?' she said. 'Nothing's too good for our Lizzie.'

Gilbert managed a smile, though he felt nothing but shame and guilt and a deepening anger directed towards himself for ever having allowed this situation to develop. Nevertheless he comforted himself that he had now taken positive steps to rectify the matter and that knowledge gave him a glimmer of comfort. The possibility that any of this unpleasantness should ever reach his wife terrified him, and his one aim now was to undo the mischief he had done. He must consider the destruction of the child as a necessary evil.

For the first time in his life he felt a sneaking sympathy for those who were forced into villainy through an unfortunate combination of circumstances. There were occasions, he told himself, when the end justified the means – and this was a case in point. Meg and this wretched child could ruin his life and he could never allow that to happen. As a doctor, he had much to offer to society and if he should be struck off the register, his talents would be a far greater loss than one puny child. Even if the baby lived beyond the first twelve months – which was unlikely – malnutrition, neglect, accident or disease would almost certainly claim her.

Meg found his silent introspection demoralizing and said, 'Give us a kiss, Gilbert, now that we're back together again. I think you do love me just a little bit – you're just too shy to say so.'

She held up her face hopefully, but he avoided her mouth and brushed his lips across her forehead as he wondered incredulously how he could ever have felt anything at all for the bedraggled creature. It had been nothing but carnal desire, he told himself desperately; he had never seen this woman as *desirable*! It was merely that she tolerated his unpardonable behaviour.

'Gilbert!' she protested with a pout. 'That's not much of a kiss! Look, give me a few more days and we could have a bit of fun the way you like it, you know what I mean. Sal's out most of the time now because her old ma's taken sick; that's where she is now. Ellie can take Lizzie out, then there'd be just the two of us again like old times. I bet you're dying for a bit, aren't you?'

'Yes,' he lied, his voice strained, and nodded in further confirmation although all his instincts cried out for flight. He had to be sure, however, that the baby would not survive, but he must also convince her that he was well-intentioned towards it so that he would never be connected with its death.

'You will remember the cordial, won't you,' he said. 'Try it tonight, perhaps, and make sure of a good night's sleep. You are looking very tired and you must get your strength back.'

'I reckon the honey'll do that,' she told him. 'That and the beef broth. It was real kind of your wife, but funny in a way – you and me and the baby and her being all generous –'

He could bear it no longer. 'I must go,' he cut in, his tone curt.

Meg tried to hide her disappointment. 'But you'll come again, won't you?' she begged. 'Promise me you'll come again.'

'I will, yes, and of course if the child is taken sick at all, you must let me know.'

'Taken sick?'

'Anything at all. You notify me. No one else.'

'If you say so.'

As he moved to leave, she put out a hand to detain him. 'What about some money?' she suggested. 'To buy milk and what-not for little Lizzie. Just a bob or two to tide me over for another few days, and then I'll be right as rain again and I'll give you what you want, like before. I swear it.'

He fumbled in his pocket, drew out a florin and put it into her hand.

'Is that all?' Her face fell. 'Gilbert Reid, you old miser! There's your own baby daughter – and I do think she looks like you, you know –'

'For God's sake!'

He gave her a second florin and without a 'Goodbye', left the room without waiting for her thanks, his one aim being to put as great a distance as possible between himself and Meg Swain. Having slammed the front door behind him, he climbed into the waiting hansom with alacrity.

As they bowled through the unsavoury streets his heart was heavy with a new problem. The child was taken care of, he had seen to that, but what was he going to do about the mother?

*

Several days after Jeff was attacked, Dora returned home from visiting Meg to find that a note had been pushed under her door. Written in an untidy scrawl, it said, 'Your fansy man isn't so fansy now! Let that be a lesson. See you at the pay-out. Sid.' Her heart contracted with fear as she stared at the words. Her 'fansy man'? Did that mean Jeff Bannerman?

'Please God, no!' she whispered. 'He wouldn't – he daren't! Would he?'

She felt as cold as ice. She would trust Sid Patten almost as far as she could throw him, yet she would not have called him a *violent* man – but then she only ever saw him at work in his job as foreman. She knew nothing about his family or friends and there were plenty of thugs in London's East End – unscrupulous, desperate men who would stop at nothing. Shoreditch, White-chapel, Hackney and Bow were notorious areas where vile crimes could be committed and people would close ranks around the perpetrators. If Sid Patten *had* hurt Jeff it might be difficult to bring him to justice, for the people of the East End viewed anyone in authority with deep distrust and the police were no exception. Informing on a criminal could prove a dangerous business for the informer. Men like Sid Patten had friends and he would no doubt have an unshakable alibi. Assaults were so common and many people would look the other way rather than become involved with the law.

'But not me!' Dora told herself fiercely. 'If Sid Patten has hurt Jeff, I'll turn him in. He won't get away with it.' She read the note again and whispered, 'If he's hurt Jeff . . .' Then she went back on to the landing and locked her door carefully behind her, her imagination running riot as she hurried down the stairs and out into the street.

'I'll turn him in,' she repeated, 'if he's harmed a hair of Jeff's head!'

The journey to Parfett Street seemed interminable, but at last she was knocking at the door of Jeff's lodgings. It was opened by Mrs Coot who was delighted to see her.

'Come on in, my dear,' she cried. 'We've been expect-ing you.' She lowered her voice a little. 'I think he was a little bit disappointed you didn't come flying round at once, but I said, "She's probably got things to do." Men are so impatient, aren't they?'

'But I didn't know until half an hour ago,' said Dora, 'when I got this note. How could I have come any earlier? Is he badly hurt? What happened?'

Mrs Coot read the note and then shook her head,

puzzled. 'That's not the note Mr Bannerman sent you,' she said. 'He wrote a nice long letter, took him most of the morning. I teased him about it. "Writing your memoirs, are you?" I asked him.' She showed Dora into the parlour and told her to sit down, then went to the bottom of the stairs and called her lodger.

'Someone to see you, Mr Bannerman. A Miss Becket!' There was an answering shout from above and Mrs Coot went back to Dora.

'Now you mustn't worry,' she warned. 'He's got a black eye and lots of bruises, but he's going to be all right.'

'But what happened? *Was* it Sid?'

'He'll tell you that himself – ah, here he comes now. You'll have lots to talk about, so I'll just pop out and make a nice pot of tea,' and she bustled out as Jeff came in.

Dora gasped when she saw him. A huge area around his right eye was purple and brown and the eye itself was half closed; his mouth was still swollen, and there was another bruise on the left side of his jaw.

'Jeff!' she cried, jumping to her feet. 'You look as though you've been run over by a steamroller! Did that swine Sid do this to you? I found this note under my door.'

They sat down and Jeff read it. 'This is probably evidence,' he said. 'May I keep it to show to the police?'

She nodded and Jeff explained exactly what had happened, adding that he had told her all about it in his letter which he had written the day after the attack.

'But I haven't got it yet,' she reminded him. 'Maybe it will come tomorrow. Oh, Jeff, I feel it's all my fault and I'm so terribly sorry. I wonder when Sid saw us together? At the strike meeting, perhaps. Oh, and you've lost a tooth! Just wait until I see him again; they might have killed you.'

'The police are looking for them both,' he told her.

'The big man who lives along the road is still unconscious and one of the brutes – either Sid or his damned brother – is responsible for that too. If the poor man dies, it could mean a murder charge. I shouldn't care to be in their shoes. I wrote to you because I was so afraid he might try to contact you. Dora, you mustn't have anything more to do with him. He's dangerous.'

Dora paled. 'But he says in this note that he'll see me at the pay-out.'

'He won't if I see him first! Don't worry too much on that account. I'll come with you. I doubt he'll dare to show his face at a public place, because he'll guess we'll show this note to the police and they are sure to be keeping an eye open for him. They went to his lodgings apparently, but he hasn't been seen since the fracas. Neither of them has been seen since, or so the story goes. It could be a big cover-up. Those kinds of people stick together.'

The door opened and Mrs Coot came in looking very upset and carrying a letter.

'It's here,' she confessed. 'I had several letters to post and . . .' She looked at Jeff. 'Oh, Mr Bannerman, whatever can I say? I know my memory isn't what it was, but this letter was so important. I can't tell you how sorry I am. I didn't forget it, but I truly thought I'd posted it with the others.'

Jeff smiled reassuringly. 'Please don't worry about it. We all make mistakes and luckily there's no harm done.'

'Well, that's kind of you. Now I'll make that tea.'

Dora said, 'May I have the letter? I'd like to read it when I get home'

'Sure you can.' He handed it to her and Dora slipped it into her pocket, then looked up at him again with a worried frown on her face. 'I do hope the police find them soon. I don't much like the thought of those two on the loose. They might come after you again to finish you off!'

'I doubt it,' he said, 'but Sid might try to see you. I wish you didn't live alone. Would your cousin Meg let you stay with her, do you think? Just until they catch him.'

Dora wrinkled her nose. 'She's offered before but to tell the honest truth, I don't think I could bear it,' she confessed. 'It's not just her and Ellie. There's her lodgers – Sal and Alf and their baby, all crammed into one room. I could stand it for a day or two, but if the police didn't pick up Sid and his brother . . .'

'Perhaps Mrs Coot could find you a bed here.'

Hastily Dora shook her head and lowered her voice. 'I couldn't afford it, Jeff, and I've never taken charity so I don't want to start now. Besides, if I leave my room empty for any length of time I'll probably find that someone else has moved in! Nothing would surprise me.'

For a while longer they discussed the attack and then Mrs Coot brought in a pot of tea for two.

'I thought I'd have mine in the kitchen,' she said with a wink at Jeff. 'I'm sure you two young people have things to talk about – oh, and I've brought you your *Times*. I was telling Mr Bannerman before you came, Miss Becket, that there's an article about you match-girls. Fancy getting into *The Times*! You're getting quite famous, you and your strike.'

While Dora poured tea into Mrs Coot's best cups, Jeff began to read aloud the article which dealt with the meeting on Mile End Waste.

'. . . about thirteen hundred of Bryant & May's girls, all of them employed in the making of wooden matches, are still on strike. Only a few of the wax match hands are at work . . .'

Dora looked up indignantly. 'Trust them!'

He read the rest of the article and then said, 'It's interesting; the newspapers are beginning to take sides.

The Link, *The Star* and the *Pall Mall Gazette* are on one side, *The Times* on the other. Left versus Right.'

'But we are in the right,' said Dora. 'I'm sure we are.'

'Not that sort of right, Dora. Right-wing politics.'

'Oh, *those*,' she responded vaguely.

Jeff opened his mouth to give her a lecture on politics, but thought better of it. Instead he said, 'Well, it's obviously attracting a lot of attention and it could attract even more. If you're going to get strike pay, you girls could hold out indefinitely.'

'Don't say that,' said Dora. 'I don't know what to do with myself as it is, with Saturday and Sunday the same as the rest of the week. I keep forgetting what day it is. I've been round to Meg's a few times – she had her baby, you know, and it's a real little pet. They're calling her Lizzie. She's a good little thing and Ellie's over the moon at being an aunt! And, wonder of wonders, the baby's father showed up!' She took a mouthful of tea and went on, 'I told you he's a doctor, didn't I? Married, unfortunately, although I doubt he'd marry Meg even if he wasn't. Life's not like it is in fairy tales, but at least he's taking an interest and his wife, poor thing, sent some little things for the baby. A rattle and a bonnet.' Her eyes clouded momentarily. 'Sad when you think about it. She can't have any children because –'

She stopped abruptly, embarrassed, afraid that already she had said too much on a delicate subject.

'Go on!' Jeff grinned. 'It's just beginning to get interesting.'

Dora gave a firm shake of her head. 'I've said too much already,' she laughed.

'You're a strange girl,' he said. 'You don't seem to belong to that crowd.'

'Well, I don't belong anywhere else.'

He shook his head. 'I don't know; I just don't think you're one of them.'

She was beginning to look anxious, so he added,

'What I mean is you're a cut above the rest. Don't look like that, it's a compliment.'

'You make me sound like a freak!' she protested.

'Of course you're not a freak. You're a very nice girl.'

'You really think I'm nice?'' She looked at him eagerly.

'*More* than nice.' He thought about it. Yes, he certainly did think she was more than nice. A *lot* more. 'I guess you're one of the nicest girls I've ever known,' he said and then swallowed nervously, awed by the significance of his remark.

Dora gave him a long cool look. 'Now *you've* said too much,' she told him with a faint smile. 'You didn't mean to say that.'

He looked into the gold-brown eyes that stared so calmly into his. 'Maybe not, but now I've said it . . .' He shrugged. 'It happens to be true.'

He stood up suddenly, held out his hands to her and pulled her to her feet so that they stood very close, each watching the other, each hopeful and yet afraid.

At last Jeff took a deep breath. 'What I really want to do is kiss you,' he told her. 'Would you scream if I did?'

She regarded him with serious eyes. 'No, I think I'd rather like it.'

Still neither moved, both astonished at the speed with which things were happening.

'Oh, Dora –'

'Jeff!'

Then she leaned forward slightly and he kissed her forehead, the tip of her nose and finally her mouth. Then he put his arms around her. When they parted they still held hands; her cheeks were pink and he was a little breathless.

'You didn't scream,' he joked. 'What a relief!'

'No, I didn't. I thought it might bring Mrs Coot rushing in and I didn't want that to happen.'

He shook his head, dazed. 'This is so amazing! I feel – hell! I don't know what I feel, but I like it!'

They both laughed and still Dora did not withdraw her hands from his.

'Let's do it again,' he said and with her smile as encouragement he drew her towards him once more. The second kiss was longer and infinitely more satisfying – so much so, in fact, that when Mrs Coot came into the room and saw what was happening, she was able to withdraw quietly before either of them was aware of her presence.

*

Amelia tutted loudly and waited for her son to glance up from the book he was pretending to read.

'I have a bill here,' she said, 'from Dr Reid who has attended the confinement of a Miss Swain. I'm sure it is a mistake. I know his wife deals with the accounts for him, and I suspect she has sent it in error; obviously it should have gone to someone else.'

'Swain? That sounds familiar.' He frowned. 'Wasn't Swain the name of that child with the "phossy jaw"? She may have a sister; it could be her.'

'Was she in a certain condition?'

'How on earth would I know a thing like that? It was ages ago, Mama; last year in fact.'

He turned a page in his book and his mother fought down a sigh of exasperation. This wretched Marion, whoever she was, was causing her son too much heartache; if he had been a few years younger whe would have accused him of 'mooning about the house', but his years entitled him to some respect. Was this Marion in love with him, or was it all a game to her? Some women, she reflected irritably, collected lovers the way others collected gloves or fans. She had racked her brains to recall anyone named Marion, but without success.

'Well, I shall call on Dr Reid later in the day and return the bill,' she told him. 'If it is this phossy girl's sister, I have certainly never agreed to pay for her confinement. The hussy will find she has presumed too much on my good nature.'

For a moment she remembered Ellie and pondered the child's fate. 'They should have operated on her face,' she reflected aloud. 'I should have insisted on it. At least she would have had a chance, then. Toothache, indeed!'

'Take her into your school, Mama,' suggested Ralph. 'Then you *could* insist.'

'I can hardly do that, dear. She is not an orphan; she has a home of her own, of a kind. I cannot go round abducting children, no matter how deserving they are. Anyway, there are plenty of equally deserving children, so I shall find no difficulty in filling the school. My problem will be to finance it year after year.' She leaned back in her chair, her expression shrewd. 'I think I have stumbled on a way of raising more money for the enterprise,' she told her son. 'If a wealthy man or woman donates a certain sizeable sum – guarantees an *annual* sum, that is – he or she may then nominate a candidate for the school. I was talking to Sir Edward the other day and he assures me that this is how some of the larger, longer-established asylums operate.'

'Is it legal and ethical?'

She raised her eyebrows indignantly. 'Ralph! What a question! Of course it is both legal and ethical. Surely you know me better than to think I would ever suggest a scheme which was not so. Sir Edward is somehow connected with an orphanage in Wanstead and I have it on his authority that this system is not only acceptable but actually desirable, because the annual sums guaranteed by the donors ensure that we shall not suddenly find ourselves short of funds. It is likely to be a very expensive undertaking and once started it must be able to continue. We can hardly turn the children out into the snow after a few years, on the grounds that we have run out of money.'

'I hope it is not going to prove too daunting, Mama.'

'I do not consider it *daunting*, Ralph,' Amelia reproved him. 'I consider it a challenge, and one I take up willingly on behalf of those less fortunate than myself. Do you know how much it will cost to feed and clothe one of our girls? A minimum of thirty pounds per annum! Yes, thirty! I have now revised the staff requirements and in addition to the resident matron we shall need a cook, maid and laundrymaid. Are you listening to me, Ralph?'

'Of course, Mama.'

'Well, I certainly hope so. You will need to know all these things.'

Suddenly she had caught his full attention. '*I* will need to know them?' he said. 'Why do you say that?'

'Because you will have to assume responsibility when I die.'

'But I have no intention of –'

She sighed. 'Ralph, please listen to me. You are approaching thirty years of age –'

'Mama! What are you saying? I'm twenty-five!'

'Don't quibble.'

'But really, I . . .'

'And so far you have done nothing useful with your life.'

'But you insisted that I travel! It was your idea.'

'I wanted you to make a name for yourself as an artist and live in Holland Park. With your talent, you could have made a fortune for yourself instead of waiting for me to die and leave you mine. There never has been such an interest in pictures. There is not an artist today who cannot enjoy a very satisfying life. You showed great talent which I have encouraged. No!' She held up a hand as he tried to interrupt. 'You studied under the best tutors, and when they advised travel I sent you abroad for further study.' She regarded him irritably. 'And what use have you made of your talent? None. You have a fully equipped studio at the top of the house, but you are never to be found in it. I don't think you have even lifted a paint-brush. Nor, I may add, did you lift it very frequently while you were away. I was very disappointed. Venice, Rome, Paris and so little to show for it. You have had your chance, Ralph; it can't go on. I have put your name forward for the committee and it has been accepted.'

Ralph's consternation was complete. 'But suppose I don't want to be on your damned committee?'

'Please don't be ridiculous, dear. I tell you that you *are* on it. You are the obvious person to take over from me, and you must be in at the beginning.'

'So much for Ralph Gaunt, artist!' he said with a rare touch of sarcasm.

Amelia ignored the comment and went on, 'It will be an exciting but highly complex undertaking, and it will be no good if you come in half-way through.' She held up an imperious hand. 'I do not want to hear any more objections, Ralph. How on earth would it look if you backed out after I have nominated you?' Ignoring his outraged expression, she continued, 'I think the children will have to attend the nearest day school for the first year or two. Ideally, of course, we should have our own teacher – I did hope we would – but they cost a lot of money. I think we would have to pay about fifty pounds per annum, and that might include a midday meal. We might get someone for less, but they would not be of the right calibre.'

Ralph said, 'Really, Mama. I must protest –'

'Protest away, dear. It will make no difference at all.' She rose abruptly. 'Now I shall call on the doctor and then go on to Mary's. I have told Cook we shall eat at eight tonight.'

Ralph jumped to his feet. 'Mama, we need to discuss this. You can't just run away.'

'*Some* of us have things to do,' she told him. 'The

devil finds work for idle hands, Ralph. Now, I must be on my way. I shall be home about seven-thirty.'

*

Marion rose to her feet panic-stricken, and stared at the housekeeper.

'Mrs Gaunt!' she stammered. 'What does she want? Did she say?' Her first thought was that Ralph's mother had somehow found out about their liaison.

'It's about an account, ma'am, sent to her in error.'

'An account! Oh, I see.' As the panic subsided, Marion put a hand to her heart which was racing. A guilty conscience, she told herself, tried to compose her features as relief mingled with curiosity. She had never met Amelia Gaunt, who obviously had the good fortune never to be ill. 'Please show her in,' she said.

As Mrs Gaunt came into the room Marion, still feeling very flustered, stretched out her hand in greeting. So this austere woman was Ralph's mother; how unalike they were, she thought.

'Mrs Gaunt. What a pleasure! How may I help you?'

Amelia looked at her severely, and held out the offending bill. 'I assume this to be an error? It concerns a Miss Swain, who has just been delivered of a child.'

Marion nodded. 'That is correct. She called my husband out in the middle of the night for a perfectly straightforward birth, but by the time he arrived the child had been born. As you see from the account, he gave her and the child the normal examination.'

'Why send it to me?'

'I thought you were –'

'Well, you are wrong,' snapped Amelia. 'I cannot think how your husband could allow such a mistake. I did not even know the woman's name, nor that she was with child, and I object to being used in this way, Mrs Reid. Of course I am not referring to you or your

194

husband; it is obviously this wretched woman who has misled the doctor.'

Marion took the bill from her. 'Mrs Gaunt, I am so sorry this has happened,' she apologized. 'I will ask my husband about it. It may be my fault.'

'He must be firm with her,' Amelia insisted, ignoring Marion's last comment. 'These unfortunate women live by their wits, you know, and will stoop to any deception. If Dr Reid is to become consultant to our school, he must learn to distinguish between fact and fiction. I have no sympathy with the young woman, however much I may sympathize with the child. According to Dr Reid, it was her ignorance which prevented Ellie from having an operation on her jaw. There can be no hope for that poor child, and the woman has much to answer for.'

'I will speak to my husband as soon as he returns,' Marion told her. 'I'm sure he will write to you himself, but in the meantime please accept our apologies.'

'I do,' said Amelia, 'but please see that such a mistake does not happen again.' And with a brief nod of her head and an indignant rustle of silks, she swept out of the room.

CHAPTER NINE

Marion left the offending bill on Gilbert's table and he found it on his return from his rounds. When he brought it into the parlour with him Marion said, 'Mrs Gaunt returned it. She thinks there has been a mistake, as she has never agreed to pay for any of Miss Swain's medical expenses, only for Ellie's.'

She had decided that if it seemed likely that Gilbert would be visiting the Swains again, she would have to tell him about the gifts she had sent. If not, she would say nothing and hope for the best.

'I didn't intend you to send her an account,' he said. 'Did she refuse to pay it?'

'Yes, I'm afraid she did – and she was rather unpleasant about it. I'm sorry, it was my fault.'

To Marion's surprise, Gilbert merely shrugged, tossed the bill on to the mantelpiece and sat down. Was that all he was going to say on the matter?

He glanced up and caught sight of her face. 'What are you staring at?' he demanded.

'I didn't think I was.'

She turned away, found *The Times* and handed it to him in silence, her mind racing. She had expected a 'Damn!' at the very least, since if Mrs Gaunt was not going to settle the account no one else would.

'What kind of day have you had?' he asked.

Again she hid her surprise and said, 'Agreeable, thank you. And you?'

He shrugged again by way of an answer and Marion picked up her needlepoint. He seemed to be in a very odd mood and she wondered if she could confess to the gifts she had sent Meg in case he learned about them for himself at a later date if he went back to the Swains.

On impulse she said, 'Gilbert, I hope you will not be too angry, but I did send something to the Swain baby. Just a few little –'

He did not raise his head from the newspaper but said, 'That was very foolish of you. They will not be appreciated, I can assure you.'

'I'm sorry, Gilbert. I just couldn't bear to think of the poor child coming into this harsh world without even a rattle or . . .'

'You are too sentimental, Marion. It was a foolish gesture and I hope you now see the error of your ways.'

Gilbert's overbearing manner always brought out the worst in her, and she struggled to keep back a sharp reply. He made her feel like a child being reprimanded by a teacher.

'It was hardly a crime,' she protested.

'That is for me to decide.' Gilbert put down the paper at last and now his expression was cold. 'I specifically told you not to visit.'

'I didn't visit. I sent them. They were only trifles –' she began.

'They were not trifles!' he corrected her. 'The elephant alone . . .' He stopped himself, but it was too late.

Suddenly Marion's heart hammered. He knew! He had been back to the Swains. He was looking at her so strangely, yet he knew about the gifts and had tried to pretend otherwise.

Suddenly he dropped the paper into his lap and covered his face with his hands.

'Gilbert . . .' she faltered, her thoughts chaotic. There was no reason for him to hide the fact of his visit – or was there?

'You knew!' she whispered. 'You *have* been to see them. Is it the baby, Gilbert? Is she ill? Did she die? Is that it?'

When he did not answer she moved across to kneel beside him. 'Did she die, Gilbert? If she did, then you must not blame yourself. You always do your best, but they have so much to contend with and so many of them die. Gilbert, you must not take it to heart.'

She put a comforting arm around his shoulder, but he immediately shook it off and then uncovered his face.

'I don't want to discuss it,' he told her. 'Please don't press me on the subject, Marion; they are *my* patients and not your concern.'

Somewhere deep in the recesses of her mind a bell rang. Once he had called the Swain woman 'Meg'; she was sure of it. So was he more closely involved with the family than she suspected? She tried to think of any reason for such an involvement coming about. Perhaps he had taken pity on them, and was treating them free of charge and did not want her to know.

'Gilbert, are you –'

'Stop it, Marion!' he snapped. 'For your own sake, stop questioning me. You will just have to trust me.'

She got to her feet and stood looking down at him, deeply disturbed and suddenly aware of a gulf between them that was widening inexorably. They were both guilty of deceit. Soon they would be strangers.

Marion turned away to hide her dismay. She had begun her married life with such high hopes, such determination, such a sense of duty towards her husband; yet now, slowly but surely, they were drawing apart – each one withdrawing to a private world the other could not share. Gilbert had not confided in her about the Swains. Did that mean that he no longer felt he could rely on her understanding? Did he believe that she would disapprove of his charity towards the family? No, she decided; there was more to it than that.

'Gilbert, we really must talk about it,' she told him. 'Don't shut me out of your life like this. We have always . . .'

He picked up the newspaper again. 'My patients are my concern,' he repeated and turned the page.

Marion regarded him helplessly. 'Is the baby dead, Gilbert? You can tell me that much, surely?'

After a slight hesitation he said, 'Yes, it is. I hope you're satisfied.'

Satisfied? At a child's death? What a strange choice of words. Why should she be 'satisfied' – unless the child was Gilbert's! Horror rendered her speechless and fear churned within her. She had tried for so long to suppress her suspicions.

She began, 'Please, Gilbert –' but he interrupted her.

'I'm sick of your prying,' he told her. 'All those questions.'

'In the circumstances, I think they are natural.'

He turned over another page and appeared to be engrossed.

'*Gilbert!*'

With a single movement he crumpled the newspaper and threw it to the floor; then he stood up, his eyes glittering with anger.

'Do not dare to raise your voice to me, Marion. I think you forget yourself.'

Before she could answer he strode to the door and opened it. After a moment Marion gathered her courage and followed him into the hall, where she found him putting on his coat.

'I shall not be in to dinner,' he told her as he reached for his hat.

'But where are you going?' she asked him.

'Out!' he replied and a moment later he had gone, banging the door behind him.

Marion was left to her thoughts, which were uncomfortable in the extreme; trembling slightly, she went back to the morning room and poured herself a small brandy which she sipped gratefully. When she felt more composed, she sent for Mrs Cobbett and told her that the doctor had had to go out unexpectedly and therefore she would be alone for dinner. Then she took several deep breaths to try to calm the frightened fluttering in her stomach and spoke to herself sternly.

'Be calm, Marion. Think it all over carefully. Don't panic.'

If only Rachel were still here, she thought. It would be such a relief to confide in someone. Why had Gilbert behaved so strangely? Was it merely that she had disobeyed his instructions, or was it the baby's death? Did he somehow feel responsible? A new and frightening thought struck her – had he been guilty of negligence? Had he laid himself open to prosecution? No, that was impossible, but even if he *had* Miss Swain would hardly take the matter to court since litigation was an expensive proceeding and according to Gilbert the family was impoverished. A charge of negligence was a doctor's nightmare.

Her own conscience began to trouble her. Perhaps if she had not been so obsessed with Ralph Gaunt, she might have been more aware of her husband's problems and able to help. Had her own indifference exacerbated the problem? She hoped not, but had to admit that this was possible and if so she must now accept a share of the blame for whatever had happened. The pleasure she had once felt in her relationship with Ralph was now dimmed by the knowledge that she had failed her husband in his hour of need, and it was not a pleasant thought. Those few carefree hours in the Zoological Garden had been purchased at too high a price.

The question which now loomed large was what to do about her association with Ralph. In her heart she knew it should end, although every instinct cried out against such a drastic step. Ralph, she knew, would not willingly relinquish the friendship between them, but he was a single man with no ties and consequently no guilt. She was a married woman and would have to take the initiative; she must go to him, or write a letter. Somehow she must convince him that they must never meet again. He was an honourable man and she was sure he would respect her feelings. But could she bear never to see him again? His light had shone so brightly upon her world that she felt she would never survive the darkness.

'Oh, Ralph!' she whispered. 'How will I live without you? I *love* you. What am I to do?'

After a long deliberation she went upstairs and began a letter to Rachel.

*

Ten minutes before 11 o'clock on July 14th Dora arrived at Charrington's Hall in Mile End, as did hundreds more of the striking match-girls, although there were fewer than had been expected for a considerable number of the girls had gone fruit-picking. She found Zoe already there and the two girls chatted excitedly, comparing notes on how they had managed financially in the intervening days, while Dora kept an eye open for Jeff and a sharp lookout for any sign of Sid Patten. By the time 11 o'clock came she had seen neither of them, but she joined in the great cheer that went up as Annie Besant arrived with three men whom Dora did not recognize. They carried the money which had been donated for the strike pay, and their manner was jubilant. Dora kept a tight hold on her ticket, for without that she knew she would be ineligible for any payment. Inside the Hall a man was arranging the chairs into sections which corresponded to the various departments within the factory.

'It's Mr Burrows,' said Zoe. 'He spoke at that first meeting – don't you remember him?'

Dora shook her head. 'I'm not very good at names,' she confessed.

At last the meeting began with a few words from Herbert Burrows, and the girls listened as he told them that the London Trades Council had offered to arbitrate in the dispute and that the girls' own committee of six would attend any discussion on their return to work. He told them, too, that they must form themselves into a union to protect themselves in the future. Dora tried to concentrate, but she was somewhat distracted by the thought of Sid's threat and by Jeff's non-appearance.

Herbert Burrows then announced that they had brought £150 which had been collected for the strikers, and this information drew forth loud and prolonged applause.

'It will be divided in the following way,' he explained. 'Girls whose earnings did not exceed six shillings will each receive four.' There was a ripple of excitement among the listeners. 'Those previously earning over six shillings will receive five . . .' He smiled as a few cheers rang out. 'Married women and widows will also receive five shillings, and the boys who have been put out of work by the action of the girls will get four shillings and sixpence each.'

When the ensuing chatter had died down, Annie Besant told them that their cause had excited a great deal of interest nationally and urged them all to stand firm. No one, she insisted, should be prepared to go back to work until a satisfactory settlement had been agreed. The audience gave her three hearty cheers and she then announced that the distribution of the money would begin. Everyone hurried to get in line in the appropriate place.

'I thought your young man was coming,' said Zoe as she and Dora waited together. 'Looks like he's not going to show up.' She was rather piqued that Dora had found herself such an eligible admirer; a newspaper reporter was quite definitely a catch.

'He'll come,' said Dora, crossing her fingers.

'Is he writing all about us?' Zoe asked. 'I've never seen anything by a Jeff Bannerman.'

'I didn't know you read the newspapers?'

'I don't.'

'Well, then, you wouldn't see what he writes, would you?'

'Well, what does he say about us, then? Is he on our side?'

'Of course he's on our side, silly,' said Dora. 'I wouldn't have a young man who thought we were in the wrong, would I? I wouldn't be walking out with a man who –'

Zoe's eyes widened. 'Walking out? What, going steady? Dora Becket, you never are!'

Dora grinned. 'Well, maybe not, but he kissed me,' she confided, '*and* I've been to his lodgings *and* he says I'm the nicest girl he's ever known, *and* I've had tea with his landlady and he –'

'And he hasn't turned up!' Zoe's tone was accusing.

'He will.'

'So what does he say about us girls, then?' Zoe demanded.

'I don't know exactly; he sends it all to America.'

America! Zoe was finally silenced. If Dora had a young man who sent articles to America, she was definitely more than 'one up'. Zoe wished *she* could meet an American . . . or even an Australian . . . instead of being courted by Bert Fisher, who had pimples and bad breath. And quiet little Dora, the dark horse, had snaffled an *American*! Dora, who wouldn't say 'boo' to a goose! Life was very unfair, Zoe reflected.

The lines of girls moved forward at a surprisingly brisk rate and still there was no sign of Jeff Bannerman. Zoe made further comments on the subject of his absence, but Dora found consolation in the fact that there was no sign of Sid Patten either.

There were still more than a dozen people ahead of her in the queue when a small, wiry man with a flattened nose came up to them.

'Your name Dora Becket?' he asked.

A greasy cap was pulled well down over his eyes and his shoulders were hunched so that the lower part of his face was hidden by the upturned collar of his jacket.

Dora hesitated, but Zoe said, 'Yes, she is. So what?'

He addressed himself to Dora. 'I got a message from someone who's taken a shine to you,' he said. 'Know who I mean? Someone who's got himself into a spot of bother all because of you.'

'Go away!' cried Dora. 'I don't want to hear any messages from him. He's a bully and a thief!' She looked round hopefully; if only she could see a policeman, she would have this wretched little man arrested and questioned, because if he was carrying messages for Sid Patten then he must know where he was hiding.

Undeterred, the messenger continued, 'He says he'll be seeing you, like he promised.'

Dora put her hands over her ears. 'I can't hear you,' she told him. 'Just go away!'

However, Zoe asked him, 'Where is he, then, since you know so much?'

The man's eyes narrowed craftily and he tapped one side of his nose. Dora, understanding Zoe's ploy, uncovered her ears and asked, 'How do we know the message is really from Mr Patten?'

'You don't – but it is.' He gave a grim laugh. 'You'll find out soon enough.'

Zoe and Dora exchanged glances. 'But you do know where he is?' insisted Dora.

The man's mouth opened to reply, but then he paused cautiously. 'Nobody knows where he is,' he announced.

Zoe pounced. 'Then if you don't know where he is, how could he have given you a message for Dora?' She turned to Dora. 'Take no notice of him; he's having you on.'

'I am not!' he protested. 'That message is from Sid, I tell you. Straight up!'

'Then where was he when he gave it you?'

He shook his head. 'Ah! You don't get round me that easy,' he told them. 'Sid give me the message and I've give it to you, and if you know what's good for you you'll heed it, too. Now I'm off.'

'Wait!' called Dora. She thought frantically, wondering how she could detain him until Jeff arrived. 'Suppose I give you a message – could you take it to him?'

'You going to make it worth my while?'

She turned to Zoe. 'He does know!' she whispered. 'If we could find out his name, we could –'

But suddenly Zoe caught sight of Jeff. 'Here comes your young man,' she told her and both girls turned to welcome the American, who looked hot and bothered.

'Crikey!' muttered Zoe. 'His face! What a mess.'

'Dora!' he cried. 'Thank heavens you're all right.' He gave her a quick peck on the cheek, embarrassed by Zoe's presence. 'I should have been here earlier, but the cabby was taken ill; he collapsed and fell off the seat. I couldn't just leave him lying in the road.'

Dora said quickly, 'Jeff, this man here –' She turned to look for him, and her face fell. 'Oh, no! He's gone!'

'Who's gone?'

Dora explained and Jeff looked thoughtful. 'But that must mean that Sid himself isn't here, so you can stop worrying on that score. Anyway, there's a policeman on the door of the Hall. I don't think Mr Patten would dare show his face if he's heard the news. Poor Mr Tredwell died this morning, so although they probably don't know it yet, those two villains are wanted on a charge of murder.'

Dora looked at him in dismay. 'Dead! Oh, the poor man! How terrible. And his poor wife!'

While they talked the queue dwindled, and then it was Dora's turn. She produced her ticket and said, 'Two seven four, please.'

A brisk finger ran down the edge of the register until it reached Dora's name. 'Dora Becket?'

'Yes.'

'Five shillings.' Five coins were placed in her hand.

'Thank you very much.'

'Don't thank me. Thank all the people who gave to the fund.' Dora nodded. 'Next please.'

Dora moved away and Zoe took her place. 'Two eight one,' she said.

'Zoe Bush?'

'That's right.'

'Five shillings for you.'

'Thanks.'

As they moved on Dora said, 'I wonder where that man went. If we could point him out to the policeman, they could question him about Sid. He must have taken fright when he saw you, Jeff.'

Jeff nodded. 'Pity, he could have proved very useful. Dora, I wish you would move in with us. Sid is still very determined to reach you, and I don't trust him. If you won't come to us, then go to Meg's place until they catch him.'

'*If* they catch him!' said Dora. 'You don't know what it's like, Jeff. What do I do if they never catch him? I can't stay in hiding for ever.'

Just then Zoe caught sight of another friend and dashed off, leaving them together, and at once Jeff took Dora's hand in his.

'Miss me?' he asked hopefully.

'Yes, a lot! Did you miss me?' He nodded.

'Your poor face! How are you feeling?'

'Better for seeing you!'

A radiant smile lit up her face. 'Oh, Jeff . . .!'

'I know,' he said. 'Aren't we lucky to have found each other!'

'I keep thinking it can't be true,' Dora confessed. 'I'm afraid I shall wake up and find it's a dream.'

'Two people sharing the same dream?' he grinned. 'Now that would be news!'

They laughed, and as they looked at each other all their problems faded instantly from their minds. When Jeff slipped his arm round Dora's waist she made no objections.

'Let's go and eat,' he said, 'and you can bring me up to date on all that happened before I arrived. I guess there were speakers.'

She laughed. 'What's it worth?'

'A plate of steak and kidney pie?'

'You're on!' she told him, and as they left the Hall arm-in-arm she thought she had never been so happy in her whole life.

*

Ellie lay awake, staring at the ceiling, and wondering if the large crack which ran across it was getting longer. It had worried her for some time now, and she had tried to measure its progress. It started above the window and went diagonally towards the door, and Ellie thought it might suddenly get bigger and bring the roof crashing down upon them. She had suggested this to Meg but her sister had scoffed at the idea, insisting that the crack was only as deep as the ceiling paper. Ellie lay on her back because to lie in any other position made the pain in her jaw worse, and from time to time she screwed up her eyes and clamped a hand over her mouth as a new wave of pain engulfed her. Earlier that morning she had felt a new small lump on the other side of her jaw, like a small speck of gravel which was painful to the touch. She knew it was the 'phossy jaw' again, and knew too that eventually the swelling could spread to her ears and maybe up around her eyes, but she comforted herself with the thought that by then she might be a ghost.

Moonlight shone in through the grimy window, casting a soft glow over the sleeping inhabitants. Alf slept alone tonight, for Sal and the baby were with her mother again. He lay huddled against the wall, his long legs drawn up almost to his chest, his breathing ragged. Meg sprawled in cheerful confusion among her threadbare blankets and little Lizzie, wide awake but silent, lay in her crib made from the bottom drawer of the chest.

Ellie's head ached and her body burned, and during the day she had become increasingly aware of a dull ache in all her limbs, so that by the time she had settled to sleep she was utterly exhausted by pain and fear. Rest, however, had brought about no improvement and now she tossed restlessly, longing for the release of sleep.

Another hour passed and she heard the church clock strike two. Moving carefully, she climbed over her sleeping sister and paused to look at the baby as she passed by. She was worried about how she would talk to Lizzie, because the baby would not be able to understand her clumsy speech the way Meg did. She wanted to teach her nursery rhymes and tell her stories. Ellie's favourite story was 'Little Red Riding Hood', which her teacher had told her in the far-off days when she had been well enough to attend school.

Lizzie stared up at her aunt and Ellie put her finger within the baby's grasp, feeling the small hand close firmly around it. She was so glad the baby had hair like Meg and did not take after the doctor for whom Ellie felt a deep and passionate hatred. He had wanted to cart her off to hospital and cut up her jaw; then she would have looked even worse than she did now, and having a jaw cut up sounded a painful process and going into hospital would be like going to the moon! Hospitals were to be avoided at all times, for she had heard that not all those who went in came out again, and if she was going to die she would prefer to do it in her own home.

It came to her gradually that she was feeling much worse. Now her eyesight was blurred and she felt light-headed. In a moment of intense clarity she saw herself ugly and in pain and with nothing to hope for, and she was filled with anguish. Scalding tears of self-pity filled her eyes and ran down her face. In a moment of deep desperation, she crawled to Meg and shook her until she woke up.

'What the hell –?' Meg demanded sleepily. She rubbed her eyes and abruptly became aware of Ellie's distress. At once she sat up and put her arm round the girl's shoulder.

'Ellie, love! What's the matter? Tell me what it is.' For a few moments Ellie's poor speech was made worse by the ferocity of her sobs, but Meg waited patiently, cuddling her and murmuring soothingly until at last Ellie calmed down enough to make herself understood.

'You feel funny?' repeated Meg. 'Whereabouts? Is it your poor old face? Those beastly old teeth! Never mind, lovey. You what? Feel hot? Do you?' She put a hand on Ellie's forehead. 'Christ! You *are* hot! Poor old you. Let's think now . . . Ah! I've got it! You shall have some of that cordial that the doctor give me for Lizzie. How about that now? The stuff what *rich* kids have when they're poorly. That'll do the trickl'

Ellie mumbled a protest, but Meg brushed it aside.

'Lizzie doesn't need it,' she assured her. 'She never gets the colic and she never cries, bless her. Why shouldn't you have it, instead of her? Little Lizzie won't mind if her auntie has a few spoonfuls of her medicine.' Scrambling out of the blankets, she fetched the bottle Gilbert had given her and a large spoon. 'Now, let's think. What did he say to give her? A spoonful in water – was that it?'

She looked at Ellie who, still shaken with the aftermath of her tears, could only shake her head helplessly.

'Well, let me think then,' said Meg. 'If a baby could have a spoonful, then you're much bigger than a baby. Say you're six times as big as Lizzie, so you could have a good bit more – say six spoonfuls, that should do it. And I won't mix it with water; that's probably just for babies.' She put the opened bottle to her nose and sniffed. 'Mm. Smells good. Now open your poor old mouth, lovey, and swallow this down. It'll take away the pain and help you sleep.'

She poured six spoonfuls of the syrup and obediently Ellie drank them down, grimacing a little at the taste.

Meg said, 'It's not too horrible, is it? Never mind if it makes you better.' She held the bottle up to the window to see how much was left.

'Nearly half gone,' she remarked. 'You'd think he'd have been a bit more generous with it, miserable old skinflint – still, there's enough there for another lot. That'll do for later if the pain comes back. Now you snuggle down and shut your eyes. You'll soon be asleep.'

Ellie did as she was told and was pleasantly surprised to find the remedy effective, for soon she felt her thoughts drifting and slid thankfully into oblivion.

Meg slept again and for some time all was quiet. A few hours later, however, Ellie woke up complaining of pains in her stomach and Meg gave her the remainder of the cordial. Half an hour later still, all the occupants of the room were rudely awakened by a piercing scream from Ellie who sat bolt upright, her eyes staring vacantly ahead as a foamy white spittle appeared at the corners of her mouth. In the thin light of early dawn, they could see that she was desperately ill. She clutched her stomach and groaned horribly, and seemed not to hear when Meg spoke to her.

'Jesus Christ!' cried Alf. 'What's up with her?' He made a grab for his trousers and pulled them on.

'How do I know?' demanded Meg fearfully. 'She was feeling poorly earlier, so I give her some of Lizzie's medicine, but she's – oh Gawd!'

With a convulsive movement Ellie retched violently and a sour smell of almonds filled the room.

Alf moved towards the water-jug. 'I'll give her a drink,' he suggested. 'She must have ate something that disagreed with her.'

'She only had kippers,' Meg protested, 'and I had some too, and I'm not ill.'

'Hers must have been off, then.'

Meg moved forward gingerly, afraid that Ellie would be sick again, but she had relapsed into a semi-stupefied condition and was lolling against the wall.

'Ellie, love, are you all right?' Meg asked. 'I'll get a towel and some water, and we'll wash you down.' She turned to Alf. 'Light the candle, will you; we could do with a bit more light . . . Ugh!' She recoiled hastily. 'I stepped in it! Never mind, Ellie, we'll soon have you . . . Alf! The candle!'

'I'm doing it as fast as I can!'

'Well, get a move on. I can't see what I'm doing.'

'He found and lit the candle stump and by its light they peered at Ellie.

'Ellie? Can you hear me?' Meg asked. She snapped her fingers in front of Ellie's face, but there was no response.

'She's real bad!' said Alf. 'Give her some more of the medicine.'

'She's had the lot already.'

He shook his head. 'I don't like it. I tell you, Meg, she's real bad.'

Meg nodded. 'Perhaps I should fetch the doctor?' she suggested.

Alf leaped to his feet. 'You're not leaving me alone with her. She might croak on me!'

Meg's mouth dropped. '*Croak?* Christ, Alf, she's not *that* bad.'

'I reckon she is. Look, you tell me where he lives and *I'll* go for the doctor.'

Alf found his shirt and pulled it on while Meg told him, and was searching for his boots when Ellie gave another piercing scream.

Meg put a hand to her heart. 'Strewth, Ellie! Don't keep doing that,' she begged. 'It frightens the life out of me!'

She and Alf stared at Ellie, who suddenly groaned and clutched her stomach. They watched in horror as she struggled to her feet, swayed precariously and then with a low moan pitched forward on to the floor.

'Ellie!' whispered Meg, hardly daring to approach the unconscious form. 'Oh, Alf! She's not –'

Alf held the candle nearer to the pathetic bundle on the floor, but they could see no sign of movement. Meg put a hand to her mouth and swallowed hard. Was Ellie *dead*? It seemed impossible, for a moment earlier she had been alive and screaming.

'She's fainted,' she said, but her voice trembled with a terrible uncertainty.

'Maybe,' said Alf. 'Maybe not.'

Meg knew she should take a closer look at her sister, but fear held her back, for once she *knew* there would be no hope and she wanted to delay the dreadful moment.

'She'll come round . . .' she began.

'I don't know . . .'

Frantically Meg tried to rally her resources, knowing she must steel herself to find out if Ellie's heart was still beating. However, her legs had turned to jelly and would not carry her nearer to her sister, and in the end it was Alf who found the courage. He put the candle on the table and moved gingerly forward to crouch beside Ellie, leaning down to put his ear to her chest.

Meg said, 'She's going to be all right, Alf,' but her voice lacked conviction.

Without answering, Alf took hold of Ellie's right wrist in a clumsy attempt to find a pulse, but after a few moments he sank back and there were tears in his eyes which he wiped away with the back of his hand.

'Gawd lummy!' he said helplessly.

'Alf!' cried Meg.

'She's gone!' he told her. 'She would have died sooner or later.'

Meg stuffed both fists into her mouth as Alf's words

echoed in her brain: 'She would have died sooner or later.' So she *was* dead. She whispered the words 'Ellie is dead,' and the realization stunned her. Slowly she groped her way to a chair and sat down. She had watched Ellie being born – it seemed like only yesterday – a lusty bawling infant, bald, ugly and red with rage. She had nursed Ellie the way Ellie had nursed Lizzie, closer to her than her overworked mother ever could be. Ellie had been part of her life for so many years that she *couldn't* be gone so suddenly, snatched away without any warning.

'Are you sure, Alf?' she whispered.

'I'm sure,' he muttered and taking out a grimy rag that served him as a handkerchief, he blew his nose loudly.

Meg eyed Ellie nervously. Was that Ellie, or was it just a dead body? She was no stranger to death, for her mother had lost five of her seven children before dying herself, but the children had all died very young, within the first two years. Ellie was different.

A thought struck her. 'If it was the kippers,' she said, 'then I could go next.'

Alf looked up. 'How d'you feel?'

'All right.' She thought about it. 'And I had a pair; she only had one.'

'It wasn't the kippers then, else you'd be gone by now.'

They continued to stare at Ellie's body. 'She must have just got sick,' said Alf. 'People get sick all the time.'

Meg said suddenly, 'She's to have a decent box. Not one of them charity ones but a good one.'

'They cost money.'

'I'll get some,' Meg told him, clinging in desperation to the idea that Ellie should be laid to rest in style. It became imperative. It was the last service she could render for her sister.

'And flowers,' she told Alf. 'She'd have liked that. Oh, Ellie!'

She was aware of a great pressure within her chest and her throat felt so tight she could hardly breathe. 'Oh, Ellie!' she cried again as the grief welled up.

In her makeshift bed in the drawer, Lizzie's small hands flailed the air helplessly, her tiny mouth drooped and she began to cry as though her heart would break.

*

Marion walked slowly back from the pillar-box in which she had posted two letters – one to Rachel and another to Ralph – while Pip tugged at her lead and strained against her collar, waiting to be noticed. Today, however, Marion ignored her behaviour and Pip continued to cough and splutter reproachfully to no avail. When they arrived back at the house Pip struggled up the steps, choking and gasping, but still received no attention from her distracted mistress until at last Marion bent down to unfasten her lead. At that moment Mrs Cobbett appeared from the kitchen with floury hands, looking agitated and none too pleased.

'Ma'am, it's that young woman again. The one who . . .' she lowered her voice '. . . *pesters* the doctor. Miss Swain, her name is.'

Marion gave a start, for Meg Swain had been in her mind almost constantly and was one of the main subjects of the letter which she had just posted to her sister. Now her thoughts whirled – presumably she had come about the baby's death, to accuse Gilbert of professional negligence, perhaps? She tried to steady her voice as she asked, 'How does she seem? Did you know that her baby died?'

Mrs Cobbett's expression changed. 'Oh, the poor little mite! Dead already! Well, it wasn't long for this world then and that's a fact. That explains the red eyes; I thought she looked a bit tearful. I let her in, ma'am, because I didn't want a scene on the steps – and you know how neighbours talk, and you were out and I didn't know what to do. She doesn't want to see the doctor; all she wants is an address – at least that's what she says, but you can't trust her sort. She says she wants Mrs Gaunt's address.'

'Thank you, Mrs Cobbett. I'll deal with it now.' Marion hoped she sounded calmer than she felt.

As Mrs Cobbett returned to the kitchen, Marion took a deep breath in an attempt to steady her fluttering nerves. There was a great deal she wanted to know, so she was glad that Gilbert was out and prayed that he would not come home until she had finished talking. When she went into the waiting room Meg jumped to her feet.

'I only want Mrs Gaunt's address,' she began breathlessly before Marion could formulate her first sentence. 'I don't want no trouble, just Mrs Gaunt's address. I know the doctor must have it. *Please*, Mrs Reid.'

She was dishevelled and her hat was lopsided. There were dark shadows under her eyes and, as Mrs Cobbett had said, there were signs of recent tears.

Marion said gently, 'I'm so sorry about your sad loss. It must have been a terrible blow.'

Meg stared at her. 'How do you know about that?'

'My husband told me. Your poor little –'

'Your husband?' cried Meg. 'But she only went this morning, and he doesn't know; nobody knows, only me and Alf, and Dora because I called in on my way and left the baby with her. I came straight here for Mrs Gaunt's address. She was sort of interested in her and I thought, that is I *hoped* . . .' Her lips trembled. 'I don't want her to go in a charity box, Mrs Reid. I want her to have a good do with flowers and that. She liked flowers.'

Marion was staring at her. 'Liked flowers?' she echoed.

Meg nodded. 'She got sick in the night. Real bad and crying with it, she was, and Ellie's not one to cry. That is, she wasn't . . .' She gulped noisily, swallowed and blinked hard. 'I thought Mrs Gaunt might pay for a proper box, seeing as how she took an interest in her and everything.'

By now Marion was thoroughly confused. Gilbert had told her the baby was dead, yet now Meg was claiming that *Ellie* had died – and within the last few hours!

She held up one hand. 'Please, Miss Swain,' she said. 'May we get something clear? You say that Ellie died during the night?' Meg nodded. 'And your baby is dead also?'

'Lizzie?' Meg looked surprised by the suggestion. 'No. She's fine, bless her, except now she's got no Auntie Ellie. Ellie loved that kid.'

Marion shook her head. Gilbert had definitely said the baby was dead, and if she *wasn't* then Marion's suspicions about him were totally unjustified and she had greatly wronged him. And, she thought, with the beginnings of panic, she had confided in Rachel! If only she hadn't posted the letter . . . but there was no way now to retrieve it, so she would have to write again to set the matter straight.

'I'm very sorry about Ellie,' she told Meg. 'How did it happen?'

'She woke me up, crying and feeling ill, so I gave her some of the medicine your husband had left for Lizzie. A bit later she woke up with a pain in her gut, and then later still she started screaming and sort of foaming at the mouth and then . . .' She faltered, reliving the moment.

Marion prompted, 'And then?'

'She fell forward on to her face and never moved again, and Alf said she was dead. I couldn't bear to look at her, not at first, but I did after, of course. We straightened her up and washed her down and laid her out, best way we could, with her hands crossed over her chest like this.' She demonstrated and Marion nodded. 'I'm getting her some violets on the way home, 'cos they were her favourites.' She sighed heavily.

Marion thought this sounded rather casual and asked, 'But you did call a doctor?'

Meg shook her head. 'Doctors are for sick people,' she explained, 'not dead people. I don't need a doctor to tell me that Ellie's dead. All I want now is the money to bury her proper.'

Again Marion tried to make sense of what she had heard. She was prepared to accept that Ellie was dead, but why had Gilbert lied if the baby was alive and well? Could Meg be lying? Was there a conspiracy on the subject?

'And your baby is alive and well?' she repeated.

Meg nodded. 'It was kind of you to send those things. Oh yes, I know it was you, 'cos your husband said so. Now if I could just have Mrs Gaunt's address, I'll be off.'

'You don't want to see Dr Reid, then?'

'No point, is there?'

Marion hesitated. 'There has to be a death certificate, Miss Swain. You will need a doctor to sign that, so wouldn't you like to wait for him?'

'No, thanks. I just want that address.'

Marion could see no harm in giving it to her, since Mrs Gaunt might well be willing to pay for Ellie's funeral, so she said, 'I'll get it for you,' and left Meg in the waiting room while she found the address in the book which was kept in Gilbert's desk. She wrote it out on a slip of paper and took this to Meg.

On reflection she was glad that the girl was not prepared to wait. If she was going to challenge Gilbert, she did not want a third person present – and certainly not Meg Swain.

Marion provided directions to the Gaunts' house and then showed Meg to the door. As she went down the steps, Marion asked, 'And the baby's father – is he proud of her?'

The question took them both by surprise, for Marion

had not intended to ask it and Meg was not prepared with an answer. Marion watched closely as Meg hesitated.

'He doesn't know,' she said at last. 'How could he? In my line, the father could be anyone.'

She kept her head averted as she spoke, and Marion felt a chill of apprehension sweep through her. 'And you have no idea?' she persisted.

Meg lifted her head and stared Marion straight in the eye. 'None at all,' she told her. 'Does it matter?'

'No. I . . .' Marion's courage failed her. 'As long as the child's well it doesn't matter, as you say.' Impulsively, she held out her hand. 'Goodbye, Miss Swain.'

An unfathomable expression crossed Meg's face and for a moment Marion thought she was going to ignore the proffered hand, but then she took it.

'Mrs Reid. I . . .' She swallowed and fell silent.

With their hands clasped, the two women looked at each other wordlessly, aware of an affinity between them . . . the moment lengthening as each one struggled to put into words emotions too intuitive for expression. With a deep sigh, Meg withdrew her hand, turned and walked away and Marion, feeling oddly bereft, closed the door behind her.

CHAPTER TEN

There were six people sitting around the table in Amelia Gaunt's morning room: the Reverend Albert Craythorne, Sir Edward Somers, May Thripp, John Foster, Ralph and Amelia herself. The first committee meeting was in session and at the appointed time John Foster, as chairman, rose solemnly to his feet, cleared his throat and consulted the paper he held in his hand.

While he waited for their total attention, he surveyed his fellow committee members with a shrewd eye. As a bank manager he was used to being heard with proper respect, and knew from past experience that a few moments spent in establishing a precedent now would pay dividends later. His glance fell first on the Reverend Craythorne, an elderly man in faded black who was fiddling with his pencil – a nervous habit which John Foster observed. He made a mental note to watch the reverend gentleman carefully, as he had not been entirely happy with his appointment to the committee. A *retired* vicar was much less valuable than one who still held sway over his congregation and could therefore donate generous collections to the school's fund. Opposite him Sir Edward Somers rested his elbows on the table as he puffed at a large cigar, and John Foster tried unsuccessfully to suppress the awe he felt in his presence. He himself felt a natural superiority over many lesser mortals, but a title was always a tricky thing with which to deal and he was glad Sir Edward did not bank with his own company, for that would further have affected the delicate balance of their respective positions, tipping it in Sir Edward's favour. He bore more than a passing resemblance to Lord Kitchener, John Foster thought enviously, aware of his personal inadequacies for his own head was bald and he had no chin to speak of. Still, *he* was chairman and not Sir Edward and this thought comforted him.

Amelia Gaunt sat on John Foster's right hand and her son, Ralph, sat between her and Sir Edward. John Foster could appreciate the fact that the young man ought to be on the committee because he stood to inherit his mother's money and influence, but he did wonder if – at his age – he had the desired qualities necessary for such important work. Ralph Gaunt appeared unimpressed by the committee and seemed to find the meeting a source of amusement, but then young people today were notoriously lacking in an appreciation of worthwhile values and it was to be hoped that he would learn. Hopefully too his mother would eventually instill in her son some of her own zeal for the project in which they were all engaged. May Thripp could be any age from sixty to eighty, so she was hardly likely to take a very dominant part in the proceedings, although she had contributed very generously indeed. At the moment she was leaning back in her chair and seemed to be thinking of something else.

John Foster cleared his throat again and began his address:

'Ladies and gentlemen, it is with great pleasure that I rise to speak to you on this momentous occasion – the very first meeting of the Harold Weston Memorial School committee. Mrs Gaunt has already made the necessary introductions and I shall merely add my hopes that we shall find ourselves a united and worthy group, able to work together for the good of the splendid cause with which we have allied ourselves.' He caught Ralph's eye and was annoyed to see that the young man was smiling at him encouragingly. 'I have been asked to present an outline of all monies pertaining to the foundation at this stage and this I will do. Firstly, however, we must appoint a managing secretary and Mrs Gaunt has put forward the name of her son, Ralph.' He swallowed hard, for secrectly he had hoped to fill the position himself but Mrs Gaunt had obviously, and un-derstandably, decided that the family should keep a tight hold on the reins. His job now was to make it sound as though Ralph had been the *only* choice. He went on, 'It is an onerous task and not one which could easily be undertaken by someone like myself who is already in full-time employment. Sir Edward's time is also heavily committed, while our reverend friend is in delicate health.' He smiled at the vicar. 'We shall appreciate whatever time he is able to give us, but would not wish to over-tax his energies. Miss Thripp will understand that we need a younger member of the committee who will be able to oversee the project for a considerable number of years.' He relaxed a little as heads nodded in agreement, congratulating himself that he had handled the matter with great subtlety. 'I therefore second Mrs Gaunt's proposal. Are there any comments, please?'

May said, 'I think Ralph will do splendidly,' and smiled fondly at her nephew. The vicar concurred. 'I am in complete agreement. It sounds a most sensible arrange-ment.'

Sir Edward blew out a cloud of expensive smoke and suggested that since the young man in question *was* so young, they might consider a probationary period to be prudent, and Ralph was the first to agree. Amelia was not particularly pleased at what she considered a slight on her son's ability, but she made no objection and a twelve-month period was agreed upon.

The bank manager then read out the accounts of money already received or pledged for the foundation and concluded, 'This amounts to a total of just under eleven thousand pounds,' whereupon there was a flutter of applause. He went on, 'We therefore have enough money to see us through the first year, but we must not allow ourselves to become complacent. There will always be additional expenses – repairs to property for instance – or larger than expected medical bills in the possible event of an epidemic; unexpected rises in the cost of fuel and food perhaps . . .' He spread his hands in a gesture of helplessness. 'I do not need to remind any of you that we have no recourse whatsoever to any public funds, so we must always bear in mind the unexpected and make proper provision accordingly. I have spoken of the donations, of the interest on investments, of the firm promise of certain legacies and of the subscription scheme which guarantees us regular annual injections of capital. The trust fund will be administered by our committee with the full cooperation of the bank of which I am currently manager; we will discuss that further at the next meeting when the details have been finalized. I also strongly recommend that twice yearly we arrange festival dinners as fund-raising events for which tickets will be sold and at which an appeal for donations will be made. This is quite usual in some of the larger asylums, and I see no reason why we should not find it equally suitable for the Harold Weston Memorial School.'

After a further eight minutes, John Foster sat down to gratifying applause and Ralph then rose to read out a list of expenses incurred to date. Amelia spoke about the furniture she had ordered and about the work in progress at their chosen premises.

The meeting was still going on when Janet tapped on the door and came in to whisper in Amelia's ear.

Amelia rose to her feet. 'Ladies and gentlemen, I have just heard the sad news of the death of one of those very children our little school will hope to support. Poor little Ellie Swain has died and I suspect that "phossy jaw" was the killer.' There was a shocked murmur from her listeners.

'I like to think that when the school is fully operational,

a few children like poor Ellie will have a greater chance of survival.' she said. 'Now, if you will excuse me a moment.'

She went outside into the hall where Meg waited forlornly. The walking had tired her and all her former jauntiness had deserted her.

Amelia asked at once about the circumstances of Ellie's death. 'Was it the "phossy jaw"?' she demanded. 'If so, I shall hold you responsible.'

'I don't know, do I?' Meg retorted.

'Don't know?' Amelia snorted. 'What nonsense! You must have some idea. Was she knocked down by a horse? Did she fall down the stairs? Did she die peacefully in her sleep?'

'She was took bad. A pain in her gut and –'

'But didn't the doctor diagnose the cause of death?'

'We haven't had no doctor.'

Amelia shook her head despairingly and said, 'I shall send Dr Reid as soon as possible to issue a proper death certificate.' She cut short Meg's protests with an enquiry into the health of the new baby, and Meg told her Lizzie was doing well.

'For how long, I wonder,' Amelia remarked severely, but Meg looked so miserable that she did not have the heart to berate her further. 'So you came to tell me of her death; poor wretched child.'

Meg took a deep breath. 'Not only that, ma'am, I came to ask a favour; to ask if you could see your way to give her a bit of a do. I'm getting her a really lovely wreath. I know this woman, Mrs Kelly her name is, as makes beautiful wreaths near Shoreditch Church. Her shop's right opposite the Mildmay Hospital. We're all putting in for it – we always do round our way.' On the way to Queen Elizabeth's Walk Meg's ideas had expanded somewhat. 'I want Ellie to go in style, ma'am, in a proper coffin – and I want a hearse, too, with horses and black feathers and all that – what my gran used to call a "splendiferous do". I saw a grand funeral once, with little kids in black walking beside the coffin and crying and –'

'Don't be ridiculous!' said Amelia. 'Such a parade would be farcical and entirely out of keeping.'

Meg's face fell. 'But it would give Ellie such a thrill to know that –'

'Don't talk nonsense,' Amelia chided. 'Nothing will give poor Ellie a thrill now. Such trappings may be regarded by some as necessary, but I consider them nothing more than a quirk of fashion. Contrary to popular belief, Miss Swain, the dead cannot possibly appreciate elaborately decorated horses. The money involved could and should be spent on the living.'

Meg's disappointment flashed into momentary anger. 'Well, thanks for nothing!' she cried. 'So much for your so-called goodness! So much for helping the poor! A fine benefactor you've turned out to be!'

Amelia was quite unruffled by this outburst. 'When I have heard from Dr Reid how Ellie died I shall find a suitable undertaker to measure her for an oak coffin. Now, I think that is all I have to say to you, Miss Swain, although no doubt you have something to say to me.'

Meg's fury had already burned itself out. 'Such as?' she enquired, her voice sullen.

'Such as "Thank you" for the coffin.'

Meg reflected. She was reluctant to give up all her lavish ideas for the funeral, but if she did *not* thank this frosty, miserly old trout then Ellie would not even have a good coffin. She thought frantically to see if there was any other way she could afford a decent coffin without accepting charity from this woman, but came to the reluctant conclusion that Amelia Gaunt's money *would* be needed.

'What sort of handles?' she demanded.

Amelia looked at her blankly. 'Handles?'

'On the coffin,' Meg insisted. 'I don't want anything

cheap and nasty. I want ... that is, Ellie would have liked ... brass. She always used to say, "When I'm dead, Meg, I want solid brass handles."'

Her expression defied anyone to challenge this invention and Amelia struggled to repress a smile, reluctantly admiring the young woman's audacity.

'Very well, then,' she agreed. 'A coffin with brass handles.'

'Solid?'

'Yes.'

A wan smile lit Meg's face. 'Then I'm much obliged to you,' she said. 'Thanks.'

'And I'm doing it for Ellie, not you,' Amelia reminded her. 'Now I am in the middle of an important meeting, so you must excuse me.'

As Meg turned to go, Amelia added, 'And do take care of the baby. Babies are not toys, you know. They need constant care and attention, food and warmth – and a lot of love.'

But she sighed as she watched Meg depart and shook her head despondently. With a feckless mother like Meg Swain, she did not overestimate the child's chance of survival.

*

The morning of Ellie's funeral dawned calm and sunny for which Meg was grateful, for now she could wear her new hat without risking the feathers. As she bent over the small oak coffin to give it a final polish, she thought how well she had managed everything in spite of Mrs Gaunt's refusal to help with more than the coffin. Gilbert Reid had been prevailed upon to contribute a guinea and this had proved invaluable, although Meg's gratitude had later been tempered by disappointment when he told her he would not attend the funeral. Amelia Gaunt had also declined the invitation, but Meg had finally become reconciled to their absence by assuring anyone who would listen that she did not want 'the likes of them' to be present, since they could in no way be classed as family or close friends. 'Ellie wouldn't have wanted it,' she had insisted until eventually she had convinced even herself. Now she rubbed away at the wood, admiring the gleam which followed her efforts and humming cheerfully. When she was satisfied that it was perfect, she breathed heavily on each of the brass handles in turn and polished them also.

Smiling down at Lizzie, who lay on the floor beside her, Meg said, 'Your Aunt Ellie would be pleased with this. Fit for a princess, this coffin is.'

She lifted the coffin lid for the hundredth time and looked fondly at Ellie, who lay straight and still in a grey silk dress which Meg had bought from a pawnbroker for eightpence. It was a little too big, but a few stitches here and there had made it passable. Meg ran a hand lovingly over the silk, revelling in its smooth surface; she touched Ellie's hair, which had been brushed away from her face and tucked under a lace bonnet donated by Alf's sister. Ellie's hands, crossed on her chest, held a small posy of wilting violets. Whenever she looked at her sister, Meg was surprised anew to see how peaceful she appeared considering the violent nature of her death and it seemed to her that, if it did nothing else, death removed all cares and woes. Even the swelling in Ellie's face appeared less pronounced, and Gilbert had set Meg's mind at rest about the "phossy jaw" by assuring her that Ellie had died of something that sounded like septer-seamio (whatever that might be), so Mrs Gaunt's cruel remarks about the "phossy jaw" could now be put down to the woman's ignorance. Mrs Gaunt might be rich, Meg told herself, but obviously she didn't know everything and she certainly wasn't as clever as she thought she was! Meg was glad Amelia Gaunt would not be at the funeral, but she *had* come up trumps over the warm-toned oak coffin with its brass handles. The lining of white satin was a joy to behold and she thought Ellie looked completely at peace lying amidst the virginal folds and pleats. Being dead seemed to suit Ellie, Meg reflected cheerfully, and she blew her a sister kiss before lowering the lid for the last time. Alf would be back at any moment and he was going to screw it down.

As the church clock struck two, Meg suddenly realized that Dora was late. She crossed to the window and looked out on the funeral carriage which had cost her so much time and effort and was now her pride and joy. Tommy Hudson's two-wheeled coster cart had been hired for the occasion and Meg had spent an hour cleaning and polishing its yellow wheels. She had wanted Tommy to paint them black, but he would not agree and there was not enough money left from Gilbert's guinea with which to bribe him. There had been difficult decisions to make, for Jed Cross had a cart with *black* wheels but a brown horse, whereas Tommy Hudson's elderly mare was black except for one leg – which Meg had managed to disguise with boot-blacking for the occasion. A dozen long black ribbons were tied at intervals along the horse's mane and two long black ostrich feathers (borrowed from a neighbour) stuck up at a rakish angle from the horse's head. The wreath, another of Meg's triumphs, had been subscribed to by all who knew Ellie and a few more who did not, and was generally declared one of Mrs Kelly's best. Meg had wanted 'Gates of Heaven' – a wreath in the shape of the pearly gates – but at thirty shillings it had been too expensive and she had eventually settled for a pink angel with white wings. At a pound, Meg thought it wonderful value, and could not wait to see the impression it would make on all who saw it.

Ellie was to be buried in the graveyard adjoining nearby Christ Church, but this had posed another problem for Meg since the most direct route to the church was very short – east along Fashion Street, left into

Brick Lane and left again into Fournier Street where the church was situated. However, Meg considered that this was much too short a journey to do justice to Ellie's funeral cortege, so she had decided that the procession should follow a longer route. They would now go *west* along Fashion Street, across Commercial Road into White's Row, back along Dorset Street and down to Flower and Dean Street; they would then turn north along Brick Lane and left into Fournier Street. She estimated that this route was close on a mile and worthy of the occasion of Ellie's passing. Anyone who was too old or infirm to manage the whole mile could join the procession at any point they considered convenient.

So much had gone into the planning of the event that Meg now prayed that it would take place without a hitch. When it was all over, family and friends would repair to the Black Horse in Dorset Street to celebrate its successful conclusion and Meg had thought no further than this point. All she wanted was to see her sister laid to rest with all the pomp and splendour she deserved and, Meg felt, if there was any justice in the world or any God in heaven she ought to have her wish granted.

By ten past two Alf had returned home, the coffin lid had been fastened down and Ellie in her grey silk finery had vanished for ever. Dora finally appeared accompanied by Jeff Bannerman who agreed, after a surreptitious dig in the ribs from Dora, to write an article about the funeral for his New York paper.

The funeral itself was timed for three o'clock and there was now no time to be lost, so the coffin was carried out into the street and laid with great solemnity in the centre of the cart. The huge pink and white wreath was laid alongside it, while neighbours and friends muttered words of respectful admiration in voices suitably hushed for the occasion. One or two of these people wore black, but those who could not do so wore black armbands. Tommy Hudson was flushed out of the pub looking much the worse for drink and hoisted on to the driver's seat of his cart. Counting the heads of those present, Meg was gratified to discover that a minimum of twenty-two mourners would accompany Ellie on her last journey. No doubt others would join them as they passed along the familiar streets en route for the church.

Tommy Hudson looked blearily at Meg. 'Is that it, then?' he demanded. 'Is this the off?'

Meg made a small adjustment to the angle of her hat and took a deep breath, savouring the moment. After a final look round, she nodded graciously. 'It's the off,' she agreed, 'and you go carefully, Tommy Hudson.'

Tommy felt vaguely that some special effort was required of him and therefore he raised his greasy cap in a salute to the assembled crowd. Settling it back on his equally greasy head, he picked up the whip and cracked it loudly so that the startled horse lurched forward reproachfully.

Ellie's funeral procession was on its way at last. As the cart swerved and rattled over the badly paved streets, the coffin shuddered so violently that it began to shift and after a few minutes a brief halt was called to straighten it and to replace the wreath which was also in danger of slipping off. They set off again, but before long the offside wheel passed over a deep pothole and once more the coffin lurched alarmingly.

'Hang on!' cried Meg, and she handed the baby to Dora and told Alf to straighten Ellie up a bit. Then she marched to the front of the cart, where Tommy sat hunched and apparently uncaring on his seat.

'It's your bloody driving what's doing it, Tommy Hudson!' she scolded. 'Why can't you look where you're going?'

He turned his head unsteadily and said, 'What?'

Silently Meg cursed her own stupidity, for she had paid him before the procession instead of after and now had no carrot with which to coax him.

'I said look where you're going,' she repeated. 'I could drive a sight better myself. For heaven's sake, Tommy – this is a *funeral*.'

The jibe about his driving registered on his befuddled brain. 'You want to drive?' he asked. ''Cos you're welcome to it!'

He belched loudly and Meg hesitated. She felt sure she could drive the cart, certainly at the slow speed at which she intended to travel, but it would not be seemly for the chief mourner to be seen on the seat of a coster's cart.

'No, I don't, and I've paid you good money to do it. Just you do it properly, Tommy Hudson – or else,' she added vaguely. Five pints of strong black porter had made Tommy truculent.

'Or else what?' he demanded.

'Or else you'll have me to reckon with,' she told him. 'Now get on with it, for Christ's sake, or we'll be late.'

Tommy sniffed loudly and made a great show of wiping his nose on his sleeve, but Meg pretended not to see this small provocation and returned to her place behind the cart where Dora gave her a quick smile and handed back the baby. The horse had dozed off during this interlude, but was roused and persuaded to move on again.

The cart, however, continued to jolt its cargo and eventually it was found necessary for Alf and Jeff to walk alongside and steady the coffin while Dora carried the wreath. Although Meg fumed inwardly, there was nothing she could do about it. For a while she trudged in simmering silence with a set face, but eventually her former good humour was restored as the procession began to attract the attention for which she had hoped and the number of mourners following Ellie to her grave increased. By the time they reached Flower and Dean Street, a quick head count put the number at thirty-three and this total soon rose still further.

'Thirty-nine!' whispered Meg, 'and more than half the route still to go!' She hugged the baby to her delightedly. 'Thirty-nine!' she gloated. 'Oh, Lizzie, your Aunt Ellie would have been so proud!'

She looked at Dora with shining eyes. 'I reckon we'll make fifty by the time we're done!' she whispered, and Dora was inclined to agree.

*

Outside the church entrance Marion waited in the hansom, anxiously twisting her fingers as the clock struck the quarter hour. In fifteen minutes' time the funeral service was due to start. Perhaps he was not going to come, she thought desperately, and wondered if she would have the courage to go through with it without him. Almost as she thought, she heard the clatter of approaching wheels and another cab appeared around the corner. It drew up next to hers and to her intense relief Ralph Gaunt descended, paid off the driver and quickly climbed up to sit beside her.

For a moment they simply stared at each other, for they had not met since the day at the Zoological Gardens.

Marion broke the silence. 'Thank you for coming. You must have thought me quite mad, but I'm so grateful to you.'

'Mad? Not at all. I was so pleased – after your first letter I had given up hope of ever seeing you again. But why here?'

She drew a deep breath and clasped her hands to still them. 'I had to come,' she told him nervously. 'It's Ellie Swain's funeral – do you remember the child with "phossy jaw"? I was afraid to come alone and I did not know who else I could ask – or trust.'

'I knew she was dead,' he said. 'The sister came to the house, and my mother has paid for the girl's coffin.'

'Yes, I know. She came to us for your address, but

Gilbert was out and I thought it could do no harm. Was your mother annoyed?'

'Of course not, although the sister wanted a full-blown funeral with horses and professional mourners and Mama jibbed at that, of course, but . . .' He stopped in mid-sentence and shrugged. 'But why do *you* want to attend?'

She hesitated for a moment and then shook her head slowly. 'Two reasons,' she told him. 'I know it sounds absurd, but the Swain family seem to haunt me. I dream about them frequently – nightmares rather than dreams. I felt I *had* to come. The other thing is . . .' She stopped.

'Out with it,' he smiled, but there was no answering humour in her eyes.

'This is going to sound most unlikely,' she began, 'and you may not believe me, but I fear Gilbert is somehow connected with the Swains. Something is very wrong, but –' she hesitated, then went on, 'I do know he has lied to me about them, and he grows angry when I try to ask him any questions. He has even forbidden me to visit them, although often he likes me to call on other patients. He told me categorically that Meg's child was dead, and then I found out from Meg Swain herself that this was not so; it was Ellie who had died.' She looked up at him. 'How could a doctor make such a mistake? And why is it that this family is so different from the others? I suspect he has been guilty of some kind of professional negligence – doctors are human and they make mistakes just like anyone else – and Meg Swain could be blackmailing him.'

Ralph drew his brows together in a frown as he considered what she had told him. 'Possible but unlikely, I'd say. It would be her word against his and, rightly or wrongly, a judge would hardly attach much credence to the word of such a woman.'

'I hope you are right,' she told him. 'But why does Gilbert behave so strangely? And the woman, Meg, looks at me with a kind of pity in her eyes as though she knows something about me – as though she is *sorry* for me. I'm not explaining this very well, Ralph, but can you see why I felt I had to come to the funeral? But Gilbert has said what a bad area it is – notorious was the word he used. So I was afraid to be here alone. Will you come with me, Ralph? It is a lot to ask – especially after that letter I sent you. Can you forgive me?'

'I confess it hurt me,' he admitted, 'but I felt I had to honour your wishes.' He smiled faintly. 'Had you been single, I would have ignored it and pursued you to the four corners of the earth! But you have a husband, and I know I have no right to come between you.'

'Oh, Ralph!' She put up a hand to touch his face lightly. 'I *had* to write in that way.'

'You said in your letter that you feel nothing towards me but friendship. Is that really true?'

She glanced quickly away and withdrew her hand. 'That was a lie,' she said in a low voice, 'but I could not encourage you to hope. That would have been most unfair.'

He caught both her hands in his. 'Then you *do* care for me, Marion? I must know the truth.'

At last she looked at him. 'Yes, I do, Ralph, but that makes no difference to what I said in the letter. We cannot have any kind of relationship – you must see that it could only lead to heartbreak.'

'But are we not entitled to a little love, so long as we are agreed it can lead nowhere? I would be willing to –'

'No, Ralph! Please don't tempt me. I know I could not – I should not . . .'

Seeing her agitation, he put a finger to her lips. 'We won't speak of it for the moment,' he said. 'Just say those words again – that you love me.'

She was startled by his choice of words. 'I did not say I *loved* you,' she protested. 'I said that I *cared*.'

'Ah!' he nodded. 'You *care* for me. That is all?'

She hesitated. 'I think that is all I should admit to.'

'Then I will accept that,' he told her, 'And be grateful for small mercies. But as for me – I'm afraid I have no such qualms and I have to confess to *loving* you!'

Marion looked at him helplessly. 'But you hardly know me, Ralph. How can you be so certain? Oh dear, I ought to try to dissuade you. Since there cannot be any kind of future for us, I don't think I should allow you to love me.'

'But I *do*,' he smiled. 'With or without your permission. Who cares about the future? I think we should live one day at a time. Tomorrow may bring heartache, but today I love you; it is as simple as that.'

'You are looking at life through rosy spectacles!' she told him.

'Try them on yourself,' he said gently. 'You will find the world a happier place.'

Marion took a deep breath and whispered, 'I love you!'

He laughed. 'There! It's said and the heavens have not come crashing down about our ears.'

She laughed too, a little shakily. 'There is still time!' she told him. 'Oh, my dear Ralph, I love you and it's no laughing matter.'

'No, it's not. Quite the reverse, if two people who love each other cannot be together sometimes. Marion . . .' They both heard the clatter of hooves and the rattle of wheels and Marion said, 'Someone's coming!'

Ralph leaned out of the cab, stared and then whistled softly under his breath. 'Well, I'm damned!' he exclaimed. 'Look at that! She's got her procession!'

Marion looked out at the approaching cortege and her face lit up. 'Oh, that horse!' she said. 'With the lopsided feathers! Poor Meg! And poor little Ellie!'

'Shall we wait in the cab until they've gone inside the church,' he suggested, 'and then join them?'

At the eleventh hour Marion's resolve faltered. 'But suppose she tells Gilbert? He would be so angry.'

'We could say that it was my idea,' Ralph proposed. 'If Gilbert finds out, we could say that I decided to attend to represent my mother, and asked you to accompany me.'

With Ralph beside her she felt suddenly courageous and told herself that the worst she would have to bear would be her husband's ill-temper.

She took a deep breath. 'Yes, I *will* attend; I'll chance it. Gilbert cannot eat me even if he does find out!'

They climbed down from the cab and, instructing the driver to wait for them, moved to stand beside the church door which had been opened in readiness.

As the cart pulled up outside, the driver sagged ominously on his precarious seat. Ralph whispered, 'He's drunk!' and Marion nodded, surprised to see so many people following the coffin; they tried to ignore the curious stares and whispered comments to which their unexpected presence gave rise. Meg and Dora both recognized Marion and nodded politely to her and Ralph, a greeting which they returned.

Four men then stepped from the crowd of mourners and hoisted the small coffin on to their shoulders with due ceremony. Just as they were about to move into the church the driver of the cart suddenly slumped down and toppled head-first on to the horse's rump. The startled animal jumped forward and as the driver fell to the ground Ralph, who was nearest, darted over to take hold of the horse's bridle in case it should decide to bolt.

Unfortunately, the abrupt appearance of a complete stranger in front of its blinkered head served only to increase the horse's panic and, balked of its forward rush, it suddenly reversed. The rear of the cart was driven against two of the coffin-bearers with such force that they were knocked off their feet and the coffin fell to the ground before the horrified gaze of all present. For a few seconds the silence was intense, then a babble of shocked voices filled the air. Meg gave a cry of anguish and, dumping the baby unceremoniously into Marion's arms, ran forward to inspect the fallen coffin.

Startled, Marion gazed down in wonder at the baby who now lay passively in her arms and thought incredulously, '*This is Gilbert's child!* She has the same skin, the same eyes.'

Gilbert had betrayed her with a common prostitute! Her worst fears had been realized and even now she was holding his illegitimate child. She felt a searing flash of anger against him for his cold-blooded duplicity, and against Meg Swain for seducing him from the paths of respectability. Of course Marion knew that many men frequented brothels and associated with such women, but a doctor was particularly vulnerable and his behaviour should be above reproach. She felt sure that Gilbert would never have acted so rashly without a great deal of persuasion – or coercion. Meg must shoulder a share of the responsibility, she decided.

It came to her also that while Gilbert had been deceiving her she had suffered hours of guilt and indecision over her relationship with Ralph Gaunt which was comparatively innocent. She had finally written to Ralph ending the friendship and had caused them both great heartache, only to find that she had made that sacrifice for a husband who had fathered a child by a woman of the streets.

Awkwardly, she moved the child so that its head rested more securely against her arm. The small body in its grubby shawl was warm against her chest and she felt a sudden tightness in her throat. This was Gilbert's child, the child which by rights should have been hers. Her senses whirled teacherously and she fought down an overwhelming urge to take the baby and run. As she gazed down into Lizzie's calm unfocusing eyes, tears blurred her own, but at that moment Meg Swain let out a roar of anger.

'That stupid sod!' she screamed. 'Just look at this

coffin! He's bust one of the corners. Oh, Tommy Hudson, I'll kill you for this!'

She turned from the coffin to see that by some miracle Tommy Hudson had not been run over by the wheels of the cart and now sat in the gutter muttering to himself, sublimely unaware of the wave of wrath about to submerge him.

'Would you believe it?' someone marvelled. 'Fell right on his head, he did. By rights he should be dead by now.'

'If I get my way, he bloody well *will* be!' cried Meg.

She stared round for a weapon and, seeing nothing suitable, snatched the angel wreath from Dora's hands and advanced furiously on the luckless Tommy Hudson who, alerted to his danger, now cowered backwards, covering his head with his hands and crying for someone to 'Hold her off!' However, in view of the enormity of his offence, nobody lifted a finger to help him but instead watched in delight as Meg raised the angel above her head and brought it down on him with all the force she could muster.

'Take that, you stupid, drunken clod!' she screamed. 'You useless, bloody . . .! I'll teach you to spoil Ellie's coffin! Take *that* – and *that*!'

Pink and white petals flew in all directions as she rained blows on his defenceless head while the mourners watched entranced.

'The angel!' Dora screamed. 'You'll ruin it! Stop, Meg, for heaven's sake!'

When at last they managed to pull Meg away, tears were streaming down her face. 'He's bust the bloody corner!' she sobbed. 'Oh, Ellie, love! I'm sorry!'

Marion watched helplessly while Dora tried to comfort her distraught cousin and the bearers raised the coffin once more. As soon as Ralph went back to Marion the neglected horse began to plod off down the road, pursued by his demoralized owner.

Marion touched Meg's arm. 'Please don't cry,' she said. 'The corner won't show; it's hardly damaged at all really.'

Meg stared at her hopefully but then, glancing down at the battered angel, her face crumpled once more and Dora took it from her and tried to straighten it.

'Look, Meg,' she said at last, 'It's as good as new. Anyway, Ellie would understand, wouldn't she? You know Ellie, Meg? She'd have loved to see you walloping poor old Tommy!' She appealed to those nearest to her and they all agreed eagerly that Ellie would indeed have enjoyed the spectacle.

'You've given her ghost a good laugh!' said Alf. 'I bet if you was to open that there coffin, our Ellie'd have a smile on her face! So come on, Meg, cheer up. There's no harm done; not as you'd notice, anyway.'

Thus encouraged, Meg managed a watery smile. At that moment the church clock sounded above them, striking the hour, and the vicar appeared at the church door anxious to start the service. Seeing him, Meg rallied marvellously; becoming once more the organizing genius, she began bullying the mourners into a neat line behind the coffin. Reluctantly, Marion returned the baby to her and at precisely two minutes past three, they followed the coffin out of the sunshine into the gloomy interior of the church.

*

When at last it was all over and Ellie had been laid to rest the mourners came out of the churchyard with brightening faces and drifted away down the road in lively, chattering groups.

Meg, still holding Lizzie, approached Marion and Ralph and said, 'Fancy a bite to eat? We're off to the Black Horse in Dorset Street – my treat. You'll be very welcome if you want to join us.'

Marion murmured a hasty excuse and Meg's face fell.

'Please yourself,' she said, 'Anyway, ta very much for coming. I think we gave her a good send-off.'

'All very splendid, Miss Swain', said Ralph. 'I congratulate you.'

Marion explained, 'This gentleman is Mrs Gaunt's son, Ralph.'

Meg's eyes widened. 'Ralph Gaunt! Well, I never. You mind you tell your ma we done Ellie proud with horses and everything and tell her ta for the coffin, too.'

'I will.'

Meg turned to Marion. 'I know you're the doctor's wife. Tell your old man all about it, won't you?' She dropped a kiss on the child's head and added slyly, 'Tell him little Lizzie's doing fine. Good as gold, bless her.'

Marion nodded, her throat dry. She had hoped to find out more about Gilbert's connection with this girl, but time was running out. 'Miss Swain,' she stammered, 'would you please tell me what Ellie died of? My husband mentioned it, but I forget.'

Meg screwed up her face in concentration. 'Septer-seamio,' she announced. 'It's when your blood goes all bad – it was because of the tooth.'

Marion turned to Ralph. 'She means septicaemia.'

'That's it!' cried Meg.

After a moment's hesitation, Marion went on, 'I was hoping to meet the baby's father – to congratulate him. She is a lovely little girl.'

Meg lowered her head quickly and fussed with Lizzie's shawl. 'I told you before – I don't rightly know who he is. Could be the sweep's kid; *could* be Prince Eddy's!' She laughed. 'Who cares who her father is, as long as I'm her ma? That's all that matters to me.' She waited but when Marion failed to respond, she went on, 'Well, if you're sure you won't join us I'd best be on my way or they'll think I've got lost. Cheerio!'

Marion watched her go with a troubled mind, but then Ralph put a hand on her shoulder. 'Time for us to go,' he told her and she followed him back to the cab. Neither spoke until the horse had jerked the hansom into motion.

'I'm no wiser than I was before,' said Marion a trifle disconsolately. 'Perhaps I shouldn't have come – and then I wouldn't have put you through all that.'

'Don't worry about me,' Ralph told her with a smile. 'I've enjoyed it. As for Miss Swain wielding the pink angel . . . well, I wouldn't have missed it for the world!'

Marion's face relaxed into a smile at the memory. 'I desperately wanted to laugh,' she confided, 'and yet at the same time it was somehow so pathetic.'

He leaned forward and took hold of her hands. 'Enough about them,' he said. 'What about us? I must see you again and if you won't agree to meet me, I shall have to bring a tent and camp on the pavement outside your house!'

Marion hesitated. 'I had made up my mind never to see you again, but now that I have . . . oh, I'm so weak-willed! I do *want* to see you again. Thinking about you is the only thing that brightens my life at the moment.'

'I feel the same way about you.'

'I was wondering . . .' she said slowly. 'Perhaps we could meet in Kingston. I have written to Rachel to ask her to invite me to stay with her. I wanted to get away from Gilbert. I was so miserable and confused. I have suggested she might pretend sickness so that Gilbert can't say "No" so easily. Isn't that dreadfully devious of me?'

'Dreadfully devious,' he agreed. 'What a terrible woman you are! And Rachel lives in Kingston?'

'Yes, in the house where we both grew up. It's quite an easy journey on the train. Could you meet me there, do you think?'

'Most certainly. It's a wonderful idea.'

Her eyes were troubled. 'I know it's deceitful, but I just had to be away from Gilbert for a while to think things over. I'm so anxious. *Fearful*, almost. Oh dear, we are nearly home; Ralph, we must not be seen together. Stop the cab, quickly; you wait here and when he's taken me home he can return for you.' They clasped hands briefly and then Ralph jumped out. Marion watched him as long as she could, but as the cab rounded the corner into Harrington Hill he was lost to view.

CHAPTER ELEVEN

Sid stood in the middle of Dora's room and surveyed it with a critical eye. Shabby but clean, he decided; she would make someone a good wife, and it ought to be him except that now he had blotted his copybook with the police and was going to have to leave the district in a hurry. His chances of persuading Miss High-and-Mighty Becket to go with him were slim – almost non-existent – for even if she had fancied him before, which she didn't, she would never consider him now that he was wanted for murder. That damned Bannerman would wed her, but Sid meant to ensure that she would not go to him as a virgin. He, Sid Patten, would be the first to sample those particular wares, he told himself grimly, and to that end he had broken into her room and was now waiting for her to return from the funeral.

His brother had already slipped the net and fled westward, making for St Ives. They had argued furiously, Jack insisting that they go together but Sid refusing to leave without dealing with Dora. Attracted to her long before she had taken up with Jeff Bannerman, he had fancied her for the qualities which set her slightly apart from the rest of the matchgirls, but when a rival had entered the arena winning her had become a challenge. Now, however, the disaster on the night of the attack on Jeff Bannerman had ruined Sid's chances, and he knew that he had lost Dora Becket; nevertheless he was recklessly determined to take her just once, with or without her consent.

Jack had warned him that his stubborn attitude would lead him into trouble; had assured him that there were plenty of girls as good as Dora Becket waiting for them in St Ives; Sid had remained deaf to his pleading, resolved to punish both the girl who had rejected him and the man who had apparently won her.

Jack was probably half-way to St Ives by now, Sid reflected, and that was where *he* would go as soon as his business with Dora Becket was over. Then the two brothers would change their names and hopefully be able to find work on one of the fishing boats. At least, that was Jack's idea and Sid, having nothing better to suggest, had agreed to go along with it. Jack had assured him that in Cornwall a man could lose himself, although Sid was none too confident, but on one thing they *did* agree – London was now too dangerous for them and a change of scenery was definitely called for.

Idly, Sid opened the lid of the tea-caddy and on impulse upended it, scattering the tea leaves over the tablecloth. Liking what he had done, he picked up the sugar bowl and swung his arm to and fro in wide movements, like a man sowing seed. There was a knob of butter on a saucer and this he smeared on the linoleum. He grinned malevolently. What right had the likes of a stuck-up cow like Dora Becket to enjoy the luxury of solitary living, he asked himself, when men like him had to share, crammed together in one room like hens in a coop.

When he had disposed in like manner of what little food there was, he turned his attention to the chest of drawers and from this he pulled out each drawer and emptied the contents on to the floor. Having exhausted these pleasures, he was just about to slump back into the chair when he heard voices and, peering from the window, saw Dora and Jeff Bannerman in the street below.

'Hell and damnation!' he muttered and cursed his luck, remembering all the time he had spent planning his revenge. Now it looked as though that weedy little runt of a reporter might spoil it for him.

As he watched, a woman called from the house opposite and Dora crossed the road to speak to her, then came back smiling. Sid strained his ears. If he was lucky, the reporter might get his marching orders for the day and then Dora would come up alone. If not, he would have to tackle them both, but at least he would have surprise on his side. He could not see directly down to the front door, but suddenly he heard one set of feet ascending the stairs and quickly moved to take up a position behind the door. So luck was with him after all! He could hear her humming cheerfully under her breath as she fumbled for her key and his mind raced. Would she notice that the lock had been forced? If so, she might guess that she had an unwanted visitor and he dared not risk that. With one smooth movement he pulled wide the door and grabbed Dora by the arm. Her eyes widened in shocked disbelief as he clapped a hand over her mouth, pulled her inside, closed the door behind him and leaned back against it. He then took a slim but wicked-looking knife from his pocket and held it up in front of her face.

'One word out of you!' he hissed. 'Just one word and I'll spoil your face with this before anyone can reach you.'

Staring triumphantly into her terrified eyes, he thought with relish that when he was finished with her she would bitterly regret rejecting him. He felt not the slightest compunction because in his eyes Dora Becket had a lot to answer for. If it hadn't been for her, he and Jack would not now be on the wrong side of the law.

For a moment she tore her eyes away from his and took in the rest of the room and he saw her lips tremble. So, she didn't like the way he had rearranged the room! Serve the bitch right! He would teach her!

'What do you want?' she asked hoarsely. 'For God's sake!' There were tears in her eyes, he noted with satisfaction, and she would have a damn sight more to cry about by the time he had finished with her.

He waved an arm to indicate the mess he had made. 'That's just a start,' he told her. 'Now for the main event.'

Her eyes darted around the room in search of a means of escape and he laughed, torn between the desire to torment her and the need to hurry. He moved slowly to one side of the door.

'Take that chair,' he instructed, 'and wedge it under the door-handle.'

For a moment he thought she was going to refuse. Her lips closed stubbornly, but leaning forward he grabbed her by the neck and ran the point of his knife lightly down the right side of her face. She gave a gasp of pain as blood sprang at once to the surface and began to trickle down her neck.

'You'll never get away with this!' she cried. 'They'll get you, Sid Patten. Whatever you do to me, they'll get you.'

'I don't think so.'

'They will!' she insisted. 'They're watching the place; have been ever since that man died.' She pointed across the street. 'There's a constable in that house.'

He laughed. 'Tell me something I don't know.'

'He'll have seen you come in!'

Sid shook his head. 'I came in the back way and that's the way I'll leave,' he told her. 'No one's going to come looking for me.'

'Mr Bannerman will be up in a moment,' she insisted. 'He was chatting to the landlady and I came on up to make a cup of tea. You should go while you still can.'

He hesitated. She could be telling the truth . . . yet he did not think so, for surely if she *was* expecting him she would hardly volunteer the fact. She would hope that Bannerman's unexpected appearance would prove her salvation.

'You talk too much,' he told her. 'Get those togs off.'

'My clothes? I certainly won't.'

Fear mingled with outrage in her brown eyes.

He leaned towards her. 'You heard me. Take them off – unless you want me to take them off for you. I just might enjoy that.'

'I won't, I tell you!'

'You will if you know what's good for you.' A lecherous smile moved his thick lips. 'Now do as I say. I may not have too much time, but I'm not leaving without what I came for.'

She swallowed. 'You'll have to kill me first,' she said, her eyes huge, her face pale, 'because I won't let you touch me. Not willingly.'

His smile disappeared, as his eyes narrowed. 'Why, you –'

She went on desperately, 'If you kill me, you'll hang.'

'That's my problem,' he told her through gritted teeth. 'Now do as I say and get those togs off.'

He stepped forward suddenly, the knife raised in his hand, but somehow she side-stepped and reaching out, frantically snatched up the only object she could reach and for a second or two he hesitated, incredulous. Was she planning to defend herself with a *teacup*?

But in that brief moment she swung back her arm and hurled the cup towards the window. It went through the top right-hand pane with a tinkle of broken glass and they both heard it smash on the pavement below. At once startled voices were raised in alarm and Sid drew in his breath in a furious hiss.

'You stupid cow!' he shouted. 'You –'

He grabbed her by the hair but she twisted her face away and kicked out frantically at his shin. From below there were shouts of 'Police!' and the sound of whistles, and footsteps pounded on the stairs. Sid made one last lunge in Dora's direction but his foot went into the butter he had so recently smeared on the linoleum and he slipped, momentarily losing his balance.

'You whore!' he screamed as fists drummed on the other side of the door. Fear filled him. He was trapped! Suddenly Dora dodged past him and tugged at the chair wedging the door shut.

Sid shouted, 'Leave that!' but it was already free and Dora threw it towards him as the door burst open and Jeff Bannerman tumbled into the room followed by a young police constable. As the constable ran towards Sid, Dora, sobbing hysterically, flung herself into Jeff's arms.

Cornered, Sid Patten gave a howl of frustration and rage . . . then swung round and before the constable could guess his intention he leaped towards the window and disappeared in an explosion of broken wood and splintered glass.

'Oh, God!' whispered Dora, white-faced and trembling.

Jeff's arm tightened round her shoulders. 'Serve him right! The world's well rid of men like that,' he told her. 'Don't think about him.'

The constable swore under his breath and then, carefully avoiding the jagged glass, leaned out to see what had happened to Sid.

'Dead as a dodo, I should think,' he said. 'Got to be, from this height. Let's hope so, anyway. Less work for us. All we do is scrape him up and bury him.'

He turned to face Dora. 'Client of yours, miss?' he asked.

Dora's jaw sagged momentarily as the insult dawned, then her eyes flashed furiously. 'Client!' she cried. '*Client!* I'll have you know I'm a respectable working girl!'

'Sorry miss,' he said. 'It's just this street –'

'I live in this street because I can't afford anywhere better, but that doesn't mean . . .' Her lips trembled with anger and shame that Jeff should be witness to her humiliation.

Jeff gave her arm a comforting squeeze and said, 'Miss Becket works at Bryant and Mays in Fairfield Road. I can vouch for her character.'

The constable nodded apologetically and, as Dora raised her head, noticed the blood trickling from the wound Sid had inflicted.

'You've had a very lucky escape, miss,' he said, and Dora nodded dumbly. 'Best get you to a doctor to put a few stitches in that gash. But first – if you'll excuse me – I must go down and check that our villain really *is* dead, though it would be a miracle if he isn't and his sort don't deserve miracles. I won't be long.'

Now that the danger was past, Dora began to shake uncontrollably as shock set in. 'He was waiting for me,' she whispered. 'And look what he's done to my poor little room.'

'We'll put it to rights, don't fret,' Jeff told her, then shook his head in bewilderment. 'I'm damned if I know how he got past the police.'

'He came in at the back door. They know all the ins and outs of these buildings; all the hidden alleys and courts. People like Sid come and go as they please.'

Gingerly she touched her gashed cheek and looked at the blood which ran down her fingers.

Jeff gave her a handkerchief and she pressed it to her face, then crossed to her chest of drawers to find a small mirror to inspect the extent of the damage. 'I'll be scarred for life,' she whispered. 'Oh, Sid Patten, I hope you rot in hell!'

Jeff pulled her closer. 'What's a scar between friends?' he said. 'I shall still love you, with or without a scar, and if I ever start to take you for granted, it will remind me how near I came to losing you. Now when the policeman has taken your statement, you're coming back with me; Mrs Coot will put you in her spare bedroom and fuss over you like a broody hen. How does that sound?'

Dora smiled shakily. 'It sounds wonderful,' she told him. 'I can hardly wait!'

*

In the small dark hours of the following morning Amelia Gaunt lay wide awake in bed, frowning, for in spite of the gloom light had dawned.

'It's Dr Reid's wife,' she whispered. 'It's Marion Reid! How stupid of me.'

She tutted softly. The doctor's wife! Now that she knew, it was so obvious and with hindsight she could see how many clues she had missed. Ralph had shown such an interest in Ellie Swain's case; had spoken so often of the doctor and his wife; had brought Marion Reid into the conversation so frequently. He had even attended Ellie Swain's funeral, presumably with the sole purpose of meeting her there.

'How could I have been so blind!' she whispered and sighing, she turned on to her right side to consider this information further. Her beloved and only son was in love with Marion Reid. She snorted indignantly and muttered, 'I won't have it!' It was out of the question for so many reasons. Firstly, Marion Reid was married. Secondly, she was too old for him. Thirdly, she was not of the same social standing. Something must be done to put an end to the ridiculous affair before it went any further.

'But what?' she demanded of the darkness.

She knew her son too well to imagine for even a moment that a direct appeal to his common sense would serve any useful purpose. If she spoke a single word against the doctor's wife, it would make him more than ever convinced that Marion Reid was the only woman in the world who could make him happy.

Restlessly, she turned again on to her back, carefully so as not to twist her spine; her back had been giving her a little trouble of late and she did not want to aggravate it. She could send him abroad again, perhaps . . . could invent a reason why it would be necessary for him to spend a few months in France. But he would probably refuse to go and anyway, now that he was on the school committee it would look odd if he suddenly went abroad.

She tried to remember what the doctor's wife looked like – surely she was no beauty. How on earth had Ralph ever become so seriously involved? He could not believe that there was any future for them, could he? Amelia did not want to be unsympathetic, but the fact was that Marion Reid was a nobody and even had she been single, she would hardly have been a suitable wife for Ralph Gaunt. He had said himself that nothing could come of it. A passing fancy Amelia could tolerate, but anything more permanent was not to be borne without protest. Her first impulse was to confront Ralph with the knowledge that she had solved the puzzle and knew the name of his ... his what? Her eyes narrowed as she wondered uneasily how far the relationship had developed. Was Marion Reid her son's *mistress*? Oh, no! That really was unthinkable! She tutted irritably. What was Dr Reid thinking of to allow such a thing to happen? Didn't he know his own wife? Could he not read the signs? A woman does not fall in love without any outward indications of her inner feelings. It must have been perfectly obvious; Dr Reid really had been most remiss.

A new thought presented itself – she could approach the doctor himself and enlist his help. Almost immediately, however, she rejected this idea as dangerous for, confronted by his wife's infidelity, he might decide to divorce her. No, she must be much more subtle. Somehow she must bring about the end of the affair without letting Ralph know that she had ever been aware of Marion's name. If he ever found out that she had meddled he would probably hold it against her for the rest of her life, and Amelia could not bear the possibility of being estranged from her son. She could be strong, but Ralph was her Achilles heel and she was the first to admit it; nothing in the world mattered more to her than her son, and she must allow nothing to break the bond which presently existed between them.

Outside the church clock struck four and Amelia thought thankfully that it would soon be dawn. Perhaps in the daylight the problem would appear less incapable of solution . . .

Suddenly she sat bolt upright and a smile lit up her face. 'Why, of course!' she exclaimed. 'He must meet someone more suitable!'

It was so simple that she was surprised she had not thought of it earlier. Ralph must meet someone younger, prettier and entirely more eligible – someone without the encumbrance of a husband. And the sooner the better! Already Amelia felt happier, for the world was full of desirable young women and she did not think it would prove at all difficult to arrange for her son to meet an attractive girl of the right age – say eighteen or nineteen. He would then fall in love with her and it was to be hoped that he would appreciate for himself the unsuitability of the doctor's wife.

Amelia sank back on the pillows again, already more relaxed as the prospect of disaster rapidly receded. She would give a dinner party and invite someone with an attractive daughter. The question now was, who should it be? May had a friend with a daughter named Evelyn, but she had recently announced her engagement which was a pity. The Reverend Craythorne was the father of three daughters, but Amelia had never met them; she doubted whether such a man could possibly have produced good-looking progeny and she had no wish for a brood of unprepossessing grandchildren. Sir Edward Somers had a daughter, but she was still in finishing school in Switzerland; action was necessary now, and Amelia could not wait for her to return. Did John Foster have any daughters? Searching her memory, she recalled meeting a dark-haired pudding of a girl, probably about sixteen, who had been instructed by her father to, 'Shake hands with Mrs Gaunt, one of our most valued clients.' Amelia had been unimpressed at the time, but a few years had pased and time could transform even the plainest girl into a presentable young woman. Certainly, thought Amelia, John Foster's daughter was worth a try.

Now, what was her name? It began with 'C'. Chloe? Clarissa? No, *Clarice*. That was it. Amelia smiled up at the lightening ceiling and gave a nod of satisfaction. Tomorrow she would send out the invitations and would ask May to come as well; this would not only swell the numbers but make the occasion look more natural. No one must suspect her motives, least of all Ralph, she thought; her brows contracted at the very idea and her smile faltered.

*

Not far away in the bedroom in Harrington Hill, Marion Reid also lay awake, concerned with a very different problem. Aware now that Gilbert *did* visit the Swains, it seemed inevitable that eventually he would learn of her attendance at Ellie's funeral, and she felt that she must tell him first so that he could not accuse her of deception. She would have to pretend a certain obtuseness with regard to his feelings on the matter and he would no doubt berate her at some length, but at least she would be guilty of nothing worse than a lapse of discretion and he could hardly judge her action as malicious.

She must bring up the subject quite naturally – perhaps the best time to do so would be at breakfast. Marion was resigned to the argument that would undoubtedly follow, but she told herself that the worst she would have to endure was her husband's displeasure. This could be alarming, however, and she later went down to breakfast with a fast beating heart. Pip was waiting for her at the bottom of the stairs with tail wagging eagerly, and Marion bent to fondle her.

'Hullo, my darling Pip!'

They both went into the dining room, where Gilbert had finished his porridge and was reading *The Times* while he waited for Kitty to bring his kedgeree.

Marion assumed a cheerful smile and said, 'Good morning, Gilbert. Did you sleep well?'

He lowered the paper and replied, 'I'm afraid not.'

'Perhaps a sleeping draught?' she suggested. 'It cannot be good for you to go without sleep.'

'No one has suggested that it is,' he said, his tone caustic as Marion sat down opposite him.

Kitty appeared with his kedgeree and placed it in front of him. 'Cook says it might need a little more salt than usual, sir,' she told him.

'Thank you.' He folded *The Times* neatly and laid it to one side of his plate.

'And for you, ma'am?' asked Kitty. 'Eggs, bacon or kedgeree?'

Marion considered. 'Just a coddled egg, please, Kitty.'

'Right you are, ma'am.'

When the maid had gone out again, Marion glanced at the clock and asked casually, 'Hasn't the postman been yet?'

'Oh yes. There was a letter for you; it's on the sideboard.'

With a beating heart, Marion rose to fetch it, but Gilbert put out a restraining hand. 'It's only Rachel,' he said. 'I recognized the writing. Plenty of time to read it later.'

Marion sat down again, hiding her frustration with an effort because she wanted to read it now, so that if Rachel *had* invited her to stay she could ask Gilbert's permission before he started his surgery. As she helped herself to stewed figs she thought frantically. She *had* to know; the suspense was more than she could bear. Perhaps she might catch him after surgery and before he went out on his rounds, but the problem was that by that time uncooperative patients could have soured his mood even further and he might not allow her to go. She had been longing for the chance to talk to Rachel and to get away from the house, but now there was the added attraction of seeing Ralph again.

Gilbert swallowed a mouthful of kedgeree and pulled a face.

'Cook was right,' he told her. 'It does need more salt. If she knows that, why didn't she add a little?'

Obligingly Marion passed the cruet.

'I see that the match-girls have gone back to work,' Gilbert continued. 'I should think so too; they've been out far too long. I blame the employers. They should have sacked them all; they've been far too lenient.'

'What happened then?' Marion asked dutifully, wondering if there would be time to read Rachel's letter after she had finished the figs and before Kitty returned with her egg.

'It seems that the London Trades Council worked out acceptable terms and the girls agreed to them. They've done quite well out of it. No more fines and a revision of their piece rates. More than they deserve, most likely. They've even been offered a separate room in which to eat their dinner.'

Marion swallowed a mouthful of figs and asked, 'Where did they eat before?'

Gilbert glanced at her with obvious irritation. 'Don't you read the paper?' he demanded. 'Those who didn't go out used to eat at the work-bench.'

So, thought Marion, Meg Swain's cousin would be back at work.

Gilbert went on, 'It's quite a victory in its way, of course – unskilled workers, women at that, winning a strike. Annie Besant will be cock-a-hoop, no doubt, and it will set an unfortunate precedent. It makes one wonder who will be next.'

Marion suddenly saw her chance and remarked, 'That cousin of Meg Swain worked in the match factory. She'll be a cock-a-hoop, too, I expect.'

'No doubt.' His tone was obviously intended to discourage further comment, but Marion pressed on.

'She seems a nice enough girl, and her young man is a newspaper reporter. They were together at Ellie's funeral.' There! It was out! Inwardly she quaked, but only her hands betrayed her and these she quickly hid in her lap.

Slowly Gilbert raised his head. 'Ellie's funeral? What do you know about Ellie's funeral?' he asked.

'I was there.' She tried to sound casual, but failed. Gilbert laid down his knife and fork and raising his table napkin dabbed carefully at his lips while Marion forced herself to meet his eyes.

'Are you telling me,' he demanded, 'that you attended Ellie Swain's funeral? Without so much as a by-your-leave?' His eyes glittered.

Marion steadied her voice. 'I did not know I required your permission,' she told him. 'I saw no reason why I should not attend. I went to Ada Goodman's funeral, and to Henry Thrush's funeral. You made no objection then.'

'But, dammit, this is different!' His voice had risen noticeably.

'Is it, Gilbert? Will you tell me why?' asked Marion.

His face flushed. 'No, I will not!' he snapped. 'I have no need to explain my every thought and action to you. It is enough that I would not have allowed it, and I'm sure you were well aware of that fact. They are a thoroughly unsavoury family and I have warned you before about them. You had no right to attend, and what is more I imagine your presence must have embarrassed them immensely.'

'I don't think so,' said Marion. 'In fact, Miss Swain was delighted to see us. She –' Horrified by her slip, she halted in mid-sentence as Gilbert pounced.

'*Us?*' he demanded. 'And who exactly is "us"?'

Her heart raced. There was no way out, she would have to tell him. As calmly as she could, she said, 'Ralph

Gaunt was also present. Apparently he did not think it unsuitable that he should be there.'

'Ralph Gaunt?' Gilbert looked somewhat taken aback. 'What in heaven's name was he doing there?'

'I don't know,' she lied desperately. 'Perhaps his mother thought that one of the family should attend since she had taken such an interest in them. She paid for Ellie's coffin, too.'

To her intense relief, this information seemed to defuse the worst of his anger. For a moment he was silent and Marion took the opportunity to say lightly, 'It was quite an event; more than fifty mourners. I was impressed.'

He pushed his plate away with the kedgeree half eaten, stood up and walked to the mantelpiece where he checked the clock's time with his gold hunter watch.

Without turning towards her, he asked, 'Did she enquire after me?'

'Who?' Marion asked innocently.

'Miss Swain.'

'No, she didn't.'

'Good.'

Feeling her courage returning, Marion said, 'I held the new baby, a dear little thing. Lizzie, her name is.'

He rounded as though stung. 'You held –?' He bit his lip. 'She had no right to . . .' He stopped abruptly, regretting his outburst, and repeated rather lamely, 'It was quite inappropriate that you should be there.'

'I'm sorry, Gilbert, but I don't agree,' Marion told him. 'I quite admire Meg Swain in some ways. She did her best to –'

He interrupted her. 'As usual you talk without knowing the facts, Marion, and you are not being objective. Women like Meg Swain are the lowest of the low. Do I have to spell it out for you? She is a *harlot*! Don't you understand? Can I not make you see her as she really is? You seem to have some romantic notion about them, but I can assure you there is nothing romantic about selling your body! *Nothing!* It is base and sordid. I absolutely forbid you to ever visit her or be in communication with her again. Do you hear me, Marion?'

'I hear you, Gilbert.'

'Then I would like your word on it.'

Marion opened her mouth to argue, but suddenly remembered Rachel's letter and the invitation which she hoped it contained, and cursed her own lack of foresight. She had provoked Gilbert further than was necessary and might have ruined her chances of gaining his permission to go to Kingston. If he would not let her go to Rachel's, she would not be able to enjoy Ralph's company, and she was quite desperate to see him again. Her mouth tightened. If Gilbert was secretly visiting Meg Swain for reasons best known to himself, then why should she not meet Ralph? Was there one law for husbands and another for wives? If so, was it *reasonable*?

'I am waiting, Marion,' he told her.

Marion hesitated. Could she make such a promise? Did she really want to see Meg Swain again? And if she broke her promise, would the heavens open? She would take the chance.

'You have my word,' she stated.

Gilbert gave her a long, hard look and she thought he was going to speak again, but instead he strode from the room, slamming the door behind him.

As soon as he had gone, Marion jumped to her feet and hurried to the sideboard where Rachel's letter waited. The address was written in her sister's familiar sloping hand and Marion opened it with eager fingers.

My dear Marion, [she read].

This letter will come as rather a shock, but I am in some distress and must throw myself on your mercy. Yesterday I fell down the stairs and my right ankle is very painful and badly swollen, although the doctor is not yet prepared to commit himself as to the extent of the damage. He suspects it may be no more than a sprain, but has ordered complete rest for at least a week.

Can you imagine me in bed for seven days? I should go quite mad with boredom. To make matters worse, my housekeeper is away for a week looking after her daughter's five children while their mother produces yet another! May I call on you for help? Could Gilbert spare you for a few days? I would be eternally grateful if you could finally make that long overdue visit to Kingston, and I promise not to be a difficult patient!

I feel so useless, but have no one to blame but myself. Regrettably, that does not make it any easier to bear . . .'

The rest of the letter consisted of snippets of news which Marion ignored. Was a sprained ankle sufficient to warrant outside help, or would Gilbert expect Rachel to manage? The absent housekeeper was a clever touch, though. She folded the letter and replaced it in the envelope; in Gilbert's present mood, he would certainly refuse, but later perhaps he might have mellowed. She would have to be patient.

'Oh, Ralph!' she whispered. 'How could I have been so foolish?' She imagined his disappointment if she had to tell him that her visit to Rachel would not take place.

'I shall do my very best,' she assured him.

＊

When Marion did show Gilbert the letter he hid his delight and, after a convincing show of reluctance, eventually agreed that she should answer Rachel's cry for help. He would have preferred to refuse in order to punish her for her attendance at Ellie's funeral, but he was eager to get her out of the house while he applied himself to the problem of Meg Swain's unwanted infant.

To Marion's immense surprise, he suggested that 'a week or so' might be a suitable period of time for the visit.

The following day when he returned from his evening rounds, Mrs Cobbett opened the door to him and helped him out of his damp coat.

'Has my wife gone?' he asked her.

'Yes, sir, and taken Pip with her. She thought she might pine and I thought so, too. Devoted to each other, those two. She left just after two o'clock, sir, and caught the two thirty-five to Kingston. Sad about poor Miss Napier breaking her ankle like that.'

'It was a sprain, I think, not a break.'

'Sprain, then,' amended Mrs Cobbett. 'I had a sprained wrist once, before I came here. Very painful that was, and so awkward because I couldn't use the hand – couldn't even comb my hair properly. It slowed me down something terrible.' She shook his coat and hung it on the hallstand.

'It will need drying off properly, Mrs Cobbett,' he reproved her. 'Take it into the kitchen and hang it somewhere warm. I have told you before that a wet coat will not dry on the hallstand.'

'Oh, I'm sorry, sir; I didn't realize it was as wet as all that. What on earth is the weather up to these days? We shouldn't be having such heavy showers in the summer.' She retrieved the coat and put it carefully over her arm. 'And I'm to look after you, the mistress says, and feed you well, so I've done you a lamb casserole for tonight and I thought a –'

'Anything,' he interrupted her. 'I'm not particularly hungry. I'll eat promptly at eight o'clock, and I don't want to be disturbed until then.'

'Very good, sir. Your paper's on the table, and your slippers are warming by the fire. I know it's not cold, but a fire's cheerful when the weather's so unseasonal. The mistress said –'

He cut short her little speech with a curt, 'Thank you, Mrs Cobbett,' and went into the drawing room, where he changed into the warmed slippers and handed Mrs Cobbett his shoes.

When she had gone, he sat beside the fire with *The Times* unfolded in his lap and stared thoughtfully into the flames. Marion had gone for perhaps a week, he reflected, and that gave him a breathing space. Plenty of time to think and to act, too, if only he could decide what was to be done. He admitted that with Ellie's death he had had a very narrow escape indeed. If another doctor had been called in to provide a death certificate, the overdose of arsenic would almost certainly have been discovered and he would have had some explaining to do. Probably he could have convinced the police that Meg had ignored or forgotten his instructions and had given Ellie an accidental overdose, but if the details had reached the newspapers the publicity would have been most unwelcome. In future he must be much more careful.

It was a pity that Mrs Gaunt seemed so interested in the family, for now that Ellie was dead a second death might arouse her suspicions and she would prove a difficult person to deceive. Whatever he planned for the baby it *must* look like an accident; two deaths would be difficult to explain away, yet he had to get rid of the child for while she lived there was always the chance that Meg would betray him either to Marion or to someone in authority. The plan must be foolproof, he thought, then shook his head in exasperation because his *first* plan had appeared foolproof. Who would have thought that stupid whore would have given the stuff to Ellie? Hell and damnation! He really did not deserve this . . . or did he? For a moment he wondered uneasily if a vengeful Fate was punishing him for his past misdeeds.

'I wish to God I had never set eyes on Meg Swain!' he exclaimed, his fists clenched on the arms of the chair –

and at that precise moment the thought came to him that he would like to be rid of Meg, too, but presumably this was out of the question. If he wasn't careful, he thought with a grim smile, he would end up wiping out the entire Swain family and that *would* cause questions to be asked. Unless, of course, they simply disappeared! Staring thoughtfully into the fire, he examined the idea more carefully. Suppose Meg could be persuaded to move right out of London? If so, where could she go to? It would need to be a long way away so that there could be no possibility of her ever returning. But how would she earn her living when she got there? There was less scope for a prostitute in a small village than in a place like London. Perhaps another town – why not Bristol or Plymouth? And could he think of a convincing reason for her to make such a move? Probably a lump sum of money would prove the only inducement. He had to admit it was unlikely she would agree to go, for her sort lived and died in the same mean streets and she would not willingly allow herself to be uprooted and taken away from her friends and family.

His thoughts took a more sombre turn. If she would not agree to disappear, then could he hire someone to kill her? No, that was too risky – the killer could turn blackmailer. With a sigh he glanced up at the clock and was startled to see that it was nearly eight o'clock. Even time seemed to be against him, but he must persevere because whatever he decided to do must be carried out while Marion was away and there was no chance that she would suddenly take it into her head to call on the Swains. He had reprimanded her about her attendance at the funeral, but something in her manner disturbed him and, sensing in her a growing defiance which had never revealed itself before, he felt he could no longer trust her to behave as a dutiful wife should. She was suspicious, too; he knew it. The sooner he was rid of Meg Swain and her wretched child, the better it would be for all of them.

There was a tap at the door and Kitty looked in.

'Please, sir, it's just on eight and the soup's on the table. Mulligatawny, your favourite.'

'I'm coming, Kitty. Thank you.'

As he stood up, another idea occurred to him – he might pay someone to steal the child. There was always a market for healthy infants and possibly he could arrange for its adoption under an assumed name. He made his way into the dining room, where a place had been laid for one at the end of the table.

Kitty, removing the lid of the soup tureen, remarked, 'All alone tonight, sir. I expect you'll miss the mistress.'

'I am sure I will,' he replied.

But privately he was delighted by the convenient timing of Rachel's accident. There was a lot to be done while Marion was away, and the sooner he made a decision the sooner he could put his plan into operation.

*

Two days later Ralph went into the morning room just before eleven and was startled to find a young woman sitting beside his mother at a small table littered with papers. They were deep in conversation, but the girl looked up as he entered and Ralph found himself staring into her intense dark eyes. Her black hair was swept back into a demure chignon at the nape of her neck; her features were delicately moulded; her skin was very pale and there was a small mole on her left cheek. He did not know that Amelia had been even more impressed with her than he was.

'Oh, Ralph,' Amelia said casually, 'I don't think you two have met. Miss Foster, this is my son Ralph. Ralph, this is Clarice Foster, John Foster's daughter. She has kindly agreed to help me out occasionally with this tiresome paper-work.'

Smiling, Clarice rose briefly to her feet and as she shook the hand he offered Ralph saw with approval that she was plump in the appropriate places and thought that she reminded him of a bird in the nicest possible way.

'A pleasure to meet you, Mr Gaunt,' she said.

Ralph returned her smile and positioned himself in front of the fireplace, his hands clasped behind his back.

'What paper-work is that, Mama?'

'Why, to do with the school, of course. There is so much to think about – estimates, bills, letters. Too much, in fact, for one pair of hands; I began to find myself overwhelmed.'

'I did not realize,' he said. 'You should have complained earlier, Mama.'

'I never complain, Ralph,' she corrected him mildly. 'It is not in my nature. I simply became aware that dealing with correspondence was beginning to take up too great a part of my day, leaving me no time for other more pressing matters.'

'My father suggested an extra pair of hands might be appreciated and asked me if I was interested,' Clarice said. 'I have just finished my last term at "Queens".'

When Ralph raised his eyebrows enquiringly she added, 'Queens College in Harley Street.'

He smiled 'I am sure you were glad to be done with the classroom. I was; I positively loathed Rugby.'

Amelia said, 'Don't talk such nonsense, Ralph. You were very happy there.'

'I loathed it,' he insisted, with a surreptitious wink for Clarice. 'It was utterly ghastly. All that boring Greek and Latin and those terrible beatings.'

'Oh dear,' said Clarice, following his lead after a brief hesitation. 'How perfectly beastly for you!'

Amelia turned wrathful eyes upon her son. 'You were never beaten. How could you say such a thing, Ralph; it's too bad. Take no notice, Miss Foster. He is teasing you.'

'Mama! Why on earth should I lie about a thing like

that?' he protested, the picture of innocence. 'I did not tell you at the time because I knew how you would worry.'

'Stuff and nonsense! Do try to be sensible for once. Whatever will Clarice think of you?'

Ralph kept his face straight, however, and went on, 'I ran away twice, but each time they caught me before I could get home and dragged me back.'

Clarice looked deeply concerned. 'You poor thing!'

'Ralph!' snapped Amelia. 'If you cannot behave, then you should take yourself off and leave us to our work.'

Afraid that he might go, Clarice smiled at Amelia and said hastily, 'I don't believe a word of it anyway.'

'But it's true!' He grinned at her.

'Then the harsh regime obviously suited you!' she countered. 'You appear to be a perfectly normal, civilized human being and Rugby must take much of the credit for that.'

Amelia regarded her warmly. 'And how was Queens, Miss Foster?'

'I have to admit I enjoyed it – apart from the beatings, that is!' She laughed. 'Actually I made a number of good friends there and I miss their company.'

Ralph regarded her with interest. 'So you are one of the new women we read so much about,' he said. 'Educated; *enlightened* even! How does the world look, Miss Foster, through your newly awakened eyes?'

Amelia exclaimed, 'Oh, really Ralph!' and a faint blush rose in the girl's cheeks at his mocking tone.

'It looks as though there is plenty of room for improvement,' she told him.

'So you think we men have made a poor job of things?'

She considered her answer before replying. 'It is far from perfect,' she said. 'There are too many people less fortunate than ourselves for whom no doubt it looks even less rosy. You will not deny that, surely?'

Amelia said, 'Now that puts you in your place, Ralph. Miss Foster *is* enlightened.'

'But what use will you make of your education, Miss Foster?' he insisted.

She had regained her composure and looked at him steadily. 'I hope to find a place with the Post Office Savings Bank as a clerk, and maybe from there I might transfer later to the Civil Service.'

Ralph said 'Good heavens!' and then, recovering, laughed lightly and reached for a nearby bowl of fruit which he offered first to Clarice and then his mother. Both declined, but after earnest deliberation he selected an apple and bit into it with relish.

'By helping your mother I hope I may redress some of the balance,' Clarice told him earnestly. 'The world really is a very grim place for many people and the Harold Weston Memorial School is a splendid project.'

Amelia now rose to her feet. 'Do please excuse me a moment, Miss Foster, but I have just remembered that Cook is taking the afternoon off and I must speak to her before she goes. I won't be long. Ralph, I hope you will stay and entertain our guest until I return.'

'Your wish is my command, Mama.'

Amelia shrugged resigned shoulders and said, 'I apologize for my son, Miss Foster. He has never really grown up; my fault, I suppose.'

Clarice laughed. 'Don't worry, Mrs Gaunt, I have a kind of cousin of whom I am very fond, but he is every bit as contrary.'

'A *male* cousin?' The words slipped out before Amelia could stop them.

'Yes. His name is Jeremy and his family visits us quite often.'

Amelia managed a smile as she departed, but once outside the door her mouth pursed with annoyance. Surely the girl was not romantically linked with this wretched cousin? That was a complication she had not anticipated. She wondered where to go now since she had no real reason to speak to Cook, but had merely wanted to leave the young people on their own. Deciding it would have to be the bedroom, she made her way upstairs looking very thoughtful.

Ralph asked Clarice, 'What is a *Kind of* cousin? It sounds intriguing.'

'Not really. My aunt married a widower with two sons, Jeremy and William; their mother had died giving birth to Jeremy, so the two boys called my aunt "Mama". Jeremy had never known his real mother, of course.'

'So you have two male cousins?'

'No. Poor William was killed at the Regatta.' Seeing that she had caught Ralph's interest, she went on, 'I always think that perhaps it was meant to happen, because otherwise it was the most cruel twist of circumstances. We had booked seats on one of the launches, you see, and should have watched the race from there, but William had left the tickets at home and we decided to go back for them. That made us late, so we found ourselves in the worst of the traffic. It seemed as though all of London was heading for Putney Bridge and by the time we finally arrived there was such a crush along the river that we abandoned the idea of finding our launch and decided instead to watch from the river-bank. Have you ever watched from there?'

Ralph shook his head. 'I've only been a few times, but then we watched with friends at The Limes.'

'Well, if you sit along the bank under the trees you soon discover that half the urchins in London are clambering about in the branches overhead. We were amused to begin with, but then one of the boys fell on to William. At first everyone laughed and then . . .' Her eyes were anguished. 'Then suddenly William toppled over. We didn't realize it then, but his neck was broken.'

'Good Lord!' exclaimed Ralph. 'How ghastly for you.'

She drew in her breath painfully at the memory. 'We

couldn't believe he was dead. The urchin ran off in a fright, I was sobbing and Jeremy was holding William in his arms, trying to rouse him. A young woman next to us laid a spray of lilac in William's arms . . . I have never liked lilacs since then. Jeremy was heartbroken, of course. If William had not forgotten the tickets – or if we had not decided to sit on the river-bank – so many "ifs".'

'And you are very fond of Jeremy?' asked Ralph gently.

Her expression changed slightly and she glanced down at her hands. 'How did you know?'

'Something about the way you spoke his name. Is he fond of you?'

'No. There is someone else.'

'I'm sorry,' he said gently, his bantering tone gone. 'Life can be very hard.'

She looked up. 'I should not have mentioned it; I don't know why I did. Please forgive me.'

'For what? For being open and honest? For sharing a sad secret? I took your confidence as a compliment, Miss Foster.'

'But I should not bother you with my troubles,' she protested.

'Why not? I might have been able to help. I would if I could.'

Her eyes darkened. 'To help him over the loss of his brother, my aunt sent him to Geneva to stay with friends and that is where he met Gertrude. The worst of it is that I know I should be glad for Jeremy's sake that he is so happy, but I am not. I'm sorry for myself and I feel cheated. I have known and loved him all my life, you see, and I assumed in the way children do that we would marry. The family used to tease us about it. My father once said, "Here comes your intended" and it has always seemed so natural and right.' Her mouth twisted into a wry smile. 'Actually, Jeremy is rather like you; not to look at, but in the way he talks. Always mocking. Never serious. And Gertrude is quite charming, and I want to hate her but I can't. If only I could be pleased for them, it would be so much easier to bear.'

She stopped breathlessly and taking out a lace handkerchief pressed it to her temples. 'Oh dear, you must forgive me. I'm talking too much.'

Ralph said slowly, 'I think the trouble lies with love itself; it is such a selfish emotion. You cannot be blamed for that, for we are all victims of our emotions. If only we could master them we would be a lot happier, but very few people can do so. I am certainly not among the fortunate few.'

Confused, she picked up a paper from the table, stared at it blankly and then allowed it to drop again. 'There used to be a potion in medieval times,' she said at last, 'which made you fall in love. What I need is an antidote to make me fall *out* of love.'

They both laughed. 'The man who invents *that* will make his fortune,' Ralph told her.

He was flattered by her confidence and he understood her feelings very well because they were so similar to his own sentiments towards Marion. He had never before admitted it to himself, but secretly he was glad that Gilbert was not a loving husband – although if he *had* been, Marion would be happily married which she most patently was not. He ought to wish her happiness within her marriage, but he could not because he wanted her to be happy only with Ralph Gaunt. Yes, he mused, love was a most selfish emotion.

Becoming aware that Clarice was watching him closely, he quickly forced a smile. 'What can I do to cheer you up?' he asked.

'Oh, please, there is no need,' she replied and as Amelia chose that moment to come back into the room, Clarice bent her head over the table and fussed among the bills, apparently intent on her work.

'I really think it is too hot to bury ourselves indoors,'

Amelia said. 'Why don't you two play a leisurely game of tennis instead and I will sit under the sycamore and watch.' Seeing Clarice's look of surprise, she went on, 'Oh yes, we have had a court for nearly a year, but I so seldom have time to make use of it. I have to admit the court is not full size, but there is a net and you may borrow my racket.'

Clarice had brightened visibly at the suggestion, but now she hesitated and asked, 'What about the letters?'

'We will do them tomorrow. Perhaps you could come earlier before it gets too hot.'

'Any time that would suit you, Mrs Gaunt?'

'Shall we say nine o'clock, then? If we allow an hour or so, then we shall have most of the day free afterwards for other things. Oh, and Ralph, I forgot to tell you – Miss Foster and her parents are coming to dinner with us on Tuesday, and I have invited your Aunt May as well.' She turned to Clarice. 'Did I tell you that May Thripp is my sister? She is also one of the school's major benefactors.'

Ralph said evenly, 'Mama, I shall be away on Tuesday, staying with friends. I am so sorry.' His heart beat a little faster. He could not, *would* not miss this opportunity to be in Kingston with Marion.

Amelia's dismay was too complete to hide and Clarice was surprised to see her face stiffen with disapproval.

'Staying with friends?' Amelia echoed. 'What friends are these? I know nothing of it; why did you not tell me before?'

'I was going to tell you, Mama,' explained Ralph. 'That is why I came in here. I didn't know until the first post came, and I had no idea you had arranged a dinner party.'

'Well, you must cancel your visit,' she told him in a tight voice. 'We cannot have a dinner party without you.'

'I'm sure I shall not be missed, Mama,' he said, with an attempt at lightness that did not fool either Clarice or his mother, 'but if I *am* an essential ingredient, may I suggest that you alter the date?'

Clarice intervened timidly. 'I am sure my parents would understand if you wish to change the date –' she began.

'But I do *not* wish to change it!' snapped Amelia.

'Then I am sorry, Mama, but I will not be here,' Ralph told her.

Amelia stared at him with shocked disbelief. Her son was *defying* her! It was so rare an occurrence that she hardly knew how to react. He was a grown man who could not be bullied, while coaxing was not her way. She had never coaxed in her whole life, she told herself, and she did not intend to start now. Searching her mind for a previous occasion on which their interests had clashed, she could not recall even one. He had always been such an *amenable* child and so willing to please. Now, however, he was obviously determined to go ahead with his own plans and she could guess what *that* meant! The 'friends' must surely include Marion Reid, although he had mentioned Kingston and the Reids lived in Harrington Hill. Her eyes narrowed as a doubt surfaced suddenly amongst her whirling thoughts. Could she possibly have been wrong about Marion Reid? Was there perhaps someone else? Another Marion? She stared straight into Ralph's eyes, but his gaze did not waver.

'My arrangement was made before your letter arrived,' Amelia insisted, 'therefore the dinner party takes precedence.'

'But I knew nothing about it,' he protested. 'Anyway, it is too late. I have written accepting the invitation and have just returned from the post-box.'

He fought down a sense of impending crisis, for his mother could be very wilful and he knew how much she hated to be thwarted. Frequently in the past he had given in to her demands in order to keep the peace between them, but on this occasion he was determined to stand firm no matter how unpleasant the consequences and a battle of wills seemed inevitable.

'I am sorry,' he repeated with great firmness, 'but I shall be away this weekend. I shall regret missing the dinner party, but if you cannot change the date . . .' – he smiled at Clarice – 'I shall be forced to forgo the honour of your company, Miss Foster, and I hope that you and your parents will forgive me.'

'Of course we will,' she assured him and earned herself a disapproving glance from Amelia.

Ralph said, 'Come, Mama, we must not squabble or we shall embarrass our visitor. You suggested tennis just now, and I think I would enjoy that. Will you join me, Miss Foster?'

He had reverted to his normal bantering tone and now he offered his arm; Clarice's face cleared as she took it. 'I should be delighted,' she told him with a relieved smile.

'Then if you will excuse us, Mama?'

Amelia, thus routed, could only manage a brief nod and as the two young people left the room, she was left to consider Ralph's uncharacteristic behaviour and to marvel at the speed with which the wretched Marion, whoever she might be, had ruined her son's disposition.

CHAPTER TWELVE

The late evening of Sunday the 27th found Gilbert Reid in a hansom cab, being driven towards Fashion Street. In his inside coat pocket he carried a wad of notes, for he had decided to try to persuade Meg to leave London. If she refused, then he was determined to resort to any stronger action which might prove necessary, and then she would have no one but herself to blame.

The worst of the day's heat had passed, leaving the night air heavy and still. Gilbert sat well back in the cab to avoid being seen, but from where he sat he could observe the dingy streets where boys ran barefoot along the pavement, chasing each other so boisterously and shouting to each other in such coarse language that he shook his head in despair. Girls with lacklustre eyes carried younger brothers or sisters in their arms or on their backs; a rusty black cat slept in a doorway, vulnerable but indifferent, and further on two dogs circled each other, alert and bristling, spoiling for a fight. In most of the doorways whores slouched in twos or threes, their cheap clothes tawdry in what remained of the daylight, but Gilbert knew that come the darkness the flare of the gaslight would endow the faded silks and trumpery feathers with a false elegance. A bulky washer-woman waddled homeward, an empty basket wedged on her hip and a tuneless whistle issuing from her fat lips.

From the upstairs window a woman shouted obscenities at another who stood in the road below, her right arm thrust upward in a threatening fist.

An elderly man sat on the ground with his back against a wall, his feet – in gaping boots – thrust out carelessly to trip the unwary passer-by.

'Oh, god!' exclaimed Gilbert. 'That a daughter of mine should ever inhabit these streets!'

A few more years and she would doubtless be carrying Meg's second child on her back, her feet dirty, her hair infected with lice. As the cab slowed to a standstill at the end of the road, he shuddered and shook his head to rid himself of the unwelcome image.

'Fashion Street, guv. Here you are.'

Gilbert leaned out. 'Go on foot to number thirty eight,' he instructed. 'Ask for a Miss Swain and tell her to come here to me. Say that a gentleman wants to see her. There is a shilling in it for you.'

The cabby descended eagerly. 'Right, guv.' He touched his forehead. 'Miss Swain?'

'Yes – and hurry yourself. I haven't got all night.'

'Well, give me a chance!' the man objected. 'I can't bloody well fly!'

But he set off along the road at a shambling gait while Gilbert drew back into the shadowy interior of the cab and patted his pocket to reassure himself that the money was still there. A few moments passed and then he heard hurrying footsteps and, glancing out, saw Meg approaching the cab, her brow furrowed with anxiety.

'If this is some kind of trick,' she was saying to the cabby, 'I'll give you the back of my hand. Since when has a gentleman wanted to see the likes of . . ..' Her eyes widened as Gilbert leaned out of the cab, a finger held warningly to his lips. She had opened her mouth but now closed it obediently.

Gilbert said loudly, 'You won't know me, Miss Swain, but I bring you a message from your brother. Step up into the cab, if you please.'

Meg obeyed, her eyes dancing with excitement.

Gilbert, fearful that the cabby might overhear their conversation, gave him the promised shilling and told him to stretch his legs if he wanted another, watching as he sauntered off.

Beaming with pleasure, Meg patted Gilbert's knee and said, 'What's going on, then? I couldn't make head nor tale of him and his, "Gentleman wants to see you." "He's up to something," I thought.'

'Listen to me, Meg,' Gilbert said urgently. 'I don't have much time, and there is something I have to tell you. I admit this will sound unlikely, but you must believe me. You have to get away from here as soon as possible, and Lizzie also. You will both be in dreadful danger if you remain in London.'

Her mouth fell open and her face was almost comic in its dismay as she stared at him wordlessly. Slowly the meaning of his words registered in her brain.

'Danger?' she cried. 'Me? What danger? What are you on about?'

'I can't tell you more than that,' he replied. 'You will have to trust me. Believe me, it is the solemn truth.'

'I do trust you, Gilbert, but how am I in danger? I just don't see it, honest I don't.'

'I know it is hard for you to grasp,' he said, 'but I am taking a terrible risk in coming here to warn you. You *must* believe me, Meg. The best thing you can do is go right away – to Bristol maybe, or Liverpool.'

'Bristol?' she wailed. 'I don't want to go to Bristol – nor Liverpool neither. I don't want to go nowhere. London's my home; London's all I know.'

'Nevertheless you *must* leave!' he insisted. 'I simply cannot guarantee your safety while you remain in London, Meg.' He lowered his voice dramatically. 'Someone wants to kill you!'

She gave a squeal and both her hands went up to her mouth fearfully. '*Kill* me!' She stared at him, then blinked. 'Kill *me*? Never! You've got it wrong somehow, you must have.' He shook his head. 'But who'd want to kill me?' she cried. 'I ain't done nothing, I swear on my mother's grave. Cut my throat and hope to die!' She licked her forefinger and traced a hasty cross in the air.

'You most certainly *will* die, Meg, if you stay here. That is what I am trying to tell you. Look, Meg –' He played his trump card, producing the money he had brought and thrusting it into her astonished hands. 'I want to help you and Lizzie, so I've brought you this to help you start a new life somewhere a long way from here. Will you be a good girl? Will you take the money and save yourself and the child? There is *fifty pounds* here, Meg! See for yourself.'

'Christ Almighty!' she whispered, leaning forward to see more clearly. She did not take him at his word, however, but slowly leafed through the notes with much licking of her fingers and whispering of numbers as she counted.

'Jesus O'Reilly! It *is* fifty!' she cried. 'Fifty beautiful smackers!'

'Now will you *promise* me you will go away?'

She hesitated, bewildered. 'But are you sure about this, Gilbert? I swear to God I've done nothing wrong, leastways not as I can reckon. And little Lizzie? Is she in danger, too?'

'Oh yes! Most certainly. You may take my solemn word for it that if you both remain in London neither of you will live to see many more days.'

She looked down at the money, ruffling it with her fingers, seduced by the promise of such a fortune. Then she looked back at Gilbert. 'Bristol?' she said. 'Where the hell's Bristol?'

He began to explain as she folded the money, pushed it into her skirt pocket and immediately took it out again while he smothered his growing impatience.

'Gilbert,' she cried, suddenly hopeful. 'Why don't we just go to the police? If we tell them about this man, they could catch him and lock him up. Couldn't they?'

He shook his head. 'If I did that, they would kill *me*,' he assured her.

'Strewth!'

She was silent for a long time, weighing up the possibility of a compromise.

Gilbert elaborated, 'They have said that if you don't go, they will kill us all.'

She looked up sharply. '*They?* So there's more than one?'

'Almost certainly. Now, for your sake and Lizzie's . . .'

'And yours,' she said sadly. 'But how did they tell you? If they *told* you, then you must have seen them.'

He thought rapidly. 'No, they wrote to me – a threatening letter.'

'Let's see it.'

'I burnt it.'

'But why? That would be *evidence*.'

'It was in the letter. I was told to burn it or there would be trouble.'

Shivering, she leaned a little closer. 'I wish you could come with me, Gilbert. We'd be a little family – you, me and little Lizzie. We could start a new life.'

He almost laughed at the prospect of Meg as a doctor's wife, but even as he framed a 'No' he had a flash of inspiration. 'I was coming to that,' he told her. 'It might just be possible later on. My wife will not live for ever. In fact, she will not live as long as one might expect, since she has a rare heart condition for which there is no cure. I have always known that I would outlive her; her mother died well before her fortieth birthday.'

Meg was regarding him wide-eyed. 'So you *will* join us there!' she cried. 'You mean it? Gospel?'

'Later, I said. Don't expect it to be for a year or two.'

'Oh, Gilbert! That'd be marvellous!'

'But you must go on ahead. You must take the money and go to Bristol. You promise?'

'Well, I suppose I'll have to but . . .' She finished the sentence with a shrug and looked at him unhappily.

Telling himself that she was about to capitulate, Gilbert leaned forward and whispered into her ear, 'Fifty pounds! Think what you can do with all that money, Meg. You and Lizzie could have a wonderful life in Bristol. Rent a decent room, eat good food — meat every day if you wanted it — buy yourself some new clothes and some for Lizzie, and have a bit of fun! You're a good girl and you deserve it.'

Slowly she thrust the money deep into her pocket. 'Suppose they kill you after I've gone?' she suggested. 'I'd never know, would I? They could. You'd never come to Bristol then.'

'They won't,' he assured her, touched by her concern for his welfare.

Suddenly she gasped. 'Is it Jack Patten? Is it? Oh, my God! I can see it all! It's because of Sid, isn't it, and because I'm Dora's cousin. Is that it?'

'I dare not tell you any more.' Let her imagine what she liked, he thought, so long as she left London.

'I bet it is!' she insisted. 'Right murdering bastards, the pair of them. I mean, look what Sid done to Dora's face and to Jeff, and what Jack done to that other man. If it *is* Jack . . .'

Gilbert counted to ten. 'Meg! Are you leaving London, or are you staying here to be murdered? It's up to you. I have done my best for you, but if you are not going, I'll have that money back.' As he held out his hand she wavered visibly.

'What about Dor?' she asked. 'Is she in danger, too? She could come with me; we could go to Bristol to-gether.'

'Dora is in no danger, whatsoever. Believe me.'

Out of the corner of his eye Gilbert saw the cabby returning along the road.

'Now!' he said. 'What is it to be, Meg? Live or die?'

She drew a long deep breath and let it out in a rush. 'I suppose I'd better live,' she said, but she did not sound too sure.

Unseen, the corners of Gilbert's mouth turned up in a brief but triumphant smile. It had been easier than he had expected and relatively cheap. Going, going, gone! He congratulated himself. It would have been a bargain at twice the price!

*

It was the first time Marion had been back to Kingston since the funeral. The house was just as she remembered it and the sight of its ivy-clad walls and large mullioned windows brought a lump to her throat. She stepped out of the cab, paid the driver and turned to take another long look at the house where she had spent her childhood. Standing on the front lawn, she shaded her eyes from the hot sun and looked up at it. The walls were of red brick and the roof was gabled, and she looked at the window of the room that had once been hers. Further along was the room they had let out to a succession of lodgers, of whom Gilbert Reid had been the most memorable.

She put Pip down on the grass and watched her race across the immaculate lawn – presumably Mr Bridges still presided over the garden. Three birds flew up suddenly and Pip's excited barking brought an elderly man into view from behind a clump of pink rhododendrons. Seeing Marion, he hobbled towards her, taking off his battered hat as he came, a broad smile of welcome on his weather-beaten face.

'Mr Bridges!' she cried.

'Miss Marion! Why, it's so good to see you again. Oh dear!' He clapped a hand to his mouth. 'Hark at me calling you Miss Marion when it should be . . .' He had stopped in front of her, but was embarrassed by his lapse of memory.

She smiled. 'It's Mrs Reid now.'

'Ah! Course it is, 'cos you wed the doctor. Well then, welcome home, Mrs Reid.'

'Thank you. It hasn't changed. The lawn looks as good as ever.'

His delight at this compliment was obvious. 'It's just knowing how to treat a lawn, ma'am,' he confided. 'What to put on —'

'When to put it on and when to leave well alone!' Marion finished for him with a laugh. 'I heard you tell Mama that when I was knee-high to a grasshopper! I was very impressed because it sounded so wise.' Seeing that he still clutched his hat she added, 'Do put your hat on, Mr Bridges. You will get sunstroke if you don't.'

He did so gratefully, then said, 'Now your late father, Miss Marion — he was a man to appreciate a good lawn, God rest his soul. He could have been a gardener, begging your pardon, ma'am. He had a feel for all growing things and a gardener needs that; it's known as having green fingers.'

Marion pointed to a large chestnut tree that grew beside the house. 'I remember when Mama wanted him to put up a swing for us. "Will it damage the branch?" he asked, and Mama had to consult with you before it could go up.' She smiled. 'That was a long time ago now.'

'Maybe, ma'am, but the swing's still there,' he told her. 'Just waiting for the grandchildren, I reckon. Miss Rachel wouldn't let me take it down. Mind you,' he went on, unaware of Marion's reaction to this indirect reference to her lack of a family, 'it'd need renewing, for the ropes have rotted and so has the seat, but it could be done.'

For a moment they watched in amusement as Pip chased her tail, then Mr Bridges asked, 'D'you recall that dachshund your grandma used to bring when she came to visit? Little varmint, that was! Always burying bones in the lawn.' He shook his head and tutted at the memory of such sacrilege. 'And what a job I had after it had gone, putting the lawn to rights.'

Marion said, 'I do indeed. Fritz, he was called. Not very original, but apt.' She smiled. 'I see what you mean, though, and I'll keep an eye on Pip.'

She called Pip and bent to pat her. When she straightened up again, they began to walk towards the front door.

'Is my sister about?' Marion asked. 'I thought she would be at the station to meet me.'

'I don't rightly know, ma'am. Best ask Mrs Draper. I know she's gone out – the mistress I mean – for I heard the carriage an hour or more ago and I reckoned she was off to fetch you back from the station.'

'I hope we didn't miss each other,' said Marion and tugged at the bell.

Mrs Draper, the housekeeper, answered the door and after greeting her with the same enthusiasm as the gardener, explained that Rachel *had* gone to meet her but had intended to call on a neighbour on the way and must have been delayed. In a way Marion was pleased, because now she had a little time to rediscover the house for herself while Rachel was out. While the housekeeper returned to the kitchen to make a pot of tea, Marion made a tour of the familiar rooms. Upstairs her old bedroom remained almost unaltered, still smelling of lavender polish and mothballs, but now the flower-sprigged bedspread was faded and the carpet more worn than Marion remembered. The grate in the fireplace was stuffed with crumpled newspaper on to which a light dusting of soot had fallen, while the once cluttered dressing table was bare except for a blue china dish of potpourri from which all the fragrance had long since departed. A bowl of yellow roses stood on the bedside table and the sash windows were wide open to let in the sunshine.

Marion gazed out of the window as she had done so many times before and stared down into the garden where once her father had stood, calling her to come down and admire the first crocus; the garden where she and Rachel had played with their various dolls, or watched the grown-ups enjoying a game of croquet. Around the neat path that bordered the lawn the lodgers had taken their evening 'constitutional', perambulating purposefully with straight backs and earnest expressions – either before or after the evening meal, depending on their inclination. Marion stooped to lift Pip into her arms and pressed her face into the spaniel's warm fur.

'I used to play out there,' she said. 'Hide-and-Seek, Tag – so many games. And we blew bubbles, I remember. Mama used to send Ellen out with a small table, a bowl of suds and two clay pipes.' Pip wriggled and she laughed. 'Sometimes other children came in to play with us, and then there were enough to play Pointers Bluff and Family Coach. Oh, Pip, you're not paying attention! You're not even listening!'

She put the dog down and Pip wagged her tail and barked.

'No,' said Marion, 'I am not taking you into the garden, and you can't go out there alone. You might run off or – perish the thought! – dig a hole in Mr Bridges' lawn! Later, perhaps. If you are good, I might find you a ball to chase.'

The landing was not as dark as she remembered, nor were the stairs as wide. Downstairs, the drawing room appeared brighter and she thought that several pictures had been removed from the walls. Her first reaction to this was a spark of resentment, but then she told herself sternly that this was now Rachel's home and she was entitled to do with it whatever she pleased. Rachel would probably remain here until she died and she must rearrange the house to suit her own tastes. Suppose Rachel had married first, thought Marion? How different her own life would have been if she had been the dutiful daughter who stayed at home to care for their parents in their declining years. Perhaps Rachel would have had a family by now, and the old house would once again ring to the shrill sounds of children at play. Now that could never happen.

She drew a deep breath and let it out slowly.

'Why did I marry Gilbert Reid?' she whispered, but then shrugged off the unwelcome doubts raised by her question and once more examined the room.

The hexagonal table was still in place in front of the window; once, in a headlong dash, she had knocked it over and broken one of the legs. Her father's anger had been considerable and she had spent the rest of the day shut in her room in deep disgrace.

Marion ran her fingers over the brocaded back of the armchair in which her grandfather had died – suddenly, in the middle of a sentence. She could still see the look of surprise on his face before he fell backwards, his sightless eyes staring up at the ceiling, his lifeless hands dangling. At four years old Marion had felt the chair to be somehow responsible for this disaster, and from then on had watched with fearful anticipation whenever an unsuspecting visitor sat down in it.

She moved slowly around the room, ignoring Pip who had jumped on to the window-seat and now cast yearning glances through the window to the garden beyond. The armchairs were the same, but the cushions were new and bright and not altogether to Marion's taste. The candles on the front of the piano were almost burned down – so Rachel had been playing it, presumably. She had shown such promise as a child and her daily scales had sounded interminable to Marion who, having shown no talent for the instrument, instead had received singing lessons from Senor Vincetti, a small plump man with dark eyes and a neat moustache . . .

Mrs Draper hurried in with the tea-tray and set it down on the circular table.

'It's Lapsong tea,' she said. 'I hope you like it. Your sister never has anything else these days.'

Marion thanked her, but before she could pour herself

a cup Rachel herself came hurrying into the room, her arms outstretched in welcome, and the two sisters were soon hugging each other enthusiastically.

Mrs Draper, her eyes moist, said, 'It's just like old times!' and retired to the kitchen to leave them together. She came back a moment or two later, however, to suggest that Pip might be interested in a large meat-bone, and as the little dog hurried eagerly after her Marion and Rachel settled down to drink their tea.

As though by tacit agreement, neither of them brought up the subject of Gilbert but talked instead of more pleasant matters, including Ralph Gaunt who was expected to arrive on Tuesday and stay overnight or possibly longer. Rachel had planned a picnic by the river, but she also promised Marion time to be alone with him, assuring her that she did not see herself as permanent chaperone.

That night, however, Rachel came into her sister's room wearing a robe over her nightdress and without more ado perched herself on the edge of Marion's bed. Pip roused herself and greeted her warmly.

'Marion,' Rachel said bluntly, 'I don't want to spoil your visit by talking about your husband, but since that is one of the reasons you have come I suggest we get it out of the way. Then we can relax and enjoy the rest of our time together. It might be difficult for you to talk about it, but I do think you should try.'

Marion sighed and nodded. 'You are right, I know, but it's so hard to know how to begin.'

Rachel said nothing while Marion searched for a way to start. At last she said haltingly. 'To tell you the truth, Rachel, I don't trust Gilbert any more and at times I am almost afraid of him. I know that Meg Swain is the cause of his ill-temper, yet when I saw her at the funeral she seemed . . . well, decent enough.'

'For a loose woman, you mean!' Rachel's tone was sharp and Marion considered the remark, her head tilted slightly to one side.

'It may sound strange to you, but forgetting what she is she seems fond of the child and in the same way I think she was fond of Ellie.' She smiled faintly. 'This will sound crazy, but I have a sneaking admiration for her. Gilbert, of course, always speaks badly of her yet cannot seem to stay away from her. He forbids *me* to visit them, though.'

'And why do you think that is?'

Marion pretended not to hear the question. 'He told me that Meg's baby was dead, but she isn't. How could a doctor make such a mistake?'

'What do you think?' said Rachel remorselessly.

Cornered by her sister's insistence, Marion took a deep breath. 'To tell you the truth . . .' she began, but her courage failed her and she reached out a trembling hand to ruffle Pip's fur. She longed to confide in someone, but could she bring herself to put her suspicions into words? It would sound so incredible and Rachel would be appalled.

The silence between them lengthened, but Rachel's gaze did not falter. 'Why not tell me what you really believe?' Rachel asked quietly. 'That Gilbert is the child's father?'

Marion gasped. 'How on earth . . .' she began.

Rachel shrugged. 'I put two and two together. You say he is no husband to you in the full sense of the word – he might well turn to someone like Meg Swain. From what you say he is a brute, but the Meg Swains of this world are used to men like that and no doubt he pays her well for her pains.'

Marion shuddered. 'Don't! I cannot bear to think about it. Oh, Rachel, can you believe that we are talking like this? That we are saying these terrible things? How did I ever get myself into this impossible situation?'

'What is more to the point is how can we get you *out* of it!' said Rachel.

Marion sighed. 'Gilbert has forbidden me to visit the

Swains again, but I am almost determined to go anyway. I just have to know.'

'But suppose Meg tells you that Gilbert is the father – what then? Can you bear to know for certain? Wouldn't that be worse than suspecting it?'

'I don't think anything could be worse than this uncertainty.'

'And would you divorce him?'

'Divorce him? Good heavens, he would never allow that! I imagine he would simply deny everything – bluff it out and accuse Meg of lying. If the truth came out, it would ruin him.'

Rachel clasped her hands around her knees and said carefully, 'You must be very careful, Marion. You say that you are almost afraid of Gilbert, but if I were you I would be *very* afraid. I would be very cautious about antagonizing him.'

'Oh, come now, Rachel!' Marion protested. 'He's not exactly an ogre. He's not going to do *me* any harm. Why should he?'

'I don't know, but I wouldn't be too sure about it. You know that I have never liked him, and the reason is that he makes me uncomfortable. When we were young he used to frighten me. I hated to meet him on the landing after dark. Oh, not for any reason; it was purely intuitive. I have always felt that he had a dark side to his nature. I suppose you will think that with hindsight it's easy to say that, but I swear to you I felt that way about him even then. That is why I didn't want you to marry him, but I knew I would never convince you and you seemed genuinely fond of him. I thought that if I told you my true feelings and you still married him, you might resent the fact that I had spoken so freely. Now I think I should have been more specific instead of just saying that I didn't think you were suited. Would my opinion have made any difference? Would it have deterred you?'

'I don't think so. I had made up my mind by then.'

Pip jumped down to the floor and removed herself to a far corner, where she settled down with a loud sigh.

Marion laughed. 'That's her way of telling us that we are keeping her from her sleep!'

However, Rachel did not smile. 'You should have children to love,' she said. 'A dog is no substitute. You always wanted children. It was what you always wanted.'

'And you always wanted a horse to ride!'

'We were both disappointed.'

Marion nodded. 'You could still have a horse. You could sell this house and buy something smaller and with the spare money . . .'

'But how will you get your children?'

Marion hastily averted her gaze and Rachel's eyes narrowed.

'Marion!' she exclaimed. 'I hope you are not thinking what I *think* you are thinking.'

'Meaning what exactly?' asked Marion, playing for time.

'Meaning Meg Swain's child.'

There was a strained silence. Marion swallowed, her throat suddenly dry, for now her sister had put into words the idea which had been slowly taking shape in her mind ever since the funeral. At last she looked up. 'That little girl is Gilbert's child,' she said evenly. 'I *know* it. She has his olive skin and his eyes. New babies have deep blue eyes, but Lizzie's are very pale. Rachel, she *looks* like him. If you saw her, you would agree with me. It's not just my fevered imagination.'

'Perhaps it is wishful thinking, then.'

'No, Rachel!' Marion shook her head vehemently. 'Lizzie is Gilbert's child and should be mine also. If I thought Meg Swain would give her up –'

'No, Marion!' cried Rachel. 'Don't even think of such a thing! The idea is monstrous!'

As her voice rose, Pip turned large reproachful eyes in

their direction but, unable to attract anyone's attention, she returned once more to her slumbers.

'Listen to me, Marion,' Rachel said forcefully. 'Even if Meg would surrender the child, which is most unlikely, you cannot seriously believe that Gilbert would agree. In order to do that he would have to admit to his relationship with a whore, and I see no likelihood of that. Do you?'

'He might want the child.'

'Oh, really Marion,' Rachel protested. 'You cannot believe that. Has he ever shown the slightest hankering for parenthood?'

Marion was forced to shake her head.

'But *I* hanker,' she whispered. 'Oh, Rachel, she is such a sweet baby and I can't bear to think of her being brought up in those terrible surroundings to a life of poverty and despair.'

'But she's the child of a *whore*!' cried Rachel. 'If it had been one of your servants, it would be more tolerable. Oh Lord! I see that stubborn look on your face that I remember so well. Marion, please do be sensible about this.'

But Marion's expression was anguished. 'I want that child, Rachel. I know all the reasons why I should *not* want her, but I still do. I want to give her a decent life; I want her to grow up in happy, wholesome surroundings; I want to educate her. Oh, Rachel, I want to *love* her. That day at the funeral when Meg put her into my arms I felt so . . .' Her voice was choked with the tears that shone in her eyes. 'It felt so *right*! As though we belonged together.'

Tears spilled down her cheeks and Rachel scrambled over the bed to sit beside her and put a comforting arm round her shoulders.

'Marion, don't cry,' she begged. 'Please don't cry.'

'I don't expect anyone to understand . . .' Marion began, but fresh tears interrupted her.

Rachel waited for the tears to lessen, cursing Gilbert for reducing her sister to such an unhappy state of mind. When at last Marion was calmer, Rachel slid briskly from the bed.

'Hot milk and a splash of brandy!' she prescribed. 'No! Not another word. Hot milk and brandy will help you to sleep. We have said enough for one night – too much, probably. You take a damp flannel and wipe your face. Freshen up, as Mama used to say.' Seeing that Marion's expression remained mournful, she added, 'Well, at least try to look grateful. Here I am trying to look after you, hobbling about on my *broken ankle*!'

At last Marion's mouth turned up in the ghost of a smile. 'Suppose Gilbert had insisted on coming with me to examine it?'

Rachel gasped. 'Good heavens, Marion! That never occurred to me!'

'Nor to me until this very moment!'

They laughed over their narrow escape and then Rachel thought it safe to leave her sister, but as she went downstairs she sighed. Gilbert would never willingly give up his wife and Meg Swain would never relinquish the child. The future for Marion looked bleak indeed.

*

The prospect of seeing Ralph again buoyed up Marion's spirits and to some extent she was able to heed Rachel's advice to, 'Forget about Gilbert and enjoy yourself.'

On Tuesday morning she helped her sister to prepare a picnic and pack it into a large hamper along with crockery and cutlery. She turned down Rachel's suggestion that she go to the station to meet Ralph's train, for she was suddenly stricken with an intense nervousness and decided to wait at the house with Rachel for his arrival.

When he did come, however, all her shyness melted away at the sight of him and when he held out his arms she ran forward into his embrace.

'Do you still love me?' he whispered and she nodded emphatically.

He shook hands warmly with Rachel and they exchanged greetings, then Mrs Draper appeared with a tray of lemonade and biscuits and Rachel told Ralph of their plans.

'We are going to Hampton Court,' she told him, 'to a favourite spot we knew as children. It's on the Ribb, actually – that's a tributary of the Thames.'

Marion laughed. 'Doubtless it will be the very spot where Rachel tried to drown me at the tender age of seven! While our nanny was dozing, she pushed me into the water –'

Rachel interrupted her indignantly. 'Oh, tell it *all*, Marion! Admit that I had good cause; there was "provocation" as the judges would say. You had taken my doll –'

'I had *borrowed* it,' Marion insisted. 'Anyway, Rachel pushed me in and there I was screaming my head off and splashing about, and along came a handsome young man who waded in to rescue me –'

'And to ensnare the affections of the nanny!'

'You are making it up!' laughed Ralph. 'I don't believe a word of it.'

'It's all true!' insisted Marion. 'They fell in love and he proposed and she accepted and we lost a very good nanny. Mama was dreadfully upset.'

'That just shows,' he said. 'You cannot be too careful!'

'It was Marion's fault,' put in Rachel righteously. 'If she had not taken my doll –'

'*Borrowed* it,' Marion amended once more.

Ralph said, 'Well, I hope you're not planning to fall in again, because I admit here and now that I'm not an expert swimmer, so the consequences could be dire!'

They all laughed and Marion went off to look for Pip who was going with them. Immediately she had left the room, Rachel asked, 'What is *your* opinion of Gilbert Reid? Marion tells me that she has confided in you about her fears.'

'Yes, she has. I'm afraid I hardly know the man, but from what Marion says I do think there is something odd going on. I don't know exactly what, but I wouldn't trust him an inch. Of course, I don't share Marion's concern about the Swains, but she worries about that wretched child.'

'I worry about *her*,' Rachel told him. 'Please do what you can to keep an eye on her. Try to prevent her from doing anything rash or dangerous.'

'I'll try, Rachel, but unhappily I have to keep my distance. If her husband were to suspect that we are involved, there is no telling what he might do. It all sounds very melodramatic, but . . .' He shrugged. 'I'll do the very best I can. I wish to God I could take her right away from there. It is a relief to know that she's here with you for a few days.'

There was no time to say more, for just then Marion came back into the room with Pip and, both dog and mistress having declared themselves ready, a few moments later they all set off.

The morning was perfect, with a clear blue sky and a light breeze which served to minimize the effects of the hot July sunshine which burned down relentlessly. Fortunately, their heads were well protected – Ralph's by a boater, Marion's by a flower-decked straw hat and Rachel's by a neat bonnet decorated with ribbons. Also, both women carried parasols.

As soon as they reached the river-bank Pip was released from her lead and scurried ahead importantly, casting occasional glances behind her to ensure that her beloved mistress was still in sight. The world and his wife were out enjoying the splendour of the riverside and to Rachel's disappointment their favourite picnic spot was occupied by a mother and three young children; however, a comfortable alternative was found in the welcome shade of an oak tree.

Ralph seated himself in the middle of the rug between

Marion and Rachel. 'This way,' he joked, 'there will be no squabbling!'

They chatted desultorily, content for most of the time to watch the changing pageant that the river presented for their entertainment.

On the glittering water a variety of small punts passed by, poled by energetic young men whose lady friends reclined gracefully against their cushions beneath lace-edged parasols. One man rowed by in an ancient dinghy while his companion played sea shanties, somewhat inexpertly, on a mouth-organ. A little further up stream a group of children swam together with occasional shrieks and screams and a great deal of good-natured banter, while on the river-bank couples strolled arm-in-arm with eyes only for each other.

An elderly man approached, walking a black labrador who eyed Pip with great disdain and totally ignored her friendly overtures. A middle-aged man jolted past in a bath-chair propelled by two boys who might have been his grandsons.

Rachel talked about her new lodger, a Mr Carruthers, who was to take up residence the following week.

'A meek little man,' she told them, 'with a moustache two sizes too big for him!'

Marion talked about Pip's weight, which was increasing, and the fact that she was hopelessly spoiled.

Ralph told them a little about his painting and explained rather sheepishly that he should have been an artist.

'But can you imagine me,' he demanded, 'sitting in the middle of a field with only cows for company? I have nothing against the beasts, but they have no eye for artistic techniques and no flair for reasoned criticism!'

Marion, listening and laughing, felt a little of the past week's tension leave her body. Here by the waterside the alarms of the past few weeks faded into insignificance and even Gilbert's extra-marital adventures appeared less probable. She sighed. If she had not married Gilbert, she and Ralph would be free to marry – but then if she had not been Mrs Reid, she and Ralph would never have met, for they had been brought together by young Ellie Swain who had only come to the surgery because of Amelia Gaunt's generosity. At the thought of this austere lady, a little of Marion's nervousness returned as she imagined how Ralph's mother would react if she ever learned of her son's liaison! Amelia Gaunt, she knew, would not approve.

After the best part of an hour had passed in this delightfully lazy manner, Rachel suggested that they might eat since it was now nearly twelve thirty and all around them baskets were being unpacked and appetizing food was being devoured.

'Why don't you two wander off for ten minutes?' she suggested. 'I can then spread out the picnic to my complete satisfaction without two pairs of hungry eyes watching my every move.'

Although both Ralph and Marion saw through her ruse, they were grateful for the chance to be alone and willingly took advantage of her suggestion. They began to stroll along the towpath together, but before they had gone twenty yards Ralph had slipped his arm round Marion's waist.

'Now we look the part,' he told her with a smile. 'Two lovers. Later on we must try arm-in-arm, and then later still hand-in-hand. We must do these things properly.'

Marion laughed. 'It all sounds marvellous. I shall be entirely happy to cooperate in your experiments!'

She could not remember when she had been so happy. The Zoological Gardens had been exhilarating, but at that time she and Ralph had not spoken of their feelings for one another. Now they knew that they loved each other, which made today even more wonderful.

She had thought long and hard since learning of Gilbert's infidelity and had finally convinced herself that in the circumstances she was entitled to enjoy her time with Ralph without feeling guilty. At least she would allow herself that small luxury. Just to be in his company, just to be within sight of him, was enough. She would not allow her feelings to lead her astray – she had no intention of breaking the commandments. They would respect the proprieties and would never be intimate. But she would no longer deny her feelings ... she loved Ralph Gaunt, and she would find no shame in that. Since she could never be his wife, she would be thankful for any time they could spend together. If that was a crime, she was guilty, but she would never stand accused of anything worse.

'I nearly did not come today,' Ralph told her suddenly. 'My mother had arranged a dinner party for this evening without first confirming that I was free to attend. It was the most frightful coincidence. It must be months since we have entertained, maybe as long as a year. Mama always claims to find dinner engagements boring. Even our own! And then to choose today of all days!'

Marion's face expressed her appreciation of his dilemma. 'Whatever did you say?' she asked him.

'I told her the truth – that I had a prior engagement. She wanted to know the whys and wherefores, naturally, and I said I had been invited to stay with friends. She couldn't say too much at the time because there was a young lady present, but afterwards –'

'A young lady?'

'Yes. Clarice Foster, to be precise, the daughter of one of the members of the committee for my mother's school project. Apparently she had offered to take some of the paper-work off Mama's hands, and they were working together. I insisted that I had already accepted the invitation, although that was not strictly true since your letter had only just arrived. Of course, later that evening when Miss Foster had departed, Mama quizzed me on the subject of my mysterious friends.'

'You did not tell her about us?'

'Certainly not! Wild horses would not drag your name from my lips! I did tell her there was a lady, however.'

Marion stopped twirling her parasol and stood stock still.

'What is the matter?' he asked.

'She knows!' Marion declared. 'Your mother knows, and she is trying to tempt you away from me!'

'But that's impossible! How could she guess that it was you? All she knows is your first name.'

Marion's consternation grew. 'She knows my *name*? Good heavens! Then –'

'Don't look like that, my love. She would never suspect it was you' – his face fell suddenly – 'would she?'

Chastened, they looked at each other. 'You may be right,' Ralph confessed. 'Perhaps she has guessed . . .'

Marion looked at him in consternation. 'She has decided that I am quite unsuitable and has introduced you to the eminently more suitable Miss Foster –'

'Damnation!' He pursed his lips. 'I do believe you are right.'

His arm tightened round her waist, but as they walked on they were both sobered by the thought of Amelia's disapproval. After a moment, he gave her a little shake and said, 'Don't be down-hearted. Forewarned is fore-armed! Now that I know what she is planning I can more easily recognize and resist her manoeuvres.'

Marion's heart was thumping, since she did not for one moment underestimate Amelia Gaunt. 'What is she like?' she asked as casually as she could.

'My mother?'

'No, Miss Foster.'

'Miss Foster? Oh, you have nothing to fear from that young lady. She is grotesquely fat, has only one eye and wears a very unconvincing wig made of –'

Marion's laugh was a trifle shaky. 'Ralph! Don't pre-varicate! I really want to know. Your mother would never choose anyone like that if she was hoping to arouse your interest. What is Clarice Foster really like?'

'Neat, dark-haired . . .'

'Very young?'

He nodded.

'Very pretty?'

'I daresay – but what does it matter? You can't imagine even for a moment that she could interest me. I love Marion Reid and that is *you*. Miss Foster is only a speck on the horizon as far as I am concerned, and you cannot be jealous of a speck. Nobody could.'

Marion was silent, longing for the ability to say lightly that of course she was not jealous of the young and attractive rival whom Amelia Gaunt had conjured up so promptly. But in her heart she was jealous – and hurt, and resentful. She *hated* Amelia Gaunt. Yet in some ways she admired her. In her shoes, Marion thought, she would probably have done exactly the same.

'I shall try not to be jealous,' she said at last.

'And I'll try not to be jealous of your husband!' Ralph said quietly.

Marion swung round to face him. 'Oh, but you mustn't be.'

His face was pale. 'You love me, but you are still his wife,' he said, 'and I have to live with the knowledge that you share his bed. That he . . .' He shook his head helplessly. 'I am *very* jealous. I cannot pretend otherwise.'

'But I don't *love* him.'

'And I don't love Clarice Foster.'

'*Touché!*' She relaxed enough to smile, then her expression changed again.

'There is something I want you to know about . . . our marriage,' she said, choosing her words with difficulty. 'Gilbert and I are not man and wife in the normal sense of the words. There were one or two occasions – many years ago. I don't want to say more except that it is his choice. Does that make you feel any better?'

He nodded. 'I am so grateful that you have told me. I hate to think . . .'

'So I shall never have a child!'

He recognized the unexpressed despair in her voice as she spoke and longed to comfort her, but what could he say? She was Gilbert Reid's wife and likely to remain so; if she had a child by another man, Gilbert would know it was not his.

'If only you could be divorced,' he said desperately.

Marion shook her head. 'Gilbert would never consider it. The scandal would be totally unacceptable. He would never divorce me, and how could I divorce him? I have my suspicions, but no proof. I'm sorry, Ralph, but we dare not think along those lines.'

They had stopped walking and now stood watching the river. A young man in a striped blazer was struggling with a punt-pole which had become stuck in the river-bed, and his antics were threatening to pull him out of the boat to the great amusement of his passengers. At the last possible moment he retrieved the pole and his balance amid loud applause from a delighted audience on the river-bank. As he took off his hat and waved it in acknowledgement, Marion laughed and the gloom was dispelled.

'Let us not think about the future,' she urged. 'Or the past. Let's just think about today; now; this minute. We're together and that's what matters.' She waved her hand. 'We have the sunshine and the river – and we have our arms around each other.'

'You are a wise old bird –' he began but then, seeing her pretended indignation, amended hastily, 'Wise *young* bird!'

'That's much better,' she told him.

Ralph stood back to look at her.

'You may be a year or two my senior,' he told her, 'but that is to your advantage. You have wisdom in your face which young girls lack. You have experience of the world and a tolerance towards other people's frailties. You have understanding and are less impatient. A whole host of qualities which only come with time. To brash, shallow young men, an older woman is infinitely more desirable. Didn't you know that?'

A faint blush tinged her cheeks. 'No, I did not,' she replied, 'and I think maybe you are just being gallant.'

'I can assure you that I am not,' he said. 'Young girls are very self-centred, you see. Miss Foster had no interest in me. She wanted to speak only of her own affairs – in her case, an ill-starred romance.'

The corners of her mouth twitched humorously. 'So now you are an expert on the minds of women, Mr Gaunt? You must have known a great many.'

He grinned. 'One or two. The Grand Tour is not only about art and language, you know! It is intended to teach a young man about life with a capital "L".'

'Tell me about them,' she asked, 'as we walk back to Rachel. She will be wondering where we are.'

'Do you really want me to?'

She shrugged lightly. 'We know so little about each other. We have to start somewhere.'

So he told her about Maxine, the art student he met in Paris, and about Carlotta who had shared his life for three months in Milan.

'Girls in Europe are not like English girls,' he explained. 'English girls want only one thing: a ring and wedding bells. On the other side of the Channel the girls flirt outrageously with almost any man, but it really means very little to them. You know that when you are gone they will forget you and someone else will take your place.'

'Isn't that rather humbling?' Marion asked mischievously.

'I found it reassuring,' he laughed. 'I didn't want to marry. Oh, and then I came back to England and met a woman with soft brown eyes and a sad mouth and she was the only one I really loved. The others were fun, you see, but this one took possession of my heart.' He looked into her wide, startled eyes and added gently, 'Her name was Marion.'

He saw the understanding dawn in her eyes as he took her into his arms and held her close. 'I never want to let you go!' he whispered. 'I want you with me always. *Always!*'

'Oh, Ralph! I wish it could be so, but –'

He kissed her before she could voice her doubts. 'I want you,' he insisted. 'I have no idea how it can be achieved, and I know it sounds impossible, but if you feel the same as I do . . .'

'Ralph, I do! Believe me! But –'

'Then we will find a way. I shall think of something, I promise you. There must be some action we can take.'

Marion shook her head. 'We shouldn't hope for so much,' she said. 'If we raise our hopes, we will be so disappointed.'

'Don't think that way,' he told her. 'Think about what might be, a year from today. Anything might have happened.'

'I thought we were going to take one day at a time,' she reminded him with a smile. 'What happened to that idea?'

'I tried that,' he replied, 'and it didn't work! I am a very impatient young man. I told you, it's one of the faults of the young. Mama used to say –'

'Don't mention your mother!' Marion broke in. 'She will never approve of me. If I *were* to obtain a divorce, she would still never accept me.'

'I'm twenty-five, for God's sake!' he exclaimed. 'I don't need her approval.' They looked at each other, then kissed again.

'Lunch!' said Ralph firmly and together they hurried back to Rachel who, having prepared the picnic, was beginning to feel hungry. A white cloth had been spread out and plates, knives and forks were arranged upon it. In the centre of the cloth was a dish of patties, a raised pie, three small jellies and a deep bowl of salad.

'Oyster patties,' Rachel told them, 'pork pie, and haddock and shrimp jellies!'

Ralph and Marion were suitably impressed and said so while Rachel, gratified, tried to look modest. For dessert there was a dish of apricot cream and a bowl of Mr Bridges' best peaches. Crusty bread rolls and a dish of butter completed the feast and in the picnic basket a large stone flagon contained . . .

'Champagne cup!' Rachel announced. 'Mrs Beeton's own recipe made with champagne, soda-water and brandy. Guaranteed to bring a flush to the cheeks and a sparkle to the eye! Now sit yourselves down, and you, Ralph, pour us all a drink. I am so hungry that I could eat a horse!'

They obeyed with cheerful alacrity and were soon raising their glasses.

'To you and Ralph,' said Rachel. 'Your happiness!'

Marion leaned over and kissed her sister. 'To all of us!' she amended and they drank to that.

CHAPTER THIRTEEN

The following week Meg Swain pushed open the door of the Angel and Crown and surveyed the throng of riotous customers with a jaundiced eye. Even on a normal day the pub would be full of drunken revellers, but today was a Bank Holiday and was therefore worse than usual, the air hazy with smoke and smelling of sweat, beer and sawdust. The noise was deafening, shrill with the laughter of women and rumbling with the raucous jokes of the men. Porters, dockers, costermongers – all dressed in their Sunday best – leaned unsteadily against the bar or sprawled around the few tables, while more sat on the floor with their backs against the wall, their heads lolling stupidly, eyes dulled with an excess of liquor. The women were little better, whispering obscenely with their heads close together, bedraggled feathers wagging crazily on their gaudy hats. Others leered at the men provocatively and sang bawdy songs, swaying with the music; some sat on the laps of a group of Grenadier Guards who hailed from the barracks at Tower Hill. A few heads turned towards Meg as she stood in the doorway with her baby in her arms.

A solitary voice called, 'Hello there, Meg, my old love! How you doing, then?'

With a toss of her head she answered, 'Bloody awful! How's yourself, ducks?' This tart reply was considered hilarious and was greeted by loud guffaws.

Another voice offered, 'Going to have a pint on me, love?' But Meg shook her head, for she had drunk enough already and had not come in search of more. She was looking for Dottie Burke, who lived at the George

Yard, buildings and was reported to be seeking a room-mate.

Since accepting Gilbert's money, Meg had had second thoughts about Bristol and had decided not to leave London – or not immediately anyway. She had spent a few nights at Dora's old lodgings, but had considered that too risky since Gilbert might be able to find her there if he took it into his head to make sure she had gone. Dora's friend, Zoe, had put her up for one night, but she lived in fear of discovery from either Gilbert or the man who was going to kill her, and was now trying to move amongst a set of people who had no obvious connection with her. She could pay well, but the money would not last indefinitely. Meg was convinced that only by keeping on the move could she hope to avoid disaster. 'Anyone seen Dottie Burke?' she asked, shouting above the din.

'I'm over here! Who wants me?'

Dottie Burke was in her thirties and, having been on the streets for much longer than Meg, had lost her youthful figure and now looked nearer fifty. Too much cheap gin had broken the veins in her nose and her hair was a most unlikely shade of red.

Following the direction of the voice, Meg elbowed her way through the crowded room until she found Dottie sitting with a young soldier who was decidedly drunk. He, too, offered to buy Meg a drink, but she shook her head and thought disparagingly that she herself had never sunk so low in the matter of 'clients'. If Dottie expected anything from him she would be disappointed, unless she managed to get him into a dark alley and went through his pockets.

Assuming a bright smile, she addressed herself to Dottie. 'I hear you want a lodger. That right?'

Dottie shook her head. 'No kids,' she said. 'Sorry.'

Meg bridled. 'What's wrong with my little Lizzie? Good as gold, she is. Never a peep out of her.'

Dottie's mouth tightened. 'You heard. No kids!'

'But why?'

'Because I hate kids, that's why. I can't stand the racket, nor the smell neither.'

Meg said angrily, 'My Lizzie don't smell! Here, take a sniff!' She thrust the baby under Dottie's nose, making her recoil so sharply that she banged her head on the wall.

'Get away, damn you!' she cried. 'I said no kids and I meant it. Sod off, can't you!'

Meg hesitated. She knew that Dottie needed a lodger to help pay the rent which was deeply in arrears, and she could afford to pay more than most, but did she want to share a room with a woman who had spoken so slightingly about Lizzie? Maternal pride urged her to tell Dottie in no uncertain terms exactly what she could do with her rotten room, but it was now nearly eleven and Meg had nowhere to sleep. She could go to a public lodging house for threepence, but there she would be seen by too many people and she was not inclined to take the risk. Somone was trying to murder her, so the fewer people who knew her whereabouts, the better. She looked round the room, hoping that perhaps she might see another familiar face, but among the sea of strange faces she recognized only one and that was Martha Tabram, another whore; she, however, was locked in the arms of a soldier and would hardly take kindly to being interrupted.

Bending down, she whispered, 'I can pay over the odds, Dottie. I'm not short of a bob or two! Pay the rent, won't it? Just for a few nights?'

Just then Dottie's soldier groaned, leaned forward suddenly, then put his head in his hands. He mumbled something incoherent and stood up, his face ashen.

Dottie muttered, 'Oh, Christ! He's took bad. Just my bloody luck!' They watched him weave his way unsteadily towards the door marked 'Men'.

Meg said smugly, 'You won't get much out of him tonight!'

Dottie swore again and Meg saw the indecision in her

eyes and waited. Eventually Dottie swallowed the remaining dregs in her mug and asked, 'Flush, then, are you?'

'I've got enough.'

'How much is enough?'

'Never you mind, but I've got plenty.'

'How d'you come by plenty? Pinched, is it?'

'No, it's not. It was given me, if you must know.'

'Pull the other leg! A bob a night, then, since you're so flush.'

At her words several nearby heads turned curiously in their direction and Meg cursed Dottie's loud mouth. No one in their right mind would advertise good fortune – there were always plenty willing to relieve them of such a burden!

'What?' cried Meg. 'A bob a night? What do you think I am? That's daylight robbery, that is!'

They regarded each other balefully, and the proprietor yelled, 'Time, gentlemen, please!' but no one took any notice.

'There's two of you,' insisted Dottie. 'And I'm doing you a favour, but if the kid yells all night, out you go!'

'She never yells, bless her,' Meg declared proudly.

Dottie shrugged. 'We'll see,' she said. 'Bob a night, then.'

'Not bloomin' likely! I'll give you sixpence.'

'Ninepence, and that's my last offer.'

'And the rest!' snapped Meg.

One or two customers were making their way towards the door and as Meg saw Martha Tabram go out with her soldier she felt a small glow of superiority. Thanks to Gilbert's money, she had no need to find work tonight.

Dottie taunted her, 'I thought you'd got a bob or two. Just swank, was it? You and your "plenty"!'

Meg tossed her head. 'What I've got is no concern of yours, Dottie Burke. I've enough for my lodgings and that's all you need to know. Are you taking us in, or aren't you? I'll give you sevenpence – take it or leave it.'

'Done!' said Dottie. 'But if he starts bawling –'

'He's a *she*!' said Meg indignantly.

'Got yourself stuck with a kid? That wasn't very clever?'

'Maybe I meant to! Maybe I'm smarter than the rest of you.'

'And maybe not!'

Dottie got up without further ado and called 'Cheerio, Fred!' to the barman who raised a meaty hand in acknowledgement and Meg, with Lizzie in her arms, followed her out into the night.

*

Next morning Meg was disturbed by a thunderous banging and woke to find herself in Dottie's room; as both women struggled into wakefulness, they regarded each other in alarm.

'What the hell's going on?' cried Dottie and without waiting for an answer, she crawled out of her tousled bed, one hand to her aching head, and scrambled over Meg to get to the door.

The noise had woken Lizzie, but although her small mouth puckered anxiously she did not cry as Meg snatched her up and held her close, convinced that the murderer had finally caught up with them.

As soon as Dottie had unbolted the door, a young woman stumbled into the room, her face chalk-white.

'Peg!' cried Dottie.

'There's been a murder!' she told them, her voice shrill with fright. 'It's Martha Tabram! Some bastard's done for her with a knife!'

Meg was on her feet instantly, her heart thumping, her thoughts whirling. This was what Gilbert had been warning her about.

'Oh, God! We'll be next!' she whispered, but Dottie and Peg paid her no heed.

304

'Done for her?' Dottie repeated. 'Martha Tabram? But she can't be dead! We only saw her last night. Who says she's dead? Where is she?'

The woman pointed through the door. 'On our bloody doorstep, that's where!' she told them. 'Up there on the landing near the stairs what we come up. Johnny Reeves found her on his way to work – lying in a pool of blood, and stabbed all over. Oh, Jesus! That's given me a proper turn, hearing that. Could have been any of us!'

Dottie turned to look at Meg, her eyes wide. 'That soldier!' she whispered. 'The one she was with last night down the Angel; the one she left with. Must have been him!' She turned to their informant who was now slumped in a chair, with one hand to her heart.

'Do the rozzers know who she was with last night? Because we saw him.'

Peg looked aggrieved. 'How the hell should I know?' she demanded. 'I haven't asked them, have I? I haven't been near them, nor Martha neither. I don't want to see her all dead and bloody. I feel bad enough already, just hearing about it. I mean, why Martha? What's she ever done to deserve that? And who'll be next?'

Meg swallowed. The murderer had obviously been looking for *her* and, not finding her, had killed Martha Tabram instead! But that didn't make sense, because the soldier with Martha Tabram had been in the same pub as her and Lizzie so he would have seen her. How could he have killed Martha by mistake? And did Gilbert Reid know it was going to happen? Oh God! She would be next, without a doubt!

She glanced at Dottie, who was pulling on her clothes as fast as she could.

'Where you going?' she asked.

'To see what there is to see!'

'Hang on! I'll come with you.'

Peg refused to go with them, but offered to stay and look after Lizzie, so within minutes Meg and Dottie were making their way downstairs to the first-floor landing where they found a large jostling crowd gathered at the spot where the body had been found. The blood had been washed away but the ground was still wet; a harassed policeman was taking down statements and everyone was talking in loud whispers.

It appeared that the luckless woman's body had also been seen earlier by one Albert Crow – a cab-driver who also lived in the buildings – but he had ignored her, thinking she was drunk. Later the police had been called in and the wheels of the murder enquiry were set in motion.

'There's going to be an identity parade,' someone told them, 'at the barracks.'

'They've taken her away to the morgue,' said another. 'For a post mortem.'

'Stabbed her all over! Ugh! It gives you the creeps!'

Meg and Dottie waited their turn to tell the policeman what they knew of Martha's companion of the previous night; then Dottie went off to her mother's to tell her all about it and Meg was left alone, a prey to her too vivid imagination. She shuddered involuntarily and decided that in the light of present circumstances, it might be wise to take Gilbert's advice after all and make her way to Bristol. Perhaps she would like Bristol; she might even like it more than London. Yes, she would take the next train. She would go before the murderer caught up with her, but first she would have to collect her bits and pieces from Dora. A few cups and saucers, two blankets, the rest of her clothes, a picture and a couple of ornaments she had won at the fair. None of them of any value, but it was all she had in the world and if she was to start a new life in Bristol, she would need them. It would all go into one big bundle and she could carry it under her arm. Unfortunately Dora would be at work now that the strike was over, but the housekeeper might give her the things once she knew how urgent it was.

She set off to walk to Parfett Street, but she was less than half-way there when she made a terrible discovery – the money Gilbert had given her had gone!

'But who could have taken it?' asked Dora later that evening as she and Jeff listened to Meg's distraught account of her accumulated troubles.

'It was there when I went to bed,' she told them. 'I slept in my shift, but I rolled up my skirt for a pillow. It was there then.'

'Could it have been Dottie?' Jeff asked. 'Did she know you had a lot of money on you?'

Miserably Meg nodded. 'I had to tell her so she'd let me doss with her,' she said, 'but I never said exactly how much. I just sort of hinted that I wasn't short of the odd bob. Mind you, she's got a voice like a bloody fog-horn! "Since you're so flush!" she said, right out loud. Anyone could have heard her. She's a stupid cow, that one.'

'She could have taken it while you were asleep,' suggested Dora, 'although it's not very likely, because you might have noticed it was missing when you woke up and then it *could* only have been her. Perhaps it was someone in the crowd, when you were talking about the murder. A pick-pocket could have taken it.' She jiggled the baby on her knee while Meg bit hungrily into a slice of bread and jam.

'It doesn't matter much who it was,' Jeff pointed out. 'You'll never get it back now, Meg, so the question is – how will you get to Bristol and what will you live on?'

Meg said, 'Gilbert'll have to give me some more money, that's all. Dora will have to go and ask him.' Dora opened her mouth to protest, but Meg hurried on, 'Well, *I* daren't go; daren't show my face! The murderer might be lying in wait anywhere. You'll have to go, Dora, tell him what's happened and ask him for –'

'But he won't believe me,' Dora protested. 'He'll think it's a trick to get more money out of him because he believes you've already gone, remember? But if he saw *you* he'd –'

'He'd kick me from here to kingdom come!' Meg told her gloomily. She swallowed the last mouthful and her face softened as she held out her arms for the baby. 'I'll give her her feed now, bless her,' she said and proceeded to unfasten her blouse while Jeff, embarrassed, hastily turned away.

'It'll have to be you, Dor,' Meg insisted. 'If you won't go, then I'm stuck here. Right here.'

The last thing Dora and Jeff wanted was for Meg to become a permanent lodger and they exchanged exasperated looks. Dora was very fond of her cousin, but she preferred her company in small doses.

'*I'll* go,' offered Jeff.

'No!' cried Meg. 'Then he'll know I've confided in someone. It'll have to be Dor, because she's my cousin and she went before. Oh, please, Dor!' Her voice took on a plaintive note, for she knew Dora had a kind heart. 'It'll be the last thing I ask you, because when I go to Bristol you'll never see me again. At least you'll know that you helped to save my life, mine and little Lizzie's, and that you helped me turn respectable – because I swear that if you help me I'll change my ways. While I'm waiting for Gilbert I'll get a proper job in a shop, or I'll sell flowers or be a barmaid. I swear it, God's honour!'

Much against her own better judgement, Dora reluctantly agreed that she would make one last approach to the doctor on Meg's behalf.

'But it must be when he's on his own,' Meg warned. 'Whatever you do, don't tell him when anyone else is listening.'

'I'll pretend I'm sick,' said Dora, 'and then wait until we're alone in the surgery.'

'I don't really like the idea of you being alone with him, Dora. I don't trust that man,' Jeff said. 'I told you before, I don't believe this story of the wife's weak heart.'

Meg shook her head. 'You don't know him as well as I do,' she said. 'It's not him I'm afraid of – leastways, not exactly. I know he'll be mad with me for not being in Bristol, but he's not the murderer and that's who I'm afraid of.'

Jeff remained unconvinced. 'Well, I reckon there's something very fishy going on there. How does he come to know so much? And if he knows you're in danger, why doesn't he just go to the police?'

'Because then it would all come out about me and Lizzie, and him coming to Bristol,' said Meg, exasperated.

'Then why don't *we* go to the police?'

The two girls stared at him blankly.

'And say what?' Meg demanded. 'Someone's trying to do me in, but I don't know who, and I was told this by somebody I can't name! They'd split their sides laughing! I mean, they'll have nothing to go on, so what could they do?'

'Meg's right,' Dora told Jeff regretfully. 'We just have to take the doctor's warning on trust. If he is sincere, he'll give her some more money.' She sighed deeply. 'I'll go and see him and I'll do my best, but don't raise your hopes too high, Meg. He just might say "No".'

*

That evening Dora sat in the waiting room leafing through a copy of the *London Illustrated News* and trying to hide her nervousness. She had come straight from the factory and was only the third patient to arrive. Opposite her a gloomy young man nursed a heavily bandaged right hand, and to her left an elderly woman wheezed asthmatically.

When the doctor walked through the waiting room to his surgery, Dora kept her head well down. He rang his bell for the first patient and the elderly woman shuffled through. Almost at once the maid came into the waiting room and went up to Dora, who looked up in surprise.

'Miss Becket? The doctor's wife would like to speak with you.'

Dora bit back a gasp of dismay, for she had made no mental provision for this. What on earth could the doctor's wife want with her?

Silently, with a fast beating heart, she followed the maid out into the hallway and along to another room where Mrs Reid rose to meet her.

'Please don't look so anxious, Miss Becket,' she said. 'I only wished to ask after Miss Swain. I called at the house a few days ago and was told she had moved away.'

Shocked, Dora regarded her speechlessly. Now what was she to say? The doctor's wife was looking at her closely and she felt sure that guilt and deception must be written on her face in large letters.

She began to stammer, 'She's gone – that is – I mean, she hasn't . . .' Dora clasped and unclasped her hands as her anxiety mounted. Why on earth hadn't she considered this possibility, she asked herself desperately?

'Miss Becket, is there something wrong? With Miss Swain or the child? I do hope not.'

'No,' said Dora. 'At least, not really.'

'The child is well?'

Dora nodded. 'They're both well.'

'Then you've seen them lately? I would be grateful if you could give me Miss Swain's address.'

'The address? Oh, no, I can't do that.' She thought frantically. 'They couldn't pay the rent and they had to leave suddenly. The landlord threatened them.'

Marion Reid frowned. 'But how dreadful!' she exclaimed.

Dora went on, 'Yes; they're staying with me – at least, they were,' she corrected herself hastily. 'But they've gone now.'

'Gone?' Mrs Reid's face fell. 'Where to?'

'To Bristol.'

To Dora's surprise, this news seemed to upset the

other woman and she turned away quickly as though anxious to hide her expression.

'Bristol!' she repeated at last. 'That's a long way away. Does Miss Swain have friends in Bristol?'

Dora nodded unhappily, wondering if she was going too far and wishing, not for the first time, that she had never agreed to come on this errand. The silence lengthened uncomfortably.

'Miss Becket, I hope you won't be offended,' said the doctor's wife, 'but I believe you are not being entirely truthful with me. Are you sure that Lizzie is well?'

'Quite sure.'

'And she and her mother are in Bristol with friends?'

Dora said nothing.

'And what is the matter with *you*, Miss Becket?'

'Me? Nothing.' Too late Dora saw the trap into which she had fallen.

'Then why are you here?' the doctor's wife demanded. 'Presumably you have come on Miss Swain's behalf – is that it? Please, Miss Becket, I would like you to be honest with me.'

Dora stared stubbornly at the carpet, her lips closed.

'Are Miss Swain and Lizzie really in Bristol?'

Another silence was broken by Dora, who suddenly burst out with, 'She's got to get away! They're after her! I know you don't understand, but I can't tell you any more.' She looked around desperately and lowered her voice. 'You've heard about the murder, I suppose? Well, it could be Meg next. She's got to go away to Bristol.'

Before the doctor's wife could comment on this outburst, Kitty came into the room. 'The doctor's waiting,' she told Dora.

Mrs Reid hesitated, then said quietly, 'You must go along then, Miss Becket.'

And Dora allowed herself to be led back through the waiting room and into the surgery.

*

Gilbert was shocked and dismayed to learn that Meg Swain was not, as he had confidently imagined, in Bristol, but wandering around London with Lizzie. He was furious to learn also that she had lost – or *claimed* to have lost – the fifty pounds he had considered well spent in his efforts to be rid of them both. To add insult to injury, the stupid slut had also confided in her cousin and her cousin's fiancé. Years as a doctor had taught him self-control and as he listened to Dora's garbled tale, his eyes expressed nothing but polite interest, while his mind wrestled with the problem of how best to deal with this new emergency. He must remain unruffled, must use his intelligence and give his instincts for self-preservation full rein. Meg Swain, he decided, had had her chance and she and the child would have to be eliminated, but there must not be the slightest shred of evidence to connect him with the deaths. The recent murder of the whore, Tabram, might prove a godsend – if only he, Gilbert, could move fast enough. For if Meg was murdered in a similar way, the police would certainly connect the two events. Gilbert did not hold the Police Force in very high esteem. In his opinion they would blunder about as usual, following false clues and arresting the wrong man; their record was deplorable. But, if they *did* succeed and made an arrest, Meg's death could be attributed to Tabram's murderer.

He wondered how much time he had. It seemed unlikely that the police would employ their best brains to look for the murderer of a down-trodden drab, so time was probably on his side but he must take no chances. Suddenly, from nowhere, came inspiration. He tapped his teeth with his pencil as he waited for Miss Becket's rambling discourse to come to an end, then laid down the pencil carefully beside his prescription pad.

'Miss Becket,' he said gently, 'I see that I shall have to take you into my confidence. What I tell you will, I trust, go no further than this room.'

She nodded, frowning uneasily, and Gilbert leaned back in his chair.

'By that I mean that even Miss Swain must not be told.' At once she was alarmed. 'Not tell Meg? Oh, but –'

'I must have your word on that, Miss Becket, otherwise I can say no more. It is in her own best interests, I can assure you.'

At last Dora nodded again and, resting his elbows on the desk and putting the tips of his fingers together, he began solemnly, his voice tinged with a convincing regret. 'Miss Becket, your unfortunate cousin is, I'm afraid, suffering from what we call delusions. Childbirth does sometimes interfere with the mind's equilibrium and this has happened to Miss Swain. To put it simply, her mind is unhinged; she is deranged. There is no truth whatsoever in her story – none at all. She is *not* in danger of her life, she has *not* been told to leave London, nor has she been given any money; therefore she has not lost any. I am sad to say that the whole story is a figment of her fevered imagination.'

Even as he finished speaking, a hideous doubt rose in his mind. Suppose she had *shown* the money to her cousin! But Dora was staring at him open-mouthed, and her confusion was evident.

'Not in danger . . .' she whispered. 'You mean . . .' Her voice faltered as she tried to make the necessary mental adjustment. 'You're saying that Meg is *mad*? Oh, but that can't be true. I'd stake my life on it!'

Gilbert shook his head. 'Please don't, Miss Becket,' he said. 'Just think for a moment. Can you give me one good reason why anyone should want to kill her? Seriously?'

'No, but – you should know! You're the one who told her – oh, no! You mean, you didn't? Then if not you . . .'

'Miss Becket, no one told her any such thing; she invented it. Please do not misunderstand me. To Miss Swain it is all true, and no doubt she would swear on the

Holy Bible if necessary – but that would not make fiction into fact. It is true only in her mind.'

'But all the rest –'

'What else is there?' he questioned sharply.

'Why, the child being yours and . . .'

'*Mine!*' He assumed an air of shocked dismay. 'My dear Miss Becket, I'm sure you do not really believe that? I can assure you that nothing could be further from the truth.'

'But you have visited her on many occasions.'

'I am her *doctor*. She is in desperate need of help and I am doing what I can, but her mental state is very delicately balanced.' He pursed his lips. 'She might even need to go into an asylum. Some doctors would already have signed the papers, Miss Becket, but I wanted to give her a little longer. I suppose I was hoping against hope . . .'

Gilbert managed to look both sincere and disappointed and trusted that finally he had convinced her. She was an attractive little thing – a great pity she was mixed up with Meg Swain, he thought in passing. If he had managed to convince her, it was because the truth was no less likely than the lie.

'What's to be done?' she asked helplessly. 'Poor Meg, I can't believe it. And the baby . . .'

'Nothing,' he told her. 'Let things go on as they are for a week or so; she will come to no harm. Do not try to disillusion her, though, but allow her to continue thinking that you believe her. The sudden truth might unhinge her altogether. I have arranged a consultation with a colleague of mine who is more experienced in this kind of situation.'

'She can stay with me –' Dora began, but he shook his head.

'Don't try to hinder her in any way,' he emphasised. 'She might come to distrust you and that would never do.'

'But the baby – is she capable of looking after the baby?'

'Certainly. For the moment at least. I assume she has shown no sign of violence towards it?'

'Good heavens, no!'

'That's what I had thought.' He stood up and held out his hand. 'I am so glad I have had this opportunity to take you into my confidence,' he told her.

'But she has no money . . .' stammered Dora.

Gilbert pretended to consider this point, then reached into his pocket and took out a sovereign. 'Give her this; it will reassure her.' He brushed aside her thanks. 'Let us hope that we can save her from herself,' he said as he held open the surgery door. 'I am taking a gamble, you understand, Miss Becket, but when a young woman's liberty is at stake . . .' He gestured helplessly as she murmured her thanks.

When Dora had gone, he sank down into his chair and dabbed his face with a handkerchief. He had been so close to disaster! At the thought of Meg's duplicity, his lips curled ominously. She had stayed in London against his wishes and she deserved all that was coming to her.

*

After the surgery ended, Kitty took a newspaper in to Marion.

'I found it on one of the chairs, ma'am,' she told her. 'The *Daily News*, it is, and there's a bit about the murder. I thought you might like to see it.'

'Oh yes, I would.'

'"*Supposed* murder in Whitechapel",' Kitty read aloud. 'Not much of a "*supposed*" about it, if you ask me, ma'am – not with all those wounds. What do they think she did – fell on a bed of nails?'

Kitty had talked of nothing else since the murder was first reported and Marion did not want to encourage her to dwell even further on such a gory subject. She held out her hand and reluctantly the maid surrendered the paper, but she was not to be silenced so easily.

'The postman says they should offer a reward for information,' she told Marion. 'He says that everyone's up in arms because the police haven't tried hard enough to catch him. He says it's just like when that other one was killed back in April . . . Emma something, her name was. They pretended to care, but they didn't really.'

'Give them time,' said Marion. 'They can't work miracles. No doubt there will be an identity parade and if it wasn't the soldier, they may offer a reward.'

Kitty tossed her head. 'They won't care,' she declared, 'because she was poor. If she had been a rich lady, it would be different. The postman says that if it wasn't a soldier what done it, then it was one of those gangs that go round picking on people. He says –'

'Kitty!'

'Yes, ma'am?'

'You really should not take everything the postman says as gospel. I daresay he knows no more than the rest of us.'

Kitty's face settled into a sulky frown. 'I was only telling you what –'

'What he thinks! I realize that, but I'm sure there is something more useful you could be doing in the kitchen.'

Kitty hesitated and then departed in an indignant swirl of petticoats, leaving Marion to read the newspaper reports for herself.

Certainly the authorities did not appear particularly alarmed, and Marion suspected that there was more than a grain of truth in the postman's theory. A murdered whore was of little interest, but the police would obviously go through the motions of an investigation. The earlier murder which Kitty referred to had been committed in the same area, but the attacker had never been caught. Perhaps the postman was right and the full resources of the Police Force were not being mobilized.

Putting down the paper, Marion took up her sewing again. She was working a cushion cover in petit-point and usually found this soothing, but now the task gave her no real pleasure and her fingers moved mechanically, her thoughts divided equally between Dora's story about Meg and the recent murder. Surely there could be no connection; probably every prostitute in London imagined herself a potential victim, which was understandable. Yet Dora had been genuinely frightened on Meg's behalf; there was no doubt in Marion's mind on that score. She had hoped to speak to her again after she left the surgery, but Cook had delayed her in the kitchen and when she came out Dora had gone.

When Gilbert returned from his rounds, Marion mentioned that she had seen Dora Becket.

'Meg Swain's in trouble, Gilbert. I truly believe that,' she told him earnestly. 'According to Miss Becket, she's in fear of her life! Someone has been threatening her, and she wants to leave London because she thinks that whoever murdered Martha Tabram is going to murder her!'

Gilbert stood in front of the unlit fire, his hands clasped behind his back, his face impassive.

'It is all a pack of lies,' he declared. 'There is no truth in it whatsoever. If you had listened to me when I advised you to steer clear of that unfortunate family, you would not now be worrying yourself to no purpose.'

'Pack of lies?' cried Marion. 'Oh, but –'

'Oh, but nothing!' he said with barely veiled sarcasm. 'I just *happen* to be Miss Swain's doctor and I know a great deal more about her than you. I have always considered her feckless, but lately I have been forced to the conclusion that her mind is disordered. Sadly, the birth of the child has exaggerated the problem; she is now suffering from a severe form of delusions and is in need of medical help'.

Marion's dismay was increasing. 'Then little Lizzie,' she stammered. 'Is she safe with her mother?'

'We must hope so. I have made an appointment to see a specialist about Miss Swain –'

'But the baby?' Marion persisted, trying unsuccessfully to hide the extent of her anxiety. 'Perhaps someone should stay with them – maybe her cousin might be willing?'

'Her cousin has a living to earn,' Gilbert reminded her. 'The strike is over and she is back at her workbench.'

'But maybe if someone helped Meg financially . . .'

'*Someone?*' His voice was hard with suspicion.

Marion improvised quickly. 'Mrs Gaunt, perhaps?'

'Possibly she might be willing, but in fact it is impossible. Miss Swain refuses to remain anywhere for more than a day or two, because she insists that she must keep on the move to avoid being found by the murderer!'

'Poor soul! She must be terrified.'

'No doubt, but then we *know* that she is in no danger because she is imagining it all.'

'She is not imagining that the Tabram woman was murdered!' retorted Marion.

'She *is* imagining that she will be the next victim. Why should she be more at risk than any of the rest of her sort? The best thing for her is to go into an institution where she can be looked after, and as soon as I can arrange a place for her I shall set about finding her. Once and for all, Marion, please understand that this matter is nothing to do with you and you are not to interfere. Miss Becket is now fully aware of the true nature of her cousin's problem and there is nothing you can do to help. *Nothing*. You could even inadvertently make things worse.'

'And the child is quite safe, Gilbert? Are you sure of that?'

'Miss Swain is not violent, Marion; there is no reason to suppose that the child is in any danger whatsoever.'

Marion finished her sewing, folded it carefully and slipped it back into its bag. 'I do so hope you are right, Gilbert. The child is quite defenceless.'

'You seen determined to look on the dark side for some reason,' he said dourly. 'For goodness' sake, put the wretched woman out of your mind.'

Marion nodded unhappily, 'I will try,' she agreed, but although she said no more she was far from satisfied.

Later that night she lay awake, examining the problem from every angle and trying to decide whether or not this latest version of Meg Swain's story was true. Gilbert had been very convincing, but one thing bothered her. If he had suspected that Meg was deranged, why had he never said so before? It would explain so much that was puzzling. On the other hand, if Meg was not 'mad' – for want of a better word – then Gilbert was lying. If only she could find Meg Swain, she thought desperately.

But suppose Gilbert was right and she, Marion, somehow made things worse; then she would never forgive herself. She frowned up into the darkness, dizzy from her reeling thoughts. One fact was indisputable – there *was* a maniac at large. He had already killed once and he could strike again.

CHAPTER FOURTEEN

The Fosters finally came to dinner on Saturday August 11th when May was also present. By half-past ten Amelia was congratulating herself on the success of the occasion and feeling pleasantly elated. The meal had proved one of the best Cook had ever prepared, and it was quite obvious from the amount John Foster had eaten that he had enjoyed every mouthful. The Fosters had been better company than she had expected and Clarice looked charming in a dress of deep violet satin trimmed with chenille and decorated with black beads. Amelia felt sure that Ralph was impressed with their young visitor, for he had paid her a great deal of attention during the meal and Clarice appeared to find his company more than a little desirable. She felt a comforting glow of achievement as she, May, Mrs Foster and Clarice relaxed in the drawing room while waiting for the men to finish their port and cigars and rejoin them.

May and Clarice were discussing the murder and the lack of progress being made by the authorities to apprehend the man responsible. Four days had passed and there had been no real developments, although an identity parade had been held at the Tower of London for the benefit of another prostitute nicknamed 'Pearly Poll', who claimed to remember the face of Martha Tabram's soldier. However, she failed to identify him and a second parade at Wellington Barracks proved equally unsatisfactory, since here she picked out two men who both had unshakable alibis.

May sighed. 'I'm coming to the conclusion that the murderer will never be found,' she said. 'I do not believe the police are in full possession of all the available facts, and that is because no one wants to help them. After the riots last November in Trafalgar Square –'

'Bloody Sunday!' Clarice interposed.

May nodded. 'I'm afraid they fell out of favour after that sordid episode – and can you wonder at it? Two innocent people killed and countless injured. Now there are poor people who would rather see the murderer go free than give information to the police.'

'That's what Papa thinks,' said Clarice. 'He says that if they were to dismiss Charles Warren –'

'*Sir* Charles Warren!' Amelia amended, her tone caustic. 'They gave him a knighthood, remember, for his part in the dreadful affair! If they were to get rid of him, we might be a little nearer to discovering the truth. Until then, no one will come forward. They will close ranks and the police will get nowhere.'

May nodded and then patted her stomach with a delicate flutter of her fingers. 'I think I have dined a little too well, Amelia,' she confessed with a laugh. 'It really was quite delicious.'

Clarice agreed eagerly.

'The girl is very keen to please me,' thought Amelia with satisfaction. 'If she falls in love with my son – and I think she may – she will want my approval.'

Clarice had looked at Ralph more than once in that certain way and had hung on his words longer than was necessary. Yes, thought Amelia, the evening had been a success in every respect; she was confident of that. The girl would make Ralph a very suitable wife: pretty without being beautiful; intelligent without being intellectual and healthy without being horsey! Amelia did so dislike horsey women. They were always off hunting and never seemed to take the slightest interest in their children or husbands.

The parents, too, would be bearable, she reflected. John Foster had the right set of standards, at least so far as she could tell, and his wife was a meek little thing who would abide by any decision her husband cared to take. If they both approved of Ralph as a son-in-law – and God knows he was eligible enough! – then all that remained was for him to become disenchanted with his wretched Marion and enamoured of Clarice instead. The happy young couple would have no financial worries, and Amelia could wave them off to a sunny honeymoon in Biarritz and concentrate her energies once more on the school.

She was brought back from this rosy vision by May's voice, which was rising querulously.

'Amelia! You are miles away!' she complained. 'I was just telling Miss Foster about your sad little protégée – the one who died, the girl with the dreadful "phossy jaw". What was her name? She sold matches.'

'Ellie Swain.'

'Her sister came to Amelia,' May went on to Clarice, 'and asked her to give the girl a "proper" funeral with horses and mules. Can you imagine! The impudence of some of those people. They would ask for the moon if they thought they could get it!'

Meg Swain's forlorn image appeared suddenly to Amelia. 'It was a preposterous idea,' she said defensively, 'but I thought the poor child deserved a decent coffin.'

'You are too soft with them,' May scolded. 'Give them an inch and they take a yard.'

However, Clarice smiled at Amelia. 'Mama is soft-hearted too,' she said. 'When our parlourmaid got married she insisted that we gave them a wedding breakfast. We hired a room for them above The Hare and Hounds and provided ale and cider and a cold collation. Papa did not really approve, but he gave in gracefully. Now she has left to have a baby – the parlourmaid, I mean; her husband drives a hansom.'

'Are you fond of children?' Amelia asked.

The girl's eyes softened. 'Oh yes! I hope to have a

large family of my own some day. I think our beloved Queen has the right idea, don't you?'

But Mrs Foster was still thinking about her departed parlourmaid. Shrugging her thin shoulders, she said, 'That's the trouble with staff today; they all want to be married. You find a suitable young girl and train her, and just as she starts to be useful around the house she meets the man of her dreams and wants to leave. I don't recall my mother having any of these problems; our maids stayed all their lives, glad of a roof over their heads and food for their . . .' She hesitated.

'Bellies,' said Clarice mischievously.

'Stomachs,' her mother amended. 'Our cook stayed with us until she died, in her sixty-ninth year. Girls are not like that any more.'

'Servants have always been a problem,' agreed May, 'and they always will be. Janet is causing me great anxiety. I know she had a fall yesterday, but she will not admit it. She has a bump on her head like an egg, but insists that she tripped over. I suspect it was another of her turns.'

Amelia was more interested in Miss Foster and had no intention of discussing servants.

'So you want a large family, Miss Foster?' she went on. 'None of this new-fangled nonsense about limiting the number of children?'

'Certainly not!' Clarice was shocked at the very idea. 'I think we should have all the children God sees fit to send us.'

'But your education?' Amelia persisted. 'And your plans for the Civil Service. Would you be prepared to give up all that?'

The girl's eyes looked straight into hers. 'If the right man came along,' she said quietly.

Her mother said, 'Poor Clarice has had one disappointment and she is in no hurry to wed. We want a love match for her.'

'I want the same for my son,' said Amelia, adding, 'A *suitable* love match,' and this time she looked directly at Mrs Foster. As their eyes met there was an immediate understanding and Clarice, catching the glance, interpreted it correctly. If she and Ralph Gaunt ever wanted to marry, they would have their parents' heartfelt approval. Her heart leaped, for she was already a little in love with him and all she needed was some small encouragement. But she would allow herself no illusions; so far, no encouragement had been forthcoming.

*

It was after midnight when the Fosters left to drive home. May, who was staying for the weekend, promptly retired to her bedroom with a glass of warm milk and Ralph wandered back from the dining room with an orange in his hand.

'You are not still eating!' Amelia teased.

'I believe I am!' he countered, removing the peel and throwing it into the empty coal-scuttle. 'They really are a very pleasant family.'

'I thought it all went very well,' said Amelia.

She has the air, Ralph thought, of a cat who has had the cream.

'Oh, Mama!' he protested with a smile. 'You don't really mean that. You have always maintained that John Foster was a crashing bore – and of course he is.'

Amelia, regretting her earlier outspoken comments, sought to amend matters. 'I must confess that I did think so at one time,' she agreed, 'but he is one of those people who improve with further acquaintance. Tonight I actually enjoyed his company.'

Ralph offered her a section of orange, but she shook her head. 'You know I cannot eat oranges; they are too acid for my stomach.'

'Belly!' said Ralph and grinned, so that she knew at once he was thinking of Clarice.

'The girl is rather outspoken,' she said with a smile, 'but I must confess I found her charming. She has such poise for one so young; she is only eighteen, you know.'

'Really? As young as that?' He laughed. 'Hardly out of the nursery!'

He is being deliberately obtuse, Amelia thought.

'Nearer to nineteen, actually,' she went on. 'I find her quite charming.'

'So you have already said, Mama.'

'Don't you agree?'

He put his head on one side, considering. 'Yes,' he said at last. 'I daresay that sums her up, Mama: a charming young lady.'

'I'm so glad that you like her.'

Ralph finished the orange and wiped his fingers on his handkerchief.

'You did like her, Ralph, didn't you?' Amelia asked.

'Certainly I liked her.'

'John Foster has suggested that it is our turn to dine with them one evening.'

'How very kind of him.'

She looked at him sharply, but his innocent expression belied the slightly sarcastic tone of voice.

'You will come, Ralph, won't you?' He made no immediate answer and Amelia said sharply, 'It would be discourteous not to accompany me.'

He did not meet her eyes and once more she reflected that he was becoming very intractable.

'Ralph! Please answer my question.' When she looked at him, all the humour had left his face and there was something in his eyes that frightened her.

'Mama, it's no good, you know,' he told her.

For a moment she lost her poise. 'No good? What is no good?' she blustered. 'I don't understand what you are talking about. I merely said –' Collecting herself quickly, she stopped in mid-sentence.

Ralph said gently, 'Clarice Foster is a very sweet girl,

Mama, but she is not for me. I know exactly what you had hoped to achieve, but you must believe me when I tell you that it won't work. It would be cruel of me to pretend a fondness for the girl which I do not feel. You know that I am attached to someone else and of course you disapprove. I understand how you must see things, and I am truly sorry.'

'But she is *married*!' Amelia cried, abandoning all pretence. 'What hope is there for you with another man's wife?'

'I have no idea,' he said sadly.

Amelia glimpsed the depth of his despair, but she wanted what was best for him and a married woman could never make him happy.

'Then give her up!' she urged. 'Let her go, Ralph, before it's too late – for her sake as well as your own.'

'I wish I could, Mama,' he said quietly. 'I really wish I could – but you see I love her, and there never will be anyone else for me. If I cannot marry her, I shall never marry anyone. Of course that must sound very extravagant to you, but it is the truth. I *love* her, Mama.'

Amelia wondered frantically whether this was the time to confront her son with the news that she now knew the identity of his 'Marion', for she had confirmed her suspicions by calling at the doctor's house while Ralph was away. There she had asked for Mrs Reid and been told that she was away visiting her sister in *Kingston*.

Taking a quick look at her son's face, she decided against it. While their affair remained illicit there was always the slim chance that it would run its course, she argued; a passion could burn itself out. Once all was revealed, however, attitudes would harden, declarations would be made and irretrievable steps would be taken. No, she thought. She would keep that information to herself for the time being and do nothing to exacerbate the situation.

'Does she love you?' she asked.

He nodded and Amelia experienced a brief flash of

resentment towards the woman who was causing her son such anguish.

'She had no right to encourage you,' she said angrily.

'*I* made the running, Mama; she did her best to discourage me. She has more to lose than I have, remember; her good name, for one thing.'

'You should have had more sense!' she cried. 'Oh, Ralph, how could you be so foolish?'

He shrugged. 'It was just a game at the beginning,' he confessed. 'I can see now that I was amusing myself and had no intention of falling in love. She wanted me to stay away, but I wouldn't and then suddenly I couldn't. I realized that I was not pretending any more and I knew she was the only woman I would ever love.'

'But her husband, Ralph? Does he still love her? Does she feel nothing for him?'

'There's nothing left between them. It's a very empty marriage.'

'But her children! What of them?'

'They have no children.'

His tone forbade further enquiry along those lines and Amelia's spirits sank even lower. So if ever he did marry her they would be childless; she allowed herself a moment's self-pity. Her only son wanted to marry a woman who could give him no children and his mother no grandchildren. There would be a scandal and heartbreak – and all for nothing! And the school! What would become of her school when Ralph died without heirs? It was unthinkable.

'Well,' she said at last, 'I don't know what to say. For once in my life I am at a loss.'

Briefly he moved to put an arm round her shoulders. 'I am truly sorry, Mama. I know that it hurts you, but I want her more than anything in the world. If you knew her as I do, you would love her too.' He kissed her lightly and then turned and went out of the room, and she heard his footsteps ascending the stairs.

'No, Ralph!' she whispered. 'I will never love her. She

is ruining your life and I cannot allow it to happen.' If Ralph would not give Marion up, then *she* must be persuaded to end the relationship for his sake.

Suddenly she became aware that her legs were trembling. She ought to go up to bed, but she knew she would not be able to sleep. 'Damn you, Marion Reid!' she muttered and sat down heavily in the nearest chair.

Time passed but still Amelia sat on, upright and grim, a prey to unhappy thoughts. She had never felt truly helpless until now and she found the experience intolerable. It was not in her nature to sit back and passively await disaster; she must *do* something.

When at last she rose to her feet it was past two o'clock, but Amelia had made up her mind on a drastic course of action. She would go to Harrington Hill and make a personal appeal to Marion Reid.

*

The fifteenth day of August dawned clear and bright, promising to be hot. In London the street smells were already noticeable and Gilbert held a handkerchief to his nose until the cab had carried him out of the city. On the outskirts of the town the air was fresher and the traffic less dense, and by the time they reached Chalk Farm they were bowling along between green fields.

He was on his way to find Alf Berry who, according to his wife, should be gathering chickweed somewhere in the fields. She had been most insistent that once at Chalk Farm he could not fail to see them.

'There'll be a dozen or more,' she had told him, 'and all with baskets over their arms. It's free there, you see, so everyone goes there. Alf aims to get there around seven, because then he's got time to cut the rest of his stuff.' She had shown a natural curiosity about Gilbert's business with her husband, but had asked no direct questions and he had told her nothing. No doubt her husband would enlighten her later, he thought.

Gilbert had instructed the cabby to look out for men working in the fields and suddenly there was a shout and the horses slowed to a walk.

'Over there, guv!' cried the driver. 'Thirty or more, I'd say. They who you're looking for?'

'Most probably,' Gilbert told him. 'Take me to the nearest gate and drop me there, but don't go away. I shall not be long and then I have to get back to London pretty smartly.'

The man did as he was told and a few minutes later Gilbert was making his way across the grass towards the group of stooping men. A ground mist lay over the fields, but somewhere above him a skylark sang and briefly Gilbert paused to appreciate the serenity of his surroundings – but then, remembering his purpose, strode on. He discovered as he drew nearer that most of the men were elderly and those who were younger were in poor health. A pathetic section of humanity, he reflected, but that should make his task easier. For such as these, money was the ultimate incentive.

As he drew nearer, some of the men straightened their backs to stare at him in surprise and one or two greeted him civilly. Others watched him suspiciously, for he was 'one of them' and not to be trusted.

'I am looking for Alf Berry,' he announced.

One of the men jerked a thumb and another yelled, 'Alf! There's a gentleman here wants to speak to you!'

A thin figure straightened up and said cautiously, 'I'm here. Who wants me?'

Gilbert hurried towards him.

Alf's basket was half full of chickweed and also contained a small ball of string. Seeing Gilbert's apparent interest, he said eagerly, 'I make the chickweed into bundles, see; a dozen most mornings. I sell 'em for a halfpenny a bunch. Larks eat it. They love it. Larks and linnets, what folks keep in cages. That's all profit, that is. No overheads.'

'I see,' said Gilbert. Realizing that some of the men were taking an inordinate interest in their conversation, he decided they would have to move out of earshot, for what he had to say to Alf Berry was for his ears only.

'The groundsel I get free, too,' Alf went on, 'from a gentleman's garden. Very decent old stick, he is; says it saves him weeding! Lives down Battlebridge way.'

Gilbert took a firm hold of the man's elbow and Alf's nervousness increased. 'I don't pinch nothing,' he protested. 'It's all above board.'

'I'm sure it is,' said Gilbert. 'I want a quiet word with you, that's all.' And he began to steer Alf away from his fellows who now watched the two of them with deepening suspicion.

'Something to your advantage,' Gilbert added.

'My advantage?' cried Alf. 'Here, what's up?'

'How would you like to earn some money? Some *real* money?'

'I would, but how –'

'Then keep quiet and listen.' Gilbert lowered his voice and his fingers tightened on the man's thin arm.

'You're hurting me!' Alf protested, and Gilbert hastily released him.

'Do you know who I am?' he asked. 'Do you recognize me?'

'You're Meg's gentleman friend.'

'I'm Miss Swain's *doctor*.'

'Doctor, then,' Alf agreed.

'Did you know that she's gone into hiding?'

Alf nodded. 'There's someone after her, someone who's going to do her in, so she's got to –'

'That's nonsense. All in her mind,' Gilbert said firmly. 'She is suffering from delusions, she needs medical attention and she must be found. I would like you to help me to find her and I would pay you well.'

Alf's mouth had dropped open with surprise. 'You mean she's off her nut? Gawd lummy! Poor old Meg.'

'Yes, it's very sad. I have to find her so that we can take care of her and the baby. Do you understand?'

'Well, of course I do, but how would I know where to look for her? She could be anywhere. And if I'm searching for Meg, how do I find time to sell my stuff?'

'You won't need to, Mr Berry. All you have to do is go round to all her old haunts – anywhere she might be – until you find her.'

'And you'll pay me for doing that?'

'Naturally.'

'But my regulars. They rely on me, see.'

'Tell them you've been ill; they'll understand that.'

Alf hesitated. 'How much would it be?' he asked at last. 'I have to know 'cos I've got a family to feed.'

'How much do you earn with your chickweed?'

'A week, you mean? Well, now – let's think. There's the chickweed and the groundsel and a few turfs – not many, but a few.'

With the help of his fingers he arrived at a figure which satisfied him. 'I make about four or five bob a week, sir. Then there's the nettles; they're threepence a bunch, but they're not what you call regular. I get 'em if I'm asked, you see; if I've got a customer for them.'

'I'll double it,' said Gilbert. 'Ten shillings a week – but you have to spend all your time looking for Miss Swain.'

'Ten shillings a week? Strewth! I'll do it, sir.'

'Well done!'

Alf frowned. 'I'll need it daily though, sir, if you find that suitable. We've got to eat, you see, and buy a penn'orth of coal to boil the kettle.'

Gilbert brought out a handful of change and selected five shillings. 'That's half one week's payment in advance,' he said, 'and I'll give you the rest at the end of the week.' He dropped the coins into Alf's hand. 'And you are not to tell Miss Swain that anyone is looking for her. Just find her and then come straight to me and tell me where she is. If you try to cheat me, I'll have you thrown into jail before you can wink.'

'Cheat you?' cried Alf. 'How could I?'

'You might find her and keep her whereabouts to yourself so as to make the payments last longer!'

At once he regretted his comments because the man's face had flushed darkly. 'I never would do such a thing!' he gasped indignantly. 'If you think that of me, then you'd best find someone else to do the job.'

'No, no!' said Gilbert quickly. 'I see that I was wrong and I'm sorry.'

Mollified by this apology, Alf nodded slowly. 'I just come and tell you where she is?'

'Yes. I live at Number 68 Harrington Hill. Can you remember that?'

The man repeated the address to Gilbert's satisfaction and pocketed the money for fear another misunderstanding might rob him of his unexpected fortune.

'And I don't tell Meg?'

'Most definitely not.'

'Right, sir. I've got all that.' Alf touched the brim of his battered hat. 'And I'll do my best to find her for you.'

'In fact, I am not the only one who wants to find her,' Gilbert invented. 'It's Mrs Gaunt also. You remember her? She takes an interest in Miss Swain because of poor little Ellie.'

Alf looked relieved. 'Oh, her! The one what paid for her coffin? Oh, that was a lovely funeral! Never seen anything like it, leastways not for one of our sort. But then you must have heard all about it from your good lady?'

'Yes, I did.' Suddenly Gilbert was longing to get away. 'Now, remember all I have told you and good luck. Let us hope for Miss Swain's sake that you find her quickly.'

'I'll do my very best, sir. You can count on it.'

Gilbert returned to the cab with a lighter heart, for it seemed that his troubles might quickly be over. As soon as Alf found Meg, Gilbert would see to it that she and the wretched Lizzie would trouble him no more.

*

An hour or so later, Alf was sitting at the kitchen table trying to convince his wife that he had had no option but to accept the doctor's offer. The money, he pointed out, would come in very handy.

'Not to mention the extra rent we have to find now that Meg's run off. It's two weeks' money for only one week's work!'

'I know that,' Sally retorted, 'but say you find Meg tomorrow? Do you get to keep the five bob, or d'you have to give some of it back? And what if it takes you weeks to find her?'

'Then I go on getting ten bob a week! What's wrong with that?'

'Nothing – except that some time it's going to come to an end and then you'll have to go back to your groundsel and stuff – and where will your customers be by then?' She shook her head despondently. 'Buying from one of the others, that's where they'll be.'

'How can they?' he argued. 'The other men have beats of their own. No one does Clerkenwell and Russell Square except me. No one else does the Strand or Covent Garden either.'

'But they could take it all over while you're off playing detective.'

Alf prayed for patience. He had come home expecting congratulations for a tremendous piece of luck, and here was Sal picking holes in it. 'If anyone takes over my beat, I just take over theirs,' he told her. 'No one can do his own beat *and* mine; there's a limit to how many roads a man can cover in a day. There's plenty of roads for all, so don't you worry on that score, Sal. I know what I'm about.'

'Well, I certainly hope so!'

He picked up one of the shillings lying on the table between them and put it in his pocket. The other four he pushed towards her. 'Take 'em, love. Get something a bit special for our tea and buy a drop of extra milk for this one.' He fondled the downy head of the baby, who clung to his trouser-legs in an attempt to retain his balance.

'Another week and he'll be walking!' Sal said proudly. 'Real forward, he is – like his father!' she added, her face breaking into a smile. Suddenly she leaned forward and laid her hand over his. 'I'm sorry, love, fussing like that, but it was a bit of a shock, and I was scared, that's all.'

Relieved, he leaned forward and kissed her. 'I know,' he told her. 'I got to admit it give me quite a turn at first, but then I thought, "Ten bob's a lot of money!" You think I did right, then?'

'Course you did.'

She picked up the money, eyed it greedily for a moment and then slipped it into her pocket. 'Well then, Alf Berry, you'd better get along and earn it!' she told him. 'I've got the floor to wash over and you'll be under my feet.'

Minutes later Alf was standing outside on the pavement, thinking about Meg Swain and wondering where to start. He spent the next seven days combing the area without success, and was forced to report his failure to the doctor who made no attempt to hide his disappointment. However, he handed over the rest of the money plus a further five shillings' advance for the following week, and cutting short Alf's thanks told him brusquely to, 'Get on with it!'

Alf was beginning to think that Meg had heard of his enquiries and was somehow keeping one jump ahead of him. If not, he reasoned, then she might have left the area altogether. His search had been as thorough as he could make it, but no one seemed to know where she was or even where she had been. He had asked all her erstwhile friends for news of her, but had drawn a blank; they were sorry to hear that she had lost her wits and promised to look out for her, but no one could help him any further. He had visited all the public houses within a five-mile radius with no results. Shopkeepers had not served her recently, nor had the street sellers. He made the rounds of the common lodging-houses, but they had no record of her unless – as one manager suggested – she was using a false name, and in the circumstances this seemed very probable.

Alf spent hours tramping through unsavoury alleyways and courts, discovering many sleazy corners whose exist-ence he had never suspected, and with great temerity he ventured into areas which few policemen dared enter alone. More than once he was evicted with threats of violence if he should dare to show his face there again.

By the end of the second week he was convinced that he would never find Meg. Whoever had killed Martha Tab-ram, he argued, might well have killed her too. He put this theory to the doctor, but he refused to consider it and sent Alf off to widen his search and redouble his efforts.

'She is out there somewhere,' he insisted, 'and your job is to find her for me.'

*

Half-way down the garden at the rear of 68 Harrington Hill a small zinc bath stood in the middle of the lawn, half filled with warm soapy water. Beside it two large china jugs held the rinsing water as Pip, with her ears well back, crouched beneath a large azalea bush. Marion advanced relentlessly towards her and finally swooped on the little dog, who began to quiver with apprehension.

'Don't be silly,' Marion told her. 'No one's going to hurt you. Anyone would think you had never had a bath before. You always survive it, and when it's all over Mrs Cobbett gives you a lovely big bone.'

These reassurances had no effect, however, and when Marion finally succeeded in lowering Pip into the water she was positively shivering with fright.

'Now that's not so bad, is it?' Marion comforted as she gently scooped soapy water over the small, drooping body. 'You do want to be a smart dog, don't you?'

Pip was entirely unmoved by this last appeal and, suddenly deciding she had suffered enough indignity, made a sudden lunge forward and upwards and somehow scrambled out of the bath, sending a shower of soapy water over her tormentor. Dripping water and impervious to Marion's shouts, she headed straight for the back door and disappeared inside the kitchen.

As Marion struggled to her feet and set off in pursuit, Kitty appeared at the door, shooing the dripping and disconsolate dog ahead of her.

'All over the clean floor!' she announced, her tone disgruntled.

'Someone must have opened the back door,' Marion told her. 'I know I shut it. Oh, Pip! Come here, you silly dog. You are only prolonging the agony.'

Once more she scooped up the spaniel and had just replaced her in the soapy water when Mrs Cobbett appeared behind Kitty.

'There's a Mrs Gaunt to see you, ma'am,' she announced. 'She's in the morning room.'

Marion's good humour vanished as a brief panic seized her. Struggling to hold Pip, she asked hopefully, 'Are you sure it is not the doctor she wants to speak to?'

'No, ma'am. She asked for you.'

Marion swallowed. 'Please tell her that I'm busy with the dog but I'll join her as soon as I can. And offer her a tray of tea, will you?'

'Yes, ma'am.'

As Kitty retreated, Marion's heart began to thump uncomfortably, and while she washed the dog she tried frantically to imagine what Ralph's mother could possibly want with her — unless it was to talk about Ralph! Anxiety made her clumsy and some of the rinsing water found its way into Pip's eyes, causing the affronted dog to give a startled yelp and leap out of the bath once more.

'Pip! You bad girl! Oh, come back *here*.'

Following her to the azalea where she had again sought refuge and pulling her clear of the bush, Marion began to towel her dry. Unintentionally, she was rougher than usual and Pip turned large, reproachful eyes on her harassed mistress so that at once Marion was full of compunction.

'Oh darling, I'm so sorry!' she cried. 'It's just that — oh, Pip!'

Hugging her, she reminded the dog of the promised bone and at the magic word Pip's gloom disappeared; her tail began to wag and a few minutes later she was towelled dry and rolling in the grass.

Marion flew into the kitchen and on the way through asked Kitty to empty the bath of water on to the flower-bed and give Pip the promised bone. Then she hurried up to her bedroom to tidy her hair, remove splashes of soapy water and prepare herself for the confrontation which she now guessed was inevitable. Before going downstairs, she took a panic-stricken look at her reflection to see how Mrs Gaunt would see her. Large frightened eyes looked back at her.

'This is ridiculous!' she told herself. 'I'm a grown woman and she can't *eat* me!'

But this fact did nothing to reduce her apprehension and she finally went into the morning room with a sinking feeling in the pit of her stomach. Mrs Gaunt was standing by the window, but she turned towards Marion with a face set in stern lines.

'Mrs Reid, I know all about your relationship with my son,' she told Marion without preamble, 'and I have come to ask you to give him up.'

Shocked by this terrifying bluntness, Marion could

only stare at the older woman while her mind strove to come to terms with the suddenness of the attack. At last she asked faintly, 'Does Ralph know you are here?'

'No, he does not.'

Marion could only shake her head as the colour drained from her face. Seeing this, Mrs Gaunt went on, 'I am sorry, but I see no point in beating about the bush since we both understand the situation. My son is in love with you – oh yes, I accept that he is. No doubt you believe you love him too?'

At least Marion found her voice. 'I do love him.'

'But you are a married woman.'

Marion could only nod.

Mrs Gaunt's composure faltered. 'You must see the harm you would do to my son, Mrs Reid, not to mention the damage you would do to your husband. The doctor's reputation is of no consequence to me, but I cannot and will not stand by and let you ruin my son's life.'

With an effort, Marion marshalled her wits. 'I can see that is how it must appear to you,' she said, 'but I have no such intention.'

'You are not a suitable person for him,' Mrs Gaunt told her. 'He should marry a younger, single girl. There is one who could make him a very good wife, and if it were not for his obsession with you, I believe he could be very happy with her. That is what he needs, and that is what I want for him.'

'You mean Clarice Foster, of course?'

Mrs Gaunt raised her eyebrows. 'You know her?'

'As soon as you introduced her to Ralph, we guessed your intention.'

'I see.' Her expression revealed little of her thoughts, but Marion could guess that she was not pleased. Her thin mouth tightened. 'If you really do love him,' she continued, 'you will release him from this impossible relationship. I don't have to tell you, Mrs Reid, that if I were to tell your husband of your –'

338

These words brought Marion's head up sharply. 'Please do not try to threaten me!' she said evenly. 'You will never *frighten* me away from Ralph.'

For a long moment both women were silent, while Marion thought, 'They are so alike, mother and son.' If only she and Amelia Gaunt had met under different circumstances, they might have been friends. Even now Marion felt no real animosity towards the older woman. 'In her place,' she thought, 'I would probably do the same.'

Mrs Gaunt changed her line of attack slightly. 'You have a duty to your husband, Mrs Reid; you took certain vows before God. Do they mean so little to you now?'

Marion took a deep breath as she tried to steady her voice. It would never do to break down in front of this austere woman, for she could expect no sympathy.

'I thought I loved him once,' she said, 'but there are certain difficulties . . . that is, there are reasons why –'

Mrs Gaunt held up a peremptory hand. 'Please!' she said. 'I have no wish to hear whatever you are about to say. Show me a marriage *without* its problems. My own was not entirely trouble-free, but I never for one moment considered admitting failure or looking elsewhere for comfort. There is always something that can be done to help a marriage if both partners are *committed* to saving it. Perhaps you should reconsider your relationship?'

'You cannot possibly understand my situation,' Marion told her, 'and certainly I do not intend to discuss it with you.'

'Have you tried prayer?'

'If God has heard mine, he has not seen fit to answer them,' Marion said with more than a trace of bitterness.

'So after one unsuccessful relationship, you intend to embark on another which you must see cannot possibly succeed.'

Marion shook her head helplessly. 'I only know that I love your son dearly and he loves me. In other circumstances we could be happy together.'

'I think not,' Mrs Gaunt snapped. 'Oh, you might run away together and be blissfully happy for a month or so, but after a year or two you would look back and see that I was right. But by then it would be too late; the harm would be done, the damage to my son's reputation irreversible. I have come to ask you to give him up because I don't think he will ever give *you* up. He is young and impetuous, but you are older and should be wiser, and somehow you will have to find the courage to tell him it is over. Tell him that you were mistaken, and you have decided to stay with your husband and give your marriage another chance.'

Marion's face paled and she burst out, 'Mrs Gaunt! You cannot know how much you are asking! You cannot expect me to *lie* to him. I can't do it!'

Mrs Gaunt's expression softened and briefly Marion saw a kind of compassion . . . then it was gone. 'You will do it if you really love him,' she said firmly. 'You will do it for *his* sake.'

Marion stared at her in horror as a terrible despair swept through her. 'You can't expect . . .' she whispered. 'No, I won't do it! I cannot give him up.'

The older woman's eyes were unrelenting. 'You can, Mrs Reid. Forget yourself for once. Put aside your own selfish feelings and do this for Ralph!'

Before Marion could answer she had left the room, and a moment later the front door closed quietly behind her.

CHAPTER FIFTEEN

Wednesday 17th August

My dear Rachel,

I simply have to write to you – I am in such a sorry state. Although I know you cannot help me, I need to talk to you and a letter is the next best thing.

I had a visit from Ralph's mother yesterday and she did not mince her words. I felt utterly worthless when she had gone, yet I am not guilty of anything more terrible than loving her son. The trouble is that I am so afraid she might be right. She has asked me outright to give him up and has almost convinced me that I will ruin his life if I do not do so.

I have not told him of her visit because . . . well, to be truthful, I cannot say why I haven't written to him except that I feel somehow diminished by her visit. Before she came I truly thought I alone had the power to make him happy. Now I begin to doubt it. I tell myself that this is probably what she had hoped to achieve, but in my heart I know she has Ralph's best interests in mind – and how can I blame her for that? We both love him in our different ways.

Ralph and I have met twice since we were with you, but on a third occasion he did not meet me at the arranged time, so I assume he was somehow delayed by his mother who no doubt suspects a rendezvous with me every time he leaves the house and is determined to keep us apart. Young Clarice, whom she produced like a rabbit from a hat, is eminently suitable for him. It is so transparent that it would be funny if it were not so terribly sad.

Poor Rachel. What do I expect you or anybody else to do about it? I have to work it out for myself, but at the moment the thought of losing Ralph breaks my heart and I can hardly bear to contemplate such a loss. My whole world revolves round him. Mrs Gaunt tried to persuade me that my best hope lay in resurrecting my marriage, but I could not tell her just how impossible that is. Gilbert is withdrawing from me more and more with each day that passes. Something is preying on his mind which absorbs him totally, so that I can scarcely get a civil answer from him. The day before yesterday he left the house *before seven* in the morning and refused to say where he was going. I feel as though I am living on the edge of a precipice, and at any moment something or someone will send me tumbling over.

Please do not answer this in case your letter falls into Gilbert's hands. I know you will forgive me for burdening you with my problems. How I wish I had never married him, but 'if wishes were horses beggars would ride'!

Please write to me in your own good time – one of your cheerful letters. I never feel quite so alone when I read them. Goodbye for now.

Your loving sister,
Marion

P.S. Pip sends her love. I bathed her and she looks very handsome.

*

A crowd had formed in the gloomy court and Meg stood at the edge of it trying to pick out a likely customer. She was aware of her bedraggled appearance and this she knew would reduce the price she could ask. With Lizzie in her arms, she pushed a way through the outer ring of men who were peering over the heads of those in front. Right in the middle of the group the men crouched or knelt on the ground, their eyes fixed steadfastly on the turn of the cards scattered on the pavement amongst the coins being wagered. There was a suppressed excitement in the air; conversation was kept to a minimum and voices were hushed to avoid attracting the attention of any curious police constable who might take it into his head to stray from his allotted beat.

'Who you shoving?'

A burly man in a loose canvas jacket glared belligerently at Meg, who gave him a bright smile in return and said, 'Sorry, *sir!*'

His face was unshaven and his eyes were bloodshot, but he was little the worse for drink and she thought he might still have some of his wages about him.

'Just watch out!' he growled and turned quickly back as a murmur went up from the crowd. One of the gamblers had lost his last shilling and was forced to retire from the game.

Meg said, 'You a betting man, then? You look as though you know what's what.'

He shook his head, but before he could speak a stir ran through the crowd as one of the players found his luck turning.

'A quid!'

'He made a bloody quid!'

'I would be a betting man,' the burly man answered, 'if I had the money.'

Meg's mouth dropped. 'You're not skint, are you?'

'Not so as you'd notice!'

He laughed, but then patted his bulging coat pocket. 'I'll pick up a bit more tomorrow,' he told her carelessly. 'Who cares? I'm set up for tonight.'

'How d'you mean – set up?'

Already she had lost interest in him, mentally writing him off as her eyes searched the crowd for a more likely prospect. Where was the man who had won the quid, she wondered. He'd be first rate as long as he wasn't

343

married. If he was, he would hardly bother with the likes of her but would spend his money on gin or beer.

'Got my supper. Nice bit of boiled ham.'

At the mention of food Meg turned back to him. Ham! She hadn't eaten all day.

'How d'you get it?' she asked him.

'Nicked it off a window-sill, easy as blinking. Stuck on a plate, cooling. I mean if people are stupid enough to tempt other folks they deserve all they get, that's what I reckon.'

He was beginning to take more interest in her, Meg realized, and she had to make a quick decision. Should she wait for something better or settle for the ham? She fluttered her eyelashes provocatively. 'My old man,' she invented, 'always liked to follow his grub with a bit of "how's your fancy"! Right keen he was.'

'Was? Where is he now?'

Meg jerked a thumb skyward. 'Chest,' she said. 'Coughed himself into an early grave, God rest his soul. Runs in the family. I should have guessed. His Ma and Pa went the same way and neither of them a day over thirty.' She saw the interest in his eyes and added, 'So I have to make a bit where I can – you know what I mean? I got little Lizzie to think about.'

In the gloom he saw only the blonde curls and trim figure. 'I told you, I'm skint,' he said regretfully.

'But I'm starving,' she told him. 'How about a quick one for a bit of grub?'

'You're on!'

'I've got no place,' she said. 'Have you?'

He nodded. 'Come on.'

On the way she told him that her name was Millie Carter. His, it appeared, was Duggie Drake.

'I'm a lumper,' he told her. 'I unload stuff from boats. Not much of a living, but I can pinch a fair bit. Get rid of it ashore at the marine stores – they don't ask questions. As long as they get it cheap enough, that's all they care about.'

In spite of the liquor he had consumed, he walked quickly with a loping stride so that Meg was forced to run alongside him as he led her through the network of dismal streets in the direction of the river.

He held open his jacket. 'See? Nice deep hems,' he grimmed. 'Hides a multitude of sins, as they say. You never heard that? I like it – a *multitude* of sins.' He rolled the words on his tongue, savouring them. 'Like one big pocket, this hem is. Tobacco, too. I smuggle that ashore for the crew.'

Meg was not really listening. 'Here, slow down a bit, can't you?' she said. 'I'm fair winded, what with carrying Lizzie an' all!'

Obligingly, he slowed his pace, but he went on talking. 'They bring it over, see, the crews do, but they can't get it ashore so easy. Me and my mates do that. You'd be surprised how flat you can squeeze tobacco. I just slip it into the hem and Bob's your uncle!'

'Fanny's your aunt!' said Meg.

'What?'

'Oh, nothing.'

They ended up at a deserted warehouse where Duggie climbed in at a broken window. Meg handed over the baby and followed him across the sill with some difficulty, scraping her shin in the process and swearing under her breath.

Upstairs, in a corner that smelt of stale beer and damp straw, Duggie had made his 'home'. Fumbling in the darkness, he found and lit a candle stub and in its feeble light Meg glanced round without enthusiasm. She opened her mouth to make an adverse comment, but remembered the ham and changed her mind.

'Is it just ham?' she asked. 'Got any bread to go with it?'

'No, I haven't,' he retorted, 'so don't go getting any big ideas. You said you'd do it for a share of the ham, and that's all you'll get.'

'Suits me then,' she said quickly. 'I was only asking.'

When she had provided a makeshift bed for Lizzie, Meg prepared to earn her supper, but fate was kind. Duggie, it seemed, had drunk a little too much. After an heroic attempt, he finally admitted defeat with surprisingly good grace – assuring her that he never had seen what other men raved about in 'the whole stupid palaver' – and settled down to divide up the boiled ham.

When it was all eaten and the time came for Meg to move out again, she pointed out that she had no money for even the cheapest lodging-house and asked him if she could stay until morning. He agreed cheerfully and together they curled up on the straw which served as a bed and pulled the one threadbare blanket over them.

Next morning he rose early to go to work while Meg was still stuggling to clear the cobwebs of sleep.

'That kid of yours,' he said. 'Good little nipper – never a sound from her all night! I nearly had a kid once. Got this girl into trouble, so I thought why not? Her and me, I mean, and the kid.' He shrugged. 'They both died when it was born, so that was that. I really missed her.'

Meg said, 'That was rotten luck. Poor old Duggie.' She held her breath, seeing the way his mind was working.

'A man gets lonely,' he went on.

Meg smoothed her clothes, picking out the stray pieces of straw. 'A woman, too,' she told him.

He moved towards the top of the steps and then paused nervously. 'You don't have to go,' he said. 'Hang about a bit. I'll be back later.'

All Meg's faith in human nature returned with a rush as she looked at him. In daylight she could see more clearly the slack mouth and childlike eyes. His eyes were short and his long arms dangled at his sides, while from his head dark hair stuck out in all directions. 'Not up to much,' thought Meg, 'but there's no malice in him.'

'Maybe I'll stay around for a day or two,' she told him with a bright smile. 'See how things go, eh?'

He nodded, grinned and was gone, clattering noisily down the wooden stairs and whistling loudly.

Meg looked down at Lizzie, who gurgled happily in her corner. 'Well!' she said. 'There's a turn-up for the books if ever I saw one. Things are looking up for us, Lizzie my love. Things are definitely looking up.'

*

Four days later Alf stopped to speak to a group of men who were unloading bales of cloth from a small boat moored beneath Waterloo Bridge. He asked if anyone had seen a woman called Meg Swain, but no one had.

'She's got a baby,' he added. 'Name of Lizzie.'

Slowly one of the men turned to him. 'What if I have seen her?' he asked suspiciously. 'Who wants to know?'

The man was twice his size and Alf wanted no trouble. He hesitated. 'A friend's looking for her,' he said at last. 'Seems they're worried about her because she had to move out when she couldn't pay the rent. Her Pa and Ma's worried sick.'

The man frowned. 'You said a *friend*.'

'Well . . . they asked a friend to look out for her, and he asked me to help.'

'Fair hair? Curly?'

Alf nodded, not sure whether to be pleased or sorry if this meant that his search was at an end. He would earn no more money, but at least Meg would be safe in the hands of the doctors.

The man looked confused. 'What name did you say?'

'Meg Swain. Well, I suppose it's Margaret Swain, but everyone –'

'About twenty, would you say?'

'Yes. You've seen her, then?' he asked eagerly.

The big man shook his head. 'I never said that,' he protested. 'I never said no such thing.'

One of the other men added. 'So sod off. We don't like snoopers.'

Nervously Alf stood his ground. 'But surely,' he began, 'if her Ma and Pa . . .' but now the burly man jerked a thumb.

'You heard what the man said. 'Op it!'

Swallowing, Alf decided that discretion was quite definitely the better part of valour. 'All right,' he said, holding up a hand to ward off further threats. 'I'm going.'

And he went on his way rejoicing, for he was not deceived. He knew that the burly man had seen Meg and all Alf had to do now was follow him. The doctor's faith in him had been justified after all, and one day poor Meg would thank him for his part in her recovery.

*

In Springfield Park on the morning of the twenty-second of August, Marion waited for Ralph with a heavy heart. Pip, retrieving a stick, was puzzled by her mistress's lack of enthusiasm, so she was delighted suddenly to recognize another admirer approaching along the path. She bounded forward to greet him and Ralph bent to pat her before moving on to where Marion sat waiting for him. She stood up as he drew nearer and Ralph's heart contracted with anxiety when he saw the expression on her face. As his arms went round her she whispered, 'Oh, Ralph! Oh, my dearest!'

'Is it Gilbert?' he asked. 'Does he know about us? Something has happened, I know it.'

For a moment she clung to him, unable to answer, then she drew back a little and her hands went up nervously to straighten her hat. Pip jumped around them barking hopefully but then, her pleas to be noticed being largely ignored, she trotted away to investigate an approaching poodle accompanied by a nanny wheeling a pram.

'What is it, Marion?' Ralph repeated, disconcerted by the agony so evident in her eyes.

When she made no answer, he indicated the seat. 'Shall we sit here?' he suggested. 'Or would you like to stroll?' But Marion gazed at him, unable to speak for the terrible ache in her heart.

There was a sudden frenzied yelping as the black poodle turned on Pip, snapping furiously, while the startled nanny struck out at both dogs in an attempt to separate them.

Ralph ran up, retrieved Pip and brought her back to her mistress, who gave her only a cursory glance.

'She's not hurt,' Ralph said reassuringly. 'Give me her lead and we'll keep her with us.'

Marion had prepared a speech, but now that the moment had arrived this deserted her and she stammered abruptly, 'We can't go on, Ralph. This has to stop.'

He was crouching beside the dog, fastening on her lead, but she heard his swift intake of breath before he stood up again. Then he said evenly, 'We'll stroll. Give me your arm.'

'I mean it,' she insisted and he noticed the tell-tale quiver in her voice. 'There's no future for us, Ralph, and the longer we go on meeting the harder it will be to part. I have thought it all out and made up my mind.'

They were walking slowly and had gone a hundred yards or more before he could trust himself to answer. 'But I have decided no such thing,' he told her, trying to keep his voice steady. 'I shall never agree to stop seeing you, and I shall never give you up.'

'I knew you would say that,' she responded, 'but you know in your heart that I am right. You realize that we can never mean anything more to each other than a few stolen meetings. I know you are free, but I have a husband and I have to be strong for both of us. I have to end it, Ralph. I *must*.'

He stopped abruptly and pulled her round to face him. 'Then tell me you no longer love me,' he challenged. 'I will agree that we must part when I hear those words.'

She could not say them. 'Ralph, I have never pretended I don't love you,' she stammered, 'but I am married and that's where my duty lies. I don't love Gilbert, but I should and the fault is mine. I made certain vows and I am bound by them.'

He looked at her suspiciously. 'That sounded like my mother!' he exclaimed. 'My God! Is that it? Has she been talking to you?'

'No, Ralph!'

The lie was unconvincing and he shook her arm roughly. 'Marion, I want the truth! Has my mother persuaded you, *bullied* you into this change of heart? Because if so . . .'

Unwilling to cause trouble between mother and son, Marion hastily tried to undo the damage. 'It was not your mother,' she insisted. 'I have known all along that there was no future for us. I suppose I just wanted to snatch a few hours of happiness and that was very selfish. You are young and you have your own life to lead. I cannot share it with you, even though nothing would give me greater happiness.'

'You can get a divorce,' he insisted. 'At least *try*.'

She shook her head. 'On what grounds? Oh, do please be reasonable, Ralph. I've told you before that I can't divorce Gilbert, and he certainly won't divorce me. I'm afraid that's out of the question; there's no point in pretending.'

They began to walk on, silent and defeated.

'I shall wait for you, then,' said Ralph. 'Gilbert is older than I am. He will die before me and then you will be free and there will be no barrier to our marriage.'

'But that might be another twenty years!' Marion cried. 'I love you too much to allow you to waste your life in such a way. Gilbert might live another *thirty* years. It's quite impossible. Oh, don't think I don't appreciate your loyalty and your devotion. I do, and I'm touched and flattered. But, my dearest Ralph, I cannot let you do it.'

'You can't prevent me from waiting for you,' he said with a painful attempt at a smile. 'I could camp out on your front steps and become a permanent feature; part of the scenery!'

Marion managed the ghost of a smile. 'I would have you moved on by a constable!' she told him.

He came to a halt and faced her once more. 'I love you, Marion, and you love me, and there *has* to be a way for us. No, don't shake your head like that. I shall think of something. I promise.'

She shook her head. 'No, Ralph. There's no way we can be together. Do you think I haven't considered every possibility? I want it as much as you do, but people cannot always have what they want and we can never be man and wife. I have made up my mind and I won't change it, Ralph. In time you will get over it.'

'If you think that, then you don't know me at all!'

'Please, Ralph,' she begged. 'Agree for my sake. If our relationship ever became public knowledge, it is I who would suffer most.'

'So you are worrying about your good name,' he said bitterly.

'Without you, it is all I have!' she replied. 'Oh, my dearest, please don't let us spoil our last hour together. It will be –'

'Our last hour?' His shocked eyes reflected his misery.

She nodded. 'This must be the last time we meet. I am quite determined on that, for both our sakes.'

Terrified by her purposeful manner, he whispered, 'You cannot stop me from writing to you!'

'I can return your letters unopened. Oh, *please!*' she burst out. 'Don't make it so hard for me!'

He caught hold of her abruptly and his fingers dug deep into her arms. 'Then don't say it, Marion!' he cried. 'Don't say that we must part.'

'Ralph, I must. Your mother –' She broke off, but too late.

His eyes hardened. 'So she *has* put you up to this! Tell me the truth, Marion. I have a right to know.'

'She only told me what I knew already,' Marion exclaimed, mortified by her slip.

Helplessly he raised a clenched fist, then lowered it. 'She has no *right* to interfere,' he cried. 'It's absolutely monstrous. Anyone would think I was a child instead of a twenty-five-year-old man. And what does she know about how I feel? How dare she judge us!'

'She only wants what's best for you, Ralph!' Marion protested. 'That's only natural and you mustn't blame her. I should have reached the same decision without her.'

'No, you wouldn't. Never! I don't believe you. I can see it all now. Oh, this is unforgivable!'

She could see now that anger was mixed with his unhappiness and wondered if that would be easier to bear.

He regarded her stonily. 'So you and my mother have decided between you that my feelings are of no account.'

'Ralph! It's not like that! Oh, for God's sake try to see –'

'What is there to see?' he demanded. 'My mother has solved all our problems by persuading you to release me from this unsuitable affair – to marry me off to Clarice, no doubt. Is that right, or isn't it?'

'No, it is not. I would have –'

'I had no idea my mother had so much power,' he told her furiously. '*She* decides we are not suited and that is the end of it.' His mouth tightened. 'So be it, then. If that's what you really want.'

To her dismay, he turned and began to walk quickly away and after a moment's hesitation she started to run after him, calling his name. 'Don't go like this,' she begged. 'Can't we please part as friends?'

When he turned his face was haggard.

'For God's sake, Marion! You are turning me away

and you want it to be *pleasant*? You are breaking my heart, ruining my life, but you want me to *forgive* you? Is that it? You want me to say that I agree so as to make it easy for you and that damned mother of mine. Well, you can go to hell, the pair of you!'

Marion watched him go in shocked disbelief, her own grief magnified by the abruptness of his departure. To part without a kind word! It hurt so much that she put a hand to her heart as though it might literally break. Anguished tears pressed behind her eyes, but she would not surrender to them; she dare not – not now, not ever. Gilbert would recognize the tell-tale signs and ask unanswerable questions.

She stood stock-still until Ralph was out of sight and then, stunned by the suddenness of her loss, she gathered Pip into her arms and clung to her, grateful for the warmth of the small body and the frantic display of affection.

'Oh, Pip!' she whispered. 'I had to do it, for his sake.' For a moment the large brown eyes regarded her lovingly, but then the dog wriggled and Marion put her down and straightened up.

'I must not break down,' she told herself severely. 'I must not think about him. I must keep busy. Somehow I must endure the rest of the day.'

But as she stumbled homeward she faced the bleak knowledge that somehow she must endure the rest of her life.

*

Amelia had spent the morning at the new school inspecting the interior decorations which had just been completed. All the walls and ceilings had received several coats of whitewash; the windows and doors had been painted; a floor covering had been laid upstairs and several coats of wax had been applied to the wooden floors downstairs. The furniture had been ordered and would be delivered at the end of the week, and crockery, cutlery and linen had all been purchased. On the following morning she would be interviewing the last three girls who had applied for the position of housemaid, while in the afternoon the cook, who had already been appointed, was to be consulted about the major cooking utensils still to be acquired.

Real progress was being made and for the first time Amelia felt hopeful that the opening of the school on October the first would now go ahead as planned. To date, six places at the school had been allocated:

Annie Cobbs, 6 years, 2 months – an orphan.

May Jenner, 5 years, 6 months – mother in prison.

Alice Bray, 8 years exactly – mother dead, father
$\qquad$ habitual drunkard.

Emmie Loosely, 9 years, 11 months – mother prosti-
$\qquad$ tute, father un-
$\qquad$ known.

Agnes Loosely, 6 years, 1 month – as above.

Jane Tibbett, 4 years, 9 months – father dead, seven
$\qquad$ other children in
$\qquad$ family.

Applications for the remaining four places were still coming in.

Amelia found it all most satisfactory and was in a cheerful mood as she waited at the front door for Lucy to let her in.

As soon as she saw the maid's face, however, she felt a shiver of apprehension.

'What is it, Lucy?'

'Please, ma'am – I'm that sorry, ma'am – but Cook says I'm to tell you Mr Ralph's gone away in a dreadful hurry and he says he's not coming back!'

Amelia gasped and put out a hand to the wall to steady herself. 'Not coming back?' she echoed. 'What do you mean? Whatever are you saying, girl?'

'It's the truth, ma'am,' Lucy told her unhappily. 'He came in round about midday and ran straight up the stairs two at a time. Cook sent me up to find out if he wanted a tray of tea, and he said he didn't want anything from this house – not ever again! Those were his exact words.'

She paused as Amelia sank down on to the nearest chair, one trembling hand held to her forehead. 'Go on!' she whispered.

'So I said what about lunch, and he told me to go to hell! He was throwing his clothes into a bag and I asked him if he was going on holiday or something and he said no, he was going away for good.' Stopping to draw breath, she noticed her pale her mistress had become. 'Should I fetch your smelling salts, ma'am?'

Amelia nodded, but then said, 'Not yet.'

Ralph had gone. Her son had gone. A terrible coldness seized her. She would never see him again. 'Did he say where he was going? she asked.

'No, ma'am.'

'Did he say if he would be travelling alone?'

She closed her eyes as she waited for the girl's answer. He had run away with Marion Reid! Her heart banged wildly against her ribs, missed a beat and began to hammer away again with a new and frightening intensity.

'No, ma'am. He didn't say.'

Amelia opened her eyes. 'Well, go on!' she cried. 'I want you to tell me everything.'

'There's nothing more to tell, ma'am,' said Lucy. 'I ran down to tell Cook, and while I was in the kitchen we heard his bedroom door slam and then we heard him running down the stairs. I rushed along the passage and he was just opening the front door. I called out to him to wait, but he took no notice – just went out slamming the door behind him.'

'I see.' Her own voice frightened her.

Lucy watched her anxiously. Everyone knew how she doted on her son. Cook had said the shock would kill her and then they'd all be out of a job!

'Should I fetch your salts now?' she suggested.

Amelia gave a slight nod and while Lucy ran upstairs, she tried to collect her thoughts. Her son was gone! He had left without a word. No note. Nothing. It *must* be connected with Marion Reid. Either they had run away together or she had told him the friendship was at an end and he had taken it badly. Yes, that was the most likely. Presumably he had learned of her own part in Marion's decision. But where had he gone? And would he *ever* come back? 'Oh, God!' she whispered. 'Oh, *please* God –' He had never behaved in this way before; it was so out of character that even now she could hardly believe it.

'Here you are, ma'am.'

Lucy handed her the bottle and, removing the stopper, Amelia held it to her nose and took a slow, deep breath. The fumes revived her at once, and as she returned the salts to Lucy Cook appeared at the end of the passage, approaching rather warily as though somehow fearing that the blame for the disaster would be laid at her door. She stood in front of Amelia, wringing her hands anxiously.

'I'm very sorry, ma'am,' she said, 'about Master Ralph. We didn't know what to do; couldn't think how to stop him.'

Amelia could not trust herself to speak. She tried to tell herself that it was impossible that Ralph had gone for good. He was angry or upset now, but later on he would come to his sensès and return home. Yes, surely he would come back before the day was over. She imagined his bed remaining empty all night, and the prospect terrified her.

She was aware that Lucy and Cook were expecting some kind of explanation and perhaps reassurance. 'Mr Ralph has had some bad news,' she said shakily. 'I'm sure he will be home later, but young men can be very hasty.'

Cook appeared unconvinced. 'I hope he won't do anything rash, ma'am,' she said. 'Lucy said his expression was terrible.'

Amelia's face was suddenly drained of all its colour as Cook's meaning dawned on her and she was overwhelmed with terror.

Tactlessly Lucy said, 'There was a young man in the paper the other day, ma'am, threw himself into the Thames because –'

'Stop it!' Amelia cried. 'For God's sake! I don't want to hear it!'

'I'm sorry, ma'am, I only thought –'

Cook turned on the maid. 'You silly girl! Get back to your work at once.' She turned back to Amelia. 'What about dinner, ma'am? How many shall I cook for?'

Amelia stared at her. 'Dinner?' she repeated. 'How many?'

'Yes, ma'am.'

'Two, of course.'

'But if –'

'*Two*, Cook! *Two!* Dinner for two as usual. Are you deaf?'

Cook drew herself up, incensed by Amelia's words, and her mouth closed into a tight, resentful line. She gave Lucy a meaningful look and they both retreated to the kitchen.

When they had gone Amelia whispered, 'Two, as usual. Yes, of course. He'll come back.'

But she knew they were empty words. Her beloved son would not come back.

She felt faint and ill and wished she had retained the bottle of smelling salts. *Would* Ralph throw himself into the Thames? That was unthinkable; Lucy was a fool. She swallowed with difficulty, her mouth and throat both dry as sand. No! He would not kill himself because he had packed a bag – relief flowed warmly, comfortingly through her – but he might at this very moment be on a train with Marion Reid heading towards an unknown future – a future in which she, his mother, would play no part at all. 'Oh, dear, God,' she cried silently. 'What have I done? Whatever have I done?'

Ralph did not come home and Amelia sat alone through the evening meal, staring at the empty seat opposite her, forcing morsels of food into her unwilling mouth, swallowing but tasting nothing. She had her pride and would not give the servants the satisfaction of knowing the depths of her despair or the extent of the panic which gripped her.

She tried to concentrate her mind on matters concerning the new school – matters which only a few hours ago had proved so engrossing. Now, however, she cared nothing for the Harold Weston Memorial School. As far as she was concerned, it could burn to the ground and she would not blink an eyelid. All that concerned her was the knowledge that her son had left her and was never coming back.

Amelia stopped believing that he would be home at any moment and no longer pretended that they would be reconciled. With the coming of night, the last of her hopes faded, to be replaced by a conviction that she would never see him again; would never even hear from him.

It was after eleven before she sent the servants to bed and 1 o'clock the following morning before she admitted defeat and made her own way upstairs.

Ralph did not come home, but at 3 o'clock the following day Clarice Foster arrived. Amelia had completely forgotten the arrangement they had made, but she welcomed the visitor gladly, thankful for some company and the chance to take her mind off Ralph's disappearance. In answer to the girl's question, Amelia told her that Ralph was away for a few days staying with friends. Then she and Clarice worked together until four-thirty.

The next day a letter arrived and she opened it with trembling fingers. The letter-heading read 'The Corona Hotel, Folkestone'.

Dear Mama, [she read]

You will no doubt understand my sudden departure. Your unforgivable intrusion into my personal life has caused me great heartbreak – I hope you will never know how much. Marion refuses to see me again and I don't know how I shall live the rest of my life without her.

I must have time to deal with this in my own way. Probably I will go to France for a few months and maybe ultimately to America. There is nothing and no one to keep me in England.

I will keep in touch, but I fear we shall never have much to say to each other again.

The letter was signed simply 'Ralph'.

*

The following day Marion was helping Gilbert on with his jacket as he prepared to set out on his morning rounds. He was later than usual and anxious to be off.

'I'll be home as soon as I can,' he told her. 'I would like lunch to be prompt today, because I have a meeting with the school committee at the Gaunts at two-thirty.'

'Do you think they will open the school on time?' she asked.

'I don't see why not.' He glanced at her, frowning a little. 'Is something the matter?' he asked. 'You look very pale. Have you been crying?'

'No,' she lied, flustered by the unexpected attention. 'I have a slight headache.'

'Perhaps a tonic would help?'

'Yes, that might help. Thank you.'

'Remind me when I return from the Gaunts.'

'I will.'

'My list? What happened to it?'

She handed him the sheet of paper on which she had written details of his house calls. He studied it briefly, then put it into his pocket.

'If there is a message from Mrs Sharp, you will have to say that I cannot call until later,' he told her. 'The baby is not due until next week, but she is convinced it will be early. She will no doubt panic at the first pains.'

'But suppose she really *is* in labour?'

'Then send Mrs Bracewell round there to see to things.'

'The midwife?'

He nodded. 'If the worst happens, she can deliver the child. She is very experienced. Now I must hurry.'

He had been gone barely an hour and Marion was sitting with Pip on her lap when Kitty announced a visitor.

'Who is it?' asked Marion. 'Not about Mrs Sharp, I hope?'

'No, ma'am. It's Mrs Gaunt.'

Marion jumped abruptly to her feet, tipping the startled dog on to the floor. 'For me, or for the doctor?' she asked.

'For you, ma'am.'

Marion hesitated, trying to hide her agitation. 'Very well. Show her in, Kitty,' she said reluctantly.

'Should I bring a tray?'

'Not unless I ring for it.'

'Right you are, ma'am.'

When Amelia entered the room Marion had to bite back an exclamation of concern at her appearance. The older woman's face was grey, there were dark lines under her eyes and she looked ten years older.

When they were both seated Amelia said, 'I have had a letter from my son.'

Marion frowned. 'A letter?'

360

'You were unaware that he had gone away?'

Marion's shocked expression answered the question for her. Amelia's hands were clasped tightly together and Marion could read the anguish in her eyes.

'He blames me,' said Amelia, tight-lipped. 'I didn't even see him. I came home and he was gone, without a word to anyone.'

Marion sat without speaking and after a moment Amelia went on, 'I don't know what happened between you – if he told you his plans – but presumably not?'

'No,' answered Marion flatly.

'But you have parted?'

Marion nodded. 'I shall not see him again. That is what you wanted, isn't it?'

Amelia said in a tight voice, 'I thought it was best for him – for Ralph, but I had no idea – he wrote to me –' She took out the letter and handed it to Marion. 'I had no idea he felt so strongly. I would never have thought – please read it.'

But Marion returned the letter without giving it a second glance. 'It is over between us,' she said. 'You were quite right. Somehow we shall survive in our own separate worlds.'

Amelia stared down at the letter in her hand. 'He is going to America,' she said. 'I shall never see him again. He is all I have and I have lost him. If only I had known –'

'How much we loved each other?' Marion's voice was harsh. 'I don't really think you would have allowed that knowledge to affect your judgement, Mrs Gaunt. But why are you here? It is over and your son is quite safe from me.'

'But if I never see him again –'

'Yes, it is a high price for you to pay, but then we are both paying also.'

Amelia's lips quivered as she studied her hands. 'You must hate me,' she whispered.

'No,' said Marion. 'I don't hate you. Perhaps in your place I would have done the same. But I have given him up, Mrs Gaunt, and I don't think you can ask any more of me.'

Amelia raised her head. 'Did you really love him?' she asked.

Marion sighed. 'I shall always love him, I'm afraid, but as you reminded me, I have a husband and that is where my duty lies.'

'Perhaps I was wrong.'

'It is a little too late for doubts. But try not to worry. Ralph is not a vindictive man and I'm sure he will come back later on, when the worst of the hurt is over.'

'But *America*! It's so far away!' Amelia looked at Marion with desperation. 'I *can't* let him go like this. Mrs Reid, you must stop him; write to him and beg him to reconsider. He might listen to you.'

To her dismay Marion shook her head. 'No, Mrs Gaunt, I won't do it. I have hurt him enough already. He is old enough to know his own mind and if he thinks a new experience in a new country will heal the heartache, then let us hope he is proved right. We have both hurt him badly; the least we can do now is to let him deal with his grief in his own way.'

Amelia looked at her in desperation. 'But just ask him to wait a little longer before he goes – a few weeks, perhaps. This decision is so hasty and ill-conceived.'

'But America may be good for him!'

Amelia rose to her feet, unable to hide her agitation. 'How can it be good for him when he is going for all the wrong reasons? Oh, Mrs Reid, please write to him. Or better still, *go* to him. I have an address in Folkestone. We may be in time to stop him.'

But Marion was not to be persuaded, although some of her earlier resentment had left her and it gave her no satisfaction to know that Amelia had unwittingly engineered the disaster.

'What could I say to him?' she asked. 'Nothing has changed between us. I am still Mrs Reid, so we could never marry. No, Mrs Gaunt, I do not think we should meddle further. I cannot pretend I would not like the chance to see him once more, but why prolong his distress just to satisfy my longing? I think we should leave well alone.'

'So you won't help me?'

'I don't believe it would be best for Ralph,' said Marion. 'I am truly sorry for you if you feel you have lost your son, but if he can find happiness elsewhere then what right have we to drag him home for your sake?'

For a long moment neither spoke, then Amelia stood up and moved to the window. At last she said heavily, 'He has a job to do here; I need him for my school. What will he do in America? How will he live?'

'He'll paint, I imagine. You wanted him to be an artist. He has been trained and he has talent; he won't starve.'

'You are determined not to help me!' Amelia cried angrily. 'Determined not to see things from my point of view.'

'On the contrary, Mrs Gaunt, I would never have sent Ralph away if I had not looked at the situation through your eyes. It was you who made me see how hopeless it was; you who demonstrated that there was no future for us together. When I watched him walk away, I wanted to die with misery. It was the hardest thing I have ever had to bear in my whole life!'

Amelia's brief flash of anger had passed. 'I had no idea,' she whispered.

'I think you did,' said Marion, her voice shaking with emotion. 'You did not mind then if *I* made the ultimate sacrifice, but now it is your turn to feel the agony of losing the one you love most in the world.' Her voice broke suddenly as tears spilled down her face, while

Amelia watched helplessly. 'I mustn't cry!' she stammered. 'Gilbert will question me on his return; he mustn't guess.'

'I am so sorry,' said Amelia. 'If I had only known –'

'Please! Just go,' Marion begged as she rang the bell for Kitty. 'I am better when I'm alone. I must not give way like this. I *dare* not!'

Seeing her stricken face, Amelia asked, 'Isn't there *anything* I can do?'

Marion shook her head helplessly and after a further hesitation Amelia left the room and Marion heard Kitty see her out. She waited until the maid had returned to the kitchen and then hurried upstairs to her bedroom to find cold water with which to bathe her face.

When she had done all that she could, she sat back from the mirror and regarded the pale face and haunted, reddened eyes with despair. Pip pushed open the bedroom door and surveyed her hopefully.

'Oh, poor Pip! Your walk. I had forgotten.'

The tail wagged.

Marion said, 'Oh, my darling Pip! Come here!' and as the dog leaped joyfully into her lap her unquestioning love and boundless affection brought a little warmth into her mistress's frozen heart.

CHAPTER SIXTEEN

Jeff sat at his typewriter, his fingers flying over the keys, so keen was he to see the well-turned phrases in his head converted into black on white. A gruesome murder in Bucks Row, following so closely on the heels of Martha Tabram's death, was beginning to look like the work of one man. Suppose he struck again? Even the *New York Times* might be interested in Jeff's ringside account. People were the same the world over, and his copy would make fascinating reading for those strong enough to stomach the horrible details. He scratched his head and re-read what he had written so far.

In the early hours of Friday morning, August 31st, another woman fell victim to the murdering fiend who stalks the streets of Whitechapel in London, England.

He glanced at his notes, scribbled from the official police description.

When found at approximately 3.45 am, the body was dressed in black woollen stockings, flannel petticoats (stamped with the words 'Lambeth Workhouse'), a brown linsey dress and matching ulster with brass buttons. A black straw bonnet lay nearby, possibly dislodged during the struggle . . .

After a moment's thought, he wrote, 'A woman cut down in the prime of life . . .'
'Hmm?'

The police had described her as aged about 45 years. Was forty-five the prime of a woman's life, he wondered, and reluctantly admitted that it was not; nevertheless he left the phrase in. This was journalism, and a little distortion of the truth (or embellishment of the facts, as he preferred to call it) was quite acceptable.

He continued, 'A woman in the prime of life, snatched from the body of her family . . .'

Yes, that was good!

'. . . the body of her family by a sadistic monster . . .'

Here Jeff paused indecisively. Did she actually have a family, he wondered? The police had been somewhat vague on the matter. Never mind. The point was academic, really, and the 'sadistic monster' was true enough anyway, he reflected. The unfortunate whore had been found in Bucks Row badly slashed and with her throat cut from ear to ear. If she *had* screamed for help, no one had heard her and certainly no one had gone to her aid. A Mrs Green whose bedroom was nearby had confessed that she slept heavily but a Mrs Purkiss, who lived opposite, had told the police that she was wide awake yet still heard nothing. Jeff sat back and frowned – then, inspired, he leaned forward and added, 'She met her maker with barely a whimper . . .'

'Ah! That's better,' he told himself.

There was a knock at the door and Mrs Coot came in with a small tray. 'A nice "cuppa" and a couple of scones straight out of the oven,' she said, setting it down beside him. 'There's a tidy knob of butter in them, so eat them before it melts.'

As he thanked her, she said, 'May I?' and leaned forward to peer at the half-finished sheet in his typewriter.

'What a dreadful thing!' she exclaimed. 'What I can't see is why? I mean, why kill a pathetic creature like that? She had no money, no jewels, nothing. Not even the four coppers for a lodging-house bed, so they say! Sheer

366

wickedness, if you ask me. Sheer, unadulterated sinfulness. The police have got to do something and quickly, or no one will be safe in their beds. It makes me go all wobbly inside just to think of it.'

'Would you like me to read what I've written so far?' Jeff asked eagerly.

'Oh yes, Mr Bannerman,' she said. 'That would be most interesting. But you eat those scones first or they'll get cold. Never the same cold as hot, I always say. I can wait, so no need to choke yourself.'

Jeff looked at her with affection as he bit into a warm scone. He had told his landlady that his return to the United States would most probably be no later than Christmas and ever since she had attempted to change his mind by appealing to his stomach, arriving at intervals throughout the day with tempting home-cooked delicacies – scones, raspberry buns, vanilla slices and buttered tea-cakes. He would – he told her – go back to his family 'looking like a hog'!

Now, in a dramatic tone, he read through the few lines he had written so far and Mrs Coot nodded sagely throughout.

'Poor woman,' she remarked when he had finished. 'We know she shouldn't be doing what she does – I mean *did* – but that doesn't mean she deserves to be murdered, does it? What was her name now? Mary something?'

'Mary Ann Nicholls, known to her friends as Polly.'

'Polly. That's right. Lovely name, I always think. I lived next door to a Polly when I was a child. Thick as thieves we were, but then she died of whooping-cough.' She sighed. 'It makes you wonder who *is* safe,' she said. 'Why, it could be me next.'

Jeff started a second scone and said, 'But you're not a "fallen woman", Mrs Coot. This murderer seems to have a grudge against such women. First that one back in April, then Martha Tabram and now Polly Nicholls. I think you're safe enough. He's not killing respectable landladies – yet!'

She laughed and then covered her mouth guiltily. 'Oh, Mr Bannerman! We shouldn't joke about it, should we? God might punish us! It's a dreadful state of affairs if women aren't safe on the streets of London. You won't catch me going out after dark; leastways, not until they catch him.'

'Let's hope they catch him soon, before he kills someone else.'

Jeff could see that she longed to stay chatting, but he glanced rather pointedly towards the clock which was a polite way of saying that he wanted to get on with his work.

'Well,' she said reluctantly, taking the hint, 'I must get on. I've plenty to do and before we know it we'll have Miss Becket home from work. I must say she's no trouble. A very nice girl, in fact – the sort you'd like for your own daughter. I'll miss you both when you go back to America.'

He shook his head slightly. 'I'm afraid she's not keen on the idea, but I can't stay over here indefinitely. I have to go, and that doesn't leave her much option. Poor Dora.'

'Oh, she'll get used to it, Mr Bannerman. I'm sure of that. It's just a matter of time.'

'I hope you're right,' he told her. 'My folks are longing to meet her.'

Having drunk the last of the tea he handed back the tray with his thanks and Mrs Coot finally departed, leaving Jeff free to turn his attention once more to the Whitechapel murders.

*

Probably the only person in the whole of London who was *pleased* to learn of the latest murder was Gilbert Reid, and for him it was the goad that finally pricked him into action. If Meg were to die now, everyone would assume that Polly Nicholls' killer had struck again. He had given up the idea of hiring a killer, for that way he would lay himself open to blackmail. He knew that he must do the deed himself and now was the ideal time, for Alf had reported her whereabouts to him so he knew where Meg was living. That was another reason for acting promptly, he reminded himself, for at any moment Meg might take it into her head to move on and then he would have lost the initiative.

Two mornings after the murder in Bucks Row he sent a message to Meg via Alf Berry, asking to meet her at eleven o'clock that same evening on the steps below London Bridge.

Ten minutes before the hour he was waiting on the landing stage where, during the day, steamers disembarked their passengers. His heart was racing but his resolve was firm as he told himself that in a few minutes it would all be over.

The tide was high and all around him in the gloom boats sighed and creaked at anchor, their shrouds furled, their masts lost in the thin mist that hung over the river. Water slapped against the looming wooden hulks moored alongside and further out on the water the splash of oars was heard as someone went about his nefarious business under the cloak of darkness. Above him he heard the sound of passing footsteps and for a moment his determination wavered, but the steps were too heavy to be Meg's and he drew a deep breath of relief and took a firmer grip on his emotions.

'It has to be done,' he told himself, and the fingers of his right hand closed round the handle of the knife as slowly but surely his courage returned.

Somewhere a clock struck eleven and a sudden panic swept through him. Suppose she did not come? He could not imagine that he could ever again screw his courage to such a pitch. He thought of Marion and wondered if she would believe his 'alibi' – that he had been delayed by a street brawl in which a man received severe injuries requiring his attentions. She might doubt his story, but she could never prove him a liar.

Out on the water a man called out and was answered by another, their voices mysteriously disembodied. Minutes ticked by, while beneath his feet the water sucked greedily at the planking. 'Where are you, Meg?' he whispered. 'You should be here by now.'

His nostrils were full of the rank river smell of sour mud, rotting wood and the stench of bilge-water. Footsteps again! He felt his whole body grow tense as the sounds, lighter than before, halted in the street above him.

Meg called, 'Gilbert? Are you there?'

She clutched Lizzie to her as she listened fearfully for a reply, for the strangely worded message had alarmed her. Why had Gilbert been so insistent that she bring Lizzie with her? Had he learned more about the devils who were after them? Was he going to offer her a safe refuge after all? It was the least he could do, she thought wearily. Anything would be better than this everlasting hide-and-seek. Another day or two and she would have to leave Duggie and move on. She called again: 'Is anyone there?'

At the thought of Duggie Drake her eyes softened. He had taken a shine to her and if she had not been on the run they might have settled down together. He was good-hearted in his way and she had a roof of sorts over her head, and food for her belly. She could have done a lot worse.

Hugging Lizzie closer, she peered into the darkness. Maybe he wasn't here yet. Maybe she was early or he was late. No, that couldn't be it because she had heard the clock strike. She tried to penetrate the darkness at the bottom of the steps, but could see no one. It was a dismal place and she shivered suddenly.

'Someone's walked over my grave,' she told Lizzie. 'Now where the hell is your Pa?'

She had slipped out before Duggie returned from the Star and Garter and did not want to be too late going home. No point in upsetting him.

On an impulse she bent down and laid Lizzie in a corner propped against the stonework of the bridge.

'You wait there,' she said. 'I won't be long.'

The nearby gaslight threw a faint glow on to the baby's serene face and Meg thought again how lucky she was. Some babies bawled all day long and half the night, too. Hers was a little angel by comparison!

Cautiously she made her way down the steps towards the water; half-way there, she paused to call Gilbert's name again and to her relief, she heard his voice.

'I'm here,' he said hoarsely.

When she reached the bottom she still could not see him and took a few more steps along the landing-stage. She was hugging herself nervously when she heard a sound behind her and as she turned, she saw a figure leaping towards her and to her horror caught the dull gleam of light on an upraised knife. Instantly aware of her terrible danger, she screamed at the top of her voice.

'Murder! Murder! Help me!'

Desperately she fought for her life, stunned by the knowledge that after all it was Gilbert Reid himself who was trying to kill her. She lashed out, kicking and flailing her arms, biting his arm and scratching his face, somewhere finding a strength she did not know she possessed to hold at a distance the arm that wielded the knife.

'Damn you, woman!' he hissed. 'I'll shut your stupid mouth once and for all!'

Briefly she broke free and, still screaming, tried to make a run for the steps, but he was too quick for her and pulled her back, grasping her by a handful of her clothing and swinging her towards the water. By this time she had no breath left with which to scream for help, for she needed every ounce of energy to avoid the wicked-looking blade which she assumed was intended for her throat ... obviously Gilbert Reid was the White-chapel murderer, and she would suffer the same ugly fate as his earlier victims.

Suddenly she fell to her knees and, catching him momentarily off balance, managed to bring him down also. As they hit the ground almost simultaneously, she heard him grunt with pain. Frantically she pulled herself free, scrambled to her feet and stepped back. She had lost her bearings, however, and did not realize how close they were to the water's edge. With a shrill scream of fright she fell backwards into the swiftly flowing river while above her, at street level, hurried footsteps converged at the top of the steps.

A man's voice cried, 'God's strewth! There's a kid here!'

Another called, 'Who's doing all the screaming?'

Leaving Lizzie, the two men ran down the steps, where they stared in shocked dismay at Gilbert's body. Fearfully, they turned it over, and saw the knife-handle protruding from his chest.

'He's snuffed it! Get a copper, quick!'

One of the men ran up the steps shouting, 'Police! Bloody murder!' and a moment later, 'Down here, constable. There's a stiff with a knife through his heart!'

'I heard a woman scream "Murder!" but there's no sign of her.'

'There's a baby, too, top of the steps.'

'Someone went in the water. Leastways, there was a bloody great splash!'

The police were very thorough, but they were baffled. They had a murdered man; someone had almost certainly fallen or been pushed into the river, and a baby had been found abandoned at the scene of the crime. When the ambulance bearing Gilbert's body had been wheeled away and the notebooks closed, the sergeant shook his head.

'It'll take a genius to sort this little lot out!' he prophesied gloomily to no one in particular.

*

Marion dreamed that she was running through a large empty house. The passages along which she ran were narrow, but very high; the rooms into which she looked were dark and spacious and without furniture or fittings; she was aware of a strong smell of mildew and her footsteps sounded on the bare boards and echoed from every direction. She called her mother's name again and again, but there was no reply. Gradually the house grew darker and the noises began – the rustle of a petticoat; the creak of a door on rusty hinges; the sighing of the wind; the ringing of a doorbell . . .

Suddenly she was wide awake and the door-bell that was ringing was her own. Startled, she glanced at the clock and saw that it was a few minutes past four; a quick look towards the window showed that it was still dark outside. Late-night disturbances were always calls for the doctor, and remembering Mrs Sharp whose child was now overdue, she had returned from her visits to Rachel to discover that Gilbert had moved into the spare bedroom and now she waited to hear Gilbert rouse himself.

She heard Kitty grumbling to herself as she made her way downstairs, but there was no sound from her husband. Marion frowned. Gilbert was normally such a light sleeper. She pulled on a wrap and went through into his room.

'Gilbert! There's someone at –'

She stopped in astonishment, for his bed was empty and quite obviously had not been slept in! As she hesitated, she remembered that she had gone to bed early the previous night, before Gilbert came home from his rounds. She had not heard him come in, so perhaps he had been delayed somewhere and had not been home.

Going to the top of the stairs, she called, 'Who is it, Kitty?' When she saw a policeman her first thought, illogically, was for Ralph's safety.

'Has there been an accident?' she cried, but even as she spoke common sense told her that if anything had happened to Ralph she would be the last person to know.

She began to hurry down the stairs, but stopped abruptly two-thirds of the way.

'What is it?' she asked. 'Is something wrong?'

The police sergeant was tall and heavily built. 'Mrs Reid?' he asked. 'Mrs Gilbert Reid?'

'Yes.' Her heart contracted with fear as intuition warned of disaster.

'I am Sergeant Paine,' he told her. 'I'm afraid I have bad news, ma'am.'

Marion put a hand on the banister to steady herself for whatever might follow.

'What has happened?'

The two women stared anxiously into the sergeant's ruddy face.

'It's your husband, ma'am. Dr Gilbert Reid?'

'Yes, yes, of course. Where is he? Has something happened?'

Unwilling to meet her gaze, the sergeant stared at a point immediately above her head.

'He is hurt, yes, ma'am. He has been involved in an accident.'

'Oh, my God! Is he in hospital?'

He shook his head. 'I am afraid it's worse than that, ma'am. Your husband . . .'

'He's not – dead?' Marion could hardly take it in. 'You're not saying he's . . .'

Was this man telling her that Gilbert was *dead*?

'He *can't* be dead!' she stammered.

'I'm sorry, Mrs Reid, but that is the case.'

Kitty cried. 'He can't be! Not the master. Oh, ma'am!'

She turned appealing eyes on Marion but her mistress seemed unaware of her presence. 'Not the master, ma'am!' she repeated.

Marion struggled for words, but none came. Gilbert was *dead*? It was impossible.

The policeman was looking apologetic as he prepared to break even worse news. 'May I suggest that you sit down,' he said, 'and that your maid makes a pot of tea? At these times most women find a cup of tea very comforting.'

As Kitty hurried dutifully towards the kitchen, Marion felt as though she might still be dreaming as she led the way into the morning room. When they were both seated, the sergeant took out a pencil and notebook.

'I'm afraid I must trouble you with a few questions as to your husband's whereabouts last night. Hopefully we can then discover how he came to be . . .'

She waited, but when he did not continue she said, 'I felt rather unwell last night, and went to bed early. My husband had not returned from his rounds.'

'And did he return?'

'Apparently not. His bed has not been slept in.'

He began to write slowly and methodically, the notebook resting on his knee. His next question startled Marion.

'Mrs Reid, did your husband have any enemies?'

'Enemies? None that I knew of. Why on earth do you ask that?'

'Your husband's body was found on a wooden landing-stage below London Bridge. I'm very much afraid he had been murdered – stabbed through the heart, in fact.'

'Oh, my God!' gasped Marion.

The room seemed to spin as her senses deserted her, but the policeman moved promptly and caught her as she fell forward from the chair. When she regained consciousness, she was lying on the floor and Kitty was bending over her, holding the smelling salts to her nose.

'Oh, thank heavens, ma'am!' Kitty cried. 'When I came in and saw you like this, I thought *you* were dead too. Now then, ma'am, can you sit up? I've made a pot of tea, but I left it and came running when the sergeant called me.'

Marion was helped back on to her chair and left under the watchful eye of Sergeant Paine while Kitty hurried away to return moments later with a tea-tray set for two. The policeman waited until Marion had recovered enough to sip her tea and then suggested that the maid should go back to bed.

When they were alone, he told Marion all that was known about Gilbert's death and she listened in stupefied dismay.

'I don't think I can help you,' she told him at last. 'My husband is – was – well known and respected in the area. I can't think of anyone who would want to hurt him.'

'Did he have any violent or insane patients? Anyone who might have killed him in a fit of insane rage?'

'Not to my knowledge. No, wait . . . there was a young woman, but she was hardly violent. Gilbert did say – but no . . . I'm sure she would never do such a thing.'

'Her name, please?'

'Meg Swain,' said Marion reluctantly. 'She was one of my husband's patients, as was her younger sister until her death. She thought someone was trying to kill her, but my husband believed that she was suffering from delusions. He was trying to arrange for her to see a specialist so that she could enter an asylum. But she was never violent. Really, Sergeant, it could not possibly be her.'

He wrote again, his lips pursed, his brow furrowed. 'Was there anyone else? Did anyone bear him a grudge, perhaps?'

'Not that he was aware of – at least, he did not tell me about it.'

The policeman tapped his fingers on the arm of his chair and said, 'Then to go back to this other young woman, Miss Swain. We might be getting near to the truth here. Just suppose that her delusions took a different direction and she came to think it was your husband who was trying to kill her?'

'But that's absurd!' cried Marion. 'Oh, I'm sorry, I don't mean to be rude, but I cannot believe that.'

Sergeant Paine shook his head reprovingly. 'In my line of business, Mrs Reid, you learn that nothing is absurd. Truth is stranger than fiction. Oh, dear me, yes! If I was to tell you some of the things that go on, you'd be amazed. Nothing is too far-fetched to be true. This Meg Swain could have turned on the one person who was trying to help her.'

'Meg would never kill anyone. I am certain of it.'

'With all due respect, Mrs Reid, we none of us can understand the mind of mad men – or women.'

He wrote again, while Marion tried to imagine Meg Swain killing her husband. It was so utterly unbelievable; so *out of character*.

Suddenly he asked, 'Can you think of any reason that might take your husband to that particular spot by the river?'

She shook her head. 'None at all.'

'Could he have arranged to meet her there?'

'I can't think why.'

'Did this young woman have a child?'

'Yes, a little girl called Lizzie. But how does –'

'So *maybe* we're getting somewhere,' he said. 'Suppose the young woman was not suffering from delusions but *was* being threatened by someone, and that someone tried to kill her? Suppose your husband intervened and was himself killed and then, because the young woman was a witness, the murderer threw her into the Thames?'

Marion looked at him, shocked by this new revelation. 'Is Meg Swain *drowned*? Is that what you are trying to tell me?'

377

He spread his hands helplessly. 'I'm only *surmising*, Mrs Reid. Anything is possible. At present we can only guess at what happened. The facts are that there *was* a woman – two men heard her screaming; there was a splash; and we have an infant without a mother.' He shrugged. 'Perhaps the baby's mother killed your husband and then threw herself into the river?'

'Sergeant, where is the child now?' Marion asked. 'I would recognize Meg Swain's daughter.'

'The baby is quite safe, ma'am,' he assured her. 'She is being cared for in the London Hospital not too far from here . . . just until we trace the relatives, assuming there are any.'

'Dora Becket!' cried Marion. 'If the child is Lizzie Swain, then Miss Becket would know; she is a cousin to Miss Swain. I don't have her address, but the people who used to live with Meg would know it.'

She shivered violently and he said, 'You've had a bad shock, Mrs Reid. Perhaps I should send for a doctor to give you a sleeping-draught? You ought to get some rest.' She nodded distractedly and he went on, 'I'm afraid that at some stage we shall have to ask you to attend the mortuary to identify your husband's body. Later today, or maybe tomorrow.'

'Oh no!' she cried. 'Is that really necessary? You already know who he is.'

'It is a formality none the less, Mrs Reid. Not a pleasant task, I know, but it will only take a moment.' He wrote the address on a slip of paper and handed it to her. 'You should bring a friend with you if possible or a relative. Most people do.'

'Rachel!' said Marion. 'She could come. That's my sister.' She put a shaking hand to her head. 'Oh God, this is all so incredible! I can hardly believe it. It's like a nightmare. Whoever would want to kill my husband?'

'I hope we shall find that out, Mrs Reid. Rest assured that we shall do all we can to apprehend the criminal so

378

that he can be brought to justice.' He stood up. 'I think you've had enough questions for one night. Shall I send Dr Sullivan to see you?'

Marion shook her head. 'I don't want to sleep; I want to *think*,' she told him. 'I need to keep a clear head in case I remember something that might help you. Now I'll see you out.'

When he had gone, she sat for a long time trying to come to terms with the fact that she would never see Gilbert alive again. Try as she might, she could not imagine him lying beside the river with a knife through his heart. Had Meg killed him? And if so, why? It was all so bizarre, so unreal. Marion wanted to cry for her dead husband, for someone should weep for him, but her eyes remained obstinately dry. She knew he deserved her pity but she had spent all her tears on Ralph Gaunt and her conscience troubled her.

When at last she went up to bed she remained wide awake until the dawn chorus began, but then slipped into an exhausted sleep. It was not until she finally roused at ten minutes past eleven that she realized that she was now a widow and that although she had a roof over her head, she had no means of support.

*

By the time Rachel arrived later the same day Marion's emotions were in turmoil. When she heard wheels rolling to a stop outside the house, she ran down the steps and threw herself into her sister's arms, and the tears she had so far been unable to shed for Gilbert found unexpected release.

As they sat together on the sofa, Rachel listened patiently while Marion tried to explain the guilt she felt. She should never have married Gilbert, she insisted; she should have listened not only to Rachel, but to the whispering of her own heart. In marrying for the wrong reason, she had doomed the marriage from the start and

Gilbert had never had a proper wife in the fullest sense of the word.

'That was hardly your fault,' Rachel reminded her, but Marion was in no mood to blame Gilbert.

She should, she protested, have tried harder; should have encouraged Gilbert; should have found a way to help him instead of withdrawing from him and pretending indifference.

'Now he's dead,' she declared miserably, 'and it's too late to help him. I failed him, Rachel, and I have only just found the honesty to admit it. All these years I have resented not having a family without lifting a finger to improve matters.'

'What could you have done?' Rachel demanded. 'He was a doctor, yet he had no solution to his own problem. How could you be expected to help? Maybe he didn't want a family, and secretly was glad of the excuse not to have one?'

Marion regarded her with a sudden glimmer of hope. 'Do you think so?'

'I certainly do,' Rachel declared firmly. 'Gilbert never struck me as a family man. As I said before, if he had wanted a family he would have found himself a wife long before he did. After all, most men marry before they reach forty. In my opinion he was more interested in his work until he suddenly realized that he was getting older and decided he did not want to remain a lodger for the rest of his life. There is nothing wrong in that,' she added hastily, 'but it doesn't really fit with the picture of a family man – not to me, anyway.'

She could see that Marion wanted to be convinced, so she went on, 'I think you suited him very well. He had no cause to complain, and you have nothing for which to reproach yourself. Nothing at all.'

'But Meg Swain? What was she to him?'

Rachel shrugged. 'Well, if Meg is drowned we shall most probably never know the answer to that – and truthfully, I think it better that we do not. Whatever she was to him, you cannot undo the past. I'm not trying to malign him now that he's dead, but we had our doubts about him for a long time where the Swains are concerned. Just because he's dead he does not automatically become a saint; maybe he only got what he deserved.'

'Rachel! That's a terrible thing to say.'

'It's true, Marion,' insisted Rachel obstinately. 'I'm not prepared to sit here while you whitewash Gilbert just so that you can revel in guilt. I won't have it. He was behaving very suspiciously long before he was killed, and we still have no idea what was going on.'

'But Meg would never kill him, surely?'

'Maybe she did not intend to. Maybe he was trying to kill *her*.'

'Oh, that's monstrous!' cried Marion. 'I won't listen to you any more.'

She put her hands over her ears, but Rachel sat beside her quietly unrepentant. When at last Marion lowered her hands and began to speak again, she was interrupted by a ring at the front door-bell.

'I suppose that will be the police again,' she said, but Rachel had already risen to her feet as Mrs Cobbett came in looking flustered. 'It's three gentlemen from the press,' she told them. 'They want to talk to you, Mrs Reid. Here are their cards.'

Marion glanced at them: Herbert Carter, Douglas Bidwell and Samuel Mayhew.

'No,' she said. 'I don't want to speak to them. I can't.'

'Let me speak to them,' Rachel suggested.

In view of their recent conversation Marion looked at her sister in alarm, but Rachel held up a hand to silence her protests.

'I promise to be very discreet,' she assured her. 'Don't worry.'

Still Marion was not happy. 'Does anyone have to speak to them?' she asked. 'Can't we just send them away?'

Mrs Cobbett put in, 'Begging your pardon, ma'am, but I don't think they will go away until they get their story. They seem very determined.'

Rachel looked at her sister until at last Marion nodded reluctantly, then she went out to the front door. The reporters – from *The Times*, the *Evening News* and the *London Illustrated News* – were none too pleased to be told that Marion was not well enough to talk to them. However, once they were convinced that Rachel was to be their only source of information, they accepted with alacrity her invitation to step into the hallway.

'Miss Thripp,' began Carter – he was from the *Evenings News* and scruffier than his companions – 'Do you know what the relationship was between the deceased and the abandoned baby's mother?'

'Do we know the baby's identity?' Rachel countered innocently.

'Well, no, but assuming it's Miss Swain's child . . .'

'Gilbert Reid was Miss Swain's doctor,' said Rachel. 'He had been concerned about her since he first met the family when Miss Swain's younger sister was suffering from "phossy jaw".'

They seized on her choice of words. '*Was* suffering?' cried Bidwell. 'Did the doctor cure her, then?' The representative from *The Times* looked at her briskly.

'No. Miss Swain refused to allow an operation on the girl's jaw and she later died of the disease.'

They scribbled furiously.

'And was he treating Miss Swain?' asked Mayhew, his pencil poised.

'I believe he attended the birth of her child, and more recently he had been concerned with the state of her mind.'

'You mean she was *mad*?' Bidwell was trying unsuccessfully to hide his delight that the story was proving so much meatier than they had expected.

Rachel gave him a frosty glance. 'My brother-in-law

believed her to be suffering from delusions – delusions of persecution. But why all these questions about Miss Swain? Have they found her body? Do we even know for sure that she is dead?'

'According to the police, your sister believes the child might belong to Miss Swain and –'

'That was only a suggestion. Until they find the body . . .'

'The river police are on to it now,' put in Mayhew.

'Then I suggest we discuss some other aspect of the case,' said Rachel firmly.

The three men exchanged exasperated looks. The bereaved widow would have been much easier to interview than this somewhat daunting sister!

'Miss Thripp,' began Carter, 'was your brother-in-law treating the Swain family free of charge?'

'I thought I said that we would not pursue –'

'But was he, Miss Thripp?'

'No, he was not. A Mrs Gaunt was paying the bills.'

'Amelia Gaunt?' The name aroused fresh interest.

Rachel nodded. 'You obviously know of her.'

'She's well known in the area; a great philanthropist.'

The questions continued for another five or six minutes and then Rachel decided she had suffered their interrogation long enough. Dismissing them politely but firmly, she sent them on their way and went back into the morning room, where Marion waited anxiously for an account of the interview.

'I think I managed that rather well,' Rachel told her with a faint smile. 'I don't think you need fear any kind of scandal. In fact – most undeservedly – your late husband may emerge as the innocent victim without a stain on his character!'

CHAPTER SEVENTEEN

That same evening Amelia Gaunt went up the steps of the Corona Hotel and into the foyer, and decided that she did not like it. Paint was beginning to peel from the outside walls and the dingy decor inside depressed her. It was not the place she would have expected Ralph to choose, but then he was scarcely himself at the moment, she reflected, and in his present state of mind was hardly likely to take much interest in his surroundings.

A young man beneath a sign saying 'Reception' asked if he could help her in any way. He too was depressing, she thought, with dull black hair and unattractive teeth.

'I certainly hope so,' she told him, looking with distaste at a small stain on the front of his jacket. 'I am looking for Mr Ralph Gaunt, who I understand is staying at this hotel.'

'Mr Ralph Gaunt? Now let me see . . .' He pulled out a battered ledger, laid it on the counter top and began to riffle through the pages. 'I've been away for a week or two,' he confided. 'Very nasty bout of influenza. Really laid me low, it did.'

'How very unfortunate for you.'

'Otherwise I could have told you straight away but — ah! Here we are. Ralph Gaunt: Room twenty-seven.'

Amelia's heart leapt with relief. She was not too late.

'If you would be kind enough to tell him that I'm here . . .' she began, but now the young man was shaking his head.

'I'm afraid he's no longer with us,' he said with suitable regret. 'Mr Gaunt left the hotel yesterday evening.'

'Left?' She could not keep the disappointment out of her voice. 'Are you quite sure?'

'I'm afraid so. The account was settled.'

'But – did he say where he was going? Did he leave any forwarding address?'

'Not that I know of, but I wasn't on duty last night. You see, this is my first day back. The doctor wasn't too happy about me returning to work so soon, but I said –'

'Never mind that!' snapped Amelia without troubling to hide her impatience. 'Perhaps I could speak to whoever saw him last.'

He frowned slightly. 'Let me see, that would probably be our Miss Fisk. I'll try to find her for you, but she may be off duty. If you will bear with me a moment, I'll make enquiries.'

He left her alone for a few moments, but then re-appeared with a middle-aged woman who introduced herself as Miss Fisk and disclosed the information that Mr Gaunt had arranged to cross to Boulogne and had left no forwarding address.

'Thank you for your help,' said Amelia. 'In that case, I will book a room for myself for tonight, and I would like you to arrange for me to cross to Boulogne as early as possible tomorrow morning. Oh, and I will take room twenty-seven if it is still vacant.'

Upstairs in the room so recently vacated by her son, Amelia began to try to work out exactly where Ralph would go in France. He knew several people – the Holloways, for example – but she thought it unlikely he would choose anyone who might prove too curious. He might, she thought, go back to one of the hotels in which he had stayed during his Grand Tour; at once she began to scribble down all that she could remember. There was Le Poisson D'Or at Avignon; he had written to her from there. Or Les Arbres – that was somewhere in Provence – the exact location would come to her later. He had also stayed briefly at Les Trois Ventes in Bordeaux.

When she could think of no more names, Amelia turned her attention to the room, trying to imagine Ralph asleep in the bed or sitting where she now sat at the small table by the window. Visualizing him hanging his clothes in the narrow wardrobe, she somehow felt nearer to him and was vaguely comforted. But she must find him before he left France and disappeared into the wilderness that was the American continent. Once there, she felt sure he would be lost to her for ever. He would not come back to England while he believed that Marion could never be his, but now things were different. The police had called on her in investigating the murder of Dr Reid, and Amelia had no qualms at all about thanking God for the doctor's timely demise, since nothing now stood between Ralph and the woman he loved. Marion might be a few years older than her son but, that said, there was now no good reason why they should not be man and wife in due course. Ralph had told her that there had been no love between the doctor and his wife, so a short period of mourning would suffice. After a decent interval, they could be married. Amelia could not see further than that, nor did she wish to. Having reconciled herself to the match, she was eager to see it established as fact.

Now her thoughts switched again to the route Ralph might travel to reach America. Would he return to England, perhaps, to take a steam packet from Liverpool? If not, whereabouts in France did one embark for America? Cherbourg, perhaps? She would have to make some enquiries. If Ralph intended to sail from Liverpool, presumably he would not move too far into the French interior. Her eyes narrowed suddenly. There was a family in Calais with whom he had been on very good terms for several years; while he was at Oxford, the son had been there too. Perhaps he would go there . . .

And Gilbert Reid! Of course! He would now be unable to act as medical adviser to the Harold Weston

Memorial School. Tonight she must write a note to John Foster. She would say that she would be away for a few days visiting a relative in France, and instruct him to begin making enquiries for someone to replace Dr Reid. She would not mention the murder specifically, for surely they would have seen the news by now. It would be in all the newspapers.

Amelia drew a slow deep breath and then another, and tried not to anticipate the trials and tribulations which might await her over the coming days. On one thing she was quite determined. She would find her son before he left for America, and she would take him back to England.

*

Just before eleven the following morning, Dan Petson made his way down the railings of the *Celestina*, his movements monkey-like, his blond hair blown by the breeze, his lips puckered in a cheerful whistle. From his vantage point he looked down on to the ships which filled St Katharine's Dock and marvelled at the seething mass of humanity which swarmed on and around them as cargoes were loaded or unloaded to an accompaniment of the screech of pulleys and winches and the raucous din of human voices raised to their loudest pitch. All was noise, colour and excitement, but as Dan landed lightly on the *Celestina*'s deck, his thoughts were elsewhere and he paid no attention to the organized tangle of furled sails, taut ropes and jutting spars, and did not see the masts that criss-crossed the air in all directions like an elaborate cat's cradle. The *Celestina* was tied up against a huge Dutch barge which in turn was moored alongside the quay, and Dan crossed from ship to ship with accustomed ease until at last he stood on terra firma.

At once he began to force his way through the milling crowd, fiercely elbowing aside clerks, seamen and porters with an equal disregard for their persons. Dodging between barrels, bales and crates, he narrowly avoided the hooves of a pair of dray horses whose driver subsequently bestowed on him a colourful and inventive selection of oaths which drew from Dan a broad grin and a rude two-fingered gesture of defiance. Sunshine was reflecting from the surface of the water but Dan, already sweating from his early morning labour, was thankful to reach the area where the huge ships cast a welcome shadow.

Glad to leave the confines of his ship and stretch his legs on land, he even managed a pert 'Good morning to you, sir!' to a passing Excise officer, who could not know that Dan carried two pounds of best Virginian tobacco stuffed between his shirt and his bare chest.

The smells of the docks were so familiar to him that he scarcely noticed the mix of tallow and old rags, hides and grass bags, tarred ropes and sun-baked wood. Spotting an erstwhile mate he cried, 'Wotcher, Charlie! How's tricks?' but the reply was drowned by the neighing of a startled horse as a sudden breeze fluttered the bunting on the nearest ship. A moment later he was past the old tavern and free of the worst of the crowd, heading for the narrow channel where the docks fronted the Thames and hoping that for once his contact would be on time. Two pounds of flattened tobacco could not be easily explained away if he was stopped by one of the eagle-eyed Excise men.

He ran the last four hundred yards but, seeing three men crouched at the edge of the water, abruptly slowed to a walking pace. It was too late to turn back – that would look suspicious – so he approached warily and as he drew nearer he saw that they were reaching out with poles for something that floated in the gently lapping water. One of the men turned at his approach.

'It's a woman,' he said. 'Give us a hand to fish her out.'

Weighed down by its sodden petticoats, the body was heavier than they expected but at last it lay on the cobbles, forlornly oozing water, while the four men studied it in dismay. The hair was matted with oil, the lifeless hands were spread wide and the fingers of one had been chewed by rats. The eyes were closed, but the mouth was fixed open in a silent scream for help. Dan crossed himself as they all stared helplessly at the sombre sight.

'Poor bitch!' said one of the men. 'What a way to die.'

*

The following day Dora was at work in the match factory. Her hands moved automatically about their allotted task, passing to and fro across the work-bench: reaching forward to grasp the lever; pulling it down on to the strip of double-headed matches to cut them in half. This done she gathered them up, took an empty box from the pile, pushed it open and filled it. The full box was tossed up into an open-sided crate at the back of the bench. When the crate was full it would be taken to another part of the factory where equally skilled hands would assemble and wrap the boxes into packets of various sizes.

There had been changes. Jerry Mills had been promoted to foreman, which pleased everyone. Dora's thoughts were, as usual, on her imminent betrothal to Jeff Bannerman and her subsequent departure from England. Try as she would, she could not believe that any foreign country would ever feel like home to her. There was plenty wrong with England, she would be the first to admit that, but she *knew* its faults and therefore could live with them. Whatever was wrong with America was a different kettle of fish, because she did *not* know that country's faults and might find them unacceptable. Also, there was a long and presumably dangerous sea journey to be undergone before they reached it, and Dora did not fancy that either. Gradually she became aware of a slight commotion at the far end of the room, and heads were turned as a policeman began to make his way between the rows, while hands paused over the waiting matches as consciences were hastily examined.

'Now what's up?' said Zoe. 'Someone's for it!'

Dora grinned. 'What have you done?' she joked.

Her smiled faded, however, as the policeman glanced back at Jerry Mills, who then pointed directly at Dora.

Zoe said, 'Cripes, Dora! It's you he's after!'

In spite of a clear conscience Dora watched him approach with apprehension and as he stopped beside her she swallowed hard.

'Miss Becket, I would be grateful if you would accompany me to the police station.'

'I haven't done anything!' Dora burst out, horribly aware of the dozens of shocked faces turned in her direction. 'I swear I haven't!'

'It's nothing like that, Miss. We would just like you to help us with our enquiries. If you would come with me . . .'

Dora shook her head vehemently. 'No! I won't come with you. Not unless you tell me why.'

She looked desperately at Zoe, who said quickly, 'Don't you go, Dor – not until he tells you why.' She turned to the policeman. 'What you nicking her for?'

Patiently he said, 'I'm not nicking anyone. There's been some trouble . . .'

Dora paled. 'It's not Jeff, is it? Not again?'

Now a small crowd had formed round them, which was growing rapidly despite Jerry's efforts to persuade the girls to get back to their work.

The policeman continued, 'Will you come with me to the foreman's office, then?'

Reluctantly Dora agreed, and as she walked away with him she was aware of the curious eyes of her workmates.

As soon as they reached the office, he asked, 'Are you related to Meg Swain, late of Fashion Street?'

'Yes, she's my cousin. What's happened to her?'

'We think she's been drowned. A body was washed up this morning by St Katharine's Dock.'

Dora stared at him. 'A *body*?' she repeated.

He nodded.

'But she had a baby. Meg can't be – is the baby drowned too? No, it can't be her.'

'We have a young child – a baby girl – that was found abandoned earlier.'

Dora shook her head firmly. 'It can't be Meg,' she insisted. 'She'd never abandon Lizzie.'

He looked unconvinced, she thought uneasily, and her relief was short-lived. 'Did your cousin know a Dr Gilbert Reid, by any chance?'

Dora nodded cautiously. Surely no one else could know that the doctor had fathered Meg's child? She must not say too much, but on the other hand she must not withhold information from the police. Her face burned with confusion.

'He, too, was found dead, Miss Becket. Murdered by a person or persons unknown.'

Her mouth fell open with shock. '*Murdered?* But how did it happen? It couldn't have been murder. An accident, maybe. Or suicide.'

'Dr Reid was murdered by a person or persons unknown,' he repeated stolidly. 'You do not stab yourself in the heart.'

'God Almighty!'

'It's a nasty business,' he agreed.

'But what's all this got to do with Meg?'

'We don't know yet, but there is reason to think that the two events may be connected. As next of kin, we would like you to identify the body. We suggest you bring a companion with you, as it's not a pleasant task. Miss Becket! Are you listening?'

Dora was staring at the floor with unfocused eyes, trying to grasp the implications of what she had heard.

Looking up, she asked, 'If it is Meg and Lizzie – where is she? The baby, I mean.'

'The London Hospital. If you would also identify the child, the authorities will have to make provision for her.'

'Provision? Like what?'

'Probably the Union.'

'No!' cried Dora. 'Not little Lizzie!'

'The only alternative is a private orphanage, but they are expensive. Unless one of the family should decide to adopt her, as sometimes happens.'

'But I'm going to America in a couple of months,' she told him. 'I'm getting married. I don't know who else . . . poor little Lizzie!'

Suddenly his face brightened. 'There is a new asylum being opened shortly,' he told her. 'The Harold Weston or something – run by the Gaunt family. There might be a place left there, although there may be a lower age limit. I could make some enquiries.'

'Did you say Mrs Gaunt?' Dora looked at him sharply. 'But she knew Dr Reid. She paid for Ellie's coffin. That's Ellie, my other cousin – Meg's sister that died.'

He was looking at her with a very strange expression on his face and immediately she wondered if she had spoken out of turn. Had she revealed anything that should have remained a secret? Thinking back over what she had said, she did not believe so.

'Rather a lot of coincidences here, wouldn't you say?' he remarked. 'I think you should come with me to the station and make a statement. What you say may enable us to shed some light on the whole sad business.'

Meg was dead! It was just beginning to dawn and Dora whispered, 'Oh Meg! Poor Meg. I'm so sorry.'

She had had such a wretched life and some might even say she was well out of it, but Dora knew better. Meg had managed to enjoy herself in her own way. They had laughed a lot . . . Meg often said that laughter was cheap enough. Dora had a sudden vision of Meg as a child dancing barefoot in the street to the music of a barrel-organ, then another of a grown-up Meg after a pint too many, giggling helplessly at one of her own bawdy jokes. She saw Meg, her face vivacious, trying on second-hand hats at a stall in the market, and mimicking the drummer in the Salvation Army band.

'It's so bloody unfair!' she cried and without warning covered her face with her hands and burst into noisy, uncontrollable tears.

*

Marion and Rachel, both in mourning black, sat together at the back of the room sharing the ordeal, their hands clasped for comfort. Their eyes were on the Coroner as he conducted his enquiry.

'You are Mr John Parker?'

'I am.'

'Occupation?'

He looked puzzled. 'What's that?'

'What do you *do*, Mr Parker?'

'Oh! I've a coffee stall in Spitalfields market. Seven days a week, come rain, come shine. Three am until –'

'Yes, yes. We have the gist, thank you.'

The Coroner glanced at a sheaf of papers on the table before him, then picked one up and studied it. High on the wall to his left was a text carved on a large wooden plaque; it said: 'What doth the Lord require of thee, but to do justly, and to love mercy, and to walk humbly with thy God.'

The premises, normally a working men's club, was doing temporary service as a Coroner's Court. Marion tried to imagine it full of cheerful men enjoying a social evening, but failed.

The Coroner went on, 'And you were the first person to find the deceased, I believe?'

'That I was, guv.'

'You will address me as "sir".'

'What? Oh! Right, *sir*.'

'Will you please describe exactly where you found the victim?'

'He was lying on the landing-stage below the steps at London Bridge. I said, "Crikey! There's a —"'

'Just answer the question, please, Mr Parker.' The Coroner consulted his notes again. 'And was there to your knowledge anyone else on that landing-stage? Anyone who could have committed the assault?'

'No, guv — I mean, sir. There was only me and him until this other chap showed up — that is Mr Hobbs — quite quick like, and I said —'

'Mr Parker!'

'Oh, sorry.'

'Please tell the jury what you discovered when you found the victim.'

'Well, I discovered he'd been done in — stabbed through the heart, to be exact.'

A murmur ran through the court, but was instantly silenced by an impatient movement of the Coroner's hand.

At the back of the room a door opened, and Dora Becket and Jeff Bannermann entered and made their way to two of the few remaining chairs.

Marion was rather surprised that Amelia Gaunt was not present, but she had received a brief note from her expressing condolences.

The Coroner asked for a knife to be shown to Mr Parker, who agreed that it looked like the knife in question, but said he had only seen the handle.

'And you saw no one, Mr Parker, who might have committed the crime?'

'Well, guv, my guess is that whoever fell in the water . . .' he began.

'We do not want to hear your *guesses*, Mr Parker. Did you or did you not see any sign of a possible murderer?'

'No, sir, I did not.'

'Thank you, Mr Parker. I have no more questions, so you may stand down.'

Mr Parker looked as though there might well be a lot more he would like to say, but he decided against attempting it and returned to his seat with the air of one who has been cheated of his rightful glory.

The other man who had been present when the body was found then took the stand. In contrast to his predecessor, he was quietly spoken and frequently had to be asked to 'Speak up!'

'Your name, please?'

'Alfred Hobbs.'

'And your address?'

'Fifty-two, Barkers Row. I'm a crock, sir.'

'A *crock*?'

'Yes, sir.' He looked apologetic. 'I deal in crockery. I swap it for old clothes.'

'I see.'

Mr Hobbs' evidence, extracted with painful slowness, corroborated Mr Parker's in every detail, and then it was the turn of the Police Surgeon.

'It was your job to carry out an examination of the deceased?'

'Yes, it was.'

'Did you find any other wound apart from the stab wound to the chest?'

'No, I did not.'

'In your opinion, was the deceased a fit man before his death?'

'Yes, he was.'

'In your opinion, could the wound have been self-inflicted?'

'It is extremely unlikely.'

'How long have you been employed as a police surgeon?'

'Seventeen years this coming October.'

'Did you find anything to suggest that a struggle had taken place?'

'Yes, I did. There were several scratches on the face of the deceased.'

Marion and Rachel exchanged surprised looks and both leaned forward intently, but although the Coroner went on to elicit the salient points of the Police Surgeon's testimony the scratches were not referred to again.

Then it was the turn of Dora Becket.

Recalling the cheerful mood of Ellie's funeral, Marion found it incredible that they were meeting again under such unexpectedly dismal circumstances.

'You are Miss Dora Becket?'

'Yes, sir.' It was almost a whisper, and the Coroner encouraged her not to be nervous.

'You have identified the body of your cousin, Margaret Swain?'

She nodded.

'Please tell us in your own words, as briefly as possible, about the relationship which existed between the deceased, Gilbert Reid, and your cousin, Margaret Swain.'

Dora swallowed and looked around the court as though searching for an escape, and Marion's heart went out to her in her awful ordeal. She also felt apprehensive on her own account, wondering what, if anything, might now be revealed. Rachel squeezed her hand sympathetically and Marion returned the pressure.

'My cousin had a sister, Ellie . . .' Dora began. 'She had "phossy jaw" and a lady called Mrs Gaunt – a very rich lady – sent her to Dr Reid for treatment, but he couldn't help her and then later she died – Ellie, that is.' She paused and the Coroner gently prompted her to continue.

'When Meg's baby was born, Dr Reid came to see her, but Mrs Gaunt wouldn't pay that bill. He visited her a few times, but –'

'For medical reasons?'

'I suppose so,' she said guardedly. 'He was very kind to her and Meg thought a great deal of him.'

'Will you tell the court how, in your opinion, your cousin's baby came to be found near the site of the crime?'

'I can't. I don't know.'

Marion thought suddenly, 'She knows much more than she's saying!'

'Do you think your cousin had perhaps arranged to meet the deceased?'

'She might have done. I hadn't seen her for some time because she was always moving on; she had got it into her head that someone was trying to kill her.'

There was another startled response from the jury as well as the rest of the court.

'Did you believe her?'

'Not at first. She seemed so normal and it sounded so unlikely, but now that she *is* dead . . .' She shrugged and fell silent.

'Miss Becket, what is your employment?'

'I work at Bryant and Mays, the match factory, in Fairfield Road.'

'That is in Bow?'

'Yes.'

'And your cousin? Where did she work?'

Dora looked at him beseechingly, but his expression did not change. 'You must attempt to answer the question, Miss Becket.'

'She was . . . unemployed.'

'Then how did she support herself and her child?'

'I don't know,' Dora replied defiantly. 'Perhaps she took in washing.'

'You don't really believe that, do you, Miss Becket?'

Dora's mouth tightened. 'She's dead, so why can't you let her rest in peace? What does it matter what she did? She was no worse than lots of others. She –'

The Coroner held up a warning finger and she closed her mouth stubbornly.

'One last question, Miss Becket,' he said smoothly. 'In your opinion, would Miss Swain have had any reason to kill the deceased?'

'Meg would never kill anybody!' cried Dora. 'Unless someone went for her – and we'd all do that.'

'That will be all, thank you. You may stand down.'

At last the moment which Marion had dreaded arrived and she was invited to take the stand. As she moved towards the front of the court her mouth was dry and there was a tight knot of fear forming somewhere within her. Whatever happened, she reminded herself, she must not reveal the extent of her own suspicions where Gilbert was concerned. It would only complicate matters. Both he and Meg were dead and nothing could bring them back.

After establishing her identity for the benefit of the jury, the Coroner began his questioning.

'Mrs Reid, what was your husband's relationship with Miss Swain – to the best of your knowledge?'

'One of doctor and patient.'

'Did your husband ever discuss his work with you?'

'On occasions. Not always.'

'Did he talk to you about Miss Swain? Did he tell you that he suspected her sanity?'

'He hinted to that effect on one occasion, but he did not like me to ask too many questions.'

'Why was that?'

'I sometimes found myself becoming rather involved with the patients.'

'Could you elaborate on that remark, please, Mrs Reid.'

'I was sorry for them and wanted to help them.'

'And that involvement applied to the Swains?'

She nodded. 'I visited them once or twice and gave a few little gifts when the baby was born. I also attended the funeral of Ellie Swain, Meg's younger sister.'

'And your husband did not really approve of these visits?'

'He thought I should be more detached from the patients. Maybe he was right.'

'In what way?'

'Very often their problems were insoluble.' She sighed deeply. 'I found it frustrating, being unable to help them.'

'But Miss Becket has suggested that your husband visited them often.'

'I suspect he did not practise what he preached.'

There was a sympathetic murmur from the crowd at this remark and the Coroner smiled at her.

'Mrs Reid, I know this is painful for you, but do you have any idea who might have killed your husband? Can you think of any motive for his killing?'

Marion shook her head slowly. 'I have asked myself those questions time and again,' she told him. 'If someone was trying to kill Meg Swain, he might have intervened . . . but then where did the killer go to – unless he *swam* away? It sounds unlikely.' She stopped and frowned. 'But then how did my husband come to be there unless . . .' She shrugged helplessly. 'I'm afraid none of it makes sense to me. I'm sorry.'

After a few more rather superficial questions, she was allowed to return to her seat. As she did so, she caught Dora's eye and gave a slight nod of recognition.

The summing-up was eventually completed and the jury instructed to consider their verdict. Twenty-five minutes later they announced their findings – that Gilbert Arthur Reid had been killed by a person or persons unknown.

CHAPTER EIGHTEEN

When Mrs Coot answered the front door-bell she found a woman on the doorstep with a pale, drawn face and large haunted eyes.

'I would like to speak to Miss Becket if that's possible,' she said. 'Is she in?'

'Certainly she is. Come in. Who shall I say wants to speak to her?'

'Mrs Reid. She knows me; we have already met.'

Mrs Coot's eyes grew round. 'Not the doctor's wife?'

'Yes.'

'The one who was –?'

'That's right,' said Marion quickly.

'Oh, Mrs Reid, you poor soul!' Mrs Coot's face crumpled sympathetically as she opened the door to admit her visitor. 'I'm that sorry about your poor husband.'

'Thank you.'

'It must be terrible for you to think of him struck down like that. However must you feel? There *are* some wicked people about.' Mrs Coot stared at the visitor with barely disguised curiosity. The wife of a murdered man in her very own hallway, and upstairs the orphaned child of a drowned woman! She had never expected so many excitements – and all since Mr Bannerman moved in.

Marion said, 'I don't have very much time, I'm afraid.'

'Oh, I'm sorry. I'll tell her that you're here. Perhaps you'd wait in the parlour.'

After a few moments Dora appeared, apologizing for the delay; she had been feeding Lizzie, she explained.

'Mrs Coot will keep an eye on her for a few moments,' she told Marion. 'Won't you sit down?'

They both seated themselves and Marion drew a deep breath.

'I think you may realize why I'm here,' she began. 'This will not be easy for me, but I feel I *must* know. It is about my husband and your cousin. I felt at the inquest yesterday that you were keeping something back.'

'I felt the same about you,' said Dora, 'but go on.'

Marion studied the pattern on the carpet, unable to meet Dora's gaze. 'I believe there was more to the relationship than doctor and patient. I suspect that they were – I don't know quite how to put this – I think my husband was . . .'

Dora gave her no help, although she knew exactly what the other woman was struggling to say.

'Miss Becket, what I am trying to say is that Lizzie may be my husband's child.'

Dora's heart sank. So she had guessed. Now she would no doubt feel responsible towards Lizzie – might try to take her away; might even have a legal right to her. It all depended on how much she knew and how much was guesswork.

'*Is* she my husband's child?' Marion insisted. 'I saw a likeness – at least, I thought so.'

Dora hesitated. If she revealed that Gilbert Reid had been Meg's sole 'client' for many months, there would be no doubt left in Marion Reid's mind.

'Look, you know what Meg was,' she parried. 'I wouldn't tell the Coroner with all those people earwigging, but you and me – we both know. It could have been anyone's kid; Meg said so herself.'

'Did my husband *think* it was his? Did Meg?'

'Does it matter?'

'Of course it matters!' cried Marion. 'If Gilbert thought the child was his, he might have had a motive for . . .'

The word hung in the air between them, unspoken but nonetheless shocking, and there was a long silence. From the expression on Dora's face, it was at once obvious to Marion that the same thought had been in her mind also.

Marion hesitated to utter the dreadful word, but Dora had no such scruples.

'Murder?' she said bluntly. 'Yes, I did wonder, though I have not spoken of it to anyone, not even Jeff. If you must know, Meg told your husband that the child was his although really she had no idea whose it was. He just happened to be the only one with any money.'

'So they were – lovers?' Marion whispered the last word.

'Hardly the word I'd have chosen,' said Dora scornfully. 'If you'd seen what he did to her! Black and blue she was, sometimes, but she still called him her "gentleman". Gentle! He didn't know the meaning of the word. Some gentleman! I begged her to give him up, but she needed the money. Your sort wouldn't understand. Lovers? Huh! There was precious little love in it, so don't go getting that idea. But I know what you mean. Yes, they *were* and he gave her money.'

'Gave?' said Marion. 'Of his own free will? It wasn't blackmail, then?'

Dora shook her head. '*Gave*,' she insisted. 'That was until he knew about the baby. Of course that didn't please him very much – in fact, it didn't please him at all. He obviously wanted to get them both out of the way, so he told her someone was trying to kill her and gave her money to leave London, but she didn't go. He *could* have decided to kill her. Who knows?'

'But he didn't, did he?' said Marion. 'The inquest found death by drowning. She hadn't been stabbed or strangled. He told me she was insane; if she *was*, then she could have killed him and then thrown herself in the river.'

Dora glared at her. 'Is that what you'd like to believe, then? That would make you feel better, would it?'

Marion passed a hand across her eyes and said wearily, 'I don't want to quarrel with you, Miss Becket, I simply want to know the *truth*! I don't think I'm being unreasonable.'

Dora did not reply immediately, but when she did her manner was less aggressive. 'For what it's worth,' she told Marion, '*I* think *he* tried to kill *her*. Something went wrong and he got killed instead – and she fell or was pushed into the river. He could have lived long enough to push her, even with a knife in his heart.' She sighed. 'But what's the use of all this wondering, Mrs Reid? We're never going to know for sure because the only ones who do know are dead. Poor Meg! She had a good heart in spite of what she was, and she did love Lizzie. Now she'll never see her grow up.'

'Miss Becket,' said Marion firmly, 'I assure you I have no intention of letting anything we have said to each other go further than this room. I wanted to know if Lizzie is Gilbert's daughter, because if she is I would wish to give her a home. I have no one now that my husband is dead, and I would like to adopt her. The idea of her going into an orphanage is quite unbearable. I could not tolerate the possibility.'

'I'm sorry,' said Dora with equal firmness, 'but you can't have her! We shall never know who her father was, but we *do* know her mother and she was my cousin. Meg and I grew up together and we were close. Jeff and I have already made up our minds to keep her; we are getting married as soon as we arrive in America.'

'America!' Marion was shaken. 'Oh, but surely – then I shall never see her again!'

'Much better that way, if you don't mind me saying so, Mrs Reid.'

'But *America*! What takes you to America?'

'Jeff comes from Seattle; he only came to England for

a couple of years. We were going at the end of the year, but now Jeff's father is seriously ill and he is needed. So we are leaving the day after tomorrow.'

Marion gasped. 'So soon?'

Dora's mouth turned down wryly. 'I know! I can hardly believe it myself. It seems like the end of the world to me, but Jeff has to go and there's no way I'm going to be left behind.' Seeing Marion's stricken expression, she added gently, 'Mrs Reid, we'll give Lizzie a good home, I promise you. Cross my heart! Jeff's family are not short of a penny or two, and Lizzie will have lots of love. She'll have grandparents to dote on her, too, and later on there will be brothers and sisters to play with. She'll have a proper family.'

'Will you ever tell her . . . about everything?'

'Most likely we'll tell her she's English and adopted, but I won't tell about the murder. I'll say her mother died of something or other – an illness. No point in upsetting her, is there?'

Marion shook her head and after a moment she rose to her feet. 'I should be going then,' she said, her voice expressionless. 'Unless . . . may I see her just once more?'

' 'Course you can. I'll bring her down.'

A few minutes later she came back with Lizzie in her arms. The baby, Marion thought, looked as tranquil as ever and was wrapped in a new shawl. With the child in her arms, Marion felt again the same unmistakable pull at her heartstrings. She *was* Gilbert's child, but Dora and Jeff would give her a happy home.

Marion held her close, then gently kissed the small downy head.

'Goodbye, little one,' she whispered. 'Be happy.'

*

Mrs Cobbett sat at the kitchen table reading the paper and punctuating her reading by frequent expressions of alarm. Yet another prostitute had been murdered – this time in Hanbury Street, a turning off Commercial Street and only a mile or so from the spot where Martha Tabram's body had been found.

'Poor creature!' exclaimed Mrs Cobbett. 'What a terrible way to die. Slashed all to pieces, if you can believe what you read.'

Kitty, cleaning the silver, shuddered. 'It's horrible!' she said. 'Makes my blood run cold just to think about it.'

'Half-past five this morning they found her.' Cook ran a finger down the column and began to read aloud for Kitty's benefit: '"The motiveless killings have led some people to express the fear that a maniac is loose on the streets of London."'

Mrs Cobbett tutted. 'He must be a maniac when you think how many people he's killed already – the Tabram woman, Polly Nicholls and now Annie Chapman. None of them with a halfpenny to bless themselves with, so where's the sense in it? And if there's no sense in it, then whoever did it must be mad. Got to be, hasn't he? Another name for a maniac. They're saying the streets aren't safe for any woman.'

'Nor for men!' Kitty reminded her. 'Look at poor Dr Reid. The maniac might have done him in – who knows?'

Mrs Cobbett said hurriedly, 'Keep your voice down, you silly girl. D'you want the mistress to hear you?'

Kitty, not wishing to be sidetracked, lowered her voice as she continued, 'Well, he might have been. Or he might have been trying to murder Miss Swain and then, when he didn't have time because the doctor arrived to save her, he pushed her in the river instead and turned the knife on poor Dr Reid.'

Mrs Cobbett was impressed in spite of herself. 'I wonder,' she said, frowning. 'I suppose it could have happened like that. I suppose the police will have thought of it. It says in here that they're "investigating every avenue".'

'Well, I wish they'd do it a bit faster!' said Kitty, gathering up the knives and plunging them into the bowl. 'I, for one, shan't set foot in the street after dark until they catch him and hang him. The butcher's boy says there's a suspect – a man who wears a leather apron. He's a bootmaker or some such, and he lives in Mulberry Road. That's not far from here. He has lots of knives, and his landlord says he's a violent sort of bloke.'

'The butcher's boy!' scoffed Mrs Cobbett, folding up the newspaper. 'What does he know about anything? Cheeky young varmint. I'll give him "suspect" when I see him!' She fetched the vegetable basket from the larder and began to select vegetables for the evening meal.

Kitty washed and rinsed the cutlery and dried it carefully, then returned it to the drawer piece by piece.

'I wish Miss Rachel was still here,' she observed. 'At least the mistress had someone to talk to when she was staying. Now all she does is sit about staring into space. I don't know where she went this morning, but when she came back her face was all blotchy as though she'd been crying her eyes out.'

Mrs Cobbett snorted. 'You'd cry your eyes out if your husband was murdered! Anybody would. Still, they say grief must out, so now's the best time for tears. When my sister lost her husband – poor old Frank, he died of apoplexy – she didn't shed a tear, not for weeks and weeks. Everyone said how brave she was, but she was only bottling it all up and it had to come out sometime.'

'And did it?' Kitty closed the dresser drawer.

'Of course it did. Months later she went into a decline; couldn't eat, couldn't sleep, wouldn't speak to anyone. It was terrible to see her. Like a skeleton she was, and nearly went out of her mind.'

'Did she die?' asked Kitty, her morbid interest aroused.

'Almost. She recovered eventually, but the doctor said it was touch and go.'

Kitty was silent, chastened by this doleful tale. 'You don't think the mistress will go like that, do you?' she asked.

'I hope not! Or where will *we* be?'

'How d'you mean?'

Mrs Cobbett shrugged. 'Well, now she's a widow she might not be able to live here. She may be in "straitened circumstances" as they say, and have to move somewhere cheaper.'

'Wouldn't we go with her? She'd still need a cook and a maid wherever she went.'

'If she could afford it,' said the cook, determined now to look on the gloomy side. She looked thoughtfully at Kitty, who waited anxiously. 'I suppose she's been provided for,' she said at last. 'People in her class always are, aren't they? Oh, well, we'll know all in good time, I suppose.'

'You could ask her,' Kitty suggested.

Mrs Cobbett shook her head. 'Let sleeping dogs lie,' she said. 'Why put the idea into her head? No, we'll bide our time. At least we know she'll do the best she can for us, not like some employers who'd turn you out as soon as look at you. If there's any way the mistress can keep us on, she will! You can take that as gospel.'

The front door-bell rang and Kitty said resignedly, 'I know! My legs are younger than yours!' She tidied herself and went to answer the door.

A few moments later she came back, closed the kitchen door and leaned back against it. There was an air of suppressed excitement about her which made Mrs Cobbett stare at her.

'What's up with you?' she asked. 'Who was it?'

'I've just seen something, Mrs Cobbett.' Kitty rolled her eyes expressively. 'You're not going to believe me!'

'What on earth are you talking about? What have you seen? Who was it?'

Kitty levered herself away from the door and came to the table, leaning on it with her face close to Mrs Cobbett's. In a low voice she said, 'It was Mr Gaunt.'

Mrs Cobbett regarded her blankly. 'So – what's so amazing about that?'

'Nothing – except that he was *kissing* the mistress!'

The cook's mouth dropped open in astonishment. 'Kissing Mrs . . . I don't believe it!'

Kitty straightened up, her eyes gleaming. 'Don't, then,' she said triumphantly, 'but it's true. He had his arms round her and he was *kissing* her. I saw it with my own eyes.'

'Gawd love us!' Mrs Cobbett stared at Kitty, fascinated by this incredible revelation. 'He must be a relative,' she suggested at last. '*Must* be.'

'He's not,' said Kitty. 'You know very well he's not. He's Mrs Gaunt's son, and she's not a relative.'

Mrs Cobbett stared at the chosen vegetables with unseeing eyes, then sat down heavily. 'Gawd strewth!' she said. 'Now I've heard everything.' She thought a moment and then went on, 'Was the mistress struggling or anything?'

'Kitty shook her head slowly and with emphasis.

'She was *loving* it!' she declared.

*

For a long moment Marion clung to Ralph.

'My dearest, *dearest* Ralph!' she whispered. 'I can't believe it and I don't deserve it! I thought I had lost you for ever. I thought – your mother said – that you had gone to America.'

When she drew back to take a proper look at him he was shocked by her haggard appearance.

'I intended to go,' he told her, 'but when I heard about Gilbert I knew I had a chance – I had to ask you one more time. Mama came after me, you know – you could say that she hunted me down!' He laughed shakily.

'She caught up with me late last night in Bordeaux and told me what had happened, and we came straight back to England. Oh, my poor sweet Marion! You look so tired and ill.'

'It doesn't matter,' she told him. 'Nothing matters now that you're here. Oh, my love, you can't imagine how much I missed you. Will you ever forgive me? I know how much I hurt you, but I thought it was for your own sake. You do know that, don't you? You do understand?'

'Of course I understand; Mama confessed all. Meddling old –'

Marion put a finger to his lips. 'Hush, Ralph. Don't speak harshly of her. After all, she brought you back to me. I could have lost you for ever.'

'But she did it for her own sake, not mine,' Ralph pointed out. 'There was nothing altruistic about it. She could not bear to lose me, so she used you to tempt me back to England. I have no illusions in that respect.'

'I don't care. It doesn't matter how or why.'

He held her close again. 'I hope you know what this means,' he teased her. 'You and me, now and for ever. There is no way you will ever get rid of me again!' He suddenly noticed Pip whining beside them, anxious to be included.

'She's been such a comfort to me,' said Marion, 'and Rachel came for a few days. She would have stayed longer, but I felt I had to learn to be on my own.'

'Not any more,' he insisted. 'Oh, I know that we must wait a while – a decent interval, as they say – but then I'm going to marry you, Marion.'

'Oh, but –'

'But nothing! I have told Mama and do you know what she said?'

Marion shook her head.

'She said, "Well, I should hope so after all the trouble I've taken to find you!"'

Marion smiled but he went on, 'I know it's a terrible thing, Gilbert dying in that way, but life goes on and we must not let the manner of his death come between us.'

There was a tap at the door and, as they drew apart, Kitty came in. 'Will you be wanting a tray of tea, ma'am?' she asked, her face determinedly innocent.

Marion looked at Ralph, who nodded and said, 'Actually, I've come straight from the ferry at Folkestone. I don't suppose you could find me a slice of cake, could you, Kitty?'

Kitty, looking at their faces, read what they would not actually tell for a good many months to come, and in spite of her good intentions to the contrary a broad grin spread over her face.

Marion said, 'Some sandwiches and cake then, Kitty, for Mr Gaunt.' She glanced at Ralph and asked, 'Will you stay to dinner?'

'I should be delighted.'

When Kitty had left the room, Marion looked at him anxiously. 'She gave us an odd look. Do you think she knows?'

He laughed. 'I don't care if she does,' he told her. 'In fact, I don't care if the whole world knows. We love each other! Nothing is going to keep us apart.' He slipped an arm around her waist and led her to the window. 'Out there is a whole new world. To everyone else it may look like the old one, but to us it's new and full of promise.' He looked at her seriously. 'We have to forget the past. Put it behind us with no regrets. We can make a new life for ourselves – just the two of us.'

'And Pip,' Marion amended with a smile, stooping to pick up the little dog.

'And Pip,' he agreed. 'Just the two of us, and Pip, and all the children!'

Marion could only shake her head, dazed by the swift reversal in her life. One moment she had been despairing and alone; now Ralph was standing beside her and her grey world was suddenly bright with colour.

*

Mrs Cobbett, now peeling apples, looked up eagerly as Kitty came back into the kitchen.

'Well?' she demanded.

Kitty kept her face straight. 'Some sandwiches and cake for Mr Gaunt,' she said, 'and –'

'Never mind that!' interrupted the cook. 'How *were* they?'

Kitty's face burst into a smile. 'They were standing by the window, *very* close.'

'Were they, now!'

'Very, *very* close,' said Kitty with a wink.

'But not kissing?'

'No, but Mrs Reid looked all flustered as though they had been, and Mr Gaunt looked like a cat with the cream!'

Mrs Cobbett shook her head in wonder.

'*And*,' said Kitty, 'he's staying for dinner.'

'Well, I don't know what to say,' said Mrs Cobbett. 'I really don't. The mistress and Mr Gaunt! It's knocked me all of a heap.'

'So perhaps they'll get married. I hope they do. I like Mr Gaunt.'

Mrs Cobbett agreed. 'A real nice gentleman.'

Kitty grinned. 'So maybe the mistress won't be in straitened circumstances after all. She'll be *rich*. Probably buy a big house and take us along. What do you think?'

Mrs Cobbett allowed herself a slow, broad smile. 'I think I ought to make those sandwiches,' she said.